"Interest in the Darkover series has been quantitatively growing. . . .

"It might be noted that the series is unique in one way: the individual novels can be read in any order . . . So grab a Darkover novel, any Darkover novel. . . ."

—Baird Searles
Science Fiction Review

THE SHATTERED CHAIN fills in an important aspect of the culture of the world beneath the bloody sun, that of the enigmatic bands known as the Free Amazons.

For it was through the Free Amazons, aloof from the restrictions and taboos of their alien society, that the Terrans first found unprejudiced allies. In THE SHATTERED CHAIN, you will enjoy the intricate unravelling of the knotty problems of Terran intruders and Darkovan aristocrats *. . . with all the marvelous color and high adventure that has made Darkover outstanding among the creations of alien planets.*

G. Barr

THE SHATTERED CHAIN

A Darkover Novel

MARION ZIMMER BRADLEY

DAW BOOKS, INC.
DONALD A. WOLLHEIM, PUBLISHER

1633 Broadway, New York, NY 10019

FIRST PRINTING, APRIL 1976

9 10 11 12 13 14

THE OATH OF THE FREE AMAZONS

From this day forth, I renounce the right to marry save as a freemate. No man shall bind me *di catenas* and I will dwell in no man's household as a *barragana*.

I swear that I am prepared to defend myself by force if I am attacked by force, and that I shall turn to no man for protection.

From this day forth I swear I shall never again be known by the name of any man, be he father, guardian, lover or husband, but simply and solely as the daughter of my mother.

From this day forth I swear I will give myself to no man save in my own time and season and of my own free will, at my own desire; I will never earn my bread as the object of any man's lust.

From this day forth I swear I will bear no child to any man save for my own pleasure and at my own time and choice; I will bear no child to any man for house or heritage, clan or inheritance, pride or posterity; I swear that I alone will determine rearing and fosterage of any child I bear, without regard to any man's place, position or pride.

From this day forth I renounce allegiance to any family, clan, household, warden or liege lord, and take oath that I owe allegiance only to the laws of the land as a free citizen must; to the kingdom, the crown and the Gods.

I shall appeal to no man as of right, for protection, support or succor: but shall owe allegiance only to my oath-mother, to my sisters in the Guild and to my employer for the season of my employment.

And I further swear that the members of the Guild of Free Amazons shall be to me, each and every one, as my mother, my sister or my daughter, born of one blood with me, and that no woman sealed by oath to the Guild shall appeal to me in vain.

From this moment, I swear to obey all the laws of the Guild of Free Amazons and any lawful command of my oath-mother, the Guild members or my elected leader for the season of my employment. And if I betray any secret of the Guild, or prove false to my oath, then I shall submit myself to the Guild-mothers for such discipline as they shall choose; and if I fail, then may every woman's hand turn against me, let them slay me like an animal and consign my body unburied to corruption and my soul to the mercy of the Goddess.

DEDICATION

for Tracy
in return for
Telling me the joke about
the spaceman, the *leronis* and
the three Dry-Towners.

PART I: ROHANA ARDAIS, Comynara

PART II: MAGDA LORNE, Terran Agent

PART III: JAELLE n'ha MELORA, Free Amazon

Twelve years elapse between
the first part and the second.

Part I

ROHANA ARDAIS,

Comynara

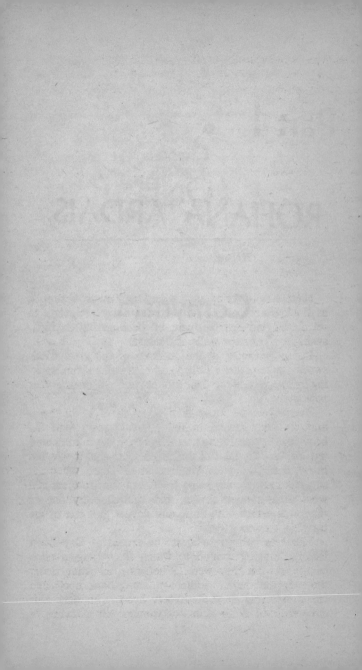

Chapter
ONE

Night was lowering across the Dry Towns, hesitating as if, at this season, the great red sun were reluctant to set. Liriel and Kyrrdis, pale in the lingering daylight, swung low over the walls of Shainsa.

Inside the gates, at the outskirts of the great wind-swept marketplace, a little band of travelers were making camp, unsaddling their mounts and off-loading their pack animals.

There were no more than seven or eight of them, and all were garbed in the hooded cloaks and the heavy tunics and riding-breeches of the mountain country, the faraway land of the Seven Domains. It was hot in the desert lands of Shainsa, at this hour when the sun still burned with some force, but the travelers still wore their hooded cloaks; and though every one of them was armed with knife and dagger, not one of the travelers carried a sword.

This was enough to alert the crowd of Dry-Town loafers, hanging around to watch the strangers pitch camp, to what they were. When one, sweating under the weight of laden saddlebags, slung back hood and cloak to reveal a small shapely head, with dark hair close-cropped as no man—or woman—of Domains or

11

Dry Towns ever wore it, the hecklers began to collect. So little goes on, ordinarily, in Dry-Town streets, that the watchers behaved as if the arrival of the strangers were a free show arranged for their benefit, and they all felt free to comment on the performance.

"Hey, there, come have a look at this! Free Amazons, they are, from the Domains!"

"Shameless bitches, that's what they are, runnin' around like that with no man to own to 'em! I'd run the lot out of Shainsa before they corrupt our decent wives and daughters!"

"What's the matter, Hayat, you can't keep hold of your own wives? Mine, now, they wouldn't run loose for all the gold of the Domains. . . . If I tried to cut 'em loose they'd come back cryin', they know when they're well off. . . ."

The Amazons heard the remarks, but they had been warned and were prepared for this; they went quietly about the business of making camp, as if their observers were invisible and unspeaking. Emboldened by this, the Dry-Town men came closer, and the jokes flew, free and ribald; and now some of them were addressed directly to the women.

"Got everything, haven't you, girls—swords, knives, horses, everything except what it takes!"

One of the women flushed and turned, opening her lips as if to reply; the leader of the group, a tall, slender, swift-moving woman, turned to her and said something, urgently, in a low voice; the woman lowered her eyes and turned back to the tent-pegs she was driving into the coarse sand.

One of the Dry-Town idlers, witnessing the little exchange, approached the leader, muttering suggestively: "Got your girls all right under your thumb, haven't you, then? Why not leave 'em alone and come along with me? I could teach you things you never dreamed about—"

The woman turned, pushing back her hood to reveal, beneath graying close-cropped hair, the gaunt, pleasant face of a woman in middle years. She said in a light, clearly audible voice, "I learned everything you could possibly teach me long before you were housebroken, animal. And as for dreams, I have nightmares like everybody else, but thanks be to the Gods, I've always waked up so far."

The bystanders guffawed. "One in the eye for you, Merach!" Now that they had turned their jokes on one another instead of on the women, the little band of Free Amazons went quickly about the business of setting camp: a booth, evidently for buying or selling, a couple of sleeping tents and a shelter to guard their mountain-bred horses against the fierce and unaccustomed sun of the Dry Towns.

One of the onlookers came forward; the women tensed against further insult, but he only asked politely enough: "May one inquire your business here, *vahi domnis?*" His accent was thick, and the woman addressed looked blank; but the leader understood, and answered for her: "We have come to sell leather goods from the Domains; saddles, harness and leather clothing. We will be here for trading at daylight tomorrow; you are all invited to come and do business with us."

A man in the crowd yelled, "They's only one thing I'd ever buy from women!"

"Buy it, hell! Make *them* pay for it!"

"Hey, lady, you going to sell them britches you're wearing so you can dress like a woman?"

The Free Amazon ignored the jeers. The man who had come to question her said, "Can we direct you to any entertainment in the city this night? Or"—he hesitated, looked appraisingly at her, and added—"entertain you ourselves?"

She said with a faint smile, "No, thank you very much," and turned away. One of the younger women said in a low, indignant voice, "I had no idea it was going to be like this! And you *thanked* him, Kindra! I'd have kicked his dirty teeth down his throat!"

Kindra smiled and patted the other's arm soothingly. "Why, hard words break no bones, Devra. He made an offer with such politeness as was in him, and I an-

swered him the same. Next to these"—she swept the
crowd of loafers with an ironic gray glance—"he was
the soul of courtesy."

"Kindra, are we really going to trade with these
gre'zuin?"

Kindra frowned faintly at the obscenity. "Why, yes,
of course. We must have some reason for staying here,
and Jalak may not return for days. If we have no apparent business here, we will be prime objects for suspicion. Not trade? What are you wearing for a head,
today? *Think*, child!"

She moved on to a woman who was piling saddlebags within the shelter, asking in an undertone, "No
sign yet of Nira?"

"None so far." The woman addressed glanced
uneasily around, as if fearful of being overheard. She
spoke pure *casta*, the language of the aristocrats from
Thendara and the plains of Valeron. "No doubt she'll
seek us out after nightfall. She would have small liking
for running the gauntlet of these folk; and for anyone
dressed as a man to enter our camp openly and unchallenged—"

"True," Kindra said, looking at their watchers. "And
she is no stranger to the Dry Towns. Yet I cannot help
being a little fearful. It goes against the grain to send
any of my women in man's dress, yet it was her only
safety here."

"In man's dress . . ." The woman repeated the words
as if she felt she must have misunderstood the other's
language. "Why, do you not all wear man's dress, Kindra?"

Kindra said, "Here you betray only your ignorance
of our customs, Lady Rohana; I beg you to keep your
voice low when we might be overheard. Do you truly
believe I wear man's dress?" She sounded affronted,
and the Lady Rohana said quickly, "I meant no offense, believe me, Kindra. But your dress is certainly
not that of a woman—not, at least, a woman of the
Domains."

Deference and annoyance mingled in the Free

Amazon's voice as she said, "I have no leisure now to explain to you all the customs and rules of our Guild, Lady Rohana. For now, it is enough—" She broke off at another outbreak of guffaws from the bystanders; Devra and another of the Free Amazons were leading their saddle-horses toward the common well at the center of the marketplace. One of them paid the watering fee in the copper rings that passed as currency anywhere east of Carthon, while the other led the animals to the trough. As she returned to help Devra with the watering, one of the idlers in the crowd laid hands on her waist, pulling her roughly against him.

"Hey, pretty, why don't you leave these bitches and come along with me? I've got plenty to show you, and I'll bet you never—*eeyah!*" His words broke off in a howl of rage and pain; the woman had whipped a dagger from its sheath, slashing swiftly upward, laying open his filthy and tattered clothing to expose bare, unhealthy flesh, a line of red creeping upward along the quarter-inch-deep slash from lower belly to collarbone. He stumbled back, staggering, falling into the dust; the woman gave him a contemptuous kick with one sandaled foot, saying in a low, fierce voice, "Take yourself off, *bre'sui!* Or next time I'll spill your guts, and your *cuyones* with 'em! Now get the hell out of here, you filthy bastards, or you won't be fit for anything but selling for he-whores in the Ardcarran bordellos!"

The man's friends dragged him away, still moaning more with shock than pain. Kindra strode toward the woman, who was wiping her knife. She raised her eyes, grinning with innocent pride at how well she had defended herself. Kindra slapped the knife out of her hand.

"Damn you, Gwennis! Now you've made us all conspicuous! Your pride in knife-play could cost us our mission! When I asked for volunteers on this trip, I wanted *women,* not spoiled children!"

Gwennis' eyes filled with tears. She was no more than a girl, fifteen or sixteen. She said, her voice shak-

ing, "I am sorry, Kindra. What should I have done?
Should I have let the filthy *gre'zu* paw me?"

"Do you really think you were in danger, here in
daylight and before so many? You could have freed
yourself without bloodshed and made him look ridicu-
lous, without ever drawing your knife. Your skills were
taught you to guard against real danger of rape or
wounding, Gwennis, not to protect your pride. It is
only men who must play games of *kihar,* my daughter;
it is beneath the dignity of a Free Amazon." She picked
up the knife where it had fallen in the dust, wiping the
remnant of blood from the blade. "If I return it to you,
can you keep it where it belongs until it is needed?"

Gwennis lowered her head and muttered, "I swear
it."

Kindra handed it to her, saying gently, "It will be
needed soon enough, *breda.*" She laid an arm around
the girl's shoulders for an instant, adding, "I know it is
difficult, Gwennis. But remember that our mission is
more important than these stupid annoyances."

She left the women to finish the watering, noticing
with a grim smile that the crowd of idle watchers had
evaporated as if by magic. *Gwennis deserved every
harsh word I gave her. But I am still glad she rid us of
those creatures!*

The sun sank behind the low hills, and the small
moons began to climb the sky. The square was
deserted for a while, then some of the Dry-Town
women, wrapped in their cumbersome skirts and veils,
began to drift into the marketplace to buy water from
the common well, moving, each of them, with the small
metallic clash of chains. By Dry-Town custom, each
woman's hands were fettered with a metal bracelet on
each wrist; the bracelets were connected with a long
chain, passed through a metal loop on her belt, so that
if the woman moved either hand, the other was drawn
up tight against the loop at her waist.

The Free Amazon camp was filled with a smell of
cooking from their small fires; some of the Dry-Town
women came close and stared at the strange women

with curiosity and contempt: their cropped hair, their rough mannish garb, their unbound hands, breeches and low sandals. The Amazons, conscious of their stares, returned the gaze with equal curiosity, not un-mingled with pity. The woman called Rohana finally could bear no more; leaving her almost-untouched plate, she got to her feet and went into the tent she shared with Kindra. After a moment the Amazon leader followed her inside, saying in surprise, "But you have eaten nothing, my Lady. May I serve you, then?"

"I am not hungry," said Rohana, stifled. She put back her hood, revealing, in the dim light, hair of the flame-red color that marked her a member of the tele-path caste of the Comyn: the caste that had ruled the Seven Domains from time unknown and unknowable. It had been cropped short, indeed, but nothing could conceal its color, and Kindra frowned as the Comyn woman went on:

"The sight of those women has destroyed my appe-tite; I feel too sick to swallow. How can you endure to watch it, Kindra, you who make so much of freedom for women?"

Kindra said with a slight shrug, "I feel no very great sympathy for them. Any single one of them could be free if she chose. If they wish to suffer chains rather than lose the attentions of their men, or be different from their mothers and sisters, I shall not waste my pity on them, far less lose sleep or appetite. They en-dure their captivity as you of the Domains, Lady, en-dure yours; and truth to tell, I see no very great differ-ence between you. They are, perhaps, more honest, for they admit to their chains and make no pretense of freedom; while yours are invisible—but they are as great a weight upon you."

Rohana's pale face flushed with anger. She said, "Then I wonder you ever agreed to this mission! Was it only to earn your pay?"

"There was that, of course," Kindra said, unruffled. "I am a mercenary soldier; within reason, I go where I am hired to go, and do what I am best paid to do. But there is more," she added in a gentler tone. "The Lady Melora, your kinswoman, did not connive at her own captivity, nor choose her form of servitude. As I understand what you told me, Jalak of Shainsa—may his manhood wither!—fell upon her escort, slew her guards, and carried her away by force; wishing, for revenge or sheer lust of cruelty, to keep a *leronis* of the Comyn enslaved and captive as his wife—or his concubine, I am not certain."

"In the Dry Towns there seems no great difference," said the Lady Rohana bitterly, and Kindra nodded. "I see no very great difference anywhere, *vai domna,* but I do not expect you to agree with me. Be that as it may, Lady Melora was carried away into a slavery she had not chosen, and her surviving kinsmen could not, or did not, choose to avenge her."

"There were those who tried," Rohana said, her voice shaking. Her face was almost invisible in the darkened tent, but there were tears in her roughened voice. "They vanished without trace, until the third; he was my father's youngest son, my half-brother; and had been Melora's foster-brother, reared as her playmate."

"*That* tale I have heard; Jalak sent back the ring he wore still on his fingers," Kindra said, "and boasted he would do so, and more, to any other who came to avenge her. But that was ten years ago, Lady, and if I were in the Lady Melora's slippers, I would not have lived to endanger any more of my kinfolk. If she has dwelled for twelve years in Jalak's household, surely she cannot be in any great need, by now, of rescue. By this time, one would imagine she must be resigned to her fate."

Rohana's pale face stained with color. "So in truth we believed," she said. "Cassilda pity me, I, too, reproached her in thought, wishing her dead rather than living on in Jalak's house as a shame to us all."

"Yet you are here now," Kindra said, and although it was not a question, Lady Rohana answered. "You know what I am: *leronis,* Tower-trained; a telepath.

Melora and I dwelt together, as young girls, in the Dalereuth Tower. Neither of us chose to remain life-long, but before I left the Tower to marry, our minds were joined; we learned to reach one another's thoughts. Then came her tragedy. In the years be-tween, I had indeed all but forgotten; learned to think of Melora as dead, or at least gone far beyond my reach, far, far beyond my touch or my thoughts. Then—it was not more than forty days ago—Melora came to me across the distances; came to me in thought, as we had learned to do when we were little maidens in the Tower at Dalereuth. . . ."

Her voice was distant, strange; Kindra knew that the red-haired woman was no longer speaking to her, but to a memory; a commitment. "I hardly knew her," Ro-hana said, "she had changed so greatly. Resigned to her place as Jalak's consort and captive? No; simply unwilling to cause"—Rohana's voice faltered—"more death and torment; I learned then that my brother, her foster-brother, had been tortured to death before her eyes, as a warning lest she seek rescue. . . ."

Kindra grimaced with horror and revulsion. Rohana went on, steadying her voice with a fearful effort. "Me-lora told me that at last, after so many years, she bore a son to Jalak; that she would die before giving him an heir of Comyn blood. She did not ask rescue for her-self, even then. I think—I think she wants to die. But she will not leave her other child in Jalak's hands."

"Another child?"

"A daughter," Rohana said quietly, "born a few months after she was taken. Twelve years old. Old enough"—her voice shook—"old enough to be chained." She sobbed, turning her face away. "For her-self she asked nothing. Only she begged me to get her daughter away; away, out of Jalak's hands. Only so— only so could she die in peace."

Kindra's face was grim. *Before I bore a daughter to live in the Dry Towns, captive, chained,* she thought, *I would lay hands on myself and the life within me, or strangle the babe as she came forth from my womb!*

But the women of the Domains are soft, cowards all! None of this showed in her voice, however, as she laid a hand on Rohana's shoulder, saying quietly, "I thank you for telling me this, Lady. I did not understand. So our mission is not so much to rescue your kins-woman—"

"As to free her daughter; that is what she asked. Al-though—if Melora can be freed . . ."

"Well, my band and I are pledged to do all we can," Kindra said, "and I think any of us would risk our lives to save a young girl from living chained. But for now, Lady, you will soon need all your strength, and there is neither courage nor wisdom in an empty belly; it is not fitting that I should lay commands on a *Comynara,* but will you not join my women now and finish your meal?"

Rohana's smile wavered a little. *Why, beyond her harsh words, she's kind!* She said aloud, "Before I joined you, *mestra,* I pledged myself to conduct myself in all ways as one of your band, and so I am bound to obey you."

She went out of the tent, and Kindra, standing in the doorway, watched her take a place by the fire, and ac-cept a plateful of the stewed meat and beans.

Kindra did not follow at once, but stood thinking of what lay ahead. If it came to Jalak's ears that anyone of the Domains was in his city, he might be already on guard. Or would he so despise the Free Amazons that he would not trouble to guard against them? She should have insisted that the Lady Rohana dye her hair. If any spy of Jalak's should see a redheaded Comyn woman . . . *I never thought she would be willing to cut it.*

Maybe courage is relative; for her, maybe it took as much courage to cut her hair as for me to draw knife on a foeman. . . .

It is worth risk, to take a young maiden from Jalak's hands, from chains to freedom.

. . . Or such freedom as any woman can have in the Domains.

Kindra raised her hand, in an automatic gesture, to her cropped, graying hair. She had not been born into the Guild of Free Amazons; she had come to it through a choice so painful that the memory still had power to make her lips tighten and her eyes grow grim and faraway. She looked at Rohana, sitting in the ring of Amazons around the fire, eating, listening to the women talk. *I was once very like her: soft, submissive to the only life I knew. I chose to free myself. Rohana chose otherwise. I do not pity her, either.*

But Melora was given no choice. Nor her daughter.

She thought, dispassionately, that it was probably too late for Melora. There could not, after ten years in the Dry Towns, be much left for her. But there was evidently enough left, of what she had been, to spur her to an enormous effort to get freedom for her daughter. Kindra knew only a little of the telepathic powers of the Comyn; but she knew that for Melora to reach Lady Rohana, over such distance, after so long a separation, must have taken enormous and agonizing effort. For the first time, Kindra felt a moment of genuine sympathy for Melora. She had accepted captivity for herself rather than allow any more of her kinsmen to risk death by torture. But she would risk anything, to give her daughter a choice; so that her daughter would not live and die knowing nothing but the chained world, the slave world, of the Dry-Town women.

Lady Rohana did well to come to me. After so many years, no doubt, her Comyn kin wished Melora dead, wished to forget she dwelt in slavery, a reproach to them.

But that is why the Free Amazons exist, in the final analysis. So that every woman may, at least, know there is a choice for them . . . that if they accept the restrictions laid upon women, on Darkover, they may do so from choice and not because they cannot imagine anything else. . . .

Kindra was about to leave the tent, to return to the fireside and have her own meal, when she heard a

small, strange sound: the whistle of a rain-bird; such a
bird as never cried here, in the Dry Towns. Quickly
she turned, nervously alert, seeing the small, slight
form that wriggled under the back flap of the tent. It
was very dark, but she knew who it must be. She said
in a whisper, "Nira?"

"Unless you think some rain-bird has gone mad and
flown here to die," said Nira, rising to her feet.

Kindra said, "Here, get out of those clothes; another
woman around our fire will never be noticed, but in
men's clothes you would collect another crowd here.
We had quite enough of that while we were off-loading."

"I heard," Nira said wryly, slipping out of her boots,
unbuckling the shortsword she wore—contrary to
Domain law—and concealing it in the clutter of the
tent. Kindra flung the younger woman a shirt and loose
Amazon trousers, saw that she was very faintly silhouetted by firelight, and turned the tiny lamp lower still
until they were in darkness. Nira was folding up her
disguise; as she stepped into her clothes, Kindra came
and asked in a whisper, "Was there any trouble? What
news, child?"

"No trouble; I passed for any trader's lad from the
mountains, any apprentice; they thought me a
beardless boy with his voice still unbroken. For news I
have only gossip of the marketplace, and some from
the servants at Jalak's door. The Voice of Jalak, who
keeps his Great House when the Lord is away, has received a message that Jalak, and his wives and concubines and all his household, will return before noon tomorrow; and one of the slave-girls told me that they
would have returned tonight, except that his Lady is
heavy with child, and could not ride so far this day.
Jalak has sent word for the midwives to be in readiness
at any time after his return, and his servants are making bets about whether this will be the son he wants
... it seems he has begotten nothing but girls, whether
by wife, concubine or slave-girl, and that he has
promised that the first of his women to bear him a son

shall have rubies from Ardcarran and pearls brought from the sea-towns at Temora. Some old midwife says that she can tell by the way Lady Melora carries her child, low and broad, that it is a son; and Jalak will do nothing to endanger her while he has this hope. . . ."

Kindra's face twisted in distaste. She said: "So Jalak is camped in the desert? How far away?"

Nira shrugged. "No more than a few miles, I gathered. Maybe we should have arranged to attack his tents. . . ."

Kindra shook her head. "Madness. Have you forgotten? The Dry-Towners are paranoid; they live by feud and combat. On the road, take my word, Jalak will be guarded so that three cadres of City Guardsmen could not come at him. In his own house he may be a little more relaxed. In any case, we cannot stand against open attack. A quick strike, a guard or two killed, and ride like hell; that's the only kind of chance we have."

"True." Nira had dressed in her own clothes again; they were about to leave the tent when Nira laid her hand on Kindra's arm, detaining her. "Why must we have the Lady Rohana with us? She rides but poorly; she will be no use at all in a fight—she hardly knows which end to take hold of a knife—and if she is recognized we are all dead women. Why did you not demand that she wait for us at Carthon? Or is she like those men who hire a watchdog and do their own barking?"

"I thought so myself at first," Kindra said, "but the Lady Melora must be warned, and ready to leave with us at a moment's notice; the slightest delay could ruin us all. The Lady Rohana can reach her mind, without warning Jalak, or rousing his suspicions as even the most cautious message could do." Kindra grinned wryly in the darkness of the tent. "Besides, which of you wants the task of caring for a pregnant woman on the journey back? None of us have much taste for it—nor any skill should she need nursing. Or do you want to try?"

Nira laughed ruefully. "Avarra and Evanda forbid

it! I stand reproved!" she said, and went to join the other women around the fire. After a moment Kindra went to join them, taking the plateful of food they had saved her (it was cold by now, but she ate without noticing), listening to the women talking softly as they cleared away the dishes, set a watch. Mentally, she checked them over.

She had handpicked this group from volunteers, and with all of them except the young girl Gwennis, she had worked before. Nira, who could pass as a man when she must, and had even, only the Blessed Cassilda knew how, learned to use a sword. *Against Dry-Towners we may need it.* By the Charter of the Guild of Free Amazons, it was not lawful for any Amazon to bear a sword. *Too threatening to the men of the Domains, for women to play with their precious toys!* Yet that law was not always honored; Kindra felt no guilt that she had allowed Nira to teach the others what she could of handling a sword. Then there was Leeanne, who had been neutered at fourteen and looked like a slim boy: breastless, hard-bodied and spare. Another who had known the neutering operation—which was illegal, but still turned up sometimes as a *fait accompli*—was Camilla, born of a good family in the Kilghard Hills; she did not use her family name Lindir, for they had long disowned and disinherited her. Camilla was nearing middle age, and like Kindra, had spent most of her life as a mercenary fighter; she was scarred with multiple knife-scars. Also Kindra had chosen Lori, who had been born in the Hellers and fought with two knives, mountain style; and Rafaella, Kindra's own kinswoman. Not all the Free Amazons were fighters, of course, but for this mission Kindra had chosen, mostly, the best fighting women she knew. Then there was Devra, who was not a great fighter, but skilled beyond anyone Kindra had ever known at reading the trackless lands of mountain or desert, so that Kindra had chosen her, warning her to keep out of any close-quarters fighting. And Fat Rima, who was altogether feminine in appearance and manner, and so heavy she could ride only the biggest horses; but Kindra knew she was skilled at making and managing a campsite, and their comfort was valuable, too, on a trip like this; and like all Amazons, Rima was completely able to defend herself. *And she has other skills that may be needed before we reach Thendara!* Kindra reflected. Then there was the girl Gwennis, and Lady Rohana.

Anyone who knew the Free Amazons, Kindra thought, could tell at once that the Lady was not one of them: her walk, her speech, her riding. But there was no one here, the Goddess be praised, who knew that much about them!

They had finished putting away the supper gear; Kindra surrendered her empty bowl, to be scrubbed with sand by Fat Rima. Rafaella brought out her small *rryl* and laid it across her knees, striking a preliminary chord or two. "Kindra, will you sing for us?"

"Not tonight, Rafi," she said, smiling to soften the refusal. "I have plans to make; I'll listen to the rest of you."

Devra began a song, and Kindra sat with her head in her hands, her mind not on the music. She knew she could trust every one of these women with her life. Lady Rohana was an unknown, but she had more reasons than the others to work at Kindra's command. The others had all volunteered; partly, at least, because like every Free Amazon from Dalereuth to the Hellers, they hated the Dry-Towners with a deadly hatred. The Domains themselves had made an uneasy peace with the Dry Towns, and kept it; there was no love lost between Domains and Dry Towns, but there was a bitter memory of the long wars they had fought, without any conclusive victory on either side. The Domains might accept the present state of truce out of political expediency; and their women with them. *The Domains live under men's laws. They accept the enslavement of the Dry-Town women because it pleases them to think how benevolent, by contrast, they are to their own*

women. They say all men must choose their own life-
styles.

But no woman who had ever cut her hair and sworn
the oath of a Free Amazon would ever accept that
compromise!

Kindra had early freed herself from a life that now
seemed to her as enslaved, as weighted with invisible
chains, as that of any Dry-Town woman who walked in
her ornamental bracelets and fetters of possession; she
felt that any woman who truly chose, and would pay
the price, could do as much. *Yes, even the women of
the Dry Towns.* Yet, for all her lack of sympathy for
any woman who bowed her head to a man's yoke, she
felt a surge of hatred and loathing for the men who
perpetuated this kind of slavery.

Should I tell them my plans now? She raised her
hand and listened. Lady Rohana, who had a sweet,
small, untrained voice, and Gwennis, who had a very
light, true soprano, were singing a riddle-song from the
Domains. Kindra decided not to disturb them. *Let
them have a night's undisturbed sleep first.* "Set good
watch around the camp," she said. "Some of these
Dry-Towners may have ideas about how Free
Amazons might like to spend their nights, and I doubt
we'd care for their notions."

Chapter
TWO

At high noon the marketplace of Shainsa lay sweltering under a direct sun, beating down on the dry stone, the sun-bleached stone walls of houses and buildings that turned blind faces to the light.

In spite of the insults and jeers that the loafers of the streets had flung at the Free Amazons, their booth, a light woven-wicker affair intended for transport on horseback, had been doing a flourishing business all morning; the mountain-tanned leather commanded a good price in the Dry Towns, where few animals could be husbanded and leather and textiles were scarce. Their stock was vanishing, in fact, so quickly that Kindra was beginning to fret; if any happenstance delayed Jalak's return, and their wares for sale were exhausted, their lingering in the town might cause some suspicion. *Must I lay the groundwork for an accident to one of the pack animals?* she wondered. Then there was a stir in the marketplace, an almost visible murmuring of rumor, and idlers, passersby and children began to drift toward the great gates. *Jalak,* she thought. *It must be Jalak returning, nothing else could create so great a stir.*

Leaving the booth in the hands of Devra and Fat

Rima, she moved idly with the crowd toward the gates, Rohana at her side. She muttered, in a tone that could not be heard six inches away, "Now, if ever, you must get a message through to your kinswoman. Tell her to be alert to move at a moment's notice; we may have only a few minutes to strike and we must take it when the occasion offers. It will not be until after nightfall; thereafter, she must be ready. Also, find out precisely where she sleeps, and if she is guarded and by how many; and where her daughter sleeps, alone or with other royal daughters."

Rohana leaned against the Free Amazon's arm, feeling suddenly sick and faint with the enormous responsibility. Now it was suddenly all on her shoulders. Someone jostled them; Kindra glared, steadied Rohana on her feet and the jostler flung a jeering phrase at them that made the Comyn woman blush with indignation, more for Kindra's sake than her own. She knew the Free Amazons were often accused of being lovers of women; she supposed some of them were. Yet all Kindra's kindness to her had been entirely impersonal, almost motherly, and Rohana felt a surge of anger that Kindra should suffer such insult on her behalf. *How absurd to be thinking of that now! As if I—or Kindra— could possibly care what some Dry-Town nothing thought of either of us!*

There was a blare of horns, a strange, hoarse fanfare. First came a dozen of his guards, in trappings so alien to Rohana as to make little impression on her except the general one of rude splendor: sashes and baldrics, elaborately gilded tunics, high headdresses. Then *cralmacs,* furred and tailed humanoids with great gold-colored eyes, wearing only their own fur and elaborate jeweled sashes, riding on the great shambling *oudhraki* of the far deserts: a legion of them, it seemed. More guards, less elaborately and ceremonially dressed this time, but armed with the long, straight swords and daggers of the Dry-Towners. Rohana thought, *Just as well that Kindra's band did not try to strike him encamped by night.* And then came Jalak himself.

Rohana had to turn away before she had more than a sight of his thin, hawk-keen face, sun-bleached under thick pale hair, fierce bristling mustachios; there were times when it seemed to her that so immense a force of hatred *must* somehow communicate itself to his object, that he could not fail to be aware of her thoughts. Rohana, a telepath since girlhood, lived with that as reality; but Jalak seemed impervious, riding amid his guards with a set, impassive face, looking neither to left nor right.

Near him rode—she supposed—a couple of his favorites, slaves or concubines; a slim girl with lint-white hair, chains jeweled, her body muffled in a scant fur smock, but her long legs bare to the fierce sun; she leaned toward Jalak and murmured and cooed to him as they passed. On Jalak's other side a thin, elegant boy, a pretty minion: too curled, too jeweled and perfumed to be anything else.

Behind Jalak and his favorites rode an assembly of women, and among them, outstanding for her flamered hair (now, streaked faintly with gray), rode Melora. Rohana felt faint. She had been prepared for this; Melora had come to her in thought. But seeing her like this, in the flesh, changed beyond recognition (*And yet, Cassilda pity us, I would have known her anywhere, anywhere* . . .), Rohana felt that her pain and pity would overwhelm her and she would sink down, fainting.

Kindra's hand closed painfully on Rohana's arm, the nails digging into the flesh; Rohana recalled herself. This was her part in the rescue, the thing only she could do. Deliberately, she reached out and made contact with her kinswoman's mind.

—*Melora!*

She felt the shock, the start and flutter. She was suddenly afraid lest Melora should see her, make some sign of recognition.

—*Betray nothing; do not look for me or try to see me, darling, but I am near you, among the Free Amazons.*

—*Rohana! Rohana, is it you?*

But Rohana, from her place in the crowd, saw—and felt a sudden, fierce pride in her kinswoman—that Melora rode on without making any visible sign; her eyes fixed, apparently, on nothing; slightly slumped in her saddle; the taut, thin, careworn face beneath the graying red hair showing nothing but weariness and pain. Suddenly Rohana was struck with fear and compunction. She thought, *She is so heavy, so near her time, the child weighs on her so. How can we possibly get her away in safety?* She sent the concerned question.

—*Can you ride, Melora, can you travel, so far in pregnancy?*

The answer was almost listless. —*It is easy to tell you do not know the Dry Towns; I would be expected to ride even closer to my time than this.* Then the answering thoughts were fierce with hate. —*I can do what I must! To be free I would ride through hell itself!*

Painstakingly, then, bit by bit, Rohana relayed Kindra's message; received Melora's answer, even while the caravan passed on, passed by the marketplace. At the rear came a few more guards, who indifferently tossed small coins, copper rings, wrapped fruits and sweetmeats into the crowd, watching with dead eyes, as the beggars scrambled for them. Kindra and Rohana, not staying to watch the painful spectacle, turned back toward their booth. Once safely inside it, Rohana relayed the information she had received.

"Jalak sleeps in a room at the north side of the building, with his favorites of the moment, and Melora; not that he has any interest, at the moment, in sharing her bed; not so she told me; but at the moment she is his most prized possession, bearing his son, and he will not let her out of his sight. There are no guards within the room, but there are two guards, and two *cralmacs* armed with knives, in the antechamber. Until this last pregnancy, Jaelle—that is her daughter—slept in her mother's room; now she has been moved to a room in the suite set apart for the other royal daughters. She complained that the noise the little ones made kept her from sleeping; Jalak is indulgent with girl-children if they are pretty ones, and allotted her a room to her own use, with a nurse there. It is at the far end of the royal children's suite, and looks out on an inner courtyard filled with blackfruit trees."

She anticipated Kindra's next question, saying, "I have the plan of the building so clear in my mind that I could draw it for you from memory."

Kindra laughed and said, "Truly, Lady, you would make a Free Amazon someday! Perhaps it is our loss that you did not choose our way, after all." She went to the women still in the booth, saying in an undertone, "Sell what you can; but what cannot be sold by nightfall, be prepared to abandon. Do not strike the booth; if we leave it standing they will expect us to be here come morning. Be sure the horses we used as pack animals are ready to be saddled for Melora and her daughter. . . ."

That afternoon seemed endless to Rohana. The worst of it lay in that she must behave exactly as usual—or at least as near to usual as was possible for her, here in the Dry Towns, far from her accustomed ways of occupying herself. She tried not to fidget visibly, knowing it would only disturb the Amazons, who seemed quite calm, selling their wares, tending their animals, idling around the camp. And yet, as the afternoon wore on, it seemed to her that she could see small signs that they were not, after all, quite so indifferent as they seemed to the coming battle. Camilla sat cross-legged at the back of the booth, sharpening her great knife to a razor edge, whistling an odd, tuneless little melody that, after a time, began to set Rohana's teeth on edge. Kindra sat drawing patterns again and again in the sand and quickly rubbing them out again with the toe of her boot. Rohana wondered how Melora was passing the time, but resisted the temptation to follow her in thought. If Melora could take some rest before sunset, let her do so, by all means!

How will she travel? She looks not more than three days from her time—if so much!

Slowly, slowly, the great red sun declined toward the hills. It seemed to Rohana that no day in her lifetime had worn away so wearily, with every hour stretching into lifetimes. *Not even the day my second son was born, when I seemed to lie for hours stretched on a rack of pain tearing me asunder . . . even then, something could be done. Now I can only wait . . . and wait . . . and wait. . . .*

Kindra said quietly, as she passed, "This day must seem longer still for your kinswoman, Lady," and Rohana tried to smile. That, at least, was true.

"Pray to your Goddess that the Lady Melora does not go into labor this day," Kindra said. "That would be the end of hope. We might still rescue her daughter, but if the Great House was ablaze with lights, midwives running here and there to attend to her . . . even that would be made more difficult than we could manage."

Rohana drew a deep breath of apprehension. *And she is so near to her time. . . .*

She tried to form, in her heart, a prayer to the Blessed Cassilda, Mother of the Seven Domains; but her prayer seemed to hang on the dead air, waiting, like everything else. . . .

And yet, as all things mortal must, even the day wore to an end. The Dry-Town women, veiled and chained, came to buy water at the well, and again they lingered, fascinated even through their scorn, to watch the Amazons moving about, tending their horses, cooking their meal. Rohana offered what help she could; it was easier if her hands were busy. She watched the Dry-Town women come and go in the marketplace, thinking of Melora, her hands weighted by the jeweled chains, her body weighted with Jalak's hated child. *She had been so light and quick, as a girl, so frolicsome and laughing. . . .*

They finished their meal, and Kindra signaled to Rafaella to take her harp, strike a few chords. She said in an undertone, "Come in close, and listen; act as if you were only listening to the music."

Rohana asked in a low voice, "Can you play 'The Ballad of Hastur and Cassilda'?"

"I think so, Lady."

"I will sing it. It is very long, and my voice," she added, with a self-deprecating smile, "is not so strong that anyone passing by would think it odd if you kept very quiet to listen to me—but not so soft that Kindra cannot talk more softly still, and be heard."

Kindra nodded, pleased at Rohana's quick comprehension of her plan. Rafaella played a short introduction, and Rohana began, hearing her own voice wavering:

> "The stars were mirrored on the shore,
> Dark was the dim enchanted moor;
> Silent were field and tree and stone. . . ."

The other women clustered in close, as if to listen to the ancient ballad; Rohana heard her own voice falter, fought to steady it. She must somehow collect herself to remember all the seemingly endless verses, string it out while Kindra gave soft, detailed instructions to every one of the Amazons. *Get hold of yourself,* she ordered and commanded herself: *This is something you can do, while they do the real work . . . the dangerous work, the fighting. . . .*

Yet they are women. I learned to think fighting was for men; I could never carry a knife, strike, see blood flow, perhaps suffer wounding, die. . . .

Sing, damn you, Rohana! Stop thinking, sing.

> "He lay thrown up along the shore,
> The sands were jeweled evermore,
> And to the shore Cassilda came
> And called him by a mortal name. . . ."

Struggling to remember the next lines, she heard Kindra, in a low, tense voice, detailing the information she had been given, pointing to the pattern she had scratched in the sand by firelight.

"Jalak sleeps here, with his favorites and Melora; there are no guards in the room, but just outside . . ."

> "Cassilda wept and paled and fled,
> Camilla knelt and raised his head,
> He left his high immortal fire
> For mortal man's entranced desire;
> White bread and wine and cherries red . . .

"—No, damn it, I skipped a verse," she said, breaking off in vexation, then realized it did not matter; no one was listening anyway.

> "Brought by her doves through morning bright,
> Camilla came, and bowed her head;
> He ate and drank by mortal light;
> And as his brilliance paled away
> Into a dimmer earthly day
> Cassilda left her shining loom:
> A starflower in his hand she laid;
> Then on him fell a mortal doom. . . ."

"Are the windows accessible by ladders?" asked Gwennis, and Kindra snapped, "They might be, if we *had* ladders. Next question, but no more stupid ones, please! We have time to kill, but not *that* much time!"

> "Into the heart of Alar fell
> A splinter from the Darkest Hell,
> And madness raging on him came,
> He cried again on Zandru's name,
> And at the darkened forge he made
> A darkly shining magic blade;
> An evil spell upon it cast. . . ."

"Devra and Rima, you will stay here, and the moment we come in sight, get moving! Be sure that the guards at the gate make no outcry. . . ." Kindra looked meaningfully at Rima.

The fat woman laid a hand on her knife, with a grim

nod. Kindra said, "Camilla, you ride lighter than any
of us; you will carry the child on your saddle. Lady
Rohana—*no, go on singing!* You must be ready to ride
close to Melora, to be alert for anything she needs; we
shall all be busy enough evading pursuit and dealing
with anyone who might come after us."

Rohana felt a shudder take her, seize her body and
shake it like a rabbithorn in the grip of a wolf. Her
voice faltered; she tried to cover it with a cough, and
doggedly went on, knowing she was garbling the words
horribly:

> "He could not see the—something—plan
> That gave a God to mortal wife,
> That earthly love with mortal man—
> Should bring to man a—something—life,
> Camilla fell without a cry—"

*Damn, damn, I've skipped two whole verses
again. . . .*

> "And Hastur, shielded by her heart,
> Knew he could die as mortals die. . . ."

"Lori, you handle the *cralmacs;* I understand you
know how they fight. Those long blades . . . anything
else? Leeanne?"

"Remember that sometimes the Dry-Towners poison
their swords. Don't neglect even a scratch. I've got
some ointment that is supposed to neutralize their
worst poisons. . . ."

> "Then Hastur son of Light had known,
> (For so had ruled the Shining Sire
> When first he left the Realm of Fire)
> Once more his star must burn alone . . .
> For on the earth he might not reign
> If he should cause one mortal pain,
> Or in that hour he must return
> To the far realms that were his own. . . ."

"We'll never be readier than now," Kindra said softly. "Finish the damn song, Rafaella, and get your dagger."

Gratefully Rohana began the last verse:

"And ever more the cloud waves break
Along the fringes of the lake,
And tears and songs still whisper there
Upon the still and misty air. . . ."

It was an unnerving experience, knowing they were all listening now, but impatient of every note, eager for her to finish. *Damn it, no more eager than I!*

"They built a city in the wild,
Fit for his rule, the kingly child,
And singing of Camilla's doom
They wrought for her an opal tomb."

She skipped the little postlude and rose impatiently, letting Rafaella put her harp away. Earlier in the afternoon she had packed the few possessions she had brought on this journey into a small bundle. Inside the tent the Amazons moved quickly and efficiently by the light of a single shaded candle, stowing food and necessary belongings in their saddlebags. Rohana watched, keeping out of their way. Devra and Fat Rima moved away toward the city gates, and Rohana felt another shudder take her; their business was to assure that those gates would be unguarded when they came back this way in a hurry, fleeing. . . .

Don't be squeamish! The guards there are Dry-Towners; they've probably deserved death a dozen times over. . . .

But they have no quarrel with any of us! There must be some good men among them, who have done nothing more than live as their forefathers have lived for centuries. . . .

Angry at herself, Rohana stifled the thought. *I hired Kindra's band to get Melora and her child away. Did I really believe it could be done without bloodshed? You cannot take hawks without climbing cliffs!*

Kindra beckoned the red-haired woman to her side. She said in an undertone, "I had thought to leave you here with these; but we shall need you, in case your kinswoman must have help—or reassurance. Come with us, Lady, but look to yourself if there is fighting; none of us will have time or thought to protect you, and Jalak's men may think you one of us and attack. Have you any kind of weapon?"

"I have this," Rohana said, showing the small dagger she carried, like all Comyn women, for personal protection. Kindra looked at it, trying to conceal her scorn. "It would be small service in a fight, I fear. But if we fail—I do not think we will fail, but nothing in this world is absolutely certain but death and next winter's snow—if we fail, at least it will keep you from falling alive into Jalak's hands. Are you prepared for that, *vai domna?*"

Rohana nodded, hoping the Amazon could not see that she was trembling. And again it flickered fleetingly through her mind, as had happened more than once during the twenty days she had been in their company, that perhaps Kindra had some small spark of psi power, that she followed Rohana's thoughts a little more than might happen by chance, for the Amazon's hard-boned hand descended briefly on her shoulder; only for a moment, a light touch, and hesitant, lest the noblewoman angrily refuse her sympathy. "My Lady, do you think none of us is afraid? We have not learned not to fear; only to go on in the face of fear, as women are seldom taught to do on our world." She turned away, her voice brusque again in the darkness. "Come along. Nira: to the front, you know the way step by step, we know it only from my Lady's drawings and maps."

Thrust to the rear of the small group of women, Rohana followed, hearing her pounding heart, so strongly it seemed to her that the thumping must almost be audible in the dusty, deserted streets. They moved like ghosts, or shadows, keeping in the lee of buildings, stealing along on noiseless feet. Rohana wondered where they had learned to move so silently, found she was afraid to speculate. For a panic-stricken moment she wished she had never begun this, that she were safe at home in Castle Ardais, on the borders of the Hellers. She wondered how her children fared without her, how the cousin who had managed her estates after her husband's death a few years ago was dealing with the business, what was happening far away in the mountain country. *This was never any place for me. Why did I ever come here? War, revenge, rescue, these are matters for men!*

And the men were content to let Melora pine away and die, captive! She hardened her resolve and stole along at the rear of the little column, trying to pick up her feet and put them down as silently as the Amazons, not to stumble against a chance stone.

The city was a labyrinth. And yet it was not very long before the women in front of her stopped, drew close together in a knot, seeing across an open, windswept square the loom of the Great House where Jalak of Shainsa ruled. The house was a great squared building of pale bleached stone, glimmering faintly by the light of a single small gibbous moon: a blind windowless barrack, a fortress, the two doors guarded by tall guards in Jalak's barbarous livery. Silently the Amazons turned, slipping through the shadows and along the side of the building. Rohana had heard Kindra's plan, and it seemed to her a good one. Every outside door into a Dry-Town house was guarded; against direct attack at the doors a couple of guards could hold it indefinitely. But if they could somehow get through the small side gateway into the courtyard, make their way through the garden—hopefully deserted, at this hour—and get into the house through the unguarded *inside* doorways, they might get into Jalak's chamber.

She had heard Kindra say, through her singing, "Our best hope is that there has been peace in the Dry

Towns for many moons. The guards may be bored, not as alert as usual."

She could see the guard at the side gate now. *Evanda be praised, no more than one.* He lounged against the wall; Rohana could not see his face, but she was a telepath, and even unsought, his thoughts were clear enough: boredom, dullness, the sense that he would welcome anything, even armed attack, to relieve the monotony of this watch.

"Gwennis." Kindra murmured. "Your move."

(When this plan had been put forward, Gwennis had protested, sullenly. "Does it have to be me?" and Kindra had said, "You're the prettiest.") Now there was no protest, the band's discipline held. As Gwennis deliberately scuffed a stone loose against the wall, Rohana felt the Amazon leader thinking, *This is the worst moment of risk. . . .*

The guard straightened, alert to the noise.

He's alert, we can't take him unawares; so we have to get him away from the gate, get him out into the center of the square, Kindra thought.

Gwennis had swiftly divested herself of knife and dagger, torn her tunic slightly down the front. She sauntered out into the moonlit square, and the guard was instantly alert, then relaxed, seeing a woman alone.

We are taking advantage of him, yes. Of the centuries-old Dry-Town contempt for women as helpless, harmless chattels. Victims, Kindra reflected bitterly.

The guard did not hesitate more than half a minute before stepping away from his post at the door, moving purposefully toward the young girl. "Hey, pretty thing—are you lonely? One of the Amazons, huh? Have you got tired of them and come looking for some better company?"

Gwennis did not raise her eyes. Rohana had heard the argument about that, too. ("I won't seduce him to his death. If he minds his own business he is safe. I won't use a feminine trick.") But the guard had already left his post, and Gwennis' silent indifference to him had provoked his curiosity; he came swiftly toward her, saying, "Ha—caught you without that knife you wear all the time, huh? Now you'll see what it's like really to be a woman. Who knows, you might even like it better. Here, come here and let me show you a thing or two. . . ." He reached for the girl, roughly pulled her against him, spun her around, one hand covering her mouth to stifle a cry . . . his words broke off in a strangled gasp. Lori's long knife, thrown with deadly accuracy, went straight into his throat. A moment later Lori herself bent over him, delivering a swift, fatal death-stroke to the great vein below his ear. Kindra and Camilla dragged him into the shadow of the wall, out of sight of any chance passerby; Gwennis scrambled up, fastidiously wiping her mouth as if she could wipe away the guard's rude touch. Kindra rummaged at the dead man's belt, found his keys and began to try them one by one in the heavy lock. *Locked on the outside, not within. Less against invaders than against the escape of one of his women. . . .*

The lock was stiff; it seemed to Rohana, quaking in the quiet street, that it creaked loudly enough to alarm the whole town, but after a moment it gave and the door swung noiselessly inward. The band of Amazons crowded inside, shrinking against the inner wall, pushing the door closed.

They stood in a quiet and deserted garden. Here in the Drylands little grew unless it was planted, except thornbush; but Jalak, tyrant of Shainsa, had spared no expense to create an oasis for himself and his pampered women and favorites. A multitude of fountains splashed, tall trees towered overhead, flowers grew in lush profusion, with a sweet, damp, rank smell. On silent feet, guided by the sketch Rohana had made after the rapport with Melora, the women threaded their way along the bricked pathway, and paused in the shadow of a grove of blackfruit trees.

"Leeanne," Kindra whispered.

As the slender, sexless figure moved away toward, Rohana knew, the chamber where Melora's twelve-year-old daughter slept with her nurse, Rohana found herself wondering incongruously how a neutered Amazon thought of herself. *Not as a woman, surely. A man? Some indefinable third thing?* She dismissed the thought impatiently. *What nonsense to be thinking about now!*

They moved toward the unguarded garden door; a moment later they were actually inside. Rohana, moving now from memory of her rapport with Melora, began to move directly toward the guarded room where Jalak slept.

Was Melora awake, alert for them, expecting them? All this afternoon she had resisted the temptation to reach out for telepathic contact with her cousin, but now she yielded; reached for rapport, more easily as the long-neglected skill came back.

—*Melora, Melora!* And suddenly, in a half-forgotten sensation of blending and merging, she *was* Melora, she . . .

. . . She lay silent, facing the wall, every muscle tense and alert, willing herself to relax, be patient, wait. . . . In her body the heavy child kicked sharply, and she thought, with weary patience, *You are so strong and lusty, little son, and, Avarra pity me, I have not even the heart to wish you more like to die. It is not your fault but your ill fortune that you are Jalak's son.* . . .

Will it truly be tonight? And the guards . . . how, how? The memory that had been with her, night and day, for ten years now of her foster-brother Valentine, broken, writhing, his fingers cut from his living body, covered in blood, after atrocities too many and too dreadful to think about. . . . *Oh, Evanda and Avarra, Aldones, Lord of Light, not Rohana, too.* . . .

No! I must not remember that now! I must be strong. . . .

Painstakingly, muscle by muscle, she forced herself to relax.

Jalak slept now, deeply: the first, sated sleep of the night. Beyond him she saw, by the dim moonlight from the courtyard window, the pale forms of the two favorites who shared his bed. They, too, slept; Danette—pale, nude, her long scattered hair enfolding her; Garris snoring a little, lying on his back, folded against Jalak's long body. At first this had infuriated and humiliated her to silent tears and passionate rebellion; after ten years she was only wearily relieved that *she* need no longer share his bed. During these months while she carried his son, Jalak, proud, and as near to kindness as he ever came, had yielded good-naturedly to her plea and allowed her to have a bed of her own, that she might sleep in peace and rest well. For years now she had been freed at night, like other Dry-Town women, from the chains she wore by day; only while she was still a rebellious prisoner had she been forced to wear them night and day. More than once, in that first faraway year, she had flown at his throat . . . ceasing only when she knew her furious resistance excited, amused, stimulated him. . . .

Poor Danette, how she hates me, how she gloated when she took my place in Jalak's bed, never guessing how willingly I would have resigned it years ago—and she hates my child worse than she hates me, she knows she is barren. If only I were. . . . I wish Garris no ill. His parents sold him in the brothels of Ardcarran when he was no older than Jaelle . . . he loves Jalak no more than I . . . perhaps less. Cruelly as the Dry-Towners treat their women, there are at least laws and customs to protect women to some degree, and not even such laws protect such as Garris. Poor little wretch . . . he still cries. . . . How slowly this night seems to pass. . . .

She stiffened, every nerve in her body alert. *What sound was that?* The next moment the door came crashing inward and it seemed all at once that the room was full of . . . *of women?* Jalak woke with a bellow, snatching up his sword where it lay ready, night and day, to his hand; he yelled for the guards . . . a yell that went unanswered. Already on his feet, he yelled again, naked, leaping at the first who came against him; they crowded him against the wall, and Rohana, seeing through her own eyes now—although she shared Melora's thought, *Where are the guards?*—saw the Amazons force him against the wall, saw him disappear behind what looked like a wall of women, slashing, darting in with their knives; saw the long ripping cut with which Kindra darted in, slashed, the tendons at the back of his knee. He fell, howling, struggling. Danette, wide-eyed, kneeling upright on the bed, shrieked.

"Garris! Garris! Get his sword! They're only women. . . ."

"Silence that bitch," said Kindra, and Camilla's rough hands muffled Danette's shrieks with a pillow. Garris sat upright, looking down at the writhing, howling Jalak with an unholy joy. . . . Rohana caught up a furred cloak from the foot of the bed, wrapped it over Melora's scanty nightgown. "Come—quickly!"

Guided between her kinswoman and the Amazon leader, Melora stumbled into the hall; her foot slipped in the blood of the guards who had been killed there. *Are they all dead? All?* Even Jalak's howls had stopped. *Dead, or unconscious from loss of blood?*

She saw through the still-open door that Garris had caught up Jalak's sword; Nira whirled, her own sword at the ready, but Garris rushed past them, not even looking at her, disappearing down the hallway, with—evidently—no thought in mind but his own escape.

Rohana hurried Melora along, out into the silent garden. It was so silent that it took her breath away; fountains splashed, trees rustled undisturbed in the wind, no sound or light to show that somewhere inside there in the Great House, eight or ten of Jalak's fighting men and perhaps Jalak himself lay dead.

None but Jalak himself had had opportunity to strike a single return stroke; but that single slash had gone to Nira's thigh and she limped, leaning heavily on Camilla's arm. Lori came and bent beside her, roughly wadding the wound with her kerchief, wrapping it hastily with the belt of her tunic. Leeanne came out of the darkness, carrying in her arms a small form in a long nightgown, barefoot. She set the little girl on her feet, and in the dim light Rohana caught a glimpse of a small, surprised, sleepy face.

"Mother—?"

"It's all right, my darling, they are my kinswomen and our friends," Melora said in a singing voice; she stumbled, and Kindra put a hand under her elbow.

"Can you walk, Lady? If not, we can carry you somehow—"

"I can walk." But Melora stumbled again and put out her hand to clutch at Rohana's arm, thinking, *For the first time in a dozen years I am outside that wall with unbound hands—walk? I could run, I could fly.* Hurrying along between them, stumbling, she lost track of where her steps were taking her. *Anywhere. Anywhere away from here. Like Garris. . . . Poor little creature, I hope they do not hunt him down for Jalak's murder. . . .*

She felt the knives of pain in her side and back, felt the weight of her unborn child dragging at her, not caring. *Free. I am free. I could die now, happy. But I must not die and delay them. . . .*

The deserted marketplace was a silent wilderness of empty stalls, deserted booths. Rima and Devra came out of the dark, near where the horses waited. "The gates are clear," Rima said, with a suggestive gesture—a finger drawn across her throat.

"Come, then. Leave everything but your own saddlebags and food for travel," Kindra said, leading Melora to a horse with a lady's saddle. "Before you mount, *domna,* get into these clothes; they may not fit well, but they will be better for riding than that nightgown."

Melora felt Rohana slip her gown over her head, under cover of the darkness; help her into the long, loose trousers, tie them around her waist; slip a fur-lined tunic over her head. The faint smell in their folds made her want to weep with recognition and thankfulness: the spices and incense used to sweeten the air in every home in the Domains. She caught back a sob, letting

Rohana help her to her saddle, slip suede boots—far too big—on her feet.

She looked around anxiously for Jaelle; saw that one of the Amazons had wrapped her in a cloak and lifted her to a saddle behind her, where she sat alert, amazed, her long straight hair streaming down her back, too excited and astonished even to ask questions.

Kindra took the reins of Melora's horse, saying, "Sit your horse as best you can, Lady; I will guide her." Melora clung to the saddle-horn (unfamiliar, after so many years, to ride astride again!) and watched, tensed against the pain of moving, as Kindra moved to the front of the little column of riders. She said in a low, tense voice, "Now ride like hell, all of you. We may have as many as five hours before the sun comes up and somebody finds Jalak in his blood; but we won't have more than that no matter how lucky we are, and from this day on for the next three dozen years, no Free Amazon's hide will be worth a *sekal* anywhere in the Dry Towns. Let's *go!*"

And they were off. Melora, clinging to her saddle, bracing herself as best she might against the jolting of her horse's gait (though she realized that Kindra had indeed provided a horse with an easy gait, the best available for a pregnant woman), looked back for an instant at the black loom of the walls of Shainsa.

It's over, she thought, *the nightmare is over. Thirteen years of it. Jalak lies crippled for life, hamstrung, perhaps dying.*

I hope he does not die. Worse, oh, worse for him to live and know that a pack of women has done this to him!

I am avenged, and Valentine! And Jaelle will live free!

They rode into the night, unpursued.

Chapter
THREE

To the end of her life, the Lady Rohana Ardais never forgot that mad ride, fleeing from the walls of Shainsa; alert at any moment for some small sound behind them that would mean Jalak—or his dead body—had been found, and the hunt for them was up.

For the first hour it was very dark, and she rode blindly after the sound of hooves from the other horses, with only dim shadows ahead. Then Kyrrdis rose, a brilliant half-circle above the horizon, so bright that Rohana knew it was not more than an hour or two ahead of the sun; and by its blue-green light she could make out the forms of the other horses and their riders.

They were traveling more slowly now. Even the swift horses from the plains of Valeron could not keep up the pace of those first hours. She wondered how Leeanne had found their road in the darkness; the Amazon's reputation as a tracker was evidently well-deserved. She could see Jaelle, a huddled, dark small form, collapsed in sleep against Camilla, clinging drowsily to the saddle. What did the child think of all this?

She was reared in the Dry Towns. Perhaps, to her, all this is quite normal: murder, midnight raids, the

stealing of women. What if her loyalty is to Jalak? Af-
ter all, he is her father.

None of us has any idea what Jaelle is like. . . . We
have thought only of Melora's wishes. . . .

Melora is a telepath. She must know her child's
heart. . . .

In the final hour before dawn they stopped to
breathe the horses; Leeanne went to the top of a
nearby hill to spy out any sign of pursuit. Rima came
and put some bread and dried meat into Rohana's
hand, poured wine into the cup at her saddle-horn.

"Eat and drink while you can, Lady. There won't be
much time for breakfast if we are being pursued.
There are a few hiding holes between here and Carthon,
and Kindra knows all of 'em, but mostly our safety lies
in a good long start. So you eat now."

Rohana chewed a mouthful obediently, although her
mouth was dry, and the stuff tasted like stale parch-
ment. She thrust it into a pocket of the unfamiliar
Amazon trousers; maybe later she could manage to
swallow it. She sipped at the wine, but it was too sour
to drink, almost; she rinsed her mouth and spat it out
again.

She led her horse slowly for several steps, hearing its
deep, panting breaths slowly quiet to normal; rubbed
its head absently, leaning against the warm, sweating
body. She thought, not for the first time since she had
undertaken this long journey, how fortunate it was that
she was hardened to long riding, hunting with hawks in
her distant mountain home. *If I were the kind of
woman who did little more than sit over her em-
broidery-frames, I would be half dead of saddle-sores.*
This made her think of Melora again (*How weary she
must be!*) and she made her way through the Amazon
crew: dismounting, slumped to rest, eating, talking in
low tones. She noted that Jaelle had been lifted down
and was sleeping heavily, curled up on someone's
cloak, and covered with another. *At least they seem to
be looking after her well. I do not suppose any of them
know much about children.*

She looked around for Melora, seeing that Kindra was helping her kinswoman out of the high saddle; but before she could approach them, Nira, the crude bandage loose around her thigh, intercepted her. "Can you dress this wound by moonlight, *domna?* It hinders my riding more than I thought, or I would wait for the light."

Rohana felt a moment's impatience; then, remembering that Nira's wound had been incurred in their service, felt ashamed of herself. "I'll try. Come here, away from the shadows, where the light is brightest." She rummaged in her saddlebag for the few items of women's gear she had brought, found a clean, unworn shift and tore it into strips. Like everything else it was gritty with the sand of the Dry Towns, but clean.

She had to cut the bandage, and then the trouser leg, away with a knife; it was stuck to the wound with clotted blood. Nira swore under her breath, but did not flinch as Rohana washed the ugly cut with the sour wine—*At least the stuff is good for something,* she thought—and bandaged it tightly, pressing the hard pad of bandage against the wound. "It should be stitched; but I cannot do that by moonlight. If it begins to bleed again, I will do what I can when it is light."

Nira thanked her. "Now, if that bastard Jalak doesn't poison his weapons—one hears such things of Dry-Town men—"

"He does not," Melora said quietly beside them, and Rohana rose, folding what remained of the torn shift, to see her cousin standing there. Her face was dim in the moonlight, but even so it looked swollen and unhealthy. "Jalak would think that a coward's way; it would mean he did not believe his blows were strong enough to kill, and he would lose *kihar*—lose prestige, you would say, be shamed before his peers, if he stooped to a poisoned blade."

Nira got up awkwardly, grimacing as she put weight on her wounded leg. Her boot crunched on sand as she drew it on. She said wryly, "That is a comforting thought, Lady, but is it fact, or is it a sentiment seemly for a loving wife?"

"It is true, on the honor of my House," said Melora quietly, but her voice trembled, "and only my own Gods know how little I was a loving wife to Jalak, or anything else but a pawn to his filthy pride."

"I meant no offense," Nira said, "but I make no apology either, Lady. You dwelt in his house a full thirteen years, and you did not die. I would not have lived to shame my kinsmen so, even though my father is no great Comyn lord but a small-farmer in the Kilghard Hills."

"You have shed blood in my service, *mestra;* could I take offense, unless my pride were as great and evil as Jalak's own? As for my own life—can you see in the darkness?" She thrust out her wrists, took Nira's fingers in her own and guided them. Rohana, watching, touching, saw and felt the rough callouses from the metal bracelets on the chains; and above them on each darkly tanned wrist, a long, ragged, seamed scar. "I will bear them to my death," she said. "And after that, I was chained day and night—chained so tight I could not feed myself and had to be fed by the women and carried to the bath and to the latrines." Her voice shook with anger and remembered humiliation. "By the time I had healed, my child had quickened in me, and I would not kill the unborn with my own death." She looked at the dark form of her daughter, huddled and lost in sleep, saying, "How did you get her away? Jalak had given her into the charge of his fiercest woman-guard. . . ."

Leeanne had come back from the hilltop in time to hear this last; she said: "There is no sign of pursuit so far; not even a sand-rat seems to be stirring between here and Shainsa. As for your daughter's nurse, Lady, she sleeps past any waking; I do not like to kill women, but she came at me with a dagger. I was sorry to kill her before the child's eyes, but I had little choice."

"I will not weep for that one," said Melora with a grimace. "Indeed I think there will be small weeping

for her, even in Jalak's house. She was my chief jailer
before Jaelle was born, and I hated her worse than
Jalak's own self. He was cruel because it was his
nature and he had been reared to be so; but she was
cruel because she found pleasure in the pain of others.
I trust Zandru will delight in her company in hell; to be
sure he will be the only one who has ever found such
pleasure. Had I ever been trusted with a weapon again,
even at table, I would have sunk it into her throat before turning it on myself." She turned to Rohana; for
the first time there was a moment to exchange a quick,
awkward embrace. *"Breda* . . . I am still not sure this
is no dream, that I will not waken in Jalak's bed."

With the touch of Melora's swollen hands in hers,
Melora's wet face pressed against her own, the rapport
wakened again; Melora's mind lay open to her, and
more: sharp physical discomfort, pain. Rohana thought,
panicked, *Can she ride? Will she go into labor here and
now, in the desert, far from help, delaying us . . . ?*

Gently, Melora loosed Rohana's hands and the contact lessened. "It is easy to see you know little of the
Dry Towns. May you never have cause to know more!
I would have been expected to ride, even nearer to my
time than this. Don't worry about me, *breda*." Her voice
broke in a sob. "Oh, it is so good, just to speak to you
in our own tongue. . . ."

Rohana was desperately uneasy about her; she was
not highly skilled in midwifery, but as mistress of
Ardais she had seen many births; she knew Melora
needed rest and care. But the Amazons, at Kindra's
signal, were already mounting again, and indeed there
seemed no choice.

Kindra came to inspect, briefly, Nira's bandaged
wound. "So far there is no sign of pursuit, but with
dawn someone will certainly find Jalak—or his corpse.
And I would greatly prefer not to fight Jalak's men, or
end my days chained in a Shainsa brothel."

Even in the dim light Melora's smile was perceptible. "It may be there will be no pursuit; most likely
Jalak's heirs have found him dead and are already

squabbling over his property and his wives, and the tenancy of the Great House. The last thing they would want would be to recapture a son of his with a valid claim!"

"Aldones grant it be so," said Kindra, "yet some kinsman of Jalak might seek *kihar* by avenging him— or some rival might want to make very sure any son with a valid claim did not survive him."

Melora gave Rohana's hands a convulsive squeeze, but her voice was calm. "I can ride as far as I must." Her eyes went to her sleeping daughter. "Can I have her with me on my own saddle?"

"Lady, you are heavy; your horse should not carry such a doubled weight," Kindra said. "Those of us who ride lightest will take turns to carry her, so that she can sleep a little longer. Can she ride? We have a spare horse for her, if she can sit alone on a saddle."

"She could ride almost as soon as she could walk, *mestra.*"

"That will do for when she wakes, then; for now, she can sleep," said Kindra, and lifted Jaelle, still sleeping, to her own saddle; she clambered up beside her, while Rohana assisted her cousin to mount. She was fearfully clumsy, and seemed unsteady in the saddle, but Rohana said nothing. There was nothing to say; Kindra was right and they both knew it. She gathered up her own reins, took the reins of Melora's horse to lead it onward across the desert.

Melora was gazing wistfully toward the sunrise. "At this hour, I always long for—oh, I don't know—some snow, or rain, anything but the eternal sand and hot dry wind."

Rohana said softly, "If the Gods will, *breda,* within a tenday you will be back again in our hills and see the snow at every sunrise." Melora smiled, but shook her head. "I can ride now, and guide my own horse, if you think it better."

"Let me lead it, for now at least," Rohana said, and Melora nodded and leaned back in her saddle, bracing herself as best she could against the motion of the beast.

The sun rose, and Rohana saw, as the miles went by under the feet of their horses, that the character of the land had changed. Flat, barren sand-desert had given way to low, rolling hills as far as the eye could see, and a low scruffy ground-cover of thorn-trees and gray feathery spicebush. At first the smell was pleasant, but after a few hours of riding through it, Rohana felt that if she ever again ate spicebread at Midwinter Festival it would choke her. Her throat was dry; she almost regretted the wine she had not been able to drink. Hour by hour Melora seemed more unsteady in her saddle, but she made no word of complaint. Indeed, she did not speak at all, riding head down, her face stony-gray with effort and patience.

As the sun climbed the light grew fiercer, and the heat. Some of the Amazons drew loose folds of their shifts or tunics over their heads; Rohana did likewise, finding the heat preferable to the direct glare. She was beginning to wonder how long Melora could continue to ride—and she herself was weary and saddle-worn almost to the point of dropping from her saddle—when Leeanne, riding ahead, turned back, held up her hand and called to Kindra, who rode quickly ahead to join her, while the others came to a gradual halt.

After a moment Kindra came riding back. "In the next ravine there is a water hole; and some rocks for shelter from the sun. We can lie there during the heat of the day." As they followed her along the path Leeanne indicated, Kindra dropped back to ride beside Rohana and Melora.

"How is it with you, Lady?"

Melora's attempt at a smile only stretched her mouth a little. "As well as I can hope for, *mestra*. But I don't deny I shall be glad to rest a little."

"So shall we all. I wish I could spare you this. But—" She sounded apologetic, and Melora gestured her to silence. She said, "I know perfectly well that you and yours have put your heads in jeopardy for me, and more. God forbid I should complain about whatever you must do for your safety and ours."

Something about the words made Rohana's breath catch in her throat. Melora had sounded, for a moment, almost precisely her old self: gracious, gentle, with the winning courtesy she had shown to her peers and inferiors alike. *She spoke as she would have spoken when we were girls together in Dalereuth. Merciful Evanda, is there really any hope that one day she will be herself again, live out her life happy and free?*

The water hole was a dull, glimmering sheet of water, less than twenty feet across; it looked pallid and unhealthy, but Kindra said the water was good. Behind it were a cluster of blackish-red, forbidding rocks, casting purple shadows on the sand, turning the omnipresent fluff of spicebush to a lavender shadow on the barren space. Even the shadow of the rocks made Rohana think more of snakes and scorpions than cool, inviting rest, but it was better than the burning glare of the Dryland sun at midday.

Rohana helped Melora to dismount, steadying her uneven steps. She guided her to a seat in the shadow of the rocks and went to lead her horse to the water, but Kindra stopped her. "Care for your kinswoman, Lady," she said, taking the bridles of their horses, and, lowering her voice, "How does she, really?"

Rohana shook her head. "So far, she is managing. There is really no more I can say." She knew perfectly well that anyone skilled in such matters would say that Melora should not ride at all. But Kindra knew that, too, and there was simply nothing to be done.

She said, "Are there any signs of pursuit?"

"So far, none," said Leeanne, and Jaelle, who had slid down from her horse, came up to them, and stopped, shyly, at a little distance. She said, "How do you know we are not pursued, *mestra?*" She spoke the language of the mountain country with a faint accent, but understandably; and Kindra smiled at the child.

"I hear no sound of hooves with my ear to the

ground; and there is no cloud of sand rising where men ride, within the distance my eyes can see."

"Why, you are as good as Jalak's best trackers, then," said the little girl in wonder. "I did not know that women could be trackers."

"Living in Shainsa, little lady, there is much you do not know about women."

Jaelle said eagerly, "Will you tell me, then?"

"Perhaps when I have time; just for now, do you know enough about horses to know that these must be watered, and cooled?"

"Oh, I am sorry—am I delaying you? Can I help, then?"

Kindra handed the small girl the reins of the horse Melora had ridden. "Walk him slowly back and forth, then, till his breathing quiets and the sweat is almost dry around his saddle. Then lead him to the water and let him drink what he will. Can you do that, do you think?"

"Oh, yes," said Jaelle, and walked off, holding the horse's reins. Kindra followed with Rohana's horse, and Rohana stood, looking after Jaelle. She seemed tall for her age, lightly built, with delicate bones, her hair flaming red, hanging halfway down her narrow back; she wore the nightgown in which she had been wakened—fine-spun Dryland linex, smoothly loomed and embroidered—although one of the Amazons had put a short jacket, much too big for her, around her shoulders. Her feet were bare, but she walked on the hot sand without apparent discomfort. Rohana could not see that the child resembled Melora, except for her flaming hair; but there was no discernible resemblance to Jalak, either.

She returned to Melora, who had stretched out her clumsy body on her riding cape, and closed her eyes. Rohana looked at her with disquiet, then composed her face hurriedly as Melora opened her eyes. "Where is Jaelle?"

"She is helping Kindra to water the horses," Rohana said. "Believe me, she's quite safe and well, and seems not over-wearied by the ride." Rohana lowered herself to the shade beside her cousin. "I wish I had even a little of her energy."

Melora stretched out her thin fingers, clasping Rohana's hand in hers as if hungry for the reassurance of the touch. "I can see how you have wearied yourself for me, too, cousin. . . . How came you into the company of these—these women? *You* have not deserted husband and children as they do . . . ?" The question was evident without words, and Rohana smiled in reassurance. "No, love. My marriage—as I knew it would be—is well enough: Gabriel and I are as happy as any other couple."

"Then how—"

"It is a long story," Rohana said, "and not easy in the telling. It seemed to me that everyone had forgotten you; I had all but forgotten myself, thinking you dead or—or resigned to your life." She added, half defensively, "It had been so long."

"Yes, a lifetime," said Melora with a sigh.

"When you came to me, at first I thought it a dream. I made the journey to Thendara and spoke to some of the Council; but they said they could do nothing, the time was not right for war with the Dry Towns, and they would send no others to die. I had all but resigned myself to thinking that nothing could be done, when by chance—or who knows, by the work of some Goddess—a little band of Free Amazons met with me on the road. They were hunters and traders, and had a mercenary soldier or two to protect them; and in talk with them, I learned that while their band did not venture into the Dry Towns, they knew of one who would. So I went to their Guild-house and spoke with Kindra; and she agreed to attempt the rescue. And so—"

"So here you are," said Melora, almost with wonder, "and here I am. It was true. I had resigned myself, and when I knew I bore Jalak's child again, and that child a son—I was ready to die." Her eyes went to her daughter; Jaelle had finished walking the horse, and was standing beside him as he drank from the water hole. "She is past twelve; at thirteen she would have been chained. I think if you had not come I would have killed her, somehow, and then myself. . . ."

Rohana saw the deep shudder that ran through her cousin's body. She put out her hand quickly to clasp Melora's. "It is past, love. All past. Now you can begin to forget."

Forget? While I bear Jalak's son? Melora did not speak the words aloud, but Rohana heard them anyway. She said very gently, "Well, for now you can rest, and you are free, and safe for the moment. Try to sleep, dearest."

"Sleep." Melora's smile was wry. "I cannot remember when I really slept last. And it seems a pity to sleep now, when I am with you again, and safe . . . and I am happy. . . . Tell me all the news of our kinfolk, Rohana. Does Marius Elhalyn still rule in Thendara? What of our people, our friends—tell me everything," she said yearningly, and Rohana had not the heart to silence her.

"That is a long story and would take many days and hours in the telling. Dom Marius died the year after you were taken; Aran Elhalyn keeps the throne warm from year to year, and as usual the Lord of Hastur is the true ruler; not old Istvan, he is senile, but Lorill Hastur, who was his heir. You recall that Lorill and his sister Leonie were with us at the Dalereuth Tower, when we were girls; I thought perhaps Lorill would move against Jalak for your sake—"

Melora sighed. She said, "Even I knew better than that; the Hasturs must think of more important things than the dues of kin, or how are they better than the Dry-Towners with all their feuds and little wars? There is peace otherwise?"

"Peace, yes . . . Lorill has brought the Terrans from Aldaran to Thendara; they are building a spaceport there, and he has defended his move before the Council; some of them fought it all the way, but Lorill prevailed, as the Hasturs usually do."

"The Terrans," said Melora, slowly. "Yes, I had

heard; men like us from another world, come on great
ships from the stars. Jalak told such tales only to laugh
at them; in the Dry Towns they do not know that the
stars are suns like ours, lighting worlds not unlike our
own, and Jalak loved to scoff at such tales and say
these so-called off-worlders must be clever rogues
indeed to fool the Seven Domains, but that no sensible
man from the Drylands would be caught so. . . ." She
shut her eyes, and Rohana thought, for a moment, that
she slept; and was grateful. Knowing that she, too,
should try to rest, she closed her eyes, but a shadow
fell across her face, and she opened them to see Jaelle
standing there, looking down at them. She said in a
whisper, "It is you who are my—our kinswoman, Lady
Rohana?"

Rohana sat up and held out her arms; Jaelle gave
her a quick, shy embrace. "How does my mother, kinswoman? Is she asleep?"

"Asleep; and very weary," said Rohana, rising
quickly to her feet. She drew the child away so the
sound of their voices would not disturb Melora.

"I will not waken her, but I wanted to see—" and
her voice trembled. Rohana looked down at the small
serious face, the wide green eyes.

Comyn, she thought; *she does not look like Melora,
but her Comyn blood is unmistakable. It would have
been wrong, entirely wrong, to leave her in Jalak's
hands; not only inhuman but wrong!*

Jaelle said, almost in a whisper, "She should not ride
now; the baby will be born so soon. . . ."

"I know that, dear. But we are not safe here, except
for a little rest. When we reach Carthon, we will be
back in Domain country; and out of Jalak's reach forever," Rohana said quietly.

"But—what will it do to her? The riding, the weariness—" Jaelle began hesitantly, then dropped her
eyes and looked away. Rohana thought, *Has she
laran?* Even in the telepath caste of the Comyn, the
Gift did not begin to show itself much before adolescence; a trained *leronis* could make educated guesses

about a child Jaelle's age, but it had been so long since Rohana had used her telepath training that she could not even guess about Jaelle. *Now, when I need to know, the Gift deserts me. . . . Why must women have to choose between the use of* laran *and all the other things of a woman's life?*

She looked down at Melora, wiped out in exhausted sleep, and thought of the time when they had been young girls together, in the Tower at Dalereuth, learning the use of the matrix jewels that transformed energies; working as psi monitors, in the relay nets that kept communications alive in the vast spaces of Darkover, learning the technology of the Seven Domains.

There had been three of them, all the same age: Rohana, and Melora, and Leonie Hastur, sister to that Lorill Hastur who ruled now behind the throne at Thendara. Rohana's family had insisted that she marry, and she had left her work in the Tower—not without regrets—and gone to marry the heir to the Ardais Domain, to supervise the great estate there, to bear sons and a daughter to that clan. Leonie had been selected Keeper; a telepath of surpassing skill, she was now in charge of the Tower at Arilinn, controlling all the working telepaths on Darkover. But Leonie had paid the Keeper's price; she had been forced to renounce love and marriage, living in seclusion as a virgin all her life. . . .

Melora had been given no choice. Jalak's armed men had seized her and carried her away to imprisonment and chains . . . rape and slavery and long suffering.

Rohana's weariness was giving her strange thoughts. *Did Jalak really change her life so much? Do any of us have choice, really? At our clan's demand, to share a stranger's bed and rule his house and bear his children . . . or to live isolated from life, in loneliness and seclusion, controlling tremendous forces, but with no power to reach out our hand to any other human being, alone, virgin, worshiped but pitied. . . .*

Jaelle's small hand touched hers lightly, and the little girl said, "Kinswoman . . . you are so white. . . ."

Rohana quickly returned to reality. She said matter-of-factly, "I have eaten nothing. And in a little while I must wake your mother and see that she eats something, too." She went with Jaelle to where the Amazons were sharing out food and drink; this time she diluted the wine with water from the well and found it sour but drinkable. Kindra went to look at the sleeping Melora and came back, saying, "She needs rest more than food, Lady; she can eat when she wakes," and looked at Jaelle, saying, "You will be sun-burned and saddle-sore if you try to ride in that night-gown, *chiya*. Gwennis, Leeanne, Devra, you are small-est, can you find the little one some clothes?"

Rohana was surprised and warmed to see how im-mediate the response was; all but the tallest of the women went at once to their saddlebags, searching, sharing out what they had: an undervest here, a tunic there, a pair of trousers (Leeanne's, and even these had to be rolled up almost to the knees). Camilla, whose feet were slender, brought out a pair of suede ankle boots, saying, "They will be too big, but laced tightly, they will protect her while she is riding and keep her feet from the sand and thornbushes." They were embroidered and dyed, evidently her own holiday gear, and Rohana was more surprised than ever; a neuter, she would have thought, could hardly have maternal feelings.

Jaelle let Rohana undress her and clothe her in the strange garments, looking around hesitantly toward her mother but forbearing to disturb her. She did say shak-ily, as Rohana belted in the bulky long trousers, and began to lace up the pretty, dyed-leather boots, "I have always been told it is not seemly for a woman to wear breeches, and—and, I am *almost* old enough to be called a woman."

"Better breeched than bare, Jaelle," Rohana said, adding more gently, "I know how you feel. Before I came on this journey, I believed nothing could force me to wear breeches and boots, but necessity is stronger than custom; and, as for seemliness—well, you cannot ride in that tattered nightgown with your bare haunches in the wind."

Camilla came and checked the fit of the boots. "If they are too loose and make blisters, child, tell me and I will find an extra pair of thick stockings. How do women manage to ride in the Dry Towns, little lady?"

"The saddle is made like this"—Jaelle demonstrated—"so that a woman can sit sidewise and her skirts are not disordered."

"And will slip and fall if her horse stumbles," said Gwennis, "while I can ride as fast and far as any man, and I have never had a fall. But in the Domains, little one, you can wear those clumsy riding-skirts your kinswoman prefers to wear."

"Clumsy they may look," Rohana retorted, "yet I ride well enough in them that I can hunt with hawks in the mountains; in a bad season, when the men cannot spare time for the hunt, the little children or sick people have never had to go without birds or small game for their table, riding-skirts or no; I ride as well in them as in these." *And I wish I were wearing them now*, she thought, but knew the Amazons would have had small sympathy for that.

Gwennis ran her hand along Jaelle's long tangled hair. "It is a pity it should snarl so."

Jaelle's eyes filled with tears; she looked up at Rohana's cropped head and said, "Do you have to cut it?"

Rohana said firmly, "No indeed. But let me comb and braid it tight, so it will not tangle while you ride." She made Jaelle sit down and began to comb the waist-length, fire-red hair. She felt again a pang at the thought of her own hair, which had been her pride, her one claim to beauty. *Gabriel will be angry when he sees my hair, hacked short like an Amazon's.* She thought defensively, as if answering her husband, *I had no choice, it was for Melora's sake.* But Jaelle's should not be sacrificed.

Kindra came and looked at Jaelle, dressed in the too-large odds and ends of Amazon garb, but she made no comment. She drew Rohana aside for a moment and said, "Do not tell the child, and do not disturb your kinswoman, but there is a small cloud of dust at the horizon. It probably has nothing to do with us—it is not in the direction of Shainsa, from which pursuit would come; but I must warn my women, and you, Lady, should be wary."

"Should we be ready to ride again?"

Kindra shook her head. "No. In the heat of the day we dare not; we would die of heat prostration as painfully as on a Dry-Towner's sword. We will hide ourselves among the rocks and hope that this dust has nothing to do with us, or with Jalak and his men; sleep if you can, Lady, but stay near to Melora and the little one, and caution her, if she wakes, to stay hidden in the shadow of the rocks." She signaled to Devra and Rima, saying, "I shall set you two on watch; Leeanne and I have been leading and tracking all the night, and Nira has lost enough blood that she needs rest. But call me at once if that dust seems to turn in our direction. Lady, go now and try to sleep. And you too, *domnina,*" she added to Jaelle.

"May I bring my bread and finish it before I sleep?" Jaelle asked, and Kindra said, "Of course," as she went away to rest. Gwennis, reaching into her pocket, smiled at Jaelle and said, "Are you hungry, *chiya?* Here is a sweet for you; suck it before you sleep, and it will keep your mouth from getting too dry in this heat."

Jaelle accepted the candy with a small, shy inclination of her head. She looked around at the Amazons with curiosity—though Rohana could see that she was trying hard to repress it and, in politeness, ask nothing. At last she said to Gwennis, "Some of you look—almost like men. Why is that?"

Gwennis glanced at Rohana; then said, "Yes; Leeanne and Camilla. They have been neutered; their bodies are not actually those of women. There are some women who feel that womanhood itself is too great a burden to be borne, and choose this way, even though the laws forbid it."

"But you are not like that," Jaelle said, and Gwennis smiled.

"No, *chiya*. It is troublesome to be a woman, from time to time—I imagine you are old enough to know so much—but all in all, I think I would rather be a woman than not, even if it were easy or simple to find anyone, in these days, who will risk the laws against that sort of mutilation. All in all I find it more pleasure than trouble."

Rohana, too, had been curious about this; like all women reared in the protective, pampered world of the Domains, she had always thought—when she had thought about the Amazons at all, which was seldom—that they were mannish women, or plain girls such as would burden their families to find any sort of husband. But, except for the two neutered women, and the mountain tomboy with the two knives, none of them were anything like that. Kindra was gentle and almost motherly, as was Fat Rima; and the others seemed none too different, clothing and cropped hair apart, from her own waiting-women. As for Gwennis, she seemed almost like a little girl herself, not much older than Jaelle, or Rohana's own daughter.

Jaelle smiled at Gwennis and said, "You would be beautiful if you let your hair grow long."

It was Rohana's own thought. Gwennis said with a kindly smile, "Why, perhaps so, little sister, but why should I want to be beautiful? I am not a dancer, or an actress, or a lyric performer, that I should need so much beauty!"

"But if you were beautiful, you could make a good marriage," Jaelle said, "and you would not need to be a soldier or a hunter to earn a living."

"But, little one," said Gwennis, laughing, "I do not want to make a marriage, not even a good one."

"Oh?" Jaelle pondered this for a moment; it was easy to see that this was a new idea to her. "Why not?"

"For many reasons. Among others," she said deliberately, "lest I should find that my husband sought to keep me in chains."

Rohana felt it like a blow; Jaelle put her hand to her mouth and bit at the knuckle. Her face went white, then a desperate, agonized crimson. She made a small strangled sound, turned away and ran to her mother's side, flinging herself down on the blanket beside her and burying her head in her arms.

Gwennis looked almost as dismayed as the child. She said, "My Lady, I am sorry, I should not have said that."

Silently, Rohana shook her head. She said at last, "She had to know."

Suddenly Jaelle has realized what this is all about. Before this it has been an adventure, safe because her mother is here; but she has not truly understood. And now—now she knows.

And a shock like this, to a girl just on the threshold of womanhood ... a girl with extraordinary telepath potential ... Rohana was not sure just how she knew this, but she was sure of it. *What will it do to her?* Slowly, Rohana went and laid herself down in the shade beside Melora and Jaelle. Melora slept heavily. Jaelle's face was buried in the blanket, her thin shoulders trembling violently. Rohana reached out to draw her close, comfort her, as she would have done with one of her own children; but Jaelle resisted her stiffly, and after a moment Rohana let her be. *I am almost a stranger to her,* she thought in despair. *I can do nothing for her. Not yet.*

Chapter
FOUR

Three days and nights had passed, and Rohana had given up expecting pursuit or capture. If there had been pursuit at all, it had taken the wrong direction or been left hopelessly behind. Or else Melora was right, and Jalak's heirs, finding him dead or wholly disabled, were busily dividing up his remaining wives and his property.

Gradually the character of the land had changed: the first days had seen dry, burning, gritty sand, broken only by scruffy thornbushes and feathery spicebush; now there were endless, trackless leagues of low, rolling dunes, covered by grayish Dryland bracken, with now and again a sharp black outcrop of rock. *As if,* Rohana thought, recalling the old tale, *when Zandru made the Drylands, even the very rocks rebelled and broke through their cover, thrusting up in rebellion ... the very bones of the world refusing to be covered in these barren leagues of desert and sand. ...*

It was nearing twilight; the fierceness of the sun was tempered by the lengthening angle of the shadow. All that day they had seen no living thing, and Kindra had cautioned them to drink sparingly from their water-skins. "Should anything delay us," she had warned, with a sharp glance at Melora, "we might not reach the next water hole this night ... and we cannot carry too much in reserve."

Melora rode just ahead of her, head down, braced stiffly in her saddle. She had not spoken since they left the site of their noonday rest, and when Rohana would have felt her forehead for fever, she had turned away, refusing the touch, refusing even to meet Rohana's searching eyes. Rohana was desperately worried about her. This trip was far too long, far too arduous for any pregnant woman. Melora had not complained; Rohana had the chilling sense that she had ceased to care. She seemed to have expended all the effort of which she was capable in making the original contact with Rohana that had resulted in her rescue; that accomplished, it seemed to Rohana that Melora no longer cared. She had not even asked any further questions about her home, about their kin, about what lay ahead when they should leave the Dryland country and return to the Domains.

The sun descended, a great blood-colored orb, blurred at the horizon with the first clouds Rohana had seen since they crossed the river at Carthon. Kindra, riding ahead, stopped to let Rohana come up with her, and pointed to the purpled sunset. She said, "Those clouds hang over Carthon; and beyond Carthon we are in the Domains again. Even if Jalak came so far, he would have to come with an army. Safety lies there. How does the Lady Melora?"

"Not well, I fear," Rohana said soberly, and Kindra nodded.

"For her sake I shall be glad when we cross the river and we can travel at a pace more fitting her condition. It goes against me, to force the pace this way, but there is no safety for any of us in this country."

"I know," Rohana said, "and I am sure Melora understands. She knows, better than any of us, the dangers for women of the Domains, here in the Dry Towns."

Kindra said, "Well, we will make camp yonder"—

she pointed to one of the great black tumuli of rock, upthrust like jagged teeth against the low horizon— "and there, if the Goddess is good to us, we will cook some hot food, and perhaps even wash the dust from our faces."

"Do you know every water hole in this territory, Kindra?"

The woman shook her head. "I have never traveled here before, but I can see the *kyorebni* circling as they do only over water. And tomorrow before midday perhaps we will ford the river, and be safe in Carthon." She grimaced. "I am hungry for hot roast meat and good hot soup instead of this unending porridge and dried meat and fruit, and some fresh-baked bread instead of hardtack."

"Me too," Rohana said, "and I shall stand surety for the best meal we can buy in the best cookshop in Carthon, believe me, once we cross the river!"

Kindra looked back and said slowly, "Pray to your Goddess, Lady, that *domna* Melora is able to enjoy that meal. Ride back to her, Lady Rohana, and reassure her that we will make camp just a little farther on. She seems almost ready to fall from her saddle." Her face, in the gathering darkness, was deeply troubled.

Rohana did as she was bidden, sighing. It seemed that never in her life had she known such prolonged and incessant fatigue. The thought of sleeping in a bed under a roof, eating hot, fresh-cooked food, bathing in a hot tub of scented water, comforts she had taken so much for granted that she never even thought about them, made her whole body ache with an almost sensuous longing.

She supposed the Amazons would think such longings soft and weak. Well, she would show them that she could endure hard living if she must; she was *Comynara* and she would be strong as any man of her caste. But she wished there were a few comforts for Melora.

Melora was riding next to Fat Rima; as Rohana neared them the big Amazon lowered her voice and said, "Look to your kinswoman, Lady. No, she has not complained, but I earned my bread for a time as a midwife in the Lake Country, and she has a look to her that I do not like."

It's good to know there is a midwife among us, at least. Rohana drew her horse even with Melora's; Melora raised her head, slowly and wearily, and her look shocked Rohana. Her face was swollen, with a dull pallor; even her tight lips were colorless. She tried to smile at Rohana, but could not quite manage it. Her face contracted in a sudden spasm of pain, and Rohana knew at once what her kinswoman had been trying to conceal.

"*Breda,* you are in labor!"

Melora grimaced. "For some hours, I fear," she said apologetically. "I had hoped we could reach a campsite near to water. I am very thirsty, Rohana," she added, in the first hint of complaint Rohana had heard from her lips.

She leaned over and took Melora's hands in her own. She said, "We are very near to water, love; can you ride just a little way farther, just a few hundred steps more? See?" She pointed through the falling dusk. "One or two of them are already dismounting; see there? Listen; I can hear Jaelle laughing."

Melora said softly, "She is like a little animal let out of a cage. I am so glad that they are so good to her. Poor little rabbit, I have had so little strength to spare for her, on this journey. . . ."

"I am sure she understands," Rohana said softly.

"I hope she does not," Melora said, and in the twilight her face twisted. They were near to the place where the others were dismounting; again Rohana heard Jaelle's light merry laugh. In the days of the journey she had quickly become a favorite with all the Amazons; laughing, chattering, full of endless questions about the world and the life before her. They had competed with one another for the privilege of carrying her on their saddles when she grew weary, saved her such tidbits and choice morsels as they could scrounge from their sparse meals, told her stories and sang songs to while away the tedium of the trip, even fashioned her small toys and playthings from odds and ends.

If nothing else, we have freed Jaelle, and she is a daughter of whom any of the Domains could be proud. Jalak's blood may be a handicap when the time comes for her to make a good marriage, but that can be overcome. She has laran, *I am sure; I will have her tested when we come to Thendara. . . .*

She slid from her horse, relinquished it to Rima, who came to lead it away, and tenderly helped Melora from her saddle. Melora's knees buckled and Rohana had to support her cousin's weight in her arms; she held her upright, but suddenly frightened, called to Kindra. After a moment the Amazon leader came from the shadows, took in the situation with one appraising glance. "So your time has come, *domna?* Well, only two things in this world are sure, birth and next winter's snow, and both come when they will and not when it is convenient. Thanks to the Goddess, we are near to water. A pity we had to abandon the tent; no child should be born with only the sky for a roof."

"Better under the free sky than in Jalak's Great House," Melora said fiercely, and Kindra held her hand for a moment. "Can you walk just a little, Lady? We will prepare a place for you to rest."

"I can do what I must," Melora said, but she leaned very heavily on her kinswoman, and Rohana felt an all-encompassing dread. Here, in the black night, in the desert, with no skilled hands to help ... *Rima had been a midwife, perhaps; but the Free Amazons renounced womanhood. . . .*

"I had hoped that I could hold out till we reached Carthon," Melora said, and Rohana realized that her kinswoman was sharing her sense of unease and dread. Rohana must somehow manage to be strong and confident.

She said, "Look. They are making a fire, we will have light, and some hot food, and there is water near," as she guided Melora's steps toward the kindled blaze. "And we are in luck; one of these women was once a midwife!"

She was dismayed, now that she could see Melora by firelight: hands and ankles swollen, eyes red and feverish. *She should have told us hours ago; we should have stopped . . . but then the child would have been born without water near. . . .*

Melora sank down gratefully on the pile of blankets that the Amazons had arranged for her. For a moment she buried her face in her hands; Rohana could hear her breathing, loud and hoarse like an animal. Then she raised her head and said plaintively, "I am thirsty, Rohana—will you bring me a drink?"

"Of course." Rohana began to rise, but Melora clutched at her hands. "No, no stay with me. Did I tell you why I suddenly knew I must escape, get Jaelle away, or kill her myself before this child was born?"

"No, dear, you didn't tell me—"

"When I found her—playing with Jalak's other little daughters—they had all of them, even Jaelle, tied ribbons about their hands, playing at being grown up, and in chains—"

Rohana felt herself shudder, deep down in the bones. She said quickly, "Dear, let me go. I will fetch you a drink; do you think you could eat a little?" She left Melora lying on the pile of blankets and went to the darkness near the water hole, kneeling to rinse the cup, trembling, glad to hide her face in the darkness.

After a little she managed to control herself and come back. Kindra said from the fire, "Tell her we will have some hot food soon, and something to drink; it may strengthen her for what lies ahead. And I think we can manage torchlight later, if we need it."

Rohana somehow managed to thank her. She came back and knelt beside Melora, who was lying with her eyes closed; Rohana held the cup to her lips, and Melora gulped it thirstily. Rohana said, "We shall have some hot food for you soon; try to rest." She went on talking, saying anything that crossed her mind, trying to sound encouraging; after a few minutes, Melora put out a hand to stop the flow of chatter.

"Breda—" She used the *casta* word for "sister"; in the intimate inflection it also meant "darling." "Don't lie to me. In memory of what we both were, once, don't try to pretend, as if I were still an outsider; what is going to happen?"

Rohana looked at the sick woman, heart-wrung. *So after all she is still Comyn, still telepath; she can read me so easily.* "What can I say to you, Melora? You know as well as I that no woman so far in pregnancy should travel so far or so fast. But other women have survived worse than this, and lived to frighten their granddaughters with the tales of what they endured. And I'll be with you."

Melora clasped her hand. "Better you than the evil crone who brought Jaelle into the world," she said, clinging to her cousin's fingers. "She would not even free my hands. . . ." She ran her fingertips, as with a long-habitual gesture, along the jagged scars at her wrists. "Jalak swore if I bore a son he would give me whatever I asked, save my freedom; I had it in my mind to ask for her head."

Rohana shuddered, was grateful when Fat Rima approached them; she said, "Here is our midwife; she will do what she can for you, *breda.*"

Melora looked up at her; she felt—Rohana sensed it—skeptical and more than a little frightened. But she said (and again, poignantly, Rohana was reminded of the lighthearted and gracious girl Melora had once been), "I thank you, *mestra;* I did not know any of the Free Amazons would choose such a womanly trade."

"Why, Lady, we earn our bread at any honest work," Rima said. "Did you truly think we are all soldiers and hunters? The Guild-house in the city of Arilinn, where I was trained, has a specialty of training midwives; and we compare everything that is known about the problems of birth from Temora to the Hellers, so we are the best of midwives; even on the great estates, sometimes, women will send for us. Now, my

Lady, let me see how far this thing has gone, and how long you must expect to wait here." She knelt, feeling all about Melora's body with gentle, expert hands. "Well, it is a strong child, and a big one, too."

She broke off as Jaelle came running toward them. The child's face was drawn and white in the firelight. "Mother—oh, Mother—" she said and burst into tears.

Rima said firmly, "Come, my child, that will not help Mother. You are almost a woman now yourself; you must not behave like a baby and trouble us."

Melora dragged herself upright, letting herself lean heavily on Rohana. "Come here, Jaelle. No, let her come to me, I know she will be good."

Struggling to fight back her sobs, Jaelle came and knelt beside her mother; Melora seized her in a fierce embrace and said, not to any of them, "It was worth it all. You are free, you are free!" She kissed the small wet face hungrily, again and again; then laid her hand under Jaelle's small quivering chin and looked at her a long time in the wavering firelight before saying, "You must go now, my darling, and stay with the other women. You cannot help me now, and you must leave me to those who can. Go, my dearest love, try to sleep a little."

Crying, Jaelle let Gwennis lead her away into the darkness beyond the campfire. Rohana heard the child sobbing softly for a long time; then she was quiet and Rohana hoped she had cried herself to sleep. The night wore on slowly. Rohana stayed with Melora, holding her hands, now and then sponging her sweaty face with cold water. Melora was still and patient, doing what she was told, trying to rest between the spasms; now and then she talked a little, and after a time Rohana, with a shudder, knew Melora had lost track of where she was and what was happening. She talked to her own mother, years dead; once she started up with a shriek, crying out curses in the Dry-Town language; again and again she sobbed and entreated them not to chain her again, or cried out, over and over, "My hands! My hands!" and her fingers went again and again to the long ragged scars at her wrists. Rohana listened, murmured to her soothingly, tried now and again to break through the delirious muttering. . . . *If Melora knew she was here and free, here with me. . . .* She tried, with all her telepathic skill, to reach her cousin's mind, but all she could feel was horror and long dread.

Blessed Cassilda, mother of the Domains . . . Evanda, Goddess of light, Goddess of birth . . . merciful Avarra . . . what she must have endured, what horror she must have known. . . .

None of the other women slept, although Kindra had ordered them all to bed; Rohana could sense, like a tangible vibration in the air, their awareness, their concern. *At times like this it is a curse, to read the thoughts of others. . . .*

Once, when Melora slept for a moment, in exhaustion, Rima met Rohana's eyes over the struggling body and shook her head briefly. Rohana closed her own eyes for a moment. *Not yet! Don't give up hope yet!*

Rima said, pityingly, "She has no strength left, I think, to be free of the child. We can only wait."

Rohana suddenly knew if she stayed there another moment she would break into hysterical screams and sobs, herself. She said thickly, "I will be back in a moment," and rose, plunging away, around the campfire, toward the crude latrine the Amazons dug at their camps. She leaned against the harsh rock-face, covering her face, struggling not to vomit or scream. After a moment, controlling herself a little, she went to the fire, where a pot had been left with the hot drink of fermented grain, which the Amazons used in place of bark-tea or *jaco,* just simmering. She dipped herself out a cup and sipped it, fighting for self-control. Kindra, tall and almost invisible in the darkness, stopped and laid a hand on her shoulder.

"Bad, my Lady?"

"Very bad." Rohana felt for a moment that the hot bitter brew would choke her. "She is not—not a woman who could ever have borne children easily; and here, without skilled help, after so much suffering—

after this hard journey—without care or comfort . . ."

Kindra's sigh seemed to come from the very depths of her being. "I am sorry, truly sorry. It is cruel that she should suffer so much for freedom, and never live to enjoy it, after so much courage. It must add greatly to her suffering, to know that even if her child is born alive, there will be none to suckle him or care for him."

A resentment she had not known she felt, against these women who had chosen to spare themselves the pains of womanhood, surged up in Rohana, out of control. She had forcibly to restrain herself from flinging the scalding contents of her cup at the older woman. She said bitterly, "You! What would *you* know of that fear for a child?"

"Why, as much as you, Lady," said Kindra. "I bore four children before I had turned twenty. I was given in marriage very young, and my first child died before I could bring him forth; the midwives said I should not try to bear another, but my husband was eager for an heir. My second and third children were daughters both, and he cursed me. I came very near to death with my fourth child—he was three days in the bearing—and this time, instead of curses, when he saw our son, he showered me with gifts and jewels. And then I knew a woman's lot in our world was wholly accursed. I was of no value; the daughters I bore him at risk of my life were of no value; I was nothing but an instrument to give him sons. And so when I could walk again, I left my children sleeping, one night, and cut my hair, and made my way alone to the Guild of Free Amazons, and there my life began."

Rohana stared at her in horror. She could think of nothing to say. Finally she stammered, "But—but all men are not like that, Kindra."

"No?" Kindra said. "I rejoice you have not found them so, Lady, but that is luck and good fortune, and no more." She glanced at the reddening sky, and said, "Hush," listening to the sounds that had changed, in the last few minutes, from long, patient sighs to harsh, gasping breaths and hoarse short grunts of effort. She said quickly, "Go to her, Lady. It cannot be long now."

There was enough light in the sky now so that Rohana, coming to kneel beside Melora, could see her kinswoman's face, strained and swollen as she fought, panting, for breath.

"Rohana—Rohana—promise me—"

Rima said, imperatively, "Don't talk, dear; pay attention now. Take a good deep breath, and hold it. Come now, dear, that's right, another nice long breath. Now, bear down— come on, hold on tight, just push—"

Rohana let Melora take her hands, cling to them with agonized strength as the inexorable process of birth seized her body, wrenching her into spasms. Rima said, in the singsong that Rohana supposed was common to all midwives, "Come on, now, sweet, that's a good girl, another nice big push, hard now. That's right, *that's* a good girl, come on now, just a little bit more—"

Rohana felt Melora's nails dig into her hand; the contact wrung her with agony. Wide open to her cousin, she felt the tearing pain wrenching at her own body, gasped with the weight of it. *Too much, too much . . . worse than when Kyril was born. . . .* She felt the smothered scream Melora was fighting back, thought in dismay, *Gabriel stayed with me; now I know how he felt . . . I know now he felt all I was enduring. I never knew . . . too much, too much. . . .*

She felt the pain ebb away, felt Melora relax for a moment. Rima said authoritatively, "Come on, now, breathe deep, get ready for the next one; a few more good ones like that and it'll be all over." But Melora ignored her, clutching at Rohana's hands. She gasped, "Rohana, promise—promise—if I die—care for my children. My baby, take my baby—"

She gasped, and arched her body again under the fierce, wrenching pain. Rohana could not speak; she reached for contact with Melora again, directly to her mind.

—I swear it, darling, by the Blessed Cassilda and by the Lord of Light. . . . They shall be as my own chil-

*dren, may the Gods seize me if I make any difference
between them and the children born of my own body. . . .*

Melora whispered, "Thank you—I knew—" She collapsed again. Over her head, dark with sweat, Rima looked up, and Rohana met Kindra's eyes. Kindra said quietly, "I had better fetch Jaelle now."

Rohana looked up indignantly; looked at the swollen, unconscious body, the spreading bloodstains, feeling the wrenching agony seize Melora again, and herself flinched before the terrifying assault on body and mind. She said in violent indignation, "How can you? Is this any place for a little girl . . . ?"

Kindra said gently, but inexorably, "It is her right, Lady. Would you wish to sleep through your mother's death-bed? Or are you still lying to yourself, Lady Rohana?" She did not wait for Rohana's answer. Rohana, kneeling, letting Melora grip her hands with that anguished death-grip, heedless of Melora's nails digging into her and drawing blood, was seized again by that moment of terror she had known at the climax of her own child-beds. . . . *Breaking, tearing, splitting, coming apart . . . dying. . . .* Rohana struggled to keep herself a little apart from Melora's terror, to give her kinswoman some strength, something to cling to outside her own agony and fear. She held Melora, murmuring endearments, whispering, "We're with you, love, we're right here, we're going to take good care of you . . ." but she did not know what she was saying.

For the first and last time Melora shrieked aloud, a long, terrible cry of anguish and dread; and then, just as the sun was rising, into the terrible silence there was another sound: a strange, sharp, shrill sound, the uplifted howling of a newborn child.

"Praise to Evanda," said Rima, holding up the naked, bloody child, feet first. "Listen to how strong he is! I didn't have to slap *this* one into life—"

Melora whispered, almost inaudibly, "Give him to me," and reached out for him, her face changing. *The never-failing miracle,* Rohana thought. Always, no matter how hard and terrible the birth, there was this moment of joy, when the face changed, alight and glowing. *Melora looks so happy, so happy; how can she?* Rohana wondered, not remembering her own happiness. Rima wrapped the baby in a fold of clean towel she had laid ready, and placed him on Melora's flaccid belly. She said matter-of-factly, "He will do well enough."

"Jalak's son," Melora whispered, and the joyous smile slipped away. "What will become of him, poor little wretch?"

Rima said sharply, "My Lady—"

Melora reached out her hands. She said, "Jaelle—Jaelle, come here and kiss me—oh, Jaelle—"

Rima cried out in consternation; blood came forth in a great gush, and Melora sighed and fell back, her face white and lifeless. And there was no sound in the sunrise except the crying of Melora's motherless children.

"Will you truly have Jalak's son to foster, Lady Rohana?" Kindra asked.

The sun was high in the camp. Jaelle had cried herself to exhaustion and was lying on the sand between them, limp, like some bedraggled little animal. Rohana was half sitting, half lying against a pile of saddlebags. She had wrapped the naked child and thrust him inside her tunic against her breasts, where he squirmed and nuzzled, already lively and seeking the nourishment he did not know would be denied him. Rohana patted the warm bundle tenderly. She said, "What else can I do, Kindra? I swore to Melora that her children should be to me as my own in all things."

Kindra said fiercely, "He is a male of Jalak's blood; do not your kinsmen and your foster-brother's blood cry out for revenge, that you should cherish him? Is there not blood-feud and a life between you and Jalak's son, my Lady?" She bared her knife, handed it to Rohana, hilt first. She said, "He cost Melora her life, so she came never to her hard-won freedom; and he is Jalak's son. Avenge your kinsmen, Lady."

Chilled, sick with horror, Rohana knew that Kindra

spoke no more than simple truth. The men of the Ardais
and Aillard Domains would have echoed her words:
Jalak's son must pay for Jalak's crimes.

She felt the child move against her body, warm and
strong. *Melora's child; and I took him up from her
dead body.* She looked at Jaelle, who was curled tight
beside them, her eyes shut in rejection. *She is Jalak's
child, too. Must she pay?*

Kindra said earnestly, "Rohana, he will die, whatever you do now. There is no nurse for him, no food,
no proper care. Don't wring your heart for him; let him
lie here beside his mother."

Slowly, Rohana shook her head. She handed back
the knife, meeting the Amazon's eyes. She said,
"Blood-feud and revenge are for men, Kindra. I am
glad to be a woman, and bound by no such cruel law.
Let this child's life, not his death, pay for my foster-
brother's death; Ardais lost a son in Valentine, so this
boy shall be called Valentine." She laid her hands, as if
in ritual, on the small squirming body, "And he shall
be foster-son to Ardais, in place of the one who died at
Jalak's hands."

Kindra put the knife away, raised her face with a
grim smile. She said, "Well spoken, my Lady. An
Amazon would say so, indeed; but I had not thought
you were so free to discard the laws of your clan and
caste."

Rohana said violently, "I hope I will always feel free to
ignore any law so cruel! It may be that he will die, as you
say; but not at my hands, and not if I can save him!"

Kindra nodded. "So be it," she said. "I will speak to
Rima; she has fostered motherless babes before this.
Our women sometimes die in bearing, too, and Rima is
skilled in all the secrets of the Arilinn Guild-house."
She rose, saying, "There is another child of Melora's
who needs your care; look to her, Lady."

She went off to join the other Amazons, who were
burying Melora in the hill behind the water hole. Rohana turned to Jaelle and began to stroke her hair
gently.

"Jaelle," she coaxed, "don't cry any more, darling. I know nothing can heal your grief, but you must not make yourself ill with crying. I swore that I would be a mother to you, always. Come, darling, look at me," she pleaded. "Don't you want to see your little brother? He needs someone to love and comfort him, too." She added, "*You* had your mother for twelve years, Jaelle; this poor little mite lost his mother before she had ever looked into his face. He has none but his sister; will you not come and help me to comfort him?"

Jaelle pulled away with a shudder of violent revulsion, her sobs rising again to a frenzy, and Rohana, in despair, let her go. Jaelle had not spoken since Melora's death; Rohana feared that in those last few moments of Melora's life, spent in terror and dread, in the fear of death, the child's mind had been roughly opened to the terrifying telepathic rapport, her latent Gift wakened in that dreadful instant of shock and agony.

No one could have blamed Melora for reaching out, with her last conscious thought, in the only way for which she still had strength—for one last, desperate attempt to touch her beloved child. But what had it done to Jaelle?

As if he sensed Rohana's desperate unease, the baby began to stir and fret and whimper inside her tunic again. She stroked him, thinking of the long leagues that still lay between them and Carthon, where she might at least find a wet-nurse for the child. For him it was a simple matter of survival; handled, fed, carefully cared for, he would survive. But what of Jaelle? She would not die, but what had that shock done to her? Only time would tell.

Perhaps the Amazons can do more for her than I. I am, in her mind, still part of that moment of terror and death. But perhaps they can comfort Jaelle and help her.

She must leave it to them, at least until Jaelle was calm and recovered her senses. After that—Rohana looked longingly at Jaelle's soft tangled hair, but dared not touch her—after that, only time would tell.

Chapter
FIVE

Twelve days later, Rohana looked down from the top of the pass that led away into the valley of Thendara.

"Jaelle," she called, turning back, "come here and see the city of your forefathers!"

Obediently the young girl rode forward, looking at the ancient city that lay in the valley below them. "This is the city of the Comyn? I have never seen so big a city; Shainsa is not half so large." She looked down with fascination and, it seemed, with dread, at the wide-flung buildings, the Comyn Castle beyond. "Tell me, kinswoman; is it true that the Comyn are descended from the Gods? My—I have heard it said, and I have heard—I have heard it denied. What is the truth?"

How deftly she avoids either her father's name or her mother's! In twelve days she has spoken of neither of them. Rohana said, "I can tell you only what I have heard myself. The story goes that Hastur, son of Aldones, Lord of Light, came to our world at Hali; and that he wooed and won Cassilda, daughter of Robardin, mother of the Domains; and thus all those of the blood of Hastur are kin to the Gods. If it be true, or only a beautiful fable, I know no more than you;

but this much is true beyond question. All those of the blood of the Hasturs, all the kin of the Seven Domains, have the *laran* powers, the psi gifts that set them apart from all other men born on this world."

"Are all of the Comyn of Hastur blood, then?"

"In the beginning, yes; although in the great days of the Towers they were separated into the seven families we now call the Domains. All are of the blood of Hastur and Cassilda. But it is sure that none of us are Gods or anything like it, my child."

Would that we were. I should know better what to do with you, little one. Rohana sighed, touching the warm sleeping weight where Melora's baby slept, tucked inside her tunic for warmth; it was cold at these heights, even in summer. Jaelle was no longer openly hostile to Rohana, but she had not turned to her for comfort, either. Nor had she been willing to touch her little brother, or so much as look at him.

Every one of the Amazons—even the two neutered women, Leeanne and Camilla—had shared the burden of the newborn child in those first dreadful days, before they reached Carthon and found a wet-nurse for him. They had all spared sugar and meal to make gruel for him, and, knowing that Rohana was exhausted and burdened with grief, had taken turns to carry him and try to soothe his fitful crying. Only Jaelle had steadfastly ignored her brother; had refused, even when urged repeatedly by Kindra, whom she adored, to hold him in her arms or even look at him.

As if her thoughts had reached him, the baby Valentine began to stir and fret, and Rohana beckoned to the wet-nurse from Carthon; she rode forward, took the child from Rohana, and opening her dress, lazily put the child to her breast. She was, Rohana thought, a singularly stupid woman—*I would not let her rear a pet dog, let alone a child*—but he throve on her milk, and for now that was all that mattered.

Should any woman alive be allowed to live so ignorant that she is no better than a dairy-animal? The Free Amazons openly despised her, and with the pride seen in the invincibly stupid, the wet-nurse treated them with contempt. Rohana—sharing their contempt for the woman, but needing her services—tried to mediate an uneasy peace.

Rohana stretched her back (the sling in which she carried the baby during the day gave her cramps in the shoulders) and tried to think ahead. She had pledged Melora that she would rear the children as her own. Her husband would not object; he had said often that he would welcome more children, regretted that Rohana had borne only three. But now reaction had set in, after Rohana's first elation at saving Melora's son alive. *What have I taken upon myself? My eldest is already almost grown; my daughter is already five, and since two of our children are sons, Gabriel agreed I need have no more. And now when I thought I was done with it, again I have all the worry and trouble of rearing a very little one! No doubt Gabriel will begin to talk, again, of having another so he will not be brought up alone.*

Am I only an instrument to give him sons? she thought, and was horrified at herself. Quickly she turned her thoughts elsewhere: *What place can we make in the Domains for the son of a Dry-Towner? And Jaelle, so cold and withdrawn, will she ever accept me?*

It was too much to expect, that she could find comfort in the child. I am a mother myself, that was the greatest comfort to me, that something remained of Melora ... but Jaelle is a child. She sees only that poor little Val robbed her of their mother. . . .

Kindra drew her horse close to Rohana's. She said, "Lady, is that where the Terrans are building their spaceport? What do they want here, these men from another world?"

"I do not know." Rohana gazed at the great dirt-colored slash beyond the city of Thendara, where, it seemed, several miles of the valley had been ripped open by their enormous machines and smoothed to an eerie, unnatural flatness. Part of the area had been paved, and buildings were sprouting in strange, unlikely shapes. "I have heard that our world is at a crossroad of their travel roads among the stars; they seem to have trade caravans between the many worlds as we have between the towns in the Lake Country. I don't know what their trade may be, no one has bothered to tell me, though I think Gabriel knows." She fancied a look of contempt from Kindra. *Why should I be content with ignorance? Oh, damn these Amazons, they are making me question everything: myself, Gabriel, my very life!*

It made her voice edgy. "These people, they call themselves the Terran Empire, came first to Caer Donn, near Aldaran, and began a spaceport—a small one, they could not build so wide in the mountains there—and dealt with the accursed Aldarans. Hastur offered them a place here to build their spaceport where the climate would be more to their liking—I have heard that to them our world seems cold—and so we can keep watch over their doings; but of course we have nothing to do with them."

"Why not?" asked Kindra. "I should think that a race which can travel from star to star as readily as I can ride from here to Nevarsin would have a great deal to teach us."

Rohana said stiffly, "I do not know; Hastur has willed it so."

"How fortunate are the men of the Domains, that they have the son of Hastur to teach them," said Kindra, her gray eyebrows lifting. "A stupid woman like myself would have felt that a race which can make trade caravans among the stars might outreach even a Hastur in wisdom."

Rohana was annoyed by the sarcasm, but she felt too deeply indebted to Kindra to take her to task for it. "I have heard it explained thus: Hastur feels there is much in their way of life that might be more of a threat than we can know at once. They have, for a beginning, leased the spaceport here for five hundred years, so that we will have plenty of time to choose what we can learn from them."

"I see," said Kindra, and was silent, thinking it over, studying the enormous slash on the horizon, where strange machines crawled and unknown shapes grew against the horizon.

Rohana, too, was silent. As they rode this last mile, it seemed that she was, in a curious way, changing worlds. For near to forty days she had lived in a world as alien to her as the world of the Terrans below; then she had grown used to it, and now she must again change worlds, make ready to reenter her own.

At first the world in which the Amazons lived had seemed hard and comfortless, strange and lonely. Then she had realized that most of the strangeness was not the physical lack of comfort at all. It was quite different. It was easy to get used to long hours of riding, to unfamiliar and ugly clothes, to bathing as one could in stream or river, to sleeping in tents or under the sky.

But it was not nearly so easy to give up the familiar support of known protections, known ways of thinking. Until she came on this journey, she had never quite realized how much all her decisions, even small personal ones, had been left to her father and brothers, or, since she married, to her husband. Even such small things as *Shall I wear a blue gown or a green? Shall I order fish or fowl for the table tonight?* had been dictated less by her own tastes and preferences than Gabriel's wishes. She had not realized, until Jaelle and the newborn Val were hers for fostering, how much even what she had said to the children or done for them had been based, openly or not, on how well Gabriel would think of her for her dealings with them.

A strange, painful, almost traitorous thought kept returning: *Now that I know how to make my own decisions, will I ever be content again to let Gabriel decide for me?*

Or, if I do go back, is it only because it is so much easier to do exactly what is expected of a woman of my caste?

They had ridden through the great city gates of Thendara now, and people came out to stare at the sight of a Comyn lady in the company of an Amazon band. Inside the city Kindra dismissed most of the Free Amazons to the Guild-house in Thendara. Accompanied only by Kindra, Jaelle, and the wet-nurse with the baby, Rohana rode on to the Comyn Castle.

In the suite that had belonged to the Ardais clan for uncountable years, Rohana summoned the skeleton staff of servants who remained there all year round—most of the Ardais retainers returned home to Castle Ardais, with their masters, when Council season was over—and ordered that comfortable quarters be found for the wet-nurse and the baby; that Kindra be treated as an honored guest; and that Jaelle, whom she introduced as her foster-daughter without going into details, be made comfortable in a room near her own, and provided with suitable clothing.

Then she dispatched a message to the Princess Consort announcing her return, and summoned her own personal maid, bracing herself for the inevitable: the woman's shocked reaction to her hacked-off hair, her completely unsuitable clothes, the state of her hands and complexion, roughened with riding and outdoor living.

It will be worse than this, when I return to Ardais. Why should I need to be always beautiful? I am not a dancer, or a lyric performer. And I have long ago made my good marriage. But there are those who would think Melora's rescue too dearly bought at the cost of my hair and my complexion!

Just the same, even while she chafed at the woman's cluckings and scoldings for getting herself in such a state, it was good to lie again at full length in a hot bath, scented with balsam; good to soothe her roughened and chapped skin with creams and healing lotions, to be dressed again in soft feminine garments.

When she was ready, word had come that the Lady Jerana would receive them; and that the Lord Lorill Hastur wished to receive the Free Amazon leader as well. When Rohana relayed this royal command—for, though veiled in exquisite courtesy, that was what it was—Kindra smiled wryly.

"No doubt he wishes to be certain I have not committed the Domains to war with the Dry Towns."

"Nonsense," said Rohana irritably. "He is Melora's kinsman too; I am sure he wants to thank you!"

"Well, Lady, whatever it is, it is for me to obey the Lord Hastur," said Kindra, "so we shall see."

When Jaelle was brought to them, Rohana drew breath in amazement at the child's surprising beauty. The grime of travel, and her ill-assorted cast-off garments, had obscured it before. She was tall for her age, her skin very pale, dusted with a few faint amber freckles; her hair had been washed and hung below her waist, the color of new copper. She had been prettily dressed in a delicate green gown, just the color of her eyes. Truly, Rohana thought, a daughter of whom any Comyn household could be proud. But would they see it? Or would they see only that she was Jalak's daughter?

The Lady Jerana, Princess Consort of Aran Elhalyn (she had been born an Aillard and was Rohana's cousin), a languid, fair-haired, spoiled-looking woman, greeted Rohana with the embrace due a kinswoman, kissed Jaelle coldly and spoke graciously to Kindra.

Why shouldn't she be gracious? It's all she has to do in life, Kindra thought.

"So this is our dear Melora's child," said Jerana, looking the girl up and down. "A pity she is Jalak's daughter as well; it will be hard to arrange a marriage for her that suits her station. Has she *laran?*"

"I do not know. I have not had her tested." Rohana's voice was cold. "I have had other things to think about."

Lorill Hastur said, "Such brilliantly red hair often indicates an extraordinary degree of psi power; if she were so gifted, she could be sent to a Tower, and the question of marriage need not arise."

Rohana thought that in any case it was too soon to worry about the marriage of an orphan only twelve years old, who had not yet recovered from multiple shocks; but she did not say so. She suspected Lorill picked up the thought anyway. He was a slightly built, serious-looking man about Rohana's own age; like many of the Hasturs, his flaming hair had already begun to turn white. He frowned in Jaelle's direction, and said tactlessly, "I suppose there is no doubt she *is* Jalak's child? Now if Melora had been already pregnant when she was captured, or if we could put it about that this was the case—"

Jaelle was biting her lip; Rohana feared she would cry. She said coldly that, unfortunately or not, there was no doubt about the girl's parentage.

"I assume Jalak is dead?"

Kindra said that they did not know for certain. "But there was no pursuit, Lord Hastur, and when we reached Carthon, there were already rumors of change in the Great House at Shainsa."

"Of course you know what troubles me," Lorill Hastur said. "Your rash act—I am speaking to you, Rohana; I know the Free Amazon only did what you employed her to do—your rash act could have plunged us into war with the Dry Towns."

Kindra's eyes met Rohana's in a brief, vindicated grin. She might as well have said, aloud, "I told you so."

"Lorill, you are Melora's kinsman, too! Should I have left her to die in slavery, and her child in Jalak's hands?"

The man looked deeply troubled. "How can I say that? I loved Melora; I cannot express my grief that she did not live to enjoy her freedom. As a man, and her kinsman, what else can I say? But the peace of the Domains is in my hands. I cannot go to war to right one person's wrongs, or I am no better than the Dry-Towners with their endless tyrannies of blood-feud and revenge. I must try to do what is best for everyone within these Domains, Rohana; Comyn and commoner alike. What of our farmers and peaceful citizens who live along the borders of the Drylands? Must they live in fear of revenge and reprisal by the Dry-Towners? And if the truces we have worked so hard to make are broken, that is all they can hope for."

Suddenly Rohana felt sorry for him. He was speaking only the truth. His personal feelings could not be allowed to conflict with his duty as Councillor. He was Melora's nearest living kinsman; the duty he had shirked, for whatever good reason, had been done instead by women. That could not be easy for a Hastur to swallow.

"Kinsman, that is of little moment now. What does matter is the guardianship of Melora's children."

"Children?" Jerana asked. "Has she others?"

"The son she died in bearing, Lady." Rohana glanced uneasily at Jaelle. Jerana should have had tact enough to send the child away before discussing her future before her; but it was not for Rohana to suggest it.

Jerana said, "Oh, they can be fostered somewhere. If Melora had lived, I suppose we'd have had to do something for them, but we can't be expected to take any kind of responsibility for the children of some Dry-Town tyrant. Put them out to fosterage somewhere and forget about them."

Even Lorill flinched at the brutal tactlessness of that. Rohana said firmly, "I pledged Melora before she died that I would rear her children as my own." *Melora knew our kinfolk better than I, it seems.*

Jerana shrugged. "Oh, well, I imagine you know best. If Gabriel does not object, I'll leave it to you." Rohana realized that Jerana was glad she could dispose of it so perfunctorily.

Lorill Hastur turned to Kindra and said, "Was it you who accomplished the rescue, *mestra?*"

"My women and I, Lord Hastur."

"We are deeply in your debt," Lorill Hastur said, and Rohana realized he was trying to soften Jerana's indifference. "You did what my kinsmen and I failed to do. What reward will you ask of me, *mestra?*"

Kindra said with dignity, "My lord, the Lady Rohana has paid my women generously; you owe me nothing more."

"Still, there is a life between us," Lorill said.

"No, for I failed. My appointed task was to restore the Lady Melora to her kin," said the Free Amazon.

Rohana shook her head. "You did not fail, Kindra; Melora died free, and she died happy. But it is for me, not you, Lorill, to offer her what extra reward she will ask."

Kindra looked up at them both, and moved to Jaelle's side. "Then, since you both offer a gift," she said, "I ask this: give me Jaelle to foster."

Lorill Hastur said, in shock, "Impossible. A child of Comyn blood cannot be reared among Free Amazons!"

Rohana, too, had felt a moment's shock at this request—such presumption! But Lorill's words angered her as much as Jerana's rudeness had done. "Fine words, Lorill. But you were willing to sit uncaring in Thendara, and let her be reared in chains by Jalak." She beckoned Jaelle to her, and said, "Jaelle, before your mother died, I swore to her that I would rear you as my own daughter, born of my body. I know she meant I should keep you in my house, bring you up as my own child. But you are twelve years old; and if my own daughter, at twelve years old, came to me and said, 'Mother, I do not want to live with you, I want to be fostered by such and such a one,' then—if her choice of foster-mother were such a one as I could trust—then I would consider carefully her wishes in the matter. You have heard Kindra ask for you, and"—she looked with angry defiance over Jaelle's head, at Lorill Hastur—"it is *mine* to decide. But will you not come with me to Ardais, and be *my* daughter?" she pleaded. "I loved your mother, and I will be a mother to you as well. You will have my daughter and her friends for playmates and sisters, and you will be brought up as your mother and I were reared, as a *Comynara*, as is fitting for our caste."

Jaelle, darling, you are all I have of Melora. . . .

The hard little face was unyielding, strangely set. "And when I am grown, kinswoman?"

"Then, birth or no, Jaelle, I will arrange for you a marriage as good as for my own daughter—" and then she knew, suddenly, that she had lost. Jaelle's face went cold.

She said, "I want only to live where I will never be in subjection to any man. If Kindra will have me to foster—" She went and laid her hand in the Free Amazon's, and said, "I do ask it, kinswoman."

Rohana thought, almost in despair, *It is too late to treat her as a little child. She has known so much that would age her before her time.*

Still, she was a Comyn daughter, and might have *laran*. She said gravely, "Kindra, she must not be neutered. Promise me that."

Kindra's face held outrage. "I see you have understood all too little of the Amazons, Lady. We do not neuter women."

"I saw the two of your band—Leeanne and Camilla—"

"*We do not neuter our women,*" Kindra repeated implacably. "Now and again, a woman will be so maddened with hate for her own womanhood that she will persuade or bribe some healer to break the law for her sake; often they come to us afterward, and we cannot cast them out; there is usually nowhere else they can go, poor souls. But women who come to us first, instead, usually learn self-respect, not self-hate. I do not think—if she is fostered among us—that she will come to such hatred." She put her arms lightly around the child's shoulders, turned to Jaelle and spoke directly to her, but not as if she spoke to a child at all; she spoke as if to an equal, and Rohana felt a strange emotion that after a moment, incredulously, she identified as *envy*.

"You know, Jaelle, you cannot, by the laws of our Guild, be accepted yet as an Amazon; even our own daughters must wait until they are legally old enough to be counted as women, to marry, or to choose. When you are fifteen, you will be permitted to make that choice; until then, you will be only my fosterling."

Lady Jerana said querulously, "I think this whole business is outrageous; can't you stop it, Lorill?"

Rohana thought, with anger she did not know she possessed, that it had been outrageous enough to discuss the girl before her face as if she were deaf, dumb, blind and feeble of wit. Lorill Hastur seemed to echo her indignation as he said, "It is Rohana's right to choose where Jaelle should be fostered, Jerana; she first consulted you, and you chose not to exercise your privilege of decision. Now I will defend Rohana's right to choose."

Oh, good for you, Lorill! She looked at him gratefully, thinking that being Chief Councillor couldn't be the most pleasant of jobs. Jerana's pretty, vapid face was spiteful.

"Well, Rohana, at least you need not worry about finding someone to marry Jalak's daughter; I have always heard that the Free Amazons are eager to find pretty young girls whom they can convert to their unnatural way of life, turning them against marriage and motherhood, making them haters of men and lovers of women. It was clever of you to let Jaelle among them. . . ."

White with anger, Rohana felt that she would like to slap Jerana's sneering mouth, silence the filthy implication of those words. Then, as she saw Kindra smiling, she knew her sojourn with the Amazons had changed one thing forever.

She would return to her old life, and the world of women. For the rest of her days she would tune her decisions to the invisible winds of Gabriel's whims, perhaps. But one thing would never be the same; and it was a difference that changed the world.

Rohana knew, now, that she was living that life *by choice;* not because her mind was too narrowly bounded to imagine any other life, but because, having known another life and weighed it, she had decided that what was good in her world—her deep affection for

Gabriel, her love for her children, the responsibility of the estate of Ardais that demanded the hand of its lady—outweighed what was difficult, or hard for her to accept.

And so nothing that any woman like Jerana might say could ever hurt her or make her angry again. Jerana was simply a stupid, narrow, unimaginative and spiteful woman; she had never had any opportunity to be otherwise. Kindra was worth a hundred like Jerana. *I am free. She could never be,* Rohana thought.

She said, almost gently, "I am sorry you feel that way about it, Jerana, but this seems to me a happy choice for Jaelle; you did not choose to foster her yourself, and since you do not love her, it is just as well. I would be selfish indeed to keep Jaelle tied to the ribbons of my sash, just to comfort me in my bereavement."

"You will give her to that—that Free Amazon, that shame and scandal to womanhood?"

Rohana said serenely, "I know her, Jerana, and you do not." She held out her arms to Jaelle and said, "I told you that if my own daughter made such a choice, I would listen to her. Be it as you wish, then." She folded Jaelle in her arms, and for the first time the little girl hugged her, hard, kissing her on the cheek, her eyes shining. Rohana said, "I give you to Kindra to foster, Jaelle. I bid you be a dutiful daughter to her; and do not forget me."

Then, letting Jaelle go, she stretched her hands to the Free Amazon. The older woman's calloused, sun-burned hands met her own; the level gray eyes looked straight into hers. She said quietly, "Lady, may the Goddess deal with me as I with Jaelle."

Rohana's mind lay open to the touch. Again, and for the last time, she felt the Amazon's immense kindness, steadiness; she knew she would trust Kindra with her life—or with this other life so precious to her. She was surprised to feel that her eyes were filling with tears.

She thought, *I almost wish I were coming with you, too. . . .*

Kindra said softly, aloud, "So do I, Rohana." There was no formal "My Lady" now; they had gone too deep for that. Rohana could not speak, even to say good-bye; she laid Jaelle's hand in Kindra's and turned away.

The last thing Rohana heard, as they left the audience chamber, Jaelle skipping along at Kindra's side, was the little girl asking eagerly, "Foster-mother, will you cut my hair?"

Part II

MAGDA LORNE, Terran Agent

Twelve years elapse between the first part and the second.

Chapter
SIX

If there was a noisier job anywhere in the Galaxy than building a spaceport, Magda Lorne hoped she'd never have to listen to it.

And a *long* job. This one, it seemed, had been building most of Magda's life. She had been born at Caer Donn, the Terran Empire's first foothold on Darkover; had been eight years old when the HQ had been moved here to Thendara; and the spaceport had been under construction ever since.

Even the violence of the autumnal storm had only dulled, not silenced, the roar of the building machines, although the mountains behind the city had disappeared into a blur of white snow, and even the old town beyond the HQ was all but invisible. Magda went through the heavy storm doors into the unmarried women's quarters and simultaneously slammed out storm and noise. Inside it was soundproofed. The lights here were yellow Earth-normal. At least this building was finished, she thought, and *quiet*. All during her brief marriage to Peter, they had lived in Married Personnel Quarters; unfinished and the soundproofing still not complete. And she wondered, sometimes, just how much the perpetual tension of the noise had contributed to the breakup of that marriage. She shrugged the thought off, opening the door of her room. *It would never have worked, no matter what the conditions. I don't think I was ever in love with Peter, and I'm perfectly sure he was never in love with me. We'd just been together too much,* her thoughts ran on the familiar track, *and not quite enough, not quite enough to get it out of our systems. When that wore off, we realized there wasn't anything else to hold us together.*

Recalling her marriage to Peter, her thoughts continued along an annoying, smooth and familiar groove. *Where is he? He's never been away so long before. I hope nothing's happened to him.*

She sternly admonished herself not to worry. Like herself, Peter Haldane was a graduate in Alien Anthropology from the Empire University; like herself he had been brought up since childhood on Cottman IV, which the natives called Darkover; and like herself, when they returned to the planet that both was and was not their home world, they had gone directly into Empire Intelligence work. The Empire might call the work they did *Intelligence* and think of it as elaborate spying, but to Magda, and Peter, and the others like them—not many, here on Darkover—it was the best training for an alien anthropologist: to mingle with the people of their world, to get to know them in a way anthropologists not reared here never could. Peter was evidently on a lengthy assignment somewhere. But this time he had been gone so *long!*

And there were the *dreams*. . . .

Magda knew she should report the dreams. In the course of her Alien Psychology credentials, she had been tested for psi potential; and had tested very high. Just the same, she was reluctant to make an official report of her recurrent dreams—all of which, without exception, warned her that Peter Haldane was in trouble—as if to do so might give them some reality. *Dreams are just dreams, that's all.* . . .

Nevertheless, when she finished shedding her heavy outer layer of clothing, she went to the communicator button.

"Personnel? Lorne here. Is that you, Bethany? I don't suppose Haldane has reported back, or sent word, has he, in the last twenty-eight?"

"Not a word, Magda," the woman in the coordinator's office replied. "I knew it; you're still carrying around a yen for Peter, aren't you? You've been on the button every twenty-eight, asking for news."

"Yen be damned," Magda said irritably. "In case you've forgotten, I've known Peter since I was five years old; we grew up together, and I worry." *And that,* she thought, cutting the connection, *is why I don't report the dreams. I'm sick and tired of every bored woman here speculating, out loud, how long it will be before Peter and I get together again! Is it going to get so bad that one of us has to put in for a transfer and leave Darkover? Damn it, I grew up here, this is my home, too!*

I wonder if Peter feels that way too? We never talked about it. We never talked much about anything, outside of bed. That was half our trouble. . . .

She still felt irritable as she took off the Darkovan outfit she wore for her work outside the HQ gates. She wore the ordinary dress of a woman of Thendara: a long, full skirt of heavy cloth, woven in a tartan pattern, a high-necked and long-sleeved tunic, embroidered at the neck, and ankle-high sandals of thin leather. Her hair was long and dark, coiled low on her neck and fastened with the butterfly-shaped clasp that every woman wore in the Domains. Magda's was made of silver, a noblewoman would have worn copper, a poor woman's clasp would have been carved of wood or even leather; but no chaste woman exposed her bare neck in public.

She hung the Darkovan clothes away, first rubbing their folds with an aromatic mixture of spices; it was as important to smell right as to look right, in the Old Town. She showered and got into Terran clothes, thin crimson tights and a tunic with the Empire emblem on the sleeve. They felt chilly, and she thought it made no sense to wear thin synthetics here and heat the buildings to a temperature that made them practical. It just made the Terrans unfit for the climate.

It's like the yellow Earth-normal lights everywhere in the HQ; it just keeps everyone from adapting to the red sun. I know, it's Empire policy everywhere; and when spaceport personnel are likely to be transferred all across the Galaxy at a few days' notice, of course maintaining a stable set of standard conditions makes sense.

But it's hard on those of us who really live here. . . .

She was trying to decide whether to have food sent to her room, or to go to the HQ cafeteria and eat in company, when the communicator summoned her again.

"Lorne here," she said, in no pleasant temper. "I'm off duty, you know."

"I know—Montray here. Magda, you're an expert on the Darkovan languages, aren't you? Isn't there a special inflection for speaking to the nobility, and a feminine mode of address?"

"Both. Do you want a capsule lecture, or a library reference? My father compiled the standard text, and I'm working on a revision."

"Neither; I want you to translate," the coordinator said, "You're our only resident female expert; and I'm mortally afraid of offending the lady by some improper form of speech. I've heard about the various gender taboos, but I don't know half enough about them, and that's a fact."

"The lady?" Magda's curiosity was piqued; noblewomen were rarely seen even on the streets of Thendara.

"A lady of the Comyn."

"Good God," Magda said. She had rarely set eyes on a single member of this royal and aloof caste; even the men of the Comyn, if they felt the need to speak with one of the representatives of the Empire—which didn't happen often—did not hesitate to summon them into Thendara instead. "One of the women of the Comyn has summoned you?"

"Summoned, nothing! The lady's in my office right now," said Montray, and Magda blinked.

She said, "I'll be there in three minutes." Her normal duties did not include working as a translator, but she could understand why Montray was unwilling to use the regular staff.

This was completely unprecedented; a woman of the Comyn, in Montray's office . . .

Magda put on her outdoor clothing. She had removed her butterfly-clasp; she started to coil up her long hair on top of her head. The Darkovans certainly knew that Terrans went, in Darkovan clothing, into the Old Town, just as the Terrans knew that a considerable number of the Darkovans who worked at construction jobs on the spaceport were paid to pass along information about the off-worlders to the Darkovan authorities. But neither side took official notice of it. It was important for Magda to look like any other Terran translator. But her bare neck prickled at the exposure.

I ought to act as if I didn't even know about the proper degree of exposure for a Darkovan woman. But she felt bare and immodest; she took the braid down and let it hang loose down her back.

The noise had shut down now to a nighttime roar; her feet, in thin shoes, slid on the slippery, sleeted sidewalks. She was glad to get into the Temporary HQ building, where Temporary Coordinator Russ Montray—Darkover wasn't important enough in the Empire, yet, to be assigned a proper Legate for liaison with the native residents—met her in the outer office.

"It's good of you to do this for me, Magda. It won't hurt to let them know we have some people who can speak the language the way it really ought to be spoken." He was a plump, balding man in his forties, with a habitual worried look; even in his centrally heated office, with the thermostat turned up to the maximum, he always looked, and was, cold. "I took the lady into my inner office," he said, and held the door for her.

He said, in his poor and stumbling *cahuenga* (the lingua franca of the Trade City), "Lady Ardais, I present to you my assistant, Magdalen Lorne, who will speak with you more easily than I can do." He added to Magda, "Tell her we are honored at her visit, and ask what we can do for her. She must want something, or she'd have sent for us instead of coming here herself."

Magda gave him a warning look; she guessed, from the flash of intelligence in the lady's eyes, that she understood Terran Standard—or that she was one of the occasional telepaths rumored to be found on Darkover. She began, *"Domna,* you lend us grace. How may we best serve you?"

The woman looked up, meeting Magda's eyes; Magda, who had spent her life on Darkover and knew the nuances, thought, *This woman is from the mountains; the women of the lowlands are more timid with strangers.* As custom demanded for all of the Comyn, she had brought a bodyguard—a tall, uniformed man in the green and black of the City Guard—and a lady companion, but she paid no attention to either of them. She said quietly, "I am Rohana Ardais; my husband is Gabriel-Dyan, Warden of Ardais. You speak our language well, my child; may I ask where you learned it?"

"I spent my childhood at Caer Donn, Lady, where the citizens mingled more with the Terrans than is the custom here; all my playmates were Darkovan children."

"Ah, that explains why you speak with the accent of the Hellers," Rohana said. Magda, studying her with the eyes of a trained observer, saw a small, slightly built woman, not nearly as tall as Magda herself. It was hard to tell her age, for there were no telltale lines in her face, but she was not young; the heavy auburn hair, coiled low on her neck and confined with an expensive butterfly-clasp of copper set with green gems, was liberally streaked with gray. She was well and warmly clad in a heavy dress of thick green wool, woven and dyed and elaborately embroidered. She bore herself with great poise, but her hands, clasped in her lap, moved nervously on one another.

"I have come here, against the will of my kinfolk, to ask a service of you Terrans. Perhaps it is foolish, a forlorn hope——" She hesitated, and Magda told her that it would be an honor to serve the Lady Ardais.

Rohana said quietly, "It is my son; he has disappeared. We feared foul play. Then a workman who is employed here in your port on one of your great buildings—surely it is no secret that many of these are paid by us to tell us what we wish to know about your people—one of these workmen, who knows my son slightly, reported to us that he had seen my son here, at work. This was some months ago; but it seemed to us, at last, that any rumor was worth investigating. . . ."

Startled, Magda relayed Rohana's words to the coordinator. "It is true that we employ many Darkovans. But—your son, Lady? Most of those we employ are put to work as common laborers, running machines, doing carpentry and building—"

"Our son is young, and eager for adventure, like all men his age," Rohana said. "To him, no doubt, it would seem a great adventure, to mingle with men from another world. He would not hesitate to work as a layer of bricks or a pavement-maker, for the sake of that. And as I say, he was seen and recognized here." She handed Montray a small packet wrapped in silk; he unwrapped it, slowly, glancing at Magda as she translated Rohana's words.

"I have brought a likeness of my son; perhaps you could ask those of your men who are responsible for the work crews of our people, when he was last employed here."

Inside the silk was a copper locket; Montray opened the clasp to reveal a miniature painting. His eyebrows rose as he looked at it.

"Take a look at this, Magda."

He handed it to her, and she looked on an elaborately painted likeness of Peter Haldane.

"I can see by your faces that you both recognize my son," Lady Rohana said. Magda's first thought was, *This is impossible, insane!* Then sanity came to her rescue. *A chance resemblance, no more. A fantastic coincidence.*

Montray was on the communicator. "Get me a personnel solido and photos of Peter Haldane, Bethany. Magda"—he turned back to her—"you can explain."

Magda tried. She could see faint beads of perspiration along the lady's hairline; whether from nervousness or from the heat of Montray's office—or both—she could not tell.

"Chance resemblance? Impossible, my child. He was recognized by the color of his hair, and that color is borne by none but Comyn, or those of Comyn blood."

"It is not rare among Terrans, my Lady," Magda said. (She had known this; Peter had made jokes of it. "On the Darkovan side they think I must be some nobleman's bastard!") "It carries among us no claim to nobility, but means only that one's parents had red hair, and a certain racial makeup." She broke off as Bethany came in, took the small solido and personnel printout that bore a color photo of Peter Haldane. She handed them to Lady Rohana without comment.

Rohana studied them a moment, then looked up, her face gone white. "I cannot understand this. Are you very sure he is not one of ours, in some disguise that has misled you?"

"Very sure, my Lady; I have known Peter Haldane since childhood."

"How can this be? One of your Terrans, so like to one of us . . ." Her voice wavered. "I can see that anyone might be deceived, if this man wore Darkovan dress. And your man is missing, too?" Not until hours afterward did Magda realize that she had not told Rohana this. "Strange. Well, I see I must search elsewhere for news of my son."

When she had taken leave of Montray, formally, she turned to Magda, lightly touching her hand. She looked at her, a long and searching look. "Somehow I think I have not heard the end of this matter," she said. "I thank you for your courtesy. A day may come when I can help you, my girl; until then, I wish you well."

Magda was almost too surprised to speak; she managed a formal word of thanks, but Rohana kindly waved her away, summoned her companion and the sweating Guardsman and departed.

Left alone with Magda, Montray exploded, "Well, what do you think of that!"

"I think the poor woman is worried to death about her son."

"Almost as worried as you are about Haldane, huh?"

"A lot more. Peter is a grown man, and entirely on his own. Why should I—"

"Damned if I know *why* you should, but you are," Montray said. "And I gather her son is a grown man, too. But on a damn feudal world like this where fighting duels is the most popular indoor sport, I gather there's real cause for concern if the man of the house doesn't come home."

"Feudal is hardly the proper description—"

"OK, OK, Magda, you're up on all the little nuances and fine points; I'm not, I don't want to be. All I want is away from this damn place; you can have my job any time I can get a transfer out—or you could, except that on a world like this a woman wouldn't be allowed to take it. I should think you'd want out, too. The point is: I understood most of what the lady was saying to you. It looks like you've made a useful contact. It's not easy for a woman to do anything much on this world, but if you have an in with someone on the top levels, in the Comyn—"

Magda found she did not want to explore this point just now. She reminded Montray, rather tartly, that she had come here in off-duty time; he told her to put in a voucher for the extra pay, and let her go.

Yet, back in her own quarters, removing her heavy clothing, she thought about what he had said. Rohana had spoken formally at first, and when she had called Magda "my child" she had spoken in the inflection normally used to a servant or an inferior—or someone like a translator. But at the end she had called her "my girl," in the intimate mode she would have used to a young woman of her own caste. Was it only random kindness?

Outside, the snow had turned to heavy sleet; Magda went to the window, drawing aside the curtains to look out through the doubled, soundproof glass into the silent raging of the storm.

You're out there somewhere, Peter, she thought. *What are you up to? If there's really any such thing as ESP, I ought to be able to reach you somehow. Damn it, Peter come home, I'm worried, damn you.*

She thought, *How Peter would laugh at me. He's somewhere, following some obscure lead he's found.* Magda knew she was a good Intelligence officer; knew Peter was considered a gifted one. A woman could not do too much in the Intelligence line on a planet like Darkover, where strong codes and taboos regulated female behavior; Magda knew that elsewhere, on a less strongly patriarchal planet, where men and women were equals, she could have had more scope for her talents. *Yet Darkover is my home. . . .*

One of the messier moments, during the tense weeks before the showdown that had ended their brief marriage, had been Peter's accusation that she was jealous, jealous because he was allowed to accomplish more than she was on a world like Darkover. And of course, it was true. . . .

Oh, Peter, come home. I'm worried. Feeling foolish, yet taking it seriously, Magda strained in concentration—as she had done at the New-Rhine-Rakakowski Institute on Terra, making her significantly better-than-chance scores on her ESP cards—to try to send a message, if such a thing were possible. *Peter, Peter, we are all worrying. At least let us know you are safe.*

But there was no sense of contact, and at last, drained and weary, feeling it had been an idiotic endeavor, Magda gave up and went to bed.

That night she dreamed of Peter Haldane, but he was laughing at her.

Chapter
SEVEN

The season drew on, and the cold thickened. Magda, who had been born in the mountains, did not mind the cold; at least, not when she could wear suitable clothing for it. But most of the Terrans burrowed indoors like animals in their winter holes, venturing out only when they must; and the crews of the starships that touched down here confined their stay to the minimum, seldom venturing out even into the port and never going into the Old Town.

Even Magda, careless of official disapproval, wore her Darkovan dress more and more around the HQ, suffering the inconvenience of long skirts and heavy petticoats for their warmth. One afternoon when she came in from a day spent in the Old Town, it was snowing so heavily that the idea of changing into the thin Terran synthetics seemed insane; she went directly to Personnel, and the station where her observations were recorded. Montray's pretty assistant, heavily sweatered, looked at her with envy. "I don't blame you for going native. I'm almost tempted to transfer to your section so I can dress for the climate! I don't know how you manage to get around in those things—but they do look warm!"

Magda grinned at her. "Usual question."

"Usual answer, I'm afraid," Bethany said soberly. "No word from Peter. This morning the boss took him off the active-duty list; he's officially reported PMOD—provisionally missing on duty. Pay suspended subject to official contact, and so forth."

Magda flinched. The mechanism was in motion for having him declared *Missing, presumed dead*.

Bethany said, trying to comfort her, "Nothing's final yet. Maybe he found a friendly place to stay and just settled in for the winter. He couldn't travel in this, even if he was all right."

Magda's smile only stretched her mouth. "It's not nearly winter yet. The time when travel becomes impossible and all business shuts down for the spring-thaw is almost four months away. The passes aren't even closed into the Hellers."

"You're joking!" Bethany looked into the raging storm and shivered. "But you should know, you've been out in it. Summers, I think you have a peach of a job—nothing to do but mix with the crowds in the city and listen to gossip. But in weather like this—I'm surprised they didn't name this planet *Winter*."

"They couldn't; there's already one called that. Read the records someday. Speaking of records, I'd better get mine set up."

"Is that really all you do—listen to gossip?"

"That, and a lot more. I take note of the fashions being worn by women, make linguistic notes on new expressions and changes in the local argot . . . languages change all the time, you know that."

"Do they really?"

"Do you use the slang expressions now that you did when you were seven years old? It doesn't matter if an agent uses some outdated expressions; people do pick up little tags of speech from their parents, and everybody tends to use expressions that were common in their own teens, when peer relationships were being established. The one thing no undercover agent on the Darkovan side can do is speak as if he'd learned the language from a book; so I work all the time keeping us all up to date. Montray gets away with it because he's meeting people as a Terran, and it's a compliment for him to go halfway by speaking their language at all; speaking it too well would be a subtle form of one-upmanship that would rouse all kinds of psychological resistances in the Darkovans he meets. They're *supposed* to be able to speak better than he does. But the agents who work on the Darkovan side can't make mistakes even in slang. And everybody has to keep up with common usage."

Bethany looked puzzled. Magda elucidated: "Well, look. For instance; there's a word which means, literally, 'entertainer,' or 'singing woman.' It's in the standard texts. But if you called a ballad-singer, or one of the soprano soloists with one of the orchestras in Thendara, by that word, her father or brother would call you out in a duel—call a man out; a woman using such a term would simply be regarded as very vulgar and ill bred."

"An *entertainer?*" Bethany repeated the word in amazement. "Why? It sounds inoffensive enough."

"Because for decades that particular word has been a polite euphemism—the kind of word you can use in front of a lady—for 'prostitute.' No respectable woman on Darkover would soil her mouth with the word *grezalis*—that's vernacular for 'whore'—and no man but a boor would use it in front of her. The respectable concert soprano is a 'lyric performer,' and don't forget it if you go to a concert in Thendara!"

Bethany shivered. "I had no idea a translator's work was so complicated."

"It's true; you have to take extra pains to avoid giving offense. One of my main jobs is to check through official speeches to make sure our translators and speech-writers avoid words with accidentally offensive connotations. For instance: you know how our standard official speeches—not just on Darkover—are full of expressions of friendship and brotherhood? Well, the commonest expression for 'friend and brother' in the *casta* language—that's the official language in Thendara—is red-flagged as an absolutely taboo term for official speeches here."

"Why, for heaven's sake?"

"Because the commonest expression meaning 'friend and brother,' if you don't get the inflection just right, can get you in an *incredible* amount of trouble. In the impersonal inflection it expresses the purest sentiments of fraternal charity and humanitarian concern, and is perfectly suitable for official and diplomatic use. Just the same it's red-flagged, because a lot of our officials simply cannot *pronounce* the language well enough, and even if they *mean* to use the impersonal inflection, they're likely to *sound* like the wrong one. And if you use that word —the same word—in the personal inflection, it means 'brother' in the sense of family intimacy and closeness, and is too familiar; while if you happen to use it in the intimate inflection, you're defining the person addressed as a homosexual—and your lover. Do you see now why it's an absolutely forbidden term in official language?"

"Good God! I certainly do." Bethany giggled. "No wonder Montray has his own private linguist to write his speeches!" The women exchanged a conspiratorial chuckle; Montray's ineptitude in the Darkovan language was a standing joke in the HQ. "And so that's why you go over all his speeches personally? You know everything about Darkover, don't you, Magda?"

Ruefully, Magda shook her head. "No, certainly not. No Terran can." *And if any Terran could, no Terran woman could.* The thought was as bitter as ever. But she put it aside.

"It would have been different, if the Terran HQ had stayed at Caer Donn. There, the Terrans and Darkovans met more or less as equals, and we could mingle with them *as* Terrans. There was no need for undercover agents. But here we have to work undercover; the Comyn have completely refused to cooperate. They leased us land for the spaceport, let us hire workmen for construction jobs and allowed us to build

from the work I know best, while an idiot like Montray needs a specially qualified linguist to write his speeches, and two more to hold his hand in case he gets lost or has to ask his way a hundred meters outside the gates! I should have Montray's job. He isn't even qualified for mine!

Montray was shivering; Magda had no sympathy for him. Montray knew what the climate was like; he had authority to dress for it, or modify the official uniform in some more suitable way, but he didn't even have the imagination for that.

I ought to get right off this damn world. There are planty of planets where I could do the kind of work I'm best fitted for.

But Darkover is the one I know best. And here, I'm only fit for a woman's job!

And I can only do even that because I'm a Terran. Darkovan women don't even do my kind of work!

At the gates of the Comyn Castle, a man in the green-and-black uniform of the City Guard asked their business. He used the derogatory mode, and Magda bristled.

Montray would not have noticed, but Magda told him stiffly that they had been personally summoned by Lord Lorill Hastur. The Guard went away, returning almost immediately; this time he spoke in the respectful mode, saying that the Lord Hastur had given orders for them to be conducted at once into his presence.

The hallways of the Comyn Castle were drafty, cold and all but deserted. Magda knew that at this season of the year, most of the Comyn had withdrawn to their own estates throughout the Domains; they gathered here only in Council Season, near midsummer. The Hastur Domain was far away on the borders of the Hellers; she supposed Lord Hastur had stayed here only because events in the capital city required his presence. She carefully studied the corridors, the hangings and ornaments, wanting to make the most of an opportunity which, for her, might never come again; no woman could hold an official post on Darkover, and she would probably never again enter the Comyn Castle.

At last they were led into a small audience chamber where Lorill Hastur awaited them: a slight, serious man, with dark red hair winged with white at the temples. He greeted them with courteous phrases, which Magda translated automatically. She had seen that the only other person in the room was Lady Rohana Ardais.

Magda would have said, if asked, that she did not believe in precognition and was skeptical about ESP. Yet the moment she saw the slender, copper-haired woman, in a dress of violet-blue, seated quietly on a cushioned bench, she *knew.*

This has to do with Peter. . . .

"My kinswoman has made the long journey from Ardais purposely to speak with you," Lorill Hastur said. "Will you explain, Rohana?"

"I came to you from a sense of obligation," Rohana said, "because you were kind to me when I came to you in deep trouble about my son." She spoke to Montray, apparently, but it was obvious that the words were meant for Magda.

"My husband and I have just received a message from Rumal di Scarp."

Magda could not quite control a shudder as she translated. "Sain Scarp is the most notorious bandit stronghold in the Hellers," she explained to Montray. (As a child, that word had been used to frighten her little friends into good behavior: "The men from Sain Scarp will get you!")

Lady Rohana continued: "Rumal hates the men of Ardais with a deadly hatred; my husband's father hanged half a dozen of his men from the walls of Castle Ardais. So now Rumal has sent us a message: that he holds our son Kyril prisoner in the *forst* of Sain Scarp; and he has named a ransom which we must pay before midwinter, or Kyril will be sent back to us"— Rohana shivered slightly—"in pieces."

Montray said, "Lady, my deepest sympathies. But

the Terran Empire cannot entangle itself in private feuds—"

Rohana's eyes blazed. She did not wait for Magda to translate. "I see you still have not understood. When, after I spoke with you, I returned to Castle Ardais, I found my son safe and well at home; he had delayed because of frostbitten feet, and came when he was able to travel. When we received the word from Sain Scarp, he was in the room with us, and he thought it a tremendous joke."

Magda turned pale, knowing what Rohana's next words would be. "I knew, then, having seen the portrait you showed me, just who is being held in Sain Scarp. Your friend," she said to Magda. "Is he your lover?" She had used the polite term, for which the nearest Terran equivalent was "promised husband"; the derogatory mode would have implied "paramour."

Magda forced her words through dread. A whole childhood spent hearing tales of bandits in the Hellers made her throat tight. "He was my"—she searched for the precise Darkovan equivalent for "husband," for there were at least three forms of Darkovan marriage—"my freemate. We have separated, but we were childhood friends and I am deeply concerned for his safety."

Montray, who had followed all this with difficulty, was scowling. "Are you certain? It is rare for any of my men to go so far into the Hellers. Could it not be some other kinsman with a resemblance to your son, Lady?"

"Rumal sent this with his message," Rohana said, and held out a man's neck-ornament on a fine copper chain. "I know it is not my son's; it was made in Dalereuth, and such work is not sold in the Hellers, nor worn much."

Montray turned it uneasily in his hands. It was a carved medallion of some blue-green semiprecious stone, encircled in finely worked copper filigree. "You know Haldane better than I do, Magda. Do you recognize it?"

"I gave it to him." Her mouth was dry. It had been shortly before their short-lived marriage; the one and only time they had traveled together to the plains of Dalereuth. She had bought it for herself, but Peter had admired it so extravagantly that Magda, who after all could not wear a man's ornament, had made him a present of it, in return for— She raised her shaking hands to the nape of her neck, touching the silver butterfly-clasp she always wore.

He took off the one I had worn, and pinned this one there . . . as only a lover would dare to do . . . and I let him. . . .

"That's pretty conclusive," Montray said. "Damn him, he knew better than to try to get into the Hellers alone. What chance is there that this bandit—di Scarp—will turn him loose, if he finds out he's got the wrong man?"

"None," Hastur said. "The mountain bandits remember all too well those first few years at Caer Donn, when Aldaran deceived the Terrans into believing it was permitted to use your weapons against them. I hope, for his own sake, that your young man does not reveal his identity."

Montray said, "Doesn't that just prove that we were right to help the Aldarans, and that you were wrong to stop us? They are still ravaging your people worse than ever, and your Darkovan Compact makes it impossible to attack them effectively. You should have let us finish wiping them out!"

"I must respectfully refuse to debate the ethics of Compact with you," Hastur said; "it has kept Darkover free of major wars for hundreds of years, and is not open to debate. We still remember our Ages of Chaos."

"That's all very well," Montray said, "but doesn't it mean anything to you that an innocent bystander may be murdered in a quarrel that is none of his, and that you are condoning their actions by making it impossible for our people to rescue him?"

"It means a great deal," said Hastur, and his eyes

glowed with sudden anger. "I might remind you that he is hardly an innocent bystander, having walked into this situation of his own free will. We did not require him—for that matter, we did not even give him leave—to travel in the Hellers. He went of his free choice and for your purposes, or his own—not ours. But we did not forbid him to go, either; and it is really none of our affair if he suffers the same fate that our own men risk whenever they go there. I might remind you, also, that there was no compulsion upon us ever to tell you of his fate. Nor do we refuse you leave to rescue him, if you can do it as secretly as he went there."

Montray shook his head. "In the Hellers, with winter coming on? Impossible. I'm afraid you're right; he knew the risks he was taking, he knew what would happen if he got caught. I'm afraid he'll have to take whatever he brought on himself."

Magda said in horror, "You're not going to—to abandon him, just write him off?"

Montray sighed heavily. "I don't like it either, Magda. But what else can we do? He knew the risks; you all do."

Magda felt her spine prickle, as if the small hairs on her body were all standing on end. Yes, that was the rule of the Intelligence service. *The first law and the last is secrecy. Get into trouble, and there's no way to pull you out again.*

"We can ransom him," Magda flared. "I'll stand surety for the ransom myself, if you begrudge it!"

"Magda, it's not that. We'd gladly pay to get him loose, but—"

"Impossible," Lorill Hastur said. "Rumal di Scarp would never negotiate with the Terrans; the moment he knew his prisoner was a Terran he would take pleasure in killing him out of hand—by means I would prefer not to describe before women's ears. Your man's only hope is to conceal his origin." He turned to Magda and said, courteously not looking at her (a gesture which spoke a great deal about the quality of Magda's Darkovan dress and manners), "Not knowing otherwise, I would have taken you for a woman of the Hellers. Does your friend speak the language, and know our customs, as well as you?"

"Better," Magda said truthfully. Her mind was racing. *We must think of something! We must!* "Lady Rohana, they evidently still believe he is your son. Can *you* negotiate with them for his ransom?"

"It was my first thought. I would gladly do this to save a life. But my husband has forbidden me, once and for all, to go near Sain Scarp on any such mission. It was only with difficulty that I won his consent to come and tell you this much."

"Magda, it's no use. The only hope would be for Peter to escape on his own," Montray said. "If *we* go, and try to ransom him, as a Terran, we are only hastening his death-sentence."

She said fiercely, "If I were a man, I would go myself and negotiate for his ransom! There is no man alive in the Hellers who would know me for a Terran! If I could use the lady's name, and negotiate as if for a kinsman ..." She turned, appealing directly to Rohana.

"Help me think of a way!"

I know she can do it, if she will. She is a law to herself, this lady of the Comyn, she will do what she thinks right and no one will forbid her. . . .

Rohana said to Hastur, "I told you this girl had spirit and strength. I will not disobey Gabriel—it is not worth the argument—but I will help her, if I can." She turned to Magda, and said, "You would be willing to go yourself into the Hellers? With winter coming on? Many men might shrink from such a journey, my girl." Again she spoke as if to a younger woman of her own caste. Magda set her chin, and said, "Lady, I was born near Caer Donn; I am not afraid of the mountains, nor of their worst weather."

Montray said harshly, "Don't be a damned fool, Magda! You're supposed to be the expert on women's customs on Darkover; but even *I* know that no woman can travel alone and unprotected! You may have guts enough—or damnfoolishness enough—but it's impossible for you to travel alone, here on this planet. You tell her, my Lady," he appealed to Rohana. "It would be impossible! Damn it, I admire her spirit, too, but there are things women just can't do here!"

"You are right," Rohana said. "Our customs make it impossible for a woman. An ordinary woman, that is. But there is one way, and only one, in which a woman can travel alone without danger and scandal. The Free Amazons alone do not accept the customs that bind other women."

Magda said, "I don't know much about the Free Amazons. I've heard the name." She looked straight into Rohana's eyes, and said, "If you think I can do it . . ."

"Once before, I employed a Free Amazon on a mission no man would undertake. It was a scandal, at the time." She looked at Lorill with a mischievous small smile, as if, Magda thought, she were evoking a shared memory. "So it will evoke no great scandal—or if it does, no more scandal than I can bear—when it is known that I have sent a Free Amazon to Sain Scarp to negotiate in my place for my son's release. And if Rumal di Scarp should chance to hear it rumored that my son Kyril is safe at Ardais, then he will only think that he has captured instead some kinsman or fosterling of our house, whom we are redeeming out of kindness or a bad conscience; and he will sneer at us for being so gullible, but he will take the ransom anyway and be glad to get it.

"I think I know enough of the Free Amazons to make it possible for you to pass as one, unchallenged. But there may be dangers by the way, child; can you defend yourself?"

Magda said, "Everyone in Intelligence—man and woman alike—is trained in unarmed combat and knife fighting."

Rohana nodded. "I had heard about this," she said, and Magda wished she knew *how* this information had come to Darkovan ears. *Probably the same way we learn things about them!*

"Go back, now," Rohana said. "Arrange for the journey, and for the ransom, and come to me at dawn tomorrow morning. I will see that you have the proper clothing and necessities, and that you know how to carry yourself as a Free Amazon."

Montray burst out, "Are you really going to do this harebrained thing, Magda? Free Amazons! Aren't they lady soldiers?"

Rohana laughed. "It is easy to see you know nothing about them," she said. "Indeed, it is comforting to think there is something you Terrans have not managed to discover about us!" Magda had to grin ruefully at that. "Yes, many of them are mercenary soldiers; others are trackers, hunters, horsebreakers, blacksmiths; midwives, dairy-women, confectioners, bakers, ballad-singers and cheese-sellers! They work at any honest trade; for one to serve as a messenger and negotiate in a family feud is completely respectable, as such things go."

"I don't give a damn whether it's respectable or not," Magda told Montray, and Rohana smiled approvingly.

"Good," she said. "Then it is settled." She gave Magda her hand, with a kindly smile. "It is a pity, but you will have to cut that lovely hair," she said.

Chapter

EIGHT

Magda woke in the gray dawn, hearing the thin patter of sleet on the roof of the travel-shelter. It was her seventh night on the road, and until now the weather had been fine.

She had till midwinter-night. With anything like reasonable weather, she had ample time. But could anyone expect reasonable weather in the Hellers, at this season?

From the far end of the shelter she could hear the soft stamping and the rustling breaths of her saddle-horse and the pack animal, an antlered beast from the Kilghard Hills, better suited to the mountain weather than any horse. She wondered what time it was; it was still too dark to see.

It did not occur to her to regret—or even to think about—her chronometer. Like all Terrans allowed to work undercover on any planet anywhere in the Empire, she had undergone a long and intense conditioning, designed to make it virtually impossible for her to act in any way not consonant with her assigned character; and there was no item, in all her luggage and gear, of off-world manufacture. This was a habit of years; everyone in Intelligence learned the almost hypnotic

121

mechanisms which meant that the moment she left the Trade City, Magdalen Lorne of Linguistics was gone, left wholly behind her; even her name was gone, packed away in a very small corner of her unconscious mind. *Magdalen* had no precise Darkovan equivalent; when she was a small girl in the mountains near Caer Donn, her Darkovan playmates had called her *Margali*.

She turned over restlessly in her sleeping bag, raising nervous fingers to her shorn head. It felt cold, strange, immodest.

Lady Rohana, in the long briefing session that had preceded her departure, had been sympathetic about that, too.

"I traveled once, in disguise, with a band of Free Amazons," she said, "and I had to cut my hair; I can still remember the shock I felt. I remember that I cried, and how they laughed at me. It was worse for me, probably, than for you: you are accountable to no one, but I knew how angry my husband would be when he knew."

Magda had asked, "And was he angry?" and Rohana smiled, a reminiscent smile. "Terribly. It was already done, so there was nothing he could do about it; but I felt his anger for almost a year, till it had grown to what he called a respectable length."

Magda heard the sleet beginning to abate and crawled out of her sleeping bag. Shivering in the fireless hut, she dressed quickly in the clothing Lady Rohana had provided: loose trousers, a long-sleeved and high-necked undertunic of embroidered linen, a fur-lined overtunic and riding-cloak. She had even measured Magda's foot and sent a servant to buy boots in the marketplace. Magda laced the high boots and led her animals outside, feeding them from the stacked fodder in the nearby shed and slipping the prescribed amount of coins into the padlocked box there. She led them one by one to the watering trough, breaking the ice there with the small hammer on her saddle. While they munched and drank, she went inside, quickly made a small fire and boiled some water, stirring it into the precooked, powdered mixture of grains and nuts that made a kind of instant porridge. Mixed with a few shreds of dried fruit, it was edible when you were used to it.

The ransom was safely hidden in her saddlebags, converted into the copper bars that were the standard Darkovan currency. In Terran exchange it was no more than a couple of months' salary for a good agent; they probably wouldn't even bother to take it out of Peter's "hazard" pay.

Why am I doing this? Peter's a grown man, able to take his own risks. I'm not his guardian. I'm not even his wife anymore. I don't love him that much, not anymore, not now. So why? But she had no answer, and it nagged at the back of her mind as she set off down the trail. She stopped at the indicator post near the travel-shelter, locating the next three shelters along this trail. One was at a reasonable distance for a large caravan with heavily laden pack animals; a second was located at a good day's ride for a party traveling at an easy pace but without much gear; the third was about at the limit of a long day's hard ride for a solitary traveler. *Maybe I can sleep there tonight. . . .* She turned from the post and started along the trail, feeling a faint unease she could not identify; then it came to her.

I'm out of character, reading the travel-post. Most Darkovan women can't read. . . . Literacy even among men on Darkover was by no means universal, though most men could spell out a placard or scrawl their own names; among women it was extremely rare, and her small Darkovan playmates at Caer Donn had been astonished and slightly shocked—and a little envious— when they discovered that Margali could read, that her own father had taught her. *Out of character. Damn it, this whole trip is out of character.*

Magda clucked to her horse, and started along the trail. Rohana had warned her: "I traveled with the Free Amazons, but not as one of them; I do not deceive myself that I know all of their ways and customs. If I were you, I would avoid any meeting with real

Amazon groups; but most of the folk in the hills where you will travel know *nothing at all* about them. So no one will question your disguise, if you are careful."

And in seven days she had not been challenged, though once she had had to share the travel-shelter with two men, traders from the far hills. By law and custom, these shelters, put up centuries ago, and kept inspected and stocked even in wartime by the border patrols, were sacred places of neutrality, and must be shared by all comers; anything else would have condemned other travelers to die of cold and exposure. By law, even blood-feuds were suspended in the shelters, as Magda had heard was the custom during forest fires. The men had glanced briefly at Magda's short hair and Amazon clothing, spoken a few formally courteous words, and ignored her entirely after that.

But since then she had met no one; the advanced season had sent most travelers home to their own firesides. The clouds had thinned and gone, and the great red sun of Darkover, which some poet in the Terran Zone had christened The Bloody Sun, was rising between the peaks, flooding the high snowfields with flaming crimson and gold. As she rode up into the pass, it seemed that a sea of flame bathed the high snowcaps, a brilliance of solitude that exhilarated and excited her.

But the sunrise subsided, and there was nothing but the lonely silence of the trail. Silence; and too much time to think, to ask herself again and again: *Why am I doing this? Am I still in love with the bastard?*

Pride, maybe, that a man who shared my bed—however briefly—should be abandoned and left to die, with no one to help him?

Or maybe, when we were growing up in Caer Donn, just the few of us among all the Darkovan children, we absorbed their codes, their ethics. Loyalty, kinship's dues. To the Empire, Peter is only an employee, expendable. To me, to any Darkovan, that's an outrageous notion, an obscenity.

She crossed the path before the sun was more than

an hour high in the sky, her ears aching with the altitude, and began to descend into the next valley. At noon she stopped at a little mountain village and indulged herself by buying a mug of hot soup and a few fried cakes at a food-stall. Some curious children gathered around, and Magda guessed, from their eagerness, that they saw very few outsiders; she gave them some sweets from her saddlebags, and lingered, resting her animals before the climb to the next pass, enjoying her first taste of fresh food since she had left Thendara.

They were all curious as kittens; they asked where she had come from, and when she told them "Thendara," they stared as if she had said "From world's end." She supposed that to these children, never out of their own hills, Thendara *was* the world's end. But when they asked her business, she smiled and said it was a secret of her patroness. Lady Rohana had given her permission to use her name. "I will give you my safe-conduct, too, under my seal. In the foothills there are many who owe service to Gabriel and to me." She had also cautioned her against any but the most casual contact with genuine Amazons, but had advised her that if she met any by chance, she would be asked for her Guild-house, and for the name of the woman who had received her oath. "In this case, you may say Kindra n'ha Mhari; she is dead these three years"—and a fleeting sadness had touched Rohana's eyes—"but she was my dear friend, and I do not think she would grudge this use of her name. But if the Gods are kind you will get to Sain Scarp, and, hopefully, back again, without using it."

She had finished eating, and was watering her animals at the village trough when she saw a pair of men riding into the square. By the cut of their cloaks she knew they were from the far Hellers; they were bearded, and wore wicked-looking knives in their belts. They looked at Magda and, she fancied, at her laden saddlebags, with a regard that made her uneasy. She cut short the watering, clambered hastily into her saddle, and took the trail out of town. She hoped they would stop there for a good, long rest, and she would not see them again.

For a long time the trail led upward between heavily wooded slopes. The ice and snow were melting in the noon sun and the trail was slushy underfoot; Magda let her horse find its own pace, and when the road grew steepest, dismounted to lead it. She paused at a bend in the trail, where the trees thinned at a giddy height, looking down at the narrow line of road far below. There she saw, with consternation, what looked like the same two men she had seen in the village. Were they following her?

Don't be paranoid. This is the only road northwest into the Hellers; am I the only one who could have legitimate business along it? She stepped to the edge, careful not to slip on the muddy, slushy cliff, and looked down at the men riding the trail. Could she even be sure they were the same two men? Yes, for one man had been riding a roan horse; they were not common at any latitude, and to see two in the mountains in the same day's ride was entirely unlikely. As if to dispel her last doubt, one looked up, apparently saw Magda silhouetted along the edge, and leaned over to speak urgently to his companion; they drew at their horses' reins, edging in toward the cliff where they would not be visible from above.

Magda felt panic grip and drag at her, a physical sensation like a cramp along her leg muscles. She hurried back to her horse, ordering herself sternly to be calm. *I'm armed. I've been combat-trained since I was sixteen, and first knew I was going into Intelligence.* On any other world, she knew, she would have been expected to take this kind of chance routinely, man or woman. Here she'd been sheltered by Darkovan custom.

If it came to a fight—she laid her hand on her knife for a moment, trying to reassure herself—it would be better to make a stand in the pass. She could defend herself better there than on the downslopes. But need it come to a fight? Terran agents were trained to avoid confrontations when possible. And she would have bet that even Free Amazons didn't go around looking for trouble.

Suddenly she knew that she could not, *could not* force herself to make a stand here and face them. She commanded herself to stay here and think it through, but even while she tried to form her thoughts clearly she was guiding her horse away down the slope, down the trail, hurrying and urging it more, she knew, than a good rider would ever do (there was a mountain proverb of her childhood, "On a steep road let your horse set the pace"), yet she knew she was almost racing downhill, hearing small stones slip and slide beneath the horse's hooves.

It was not long before she realized she could not go on like this; if one of her animals should fall and break a leg she would be afoot and stranded. She drew the horse to a stop, patting its heaving sides in apology. *What's wrong with me, why did I run away like that?* Behind her, the road to the pass lay bare and unoccupied. *Maybe they weren't following me at all....* But she felt the vague unease, the "hunch" she had learned, in years of successful agent work, always to trust; and it said, loud and clear: *run, hide, disappear, get lost.* The woman who had trained her, far away on another world, had said: "Every good undercover agent is a little psychic. Or they don't survive long in the service."

Now what? She couldn't outrun them, burdened as she was with luggage and pack animal. Sooner or later they would come up with her, and then it would come to a fight.

She looked at the ground, covered with melting snow and mud, an amorphous trampled brownish mess. *Lucky. In new snow they'd see my tracks ... and see where I left the trail, which would be worse. ...* But in the running, muddy water and slush all tracks vanished as fast as they were made. She turned aside from the road, leading the animals through a small gap in the trees; turned back to obliterate, with a quick hand, the marks in the snow where she had crossed the edge; led them some distance from the road and tethered them in a thick grove of evergreens, where they could not be seen.

Then she slipped back, found a concealed vantage point where she could conceal herself between trees and underbrush, and gnawed nervously on some dried fruit as she waited to see the success of her trick.

It was nearly an hour before the riders she had seen came down the slopes, hurrying their mounts as much as they could in the mushy trail underfoot. But neither of them even glanced in Magda's direction as they hurried past. When they were out of sight, she crawled shakily from her hiding place. She noted peripherally that her knees were weak and trembling, and that the palms of her hands were clammy and wet.

What's the matter with me? I'm not behaving like a trained agent—or even like a Free Amazon! I'm behaving like a—like a bunny rabbit!

And why am I panicking now, anyway? I did the sensible thing. Any of our agents, man or woman, on any world, in that situation, would have done just what I did. Kept out of trouble. . . .

Yet she knew, no matter how she tried to rationalize it, that her flight had not been a considered thing, based on her standing orders to avoid a fight where possible. It had been, quite simply, a rout. *I panicked. That's the long and short of it. I panicked, and I ran.*

I behaved like . . . like. . . . Realization flashed over her. *Not like a Terran agent. Not like a Free Amazon. Like an ordinary, conventional Darkovan girl.*

The kind I've taught myself to be, in Thendara. The kind I was brought up to be, in Caer Donn. . . .

The short winter day was drawing to a close, and she thought, *I'll camp here tonight, in the woods; I'll let them get a good, long start. By tomorrow they'll have gone through two or three of those little villages, and with luck they'll think I just found a place to stay in a village, and give up.*

Or, possibly, they were respectable traders on their

own lawful business and in a hurry to get home to their wives and children, she considered.

She put up her small tent. It was a compromise, the maximum possible protection in bad weather combined with the minimum possible in weight and size; a combination of an undersized tent and an oversized sleeping bag. It was the standard Darkovan traveler's model. She knew already that no sane person ever spent a night outdoors. if he could possibly help it, which was why the roads were lined with the travel-shelters and huts and why they were sacred places of neutrality.

But she spent that night in the open anyway. By good fortune the weather kept fine, even the predawn snowfall unusually light; but Magda knew, as she emerged shivering, this was a bad sign. Clouds scudded thick and black, away north, and a high wind had already begun to toss the tips of the evergreens, promising a severe storm on the way.

In the lonely silence of the trail she went over and over her failure. However she rationalized it, it *was* a failure; she had panicked.

I've taught myself always to behave that way, whenever I step on the Darkovan side. It was the standard Intelligence conditioning: build yourself a *persona,* a character for whatever planet you're working on, and never step out of it, even for an instant, until you're safely back inside the Terran Zone.

But the personality I built for myself in Thendara won't work here. Because of the particular society on Darkover, and the way women live. It was different for the men. But I was the only woman; and I never realized how far I had come from ordinary agent's training. . . .

She tried to think it through, to analyze just what basic changes she would have to make in her basic Darkovan *persona* for this assignment, but the attempt made her so overwhelmingly anxious that she had to give up the effort. *The trouble is, I've been trained never to think of Terra outside the Zone.* Now she was trying to bring a process as automatic as breathing under voluntary control; and it wasn't working.

I can't be a Free Amazon. I don't know enough about them. Even Lady Rohana said she didn't know enough about them. So I can be only my basic Darkovan persona, pretending to be a Free Amazon. Lady Rohana seemed to think it would be effective enough to fool people who didn't have much to do with Free Amazons; but I'd just better hope I don't meet any real ones!

This caused another of those weird small repercussions which, for years, she had thought of as "hunches" and learned to trust. Oddly, this one iced her blood; she had physically to pull her cloak tighter about her shoulders against the sudden runnel of cold down her spine. *It would be just my luck, to meet a couple!*

Peter always said I had a talent for bluffing. Better get used to thinking of him by his Darkovan name.

She had a sudden moment of blank terror when the name refused to come to her mind, when she wholly blanked on it. It lasted only a few seconds, and the panic ebbed away as the name came back to her. *Piedro. That's in the Hellers. In the lowlands they'd call him Pier . . . why did I blank on it like that?*

It was an hour past noon when she passed one of the shelter huts; it was empty, and she hesitated, tempted to stay there overnight. But she had already lost half a day, and always, at the back of her mind, was the thought of the midwinter deadline. She must not only be at Sain Scarp by midwinter, but she must leave some leeway for return to Thendara before the winter storms closed the passes. *I can't see us camping on Rumal di Scarp's doorstep all winter.*

Nor did she particularly want to spend the winter cooped up anywhere, alone with Peter. *Once I used to daydream about something that would isolate us, so we had time only to be alone together. . . . Even now, it might be . . . pleasurable. . . .* Exasperated, Magda told herself to snap out of it. She wondered, half annoyed, if Bethany had been right all along; *was* she still half in love with Peter? *I should have taken another lover right away, after we separated. God knows I had enough chances. I wonder why I didn't.*

She checked the notice board, and discovered that there was another shelter just about half a day's ride distant. As she turned her back on the shelter she felt again the curious, almost physical prickling of the "hunch," but told herself fiercely not to be superstitious. *I'm afraid to go on, so I find reasons, and call it ESP!*

The trail steepened and grew rough underfoot; by midafternoon the thickening clouds lay so deep on the mountain that Magda was riding through a thick white blanket of fog. The dim gray world was full of echoes; she could hear her horse's hooves sounding dimly, behind and before her, like invisible, ghostly companions. The valley was gone, and the lower slopes; she rode high and alone, on a narrow trail above the known world. She had never been afraid of heights, but now she began to be afraid of the narrowness of the dim trail, of the white nothingness that hemmed her in on every side and might hide anything—or worse, nothing. Her mind kept returning to the cliffs and crags below, where an animal, putting a foot down wrong, might step off the trail, go plunging down the mountainside to be dashed to death on the invisible rocks far below. . . .

As the darkness deepened, the fog dissolved into fine rain and then into a thick, fast-falling snow, wiping out trail and landmarks. The snow froze as it fell, and the slush underfoot crunched and crackled under her horse's hooves; then the wind began to howl through the trees and, where they thinned, to roar across the trail, driving icy needles of sleet into her face and eyes. She pulled up her cloak's collar and wrapped a fold of her scarf over her nose and chin, but the cold made her nose run, and the water froze on her nose and mouth and turned the scarf to a block of ice. Snow clung to her eyelashes and froze there, making it impossible to see. Her horse began to slip on the icy trail, and Magda dismounted to lead it and the faltering pack animal, glad of the knee-high boots she was wearing; a woman's soft low sandals or ankle-high, tied moccasins would have been soaked in a moment.

I should have stayed in that last shelter. That was what that hunch was all about. Confound it, I ought to listen to myself!

Her feet were freezing, and she was seriously beginning to wonder if her cheeks and nose were frostbitten. Normally cold did not bother her, but she was chilled now to the bone; her thick fur-lined tunic and cloak might have been dancing silks.

She sternly told herself not to be frightened. The woman who had trained her in Intelligence work had told her that human stock was the hardiest known in the Empire. Man's home planet, Terra, had contained extremes of temperature, and, before civilization, ethnic types had developed who could, and did, live in unheated houses made of ice blocks, or on burning deserts sufficient to blister the skin. She could survive outdoors, even in this storm.

But frostbite could delay me, beyond the midwinter deadline.

The light of her saddle-lantern glinted on one of the small arrow-shaped signs of a travel-shelter. Her antlered pack beast threw back its head and whickered. Magda turned off the trail and trudged down the narrow path, leading toward the dark building she could just see. The road crunched with rutted and frozen sleet, much trampled. As she came through the trees, she saw the loom of two buildings; it was one of the large shelters, with a separate building for animals. Then she swore softly to herself. Through the crack of the door a faint light was visible: the shelter was occupied.

Oh, damn. I should go on. Why take chances? But the next shelter might be another half-day's ride away; and she was soaked, chilled and freezing. Her cheeks felt numb beneath her hand, and her eyes smarted. *Just to get out of the wind for a minute or two....*

While she delayed, her horse and pack animal had made up their own minds; they tugged at the reins, plunging ahead of her inside the dark barn. There was a good, dusty smell of fodder and hay. It seemed warm and pleasant. She set her saddle-lantern in a safe place, and set about unsaddling the horse, off-loading her pack beast. *I wouldn't have the heart to take them out in this storm again.* Several horses and pack animals were already chomping on fodder and grain; Magda fed her animals, then sat down by the light of the saddle-lantern and pulled off her boot. She drew a sharp breath of dismay as she saw the whitish patches along the reddened flesh under the wet stocking. *I need fire,* she thought, *and something hot to get the circulation going.* She had lived on Darkover much of her life, and knew the danger signs. There could be no question, now, of camping outdoors.

She would simply have to rely on the traditional neutrality of the travel-shelters, and on the disguise she wore. After all it had excited no comment or question from the traders she had met that other night.

She gathered up her saddlebags and started into the main building. Almost automatically she drew up her cloak collar to cover her bare neck; then, self-consciously, put it down where it belonged. Her Amazon's dress and short hair were the best protection in this situation; ordinary female dress and manners would make what she was doing unthinkable.

She pushed the door open and stepped into the light of several lanterns. There were *two* parties of travelers in the long stone-floored room, one at each end, around the fireplaces. As she saw the men near the door, her heart sank; she almost wished she had taken her chances in the woods. They were a party of big, rough-looking men, wearing strangely cut cloaks, and Magda fancied there was something more than impersonal curiosity in their eyes as they turned to look at the newcomer.

The laws of the road meant it was for Magda to speak first. She spoke the formal, almost ritual words, hearing her voice, light and almost little-girlish in the huge echoing room:

"As a late-comer I crave leave from those who have come before to share shelter."

One of the men, huge and burly, with fierce-looking reddish-gold moustaches, spoke the formal greeting, "Be welcome; enter this neutral place in peace, and go in peace." His eyes rested on her with a look that made her skin crawl. It wasn't just that the man was unshaven, and his clothes far from clean; that could be bad weather and traveler's luck. It was something in his eyes. But the laws of the travel-shelter should protect her. She clutched her saddlebags and edged past. Both fireplaces had been preempted, but she could build a small fire near the stone shelving along the center wall. She need not even struggle with tinder; she could borrow a light. (But not, she resolved, from the big man with the moustaches!)

At the far end, five or six figures were gathered; they turned when Magda spoke, and one of them, a tall, thin figure, lean to gauntness, came toward her.

"Be welcome, sister," the figure said, and Magda heard the voice in astonishment. A woman's voice, low-pitched and almost husky, but undeniably a female voice. "Come and share our fire."

Zandru's hells, thought Magda, involuntarily calling on a Darkovan God in her dismay, *what now?*

They're Free Amazons.

Real ones!

The tall gaunt woman did not wait for Magda's acquiescence; she said, "I am Camilla n'ha Kyria, and we are traveling on a mission to Nevarsin. Come, lay your things here." She relieved Magda of her saddlebags, led her to the fire. "You are half frozen, child! You had better get out of those soaked things, if you have dry ones to put on; if not, one of us can lend you something, till your own garments have felt the fire." She pointed to where the women had strung cords and hung spare blankets over them for privacy; by the light of the lantern they had hung there, Magda saw the stranger, Camilla, clearly. She was tall and emaciated, her face deeply lined with age—and what looked like knife scars—and her hair all gray. She had taken off outer cloak and tunic, wearing only the embroidered linen undertunic of a Thendara woman; beneath it her body was so spare and flat that Magda knew her for what she was: an *emmasca,* a woman subjected in adolescence to the illegal neutering operation.

Magda went behind the curtaining blankets, and got out of her wet clothing, slipping into spare trousers and tunic. She was glad of the privacy of the blankets, less because of the rough-looking men at the far end—they could hardly have seen her in the dim shelter—than because of the other women. Had Lady Rohana been right about every detail of her clothing and gear?

A slight woman, with hair the exact color of new-minted copper bars, put her head around the blankets. She said, "I am Jaelle n'ha Melora, elected leader of this band. Are your feet frozen?" She bent down to look carefully at Magda's feet and toes.

"No, I don't think so," Magda said, and Jaelle touched one foot with careful fingers. "No, you were lucky. I was going to say Camilla has some medicine for frostbite, if you need it, but I think even your cheeks are all right; you got out of the wind just in time. Put your stockings on, then, and come to the fire."

Magda gathered up her wet clothes and hung them on the poles the women had rigged there for drying their own garments. On a small grille over a bed of coals, some small birds were roasting, and they had slung a hook and kettle, in which some kind of hot steaming soup was cooking. It smelled so good that Magda's mouth watered.

Jaelle said, "May we know your name and Guild-house, sister?"

Magda gave her alias, and said she was from the Guild-house at Temora; she had purposely chosen the farthest city she knew, hoping that the distance would cover any small differences in dress and manners.

"What a night for travel! I do not think there will be so much as a bush-jumper stirring in these hills between here and Nevarsin," Jaelle said. "Have you journeyed all the way from Temora? Surely your clothes are of Thendara make; that leatherwork and embroidery is found mostly in the Venza hills."

There was nothing to do but brazen it out. Magda said, "They are indeed; such warm clothing cannot be bought on the seacoast—it is like trying to buy fish in the Dry Towns. My patroness was generous in providing me with clothing for my journey, and well she might be, sending me into the Hellers at this season!"

"Will you share our meal?"

Prudence dictated having as little to do with the strange women as possible. Yet they seemed to take it so much for granted that it might cause comment and arouse suspicion. Besides, the food smelled too good, after days of powdered porridge, to refuse. She made the usual polite reply: "Gladly, if I may be allowed to contribute my share."

Jaelle gave the expected answer, "It is not necessary, but will be welcome," and Magda went to her saddlebags for some confectionery with which she had provided herself for just such an occasion. The woman who was cooking accepted the sweets with a little cry of pleasure. "These, too, are made in the Thendara valley. I have not tasted this sort for years, and I am afraid we shall all be shamefully greedy! Except for Jaelle, who hates sweets like a true Dry-Towner!"

"Shut your silly face," said Jaelle, turning harshly on the cook, and the older woman bridled and looked sullen. Magda could see now that all the women were older than Jaelle, though most of them seemed young, except for Camilla. *So young; and their elected leader. She is younger than I, I am sure! And beautiful. I don't think I have ever seen any woman so beautiful!* Jaelle, like the rest, wore the shapeless Amazon clothing: loose trousers, tunic; but this did not conceal the slender, feminine body, the delicate poise of the flame-colored head on her shoulders, the features delicate and pale, and so regular that they would have been almost ordinary, except for the eyes, which were very large and framed in thick dark lashes.

"You have met Camilla," Jaelle said. "That is Sherna"—she pointed to the woman who was cooking their meal—"and that is Rayna, and that is Gwennis. And in a few minutes, we will have something to eat. Oh, and there are two latrine closets in this shelter; we have taken this one"—she pointed—"for our own use, so that you need not go down among the men to . . ." She spoke, with complete insouciance, a word Magda had never heard a Darkovan woman speak; she had seen it only in textbooks, for no man would have used it before her.

I'd better not talk much. Among themselves, at least, they don't use the euphemisms thought polite for women!

She noticed, too, that a roughly printed sign hung on the outside of the latrine the women had preempted, warning the men away. The trained anthropologist made another assumption at the back of her mind: *They expect me to know how to read. And some of them, at least, can write.* That, too, was a faint shock.

"Here, come and eat." Sherna ladled hot soup into Magda's own cup; divided one of the roast birds with a knife and handed her a share. Like the others, Magda sat on her unrolled blankets to eat. She told herself not to be nervous; she had eaten in Darkovan company often enough before this.

The Amazon Jaelle had pointed out as Gwennis— Magda thought she must be about thirty, a slender pretty woman in a blue linen undertunic—asked, "May we know the nature of your mission, Margali, if it is not secret?"

Magda had begun to suspect that among strange bands of Amazons this kind of polite interrogation was customary. In any case, after accepting the invitation to share their fire and meal, she could not retreat into churlish silence. *I was a damn fool. I should have camped in the woods.* But outside the walls of the shelter she could still hear the howling of the storm, giving her the lie.

"It is not secret, no; but it is a family matter of my patroness."

Rayna, a tall, slender woman with hair so curly that it frizzled all about her head like a small halo in the firelight, said, "And no doubt you will be proud to name her for us?"

Lady Rohana foresaw this. Bless her; I'd never have dared to name her without her permission. "It is my privilege to serve the Lady Rohana Ardais on a mission to Sain Scarp."

Camilla, who was sitting next to Jaelle on her rolled-out blankets, pursed her lips and glanced quickly at the rough-looking men, now sitting around their fire and talking loudly as they gobbled food from a big kettle.

Magda thought, *Can those men be bandits? Is it possible they are from Sain Scarp?* The thought set her to prickling with her "hunch" again; she did not hear Jaelle speaking to her and had to ask her to repeat what she had said.

"I said: the Lady Rohana, is she still so very lame from that fall she took from her horse? Poor old woman, and so soon after losing her husband, too; what a tragedy!"

After an incredulous moment, Magda realized what was happening. Nothing to do but brazen it out boldly. She set down her plate with a good display of offended pride.

"You have had later news than mine, or you are testing me, *sister*." She spoke the customary address with heavy irony. "When last I saw the Lady Rohana she was hearty and strong, and to call her old would have been grave insult; I do not think she is twenty years older than I. As for her husband"—she rummaged quickly in her mind for his name—"I have not been privileged to meet dom Gabriel, but she spoke of him as alive and well. Or is there another Lady Rohana in the Ardais Domain whom I have not been privileged to know and serve?"

Jaelle's lovely face looked troubled now, and contrite. She said, "You must not be angry with me, Margali; the Lady Rohana is my kinswoman, and the only one of my kin who has been kind to the family disgrace. As you can guess, her honor is dear to me, and I would not hear her name bandied about without her leave. I beg you, give me pardon."

Magda said stiffly, "You had better see the safe-conduct I carry."

"Oh, please"—Jaelle looked very young now— "don't trouble yourself. Sherna, pour her some wine. Drink with us, Margali. Don't be angry!"

Magda accepted the wine, sweat breaking out on her palms; she wiped them furtively on her tunic. *Just my luck. But I managed that one. What else are they going to throw at me?* She sipped the wine, nibbling at some sweets and the nuts Rayna was passing around; they had been pickled in something tart and highly spiced, and she noticed that Jaelle, who had refused Magda's confectionery, ate the spiced nuts with relish.

She's young. But I'd better not underestimate her!

A burst of noise from the men around the other fire interrupted her, and she twisted around to look at them. They were drinking hard, passing a bottle from hand to hand and laughing uproariously; loud enough to drown out the howling of the storm outside. She strained her ears to listen, thinking, *If they are from Sain Scarp, they might know something of Piedro. . . .*

Camilla's hand came down on her wrist like a vise; Magda almost cried out with the pain of it. "*For shame,*" said the old Amazon, in a voice that cut like a knife. "Is this how Temora House teaches her daughters to behave, shameless girl, staring at drunken men like some harlot of the streets? Turn your back on them, you ill-mannered brat!"

Magda pulled her hand free of the wiry old fingers. Her eyes filled with tears of outrage and humiliation.

She said in a whisper, "I was only wondering if they are bandits. ..."

"Whatever they are, they are nothing to us." The old woman spoke with firm finality. Magda rubbed her wrist, wondering if there would be a bruise.

I'm doing everything wrong. I'd better keep my mouth shut, and go to bed as soon as I can. She lay back on her unrolled blankets, pretending sleep. The drunken laughing and singing of the bandits went on. Around the women's fire there was a little more soft-voiced conversation, some quiet laughing and joking— they were teasing Sherna about something that had happened at midsummer-feast. Magda understood none of it. The women waterproofed their low suede ankle-boots, tidied saddlebags, cleaned and put away eating utensils and began to ready themselves for bed.

Someone said, "I wish Rafi were here with her harp; we could have a song, better than that noise!" She flicked a quick, oblique glance over her shoulder at the drunken crew at the far end, but, Magda noted, did not turn to look. Amazon etiquette?

Camilla said, "Rafi was with me when we punished those two women in Thendara city. You are new-come to us, Rayna, Sherna, you have not heard? You, Margali, you came here from Thendara; has the tale made the rounds yet in the marketplace?"

"What tale?" Magda did not dare to pretend sleep too deep to answer.

"You have not heard, either? Well, it came to our ears that in the Golden Cage—you know of the Golden Cage?" she asked, waiting, and Magda nodded. The Golden Cage was a notorious brothel not too far from the Terran Zone; she knew that it was patronized by spacemen and Empire tourists sometimes.

"It came to us that there were two *entertainers*"— she spoke the polite term with irony—"who had cut their hair short and were nightly presenting an exhibition of a particularly indecent sort—I am sure that every one of you can imagine the details—which the old freak running the place announced as 'Love Secrets of the Free Amazons.' So Rafaella and I—"

"Dear aunt," said Jaelle, yawning, "I have known since my fourteenth year, and so have we all, that there are lovers of women in this world, and that there are pretended lovers of women, and that some men have nothing better to do with their manhood than indulge in naughty fantasies about them. Do you think we are so bored that you must entertain us with dirty stories, Camilla dear?"

"Then you haven't heard how we punished those bitches for pretending to be Amazons, and bringing scandal and disgrace to our name? Can you guess, Margali?"

Magda said "No," not trusting herself to say any more. *This is being told for my benefit. Somehow I've given myself away. That old* emmasca *has eyes like a gimlet.*

Camilla said, savoring the words, her eyes lingering on Magda, "Why, Rafi and I went there by night when their leering audience had gone, we dragged those shameless wenches out into the main square, we stripped them naked and shaved their heads bald as an egg, and their private parts, too, and smeared them in pitch, and rolled them in wood shavings."

"I should have been there," said Jaelle, her eyes glistening with savage relish. "I would have put a torch to them and watched them sizzle!"

"Oh, well, we left them there in that state to be found by the guard; somehow I do not think, after being so shamed, that they will pretend to be Amazons for their filthy charades. What do you think, Margali?"

Magda tried to make her voice steady, but there was a lump in her throat, and she knew what caused it: stark fear. She said, "Probably not; but I have always heard that a *grezalis* follows her trade because she is too stupid to learn any other, so it may have been a lesson wasted."

"You were too hard on them," said Sherna. "It is the foul old pervert who runs the place that I would have treated so. He staged that filthy show; it was not the women's fault."

"On the contrary, I think you were too easy on them," Jaelle said. "Shaming such women is useless; if they were not dead to shame, they would never have been in such a place."

"All women are not made harlots of their free will," Sherna argued; "they must earn their bread somehow!"

Camilla's voice was harsh, rasping like a file. "There is always an alternative," she said, in a voice that effectively shut off comment.

Magda, watching the grim old face, wondered again, *What kind of awful experience could make a woman hate herself so much that even neutering seems preferable to retaining any trace of female function?* The neutering operation had been illegal on Darkover for centuries; not even the strictest enforcement of the laws had managed to stamp it out.

Jaelle yawned again, asking Rayna, who was the tallest, to put out the lantern. Another woman banked the fire so it would keep a few coals through the night. Magda pillowed her head on her saddlebags as she saw the others doing, laid the knife from her boots beside her head.

Now that the danger seemed over, and the acute fear of discovery had subsided, she found herself elated. She had learned more about Free Amazons in one evening than twelve years on the Darkovan side had taught all the agents. She knew that because before leaving her post she had read through everything actually known about them, including folklore, rumors and dirty jokes, and it all fitted on a printout she could hold in one palm. *If I carry this off, I'll have something to brag about for the rest of my life; that I could spend the night with them and get away undetected.*

One after another, the Amazons dropped off to sleep. Old Camilla snored very softly. Sherna and Gwennis, who lay side by side, talked for a few minutes in whispers, then slept. Magda, in spite of the long day's hard riding, was too tired and tense to sleep.

The noise around the other fire did not subside, but grew louder; Magda wondered if it was deliberate, a way of expressing hostility the men dared not show. There was loud talk, drunken singing, some of the songs of such a bawdy nature Magda knew they would never have been sung directly before any woman with the slightest pretense to respectability.

For a time she listened, then grew bored and irritable. Were there no laws of polite use for the shelters, to determine how late one party might continue to carouse when sharing a shelter with another group of travelers? Damn them, were they going to keep up that racket all night? It was surprising the Amazons put up with it, but then, their code evidently forbade them to take notice of the band of men.

The songs came to an end; there was a brief lull, a minor fight broke out and was settled, and in another lull Magda heard one of the men say loudly ". . . held at Sain Scarp . . ."

Magda went tense, straining herself to hear even one more word, but the loud drunken talk started up again. *They do know something about Peter! If I could only hear!*

Blurred by the conversation she seemed to hear the word *Ardais*—she was never sure—and her resolve stiffened. She *must* hear! The Amazons were all sleeping now. She would slip very quietly along the dark wall. . . . She had partially undressed; she sat up and drew on trousers and undertunic in the dark; slid quietly from her blankets and went barefoot along the wall, clinging to the shadows. She could see Jaelle sleeping on her stomach like a child, her face on her bent arm. Magda tiptoed toward the far end of the room, holding her breath; was rewarded by hearing one of the men say ". . . Ardais cub . . ." and ". . . send him back at midwinter . . ."

"And what answer did the lady . . ."

"You think he tells me all that? All I can . . ." It was drowned out in a burst of drunken laughter, then one of the men stiffened.

"What's that?"

"Mouse or rat, probably. Pass me the jug, you——"

Magda froze, but the first speaker got up, suddenly strode straight toward where Magda huddled in the shadow; she turned to slip away, missed her footing and fell full length. Above her she heard a great shout of laughter. The next minute hard hands came down on her and she was picked up bodily and carried into the center of the circle of men.

The man holding her set her on her feet, guffawing loudly.

"Some mouse or rat, Jerral!"

Magda saw that her captor was the big burly mustachioed man whose eyes had frightened her when she first came into the shelter. He bent toward her, taking her chin in his ham-sized hand.

"Tired of sleeping alone, *chiya?*" He used the word for "little girl," which in family intimacy is affectionate; elsewhere, contemptuous. "Which one of us you got the hots for, hey? Bet it's me; saw you looking at me before."

Magda was wildly trying to get her breath, to *think*. She *would* not, she *could* not struggle and plead with these men!

"Yeah, we've all heard about the Free Amazons," said a big, black-bearded man, digging Magda's captor in the ribs with a wicked leer. "Let's wake up the rest of the girls and get them to join the party! What about it, little rabbit, did you come to ask if there was a drink for you here?"

Oh, God, what have I done? I've been responsible for breaking the shelter-truce, if I've involved the other women in this, made these men think. . . . Furtively she felt for her knife; realized, in horror, that she had left it lying by her saddlebag.

"What's wrong, *chiya?* Not a word to say? Well, we'll loosen up your tongue, soon enough," said the big man who had grabbed her, and she felt his fetid, drunken breath hot on her face, the evil, bristling mustachios brush her cheek. He jerked her undertunic down around her shoulders. "Hey, a pretty one, too. Stop shoving, Rannar, you'll have your turn soon enough—I caught this one. You want a girl, go wake up one for yourself!" He ran his hands down her bared body. Magda jerked away, caught him by the arm, tried to wrench him in a judo throw; he sidestepped, with a leering shout. "Hey, pretty, I know a trick worth two of that! So you're a fighter, too? We can *really* have some fun with this one," he said, leering. Magda's arms felt numb.

What's the matter with me? She felt him take her shoulder, twisting it cruelly; she could not keep back a cry of pain.

"Now let's not have any more nonsense, precious. Just be a good little girl and we won't hurt you, no, we won't hurt you at all," he muttered, running his hot hands down across her breasts. She backhanded him, hard, across the mouth; rearing back in drunken rage, he struck her a blow that flung her, half stunned, to the floor. "Damn it, you bitch, none of that! Hold her, Rannar—"

She fought and struggled, gasping, silent, afraid if she opened her mouth that some word of Terran Standard would escape her. The men clustered around, shouting encouragement to the men who held her. Magda had been trained in unarmed combat since her sixteenth year; she tried to catch her breath, to find the strength to strike effectively, but she found herself held too hard.

Why can't I defend myself? How did I get this far? Suddenly, as a drowning man's whole life is said to flash before his eyes, Magda knew the answer. *I've psyched myself, for years, into behaving like a normal Darkovan girl. And they're too timid to fight—they expect men to protect them. I'm conditioned to that, and it canceled out my Terran agent's training. . . .*

She hardly knew it when she started to scream. . . .

Chapter

NINE

Suddenly a light flared in Magda's eyes; a torch came down, blinding the man who held her. He reared back, yelling. Then there were half a dozen knives, it seemed, bared and leveled at Magda's captors.

"Let her go," said a low, level voice; Magda saw Jaelle's face above the torch. The man who held her backed away; Magda pushed the other man aside, pulled herself free and scrambled to her feet, clutching her torn tunic around her. The mustachioed man yelled something obscene, rushed forward, grabbing up his sword; there was a blur of blades, a clash, a howl, and the man fell, clutching at a slash across his thighs. Magda saw blood on Jaelle's knife. One of the women helped Magda to gather her torn clothing around her, while the men clustered together, muttering.

"Look out," Gwennis said sharply; the women fell back, braced, knives like a wall in front of them. Magda, thrust unregarded to one side, watched the slow, grim advance of the bandits, the unflinching barricade of the women's knives. Everything seemed sharply focused as she stood there waiting for the clash: the rough, menacing faces of the men, the equally unyielding faces of the women; the torchlight, the dark shadowed beams, even the patterns of the stone-flagged floor, seemed etched forever on her memory. Later she never knew how long that taut, sharply focused *waiting* lasted—it felt like hours, days—for the inevitable rush, clash of swords, tension drawn tighter, tighter. She felt like shrieking, *Oh, don't, don't, I didn't mean* . . . and physically raised her hands to cover her mouth so that she would *not* cry out.

Then one of the men swore roughly, dropped the point of his sword. "The hell with all this. Not worth it. Put your knives down, girls. Truce?"

None of the women moved, but the bandit leader— the big, black-bearded man who had held Magda down—gestured to his men, and one by one they lowered their swords. When the last one was down, the women slowly relaxed, letting the points of their knives drop toward the stone floor.

Jaelle said, "You have broken shelter-truce by laying hands on one of ours. If I reported this at a patrol station you could all be outlawed, with any hand free to kill you for three years." The strange beauty of her face in the torchlight, copper hair haloed around her pale features, made a strange contrast to her hard words. The leader said drunkenly, "You wouldn't do that, would you, *mestra?* We weren't hurting her none."

"We could all see how much pleasure she took in your advances," Jaelle said dryly.

The mustachioed man said thickly, "Ah, hell, she came to *us;* how'd we know she wasn't looking for a bit of fun?" The wound across his thighs still oozed blood, but Magda could see now that it was no more than half an inch deep: painful perhaps, and humiliating, but not disabling or dangerous. Jaelle wasn't even trying to kill him.

Jaelle swung around to Magda; her eyes glinted like green fire by torchlight, and Magda felt sick with shame and dread. *I am responsible for all this.*

"Did you come to them of your free will? Were you looking, as he says, for a bit of fun?"

Magda whispered, "No. No, I didn't." She could hardly hear herself speak.

"Then"—the Amazon leader's voice was a whiplash that cut—"what were you doing that they could think so?"

Magda opened her mouth to say, "I wanted to hear what they were talking about," but stopped before a single word could get out. Camilla had warned her: spying on men was not proper behavior for an Amazon. She could not disgrace these women, who had protected her without any obligation to do so, by bringing shame or contempt on them. They had welcomed her to their meal and fireside; dressed as an Amazon, she had violated one of their strictest codes of behavior. Now she knew she must lie, quickly and well, a lie that would not involve the Amazons in her misbehavior. She said shakily, "I—I had a cramp, and I turned the wrong way in the darkness, looking for the privy. When I saw I was wrong I tried to get away before they saw me, and I slipped and fell."

"You see?" said Jaelle to the men. Her eyes flicked Magda's face like the blow of a whip.

She knows I'm lying, of course. But she knows why. It was all the amend she could make.

Jaelle said, "You have broken shelter-truce, for which the penalty is three years' outlawry. And you have attempted to rape a woman here, for which *our* penalty is castration. Think yourselves lucky that your man did not succeed. And now gather up all that is yours, and be gone. By law we need not share shelter with outlaws and rapists."

Blackbeard said, and the drunken dismay in his voice was actually comical, "In this storm, *mestra?*"

"You should have listened to the voice of the storm before you broke shelter-truce," Jaelle said, and her face was like stone. "Outside, like the dirty animals you are! And if one of you sets foot over the threshold while we are still here, I swear, I will cut out his *cuyones* and roast them over the fire there!" She gestured with her knife. "Out! No more talk now! Out!"

Fumbling, drunken, muttering obscenely, they gathered up their belongings; grumbling and angry, but before the gleam of the women's knives, their massed, indomitable *waiting,* they went. When the door had closed behind the last of them, Jaelle said, "Rayna, Gwennis, go and be sure they do not disturb our horses and gear." She handed the torch to Sherna, and came slowly toward Magda. "You. Are you hurt? Did they do anything worse than tear your clothes and maul you?"

"No." Magda's teeth were chattering with shock and reaction. *I've been false to everything. To the Amazons, by behaving immodestly before men. To the mission I came on, by not finding out what I risked so much to know.* She felt sick, shamed, exhausted with the violence of her emotions.

Jaelle put an arm around Magda, supporting her. The action was not kind, but contemptuous. She said, "Give her some wine before she finishes this by falling in a faint at our feet!"

She shoved Magda down on a bench; Camilla held a cup to her lips. Magda pushed it away. "I don't want—"

"Drink it, damn you!" Camilla forced the cup against her mouth; Magda gulped, choked, swallowed again. Camilla said viciously, "You! I warned you, you bitch! Who let you out of the Guild-house in this state, with no notion of how to behave? If they had not all been as drunk as monks at midwinter-feast, it would have come to a fight, and we could all have been raped, or killed. You deserve to be beaten and sent back to the Guild-house!"

Sherna had built up the fire again; the women came in from the barn, and Rayna said, "They have gone; good riddance. I hope they freeze in the storm."

Jaelle was standing with her back to the fire, looking formidable. Camilla shoved Magda toward her.

"Jaelle, you are our chosen leader; it is for you to deal with her. If you say so, I will beat her bloody for you; it would be a pleasure!"

Jaelle said at last: "Let her go, Camilla; if I decide she should be beaten, I can do it myself. Well," she said to Magda, "what have you to say for yourself?"

It's not over yet. I've got to go on bluffing. She said, with a spurt of defiance. "You are not *my* chosen leader. Do I owe *you* an explanation of my conduct?"

Jaelle said angrily, "You could have involved us all in your stupidity—or your wantonness, whatever it was! What is one of our first basic rules? Never get yourself *into* anything you can't get yourself out of again! No one forces a woman into danger; but having taken a risk, you should be able to meet it. Now you have reinforced one of the old dirty stories about us, that we fight only in wolf packs and never meet our enemies fairly! Yes, damn you, I think you owe me an explanation; not me alone—all of us."

That was fair enough. She said at last, truthfully, "I heard a part of what they were saying; and it seemed to me that it bore on the business that brought me into these hills. I felt I had to hear it."

Jaelle considered that for a moment, frowning. Magda noticed, incongruously, something she had not seen until that very moment; Jaelle, standing there so secure and confident, was wearing nothing but her underwear. They all were. And somewhere at the back of her mind, the trained anthropologist, never off duty, was making notes: *So that's what Free Amazons wear for underwear.*

Old Camilla's voice was sharp. "Don't listen to a word she says, Jaelle. Men's boots, with a knife in them? And who let her out of the Guild-house in this shape, to disgrace us all? Any girl from the Guild-house, even a girl of fifteen, would know how to defend herself against rape, even unweaponed. There is something wrong here!"

"Yes, very wrong," said Jaelle. "Someone has behaved irresponsibly, allowing her to go about alone before she knew how to behave. You shame whoever took your oath," she said to Magda. "Who was she? Name her to us; she is responsible for your conduct!"

God help me, now I'm in for it! Well, the woman is dead, so Rohana told me, and it won't involve any living person in trouble. She said, "I took the oath at the hands of Kindra n'ha Mhari."

"You lie!" Jaelle raised her arm and struck Magda a blow that made her head ring. She slapped her again and again across the face. "You lie, you bitch," she said, trembling. "Kindra n'ha Mhari was my foster-mother; I dwelt with her seven years before her death, and every one of her oath-daughters is known to me by face and name! How dare you slander a dead woman? You lie, lie, *lie!*"

Magda's head was pounding with the pain of the blows. What now? *What now?*

Old Camilla thrust her face at Magda; she was white and shaking. She said, "If you were a man, I would call challenge upon you. Kindra n'ha Mhari took me in when I was alone and desperate; I have been a member of her band for thirty years, and I loved her as a twin sister! I don't know who or what you are, that you think you can misuse her name, but you will not do so again! Rayna, Gwennis, get her saddlebags; we will see if there is something in them to give us a clue to this filthy bitch of an impostor!"

Rayna got down and started to go through Magda's belongings by torchlight. Finally she pulled out the safe-conduct, handed it to Jaelle.

"It bears the Lady Rohana's name and seal. A forgery, no doubt, but you had better see it, Jaelle."

Jaelle turned it curiously in her hands, held it closer to the fire to see better. "Light the lantern, Rayna; we need light for whatever is going to happen," she said. "I cannot read in this murk." When the lantern was lighted she stood examining it for some time and finally said, "It is not a forgery; I know my kinswoman's handwriting too well for that. And the seal is genuine." She read aloud: ". . . Call upon all those who owe loyalty to the Domain of Ardais to give such aid as is in their power . . ."

"Stolen," said Camilla, her mouth lifting in a sneer.

"No, for it bears her name and a good description." She went to Magda and handed her the safe-conduct. "Did my kinswoman truly give this to you?"

"She did."

"No one can force Rohana to do anything she does not want to do," Jaelle said, "and I have never known her to lend her name to any wickedness. Are you truly on a mission in her name?"

Magda nodded. Jaelle said, "But you are not an Amazon, are you? How came you to try to pass yourself off as one, Margali—if that is truly your name?"

"It is the name I bore as a child." Magda blinked, for a moment afraid she would cry. But she spoke without faltering. "My mission is an honorable one, and it was the Lady Rohana who suggested to me that I dress and bear myself as an Amazon." She raised her head, still stinging with Jaelle's blows. "I have disgraced no one! If I had avoided your camp, no harm would have been done; but in this storm I did not want to sleep out of doors."

"No," said Jaelle. "You narrowly escaped frostbite as it was. So you thought you could get through the night without betraying yourself—"

"And then it seemed to me that those men knew something of importance to my mission. Something so important that nothing else seemed to matter."

"What prompted you to wear men's boots? Was it only ignorance?"

"Lady Rohana provided the boots," said Magda, "but I knew no better."

Camilla laughed suddenly. "I told the Lady Rohana that her ignorance of our customs would make trouble sometime; but it came many years later than I thought it would! Well, she meant well; I suppose if you had met no real Amazons you might have passed, indeed, as one of us."

Jaelle said curiously, "But, were you not afraid to travel in the Hellers, alone, and with winter coming on?"

A few hours ago Magda would have said, "No, I

was not afraid." Now, having tasted fear, she was more honest with herself. "I was afraid, yes. But it seemed to me that my mission was more important than fear."

For the first time Jaelle's eyes were a little kinder. "So you felt the dress of an Amazon would protect you? Well, the disguise even deceived us, for a little while, and it seems to me that in general you tried to conduct yourself in such a way as to bring no disgrace upon our dress and name. It is not your fault you failed. But what put it into your head to come alone on such a mission, my girl? Was there no man to whom you could turn, no relative, no father, no warden, overlord or guardian? What is the mission on which you must travel alone?"

Having no better idea, Magda told the truth; or as much of it as she dared. "A near kinsman"—(*A husband is related, damn it, related by marriage at least* ...)—"is held at Sain Scarp for ransom; if he is not ransomed by midwinter, he will be tortured and killed."

"And no man in your family or household would help you? But I do not understand this," Jaelle said. "If you had the right to appeal to the Lady Rohana, you would have had an equal right to appeal to her husband or to her sons for their aid."

Magda said steadily, "I have no right to appeal to the Lady Rohana. She aided me out of kindness and charity, because I had none other to help me."

"Ah, that is like her," said Jaelle. "No lame dog of the mountains ever came limping in vain to her doorstep." She sighed and yawned, covering her mouth with a small hand, so graceful it was hard to believe she had wounded a man, had beaten Magda with those same small hands. "Well, I am not your guardian, and your affairs are none of my business; normally I would feel bound to help anyone under the shelter of my kinswoman's patronage. But there is a more serious point at issue here. It seems to me, truly, that you have shown a spirit almost worthy of a true Amazon, venturing alone into the Hellers in the decline of the year, instead of calling upon some man for protection. You were stupid, yes, and you were unlucky; but if stupidity were a crime, half the human race would be outlawed at every crossroad, and—how says the proverb? *If ill luck were cheese, dairy-women would go wanting work.* Just the same"—she frowned—"no one may be allowed to impersonate a Free Amazon. Camilla has told us how one such impersonation was punished!"

Magda shuddered, but forced herself to say boldly, "You have said it yourself: I did nothing to disgrace you. And I know that Lady Rohana was allowed to travel with your band, dressed as one of you."

"True. But the law requires that before this is allowed, the woman must have the permission of the elected leader, and the consent of every one of the women who is to travel in their company."

"Then give me such permission," Magda challenged, and Jaelle broke into an unexpected smile.

"I almost wish the laws of our Guild permitted it," she said half aloud. "A thousand pities Rohana did not know how inflexible is that law. Had she sent for me, and asked that leave, *before* you had shown yourself in Amazon's dress, I almost believe—" She sighed, and said, "Well, the law does *not* allow me to give you that permission once you have invaded the privacy of my women in disguise: unknowing, perhaps, in ignorance of your crime, but invaded nonetheless. There was a day—and if we are not vigilant it could come again on Darkover—when we were invaded constantly by enemies, spies, seeking to learn something of our ways and weaknesses, or to carry tales about us, hoping to slander us to our disadvantage. The penalty for a man who invades us in disguise is death or mutilation, as we may choose and as circumstances dictate. For a woman the penalty never changes. Before you depart from us, the lie must become truth: You must take the oath of the Free Amazons, here and now."

Magda's first reaction was, *Oh, is that all?* Jaelle saw the relief in her face, for her voice hardened. "Don't dare to take it lightly," she said, "for if you swear it, and later betray it, any Free Amazon on Darkover may kill you where you stand; you are a dead woman the moment you put your nose out your own window!"

It flashed across Magda's mind: *An oath under duress is not valid.* That was the Terran Magda; in the next moment the Darkovan girl Margali, who had grown up at Caer Donn, absorbing the way of life, the codes, the beliefs of her Darkovan playmates almost more deeply than those of her parents, thought, *An oath I cannot betray; how can I do this?*

The conflict was terrible; she felt as if she were being wrenched apart. *I have come and gone between two worlds with impunity; now I must pay the price, and I do not know if I can!* She put her hands over her face, in a futile attempt to conceal her emotions. *If I refuse, will they kill me here and now?*

"Will you take the oath?"

Magda said, "What choice have I?"

"None, I fear. I owe it to my women, and to every woman of the Guild, that none shall invade us and carry our secrets outside. If you will not swear, we will simply have to carry you, as prisoner, back to the nearest Guild-house, and there keep you until you are willing to be sworn, or until midwinter-night when all our Guild meet in reunion and our judges can hear your story and decide what is to be done with you. It may be that no penalty will be exacted, that you will be sworn to secrecy about what you have seen and you will be allowed to depart."

"To that much I will swear willingly," said Magda, and meant it.

"But I am not empowered to take *that* oath from you. That can be given only by a judge, and at midwinter-night, and only after hearing everything that bears upon the case; if, for instance, you had several young children and there were none else to assume their care, or you had already sworn a Keeper's oath to a Tower. If you prefer, then, we can take you now to Neskaya Guild-house—it is only a tenday ride from here—and leave you to be judged at midwinter."

And by that time Peter would be dead by torture!

I guess I'll have to take their damned oath. It will give me time to decide what to do. . . .

Probably all it entailed—she remembered the few Darkovan oaths whose content and form she had heard—was a pledge not to harm any Free Amazon, and not to betray any of their secrets. *And I don't know any of them, so that's safe enough to promise! I can do that much honorably.*

But if there is more? She felt a kind of despair. "I will take the oath," she said, fighting to keep her voice steady.

Jaelle nodded. "I thought you would," she said. "Come, let us get it over with, then; we are all weary, and you more than any, I should imagine. Come here to the fire and stand among us."

Magda obeyed. Jaelle was standing directly before the fire, her back to the flames; Magda noticed again how very young she looked. How old could she be? Twenty-two, twenty-three . . . hardly more than that! The women made a circle around them. Camilla came to Jaelle and said in an undertone, "You are young for this; do you want me to take her oath?"

Jaelle patted the lined old cheek. "Dear aunt, you are always ready to spare me or shield me, but if I am old enough to be elected leader of a band, surely I am old enough to punish intruders, or to take an oath."

She said to Magda, "Bare your breasts before us."

Startled, confused, Magda fumbled with the laces of her torn tunic. Part of her, at this moment, the trained agent who never stopped taking mental notes for later use, was excited—the graduate anthropologist participating in an unusual and secret tribal custom; but the rest of her was just a frightened girl, ashamed as any girl reared in Caer Donn would have been ashamed, to stand with her body bared before strangers. She fumbled with the laces; Sherna came and pulled the tunic down so that she stood before them, bare to the waist, shivering. She clenched her fists at her sides, resisting the impulse to cover herself with her hands, as one by one the women came and solemnly inspected her bare breasts.

This must have been an ancient way of making sure they were not invaded by men in disguise. I'll bet there was a time when the candidate—or the intruder—had to strip herself bare, head to foot. She bit her lip hard to keep from breaking into nervous laughter—or tears. *I feel like a horse in the market!*

When every one of the women had looked her over, Jaelle said, "Have we all verified that this is in truth a woman, and not a man come in disguise to mock us? If there are any doubts we shall have this one stripped naked; any of you has the right to demand it." Magda was no longer able to be elated at this verification of her guess; she stood shivering, her eyes cast down. But no one demanded it, and Jaelle nodded.

"So be it; we accept you as a woman. Now, you have cut your hair and come among us of your free will; so I call upon you to repeat the oath given in the days of Varzil the Good, to the Guild of Free Amazons, in accordance with the Charter kept at Nevarsin. In the presence of these witnesses, repeat after me: From this day forth I renounce the right to marry save as a freemate. No man shall bind me *di catenas* and I will dwell in no man's household as a *barragana.*"

Stumbling over the words, Jaelle prompting her at intervals, Magda repeated the words. "No man shall bind me . . ." *Nothing,* she thought, *is less likely than that I should ever want—or any Terran-born woman should be allowed—to marry di catenas, by the old religious ritual. And a* barragana *is simply a kept woman, a concubine.*

"I swear that I am prepared to defend myself by force if I am attacked by force, and that I shall turn to no man for protection."

Magda repeated the words; again, feeling that she was actually disintegrating. *Two of me—the Terran Magda, the Darkovan Margali—and they're breaking apart! Who am I? Who will I be after this?*

". . . Turn to no . . . no man for protection. . . ."

I've been taught to defend myself since I was sixteen years old. On any other world I would have been doing it all along. Here I was sheltered, and when I finally had to try, I couldn't. Without Jaelle's band I'd have been beaten up and probably gang-raped. I might have survived it—people do—but it would have been a hell of a thing to live with!

"From this day forth I swear I shall never again be known by the name of any man, be he father, guardian, lover or husband, but simply and solely as—" Jaelle broke off. "What was your mother's name?"

Magda rummaged wildly in her mind for the Darkovan equivalent of "Elizabeth." *What's wrong with me? I heard it often enough. I'm disintegrating!* She said, after a perceptible pause, "Ysabet."

". . . As Margali *nikhya mic* Ysabet," said Jaelle, speaking the words in full without the common abbreviation, and Magda repeated them, biting her lip, fighting for self-control. Nothing so far in the oath had troubled or frightened her, but this did. Known only as Margali n'ha Ysabet. *Oh, Dad, do I have to give up your name, too? I didn't mind giving up Peter's, when we separated. But you, Dad, do I have to renounce you, too?* The face of David Lorne, graying, gentle, scholarly, seemed to swim in her mind, to shake his head at her in reproach. *Oh, God, Peter, are you worth this?* Margali n'ha Ysabet . . . Magdalen, daughter of Elizabeth. No more than that?

"From this day forth I swear I will give myself to no man save in my own time and season and of my own free will, at my own desire; I will never earn my bread as the object of any man's lust."

Well, no woman in her right mind would object to swearing an oath not to become a prostitute. Then she suddenly felt troubled. If a woman had no occupation of her own, that could also mean—a wife?

"From this day forth I swear I will bear no child to any man save for my own pleasure and at my own time and choice; I will bear no child to any man for house or heritage, clan or inheritance, pride or posterity; I swear that I alone will determine rearing and fosterage of any child I bear, without regard to any man's place, position or pride. . . ."

The Terran Magda thought, *Well, that makes sense.* But the girl reared in Caer Donn discovered that she was choking as she spoke the words. *Peter wanted a child. I didn't, then, but I was ashamed of not wanting it; I was almost as disappointed as he, to find I was not pregnant. I wanted so to please him. I knew I'd failed him—and now I can never . . . never make it up to him. . . .* She heard herself, to her own shame and horror, sob aloud. *He wanted that so much, and I failed him in that, I failed him in everything. . . .*

Jaelle waited for her sobs to quiet, repeating inexorably, ". . . Any man's place, position or pride. . . ."

Magda repeated the words, but found that she was crying as she spoke them. She ordered and commanded herself to be calm. *What's happening to me? Why am I coming apart like this?*

"From this day forth I renounce allegiance to any family, clan, household, warden or liege lord, and take oath that I owe allegiance only to the laws of the land as a free citizen must; to the kingdom, the crown and the Gods."

Magda repeated the words mechanically. She was almost too exhausted by emotion to hear them or understand their sense.

"I shall appeal to no man as of right, for protection, support or succor: but shall owe allegiance only to my oath-mother, to my sisters in the Guild and to my employer for the season of my employment."

And what of my loyalty to the Empire? Magda repeated the words, forcing them past the lump in her throat.

"And I further swear that the members of the Guild of Free Amazons shall be to me, each and every one, as my mother, my sister or my daughter, born of one blood with me, and that no woman sealed by oath to the Guild shall appeal to me in vain. . . ."

Magda discovered that her throat was thick again with unshed tears. She thought, *My mother is long dead. I never had a sister, and I shall never have a daughter. Yet I swear. . . .*

Jaelle reached out her hands, clasped Magda's cold hands in her own. She said quietly, "Margali n'ha Ysabet, I accept you before the Goddess as oath-daughter; henceforward you shall be as daughter and sister to me and to every one of us in the Guild. Here in the presence of these witnesses, I declare that you are from this moment sealed by oath to the Guild of Free Amazons, subject only to our laws, and I give you freedom of the Guild: and in token I exchange with you this greeting." She drew Magda close and solemnly kissed her on the mouth. "Kneel," she said softly, "and repeat: From this moment, I swear to obey all the laws of the Guild of Free Amazons and any lawful command of my oath-mother, the Guild members or my elected leader for the season of my employment. And if I betray any secret of the Guild, or prove false to my oath, then I shall submit myself to the Guild-mothers for such discipline as they shall choose; and if I fail, then may every woman's hand turn against me, let them slay me like an animal and consign my body unburied to corruption and my soul to the mercy of the Goddess."

Too late to retreat. Numb, desperate, Magda heard herself stumble through the words that condemned her to betray someone. *Whatever I do now, I am forsworn. What shall I do, what shall I do?*

Jaelle raised her to her feet, hugged her close. "Don't cry, my sister," she said softly, using the word in the intimate mode. "I know, it is a great and solemn step to take, and few of us have taken it without tears."

Camilla wrapped her in her tunic. "Poor little thing, you are chilled to the bone! Jaelle, how could you let her go through that long oath, standing there almost naked? When we had once seen her, you might have stopped to let her cover herself!" She wrapped a blanket over the tunic, drew her to the fire.

Jaelle laughed in apology and said, "Forgive me, Margali; I had never accepted an oath before, I was nervous, afraid I should forget some of the words—"

"Drink this, it will stop your shivering." Gwennis handed her the cup they had given her before, which she had not finished. She heard her teeth chattering against the rim of the cup; she sipped slowly, trying to get control of herself. They all crowded around her, hugging her, comforting her. Rayna murmured, "Don't feel bad, we all cry, you didn't cry nearly as much as I did!"

Jaelle said, "Now you must forgive us for being so rough with you before; now we are all your sisters. From tonight, every Amazon is your sister, but those who witnessed your oath are your family, and special, always." She looked affectionately around the circle, saying, "Are you not? Camilla cut my hair for me, nine years ago."

Gwennis said, in an undertone like a private joke, "How dare you chide her for crying, Jaelle? *You* didn't cry, I remember!"

"But I was fostered among you," Jaelle said. "Now we will finish this bottle of wine in our sister's honor, then we must all sleep. Tomorrow we must think how best to send her to the Guild-house, but for tonight we will celebrate."

They are all so kind to me now. I don't deserve it. Magda, calm now and exhausted, asked Gwennis, "Where am I to be taken?"

"To Neskaya Guild-house, or perhaps to Thendara, which is our own house," said Gwennis. "Every new-made Amazon must spend half a year in the Guild-house, learning our ways and unlearning the vicious old ways you have been taught since girlhood—all the things you were taught about seemly behavior for a woman. Your childhood put chains on you; there you will be taught to free yourself, to be what you best can be."

Oh, God! I took this oath to escape being sent to the Guild-house, to gain time! Am I forsworn for nothing, then?

Each of them had something to say to her. Sherna, who was a plump and pretty girl, came and knelt beside her. "I came to the Amazons two years ago, when I fully realized that I had no share in my father's estate; all my brothers shared, but not I; for me there was nothing ahead but marriage to some man who could help my brothers to manage my father's lands. They refused two men I liked because, they said, they would not dwell under one roof with them; and would have forced me on a friend of theirs. So when I knew I had no right to refuse, but could be made to marry at their wish and not mine, I cut my hair and came to the Guild-house. Do you know what I feared most?" She grinned, such a droll grin that Magda had to smile. "I feared they would tell me I could never lie with a man again! But, I thought, better that than marry to please my brothers. . . ."

Jaelle sat beside her. "It is customary for oath-mother and daughter to exchange gifts. I have no gift for you, Margali; I had not foreseen this. I must think of something."

They're so kind to me. So overwhelmingly kind. They act as if I were their long-lost sister. The oath means so much. . . .

Magda said, "My mission—I had told you it was life and death. . . ."

Jaelle said, "We will discuss that in the morning. It may be that you owe no loyalty to any man, even to a kinsman. But for now we must all sleep."

The women finished their wine and went to their sleeping rolls again. Rayna put out the lantern. It was very quiet, except for the diminishing, faraway howl of the storm. Camilla, who lay next to Magda, reached out her hand in the darkness and patted her gently on the cheek.

"You were not the first to shiver through the oath," she said. "When my oath was taken, I—you know I am *emmasca*—I had nothing like to a woman's form, and so three of the witnesses refused to believe I was not a man and I had to be stripped. Kindra was so distressed by that, that she, too, forgot to have me covered afterward. I was so humiliated, I wept for hours; but it was half a lifetime ago, and now I can laugh about it. Someday you will laugh, too, sister. Sleep well."

"You, too—sister," Magda said with difficulty. It was the first time in her life that she had ever spoken the word in the intimate mode.

One by one the women dropped away into sleep. Magda was almost too weary to think straight. *I can't go to a Guild-house and let Peter die by torture! An oath under duress is not valid ... my first loyalty is to the Empire.*

She was very weary; sleep began, against her will, to steal over her. Bits and pieces of the oath seemed to echo in her mind. *Bear no child except at my own will ... did I want Peter's child, then? If not, why did I cry that way? Or did I only want to want it ... because I had failed him so?*

She thought, at the very edge of sleep, that she would rather like to go to a Guild-house, if it were not for her mission. *I could be as strong and effective here, as an Amazon, as on any planet where women are free.*

Whatever I do, I am forsworn. I can betray my oath to my sisters—or betray my first allegiance to the Empire. All my life, never knowing it, I have been two women: one Terran, one Darkovan. And now I am torn. I must betray someone, or Peter dies by torture.

Is Peter worth the sacrifice of my integrity? Can I give up that, too? With a life at stake?

Sleep took her suddenly, and she plummeted into it like bottomless darkness.

She dreamed of Peter Haldane; he was lying in the dark, on stone; cold and alone and frightened. And it seemed to her that as he had done only once or twice in the brief term of their love, he held out his hands to her, laid his head against her breast: off guard, vulnerable, no longer concerned to keep up the mask of strength, of masculine infallibility. She kissed him and soothed him in her dream, and he whispered to her, "You are the only one I can trust, Mag. I trust you. Everybody else is out to cut my throat, but you don't compete. I'm not afraid of you, Mag, you're the only one I'm not afraid of." And she wanted to cry but knew she could not, that it was for her now to be strong enough for both of them. . . . In the dream she wiped away his tears and comforted him, saying, "Darkover is not an easy world for men, either." But when she woke she was alone, in her lonely and solitary bed.

Chapter

TEN

Magda woke late; it was full daylight in the shelter, and the Amazons had built up the fire and were cooking breakfast. She closed her eyes, pretending sleep, knowing that she could delay the decision no longer.

I took the oath to gain time. I do not want to break it. I have learned—and learned too late—that I am almost more Darkovan than Terran, and an oath is sacred. But that does not matter now. I cannot let Peter die, alone and by torture. I am an agent of Terra, and Peter is my colleague.

Once she had formulated that clearly, all the emotional reasons on the other side surged up inside her; but she forced them down with a great effort, her face set in rigid calm. *I have made my decision. I will not even think about any other possibility.*

Even if it's a wrong *decision?*

Stop that! No more wavering!

She set about wondering how she could carry it out. They were planning to send her to the Guild-house at Neskaya, which was a good long way from here. But it was in a different direction from Nevarsin, which was their immediate mission. Surely they would not alter their route to take her to Neskaya; one or, at the most,

two would be detailed for that. She would pretend submission until they were off guard and trusted her—
How skillful I am at betrayal!—then slip away and take the fastest route back to Thendara. *They will be looking for me at Sain Scarp, and if I go directly there, having betrayed my oath to them, they will have a legal right to kill me on sight, and Peter will die, under torture. Once in Thendara—what then?*

All I can do is to tell Montray I've failed, that—literally—he sent a woman to do a man's job, and on this world, a woman couldn't handle it. He will have to send someone else. There will still be time, just barely.

And what's ahead for me, on this world, after that?
Nothing. . . .

Magda accepted the fact that this meant exile from her own world, which was Darkover. She could never again take up her old work in Thendara; once she stepped into the Darkovan zone, any Free Amazon was legally entitled to kill her on sight. She would have to put in for a transfer, go somewhere else.

To a planet where a woman can have something genuine to do. She thought, bleakly, that at least her coup with the Free Amazons—*I've quadrupled all existing knowledge about them*—would bring her an offer worthy of her capabilities.

The thought of leaving Darkover brought sharp, tearing pain, almost a physical agony. But there was no other way. She knew she could no longer endure the ordinary life of a woman on this world, nor the limited work that a woman could do here for the Empire.

If I could live here as a Free Amazon . . . but the price of keeping her oath was Peter's death by torture.

He is Darkovan, too. Would he accept his life, knowing I had bought it by oath-breaking and the sacrifice of integrity? The thought was too painful to endure. Magda forced herself to get up, to break off the endless, useless self-questioning.

Jaelle, already dressed, was standing by the fire, making up a hot drink from roasted grain; Magda had tasted it a few times in Caer Donn. She dipped up a cup for Magda, and said, "I made them let you sleep; you must have been wearied to death. The others are out with the horses, making ready to go. This morning you and I take the road for the Guild-house, where your name will be written on the rolls of the Charter."

Magda said, in a last desperate attempt to get through to her, "I have told you my mission is life and death; my kinsman will die by torture if I do not ransom him at midwinter."

Jaelle looked sympathetic. But she said, "By oath, sister, you renounced loyalty to any man, and to any household, family or clan. Your loyalties are to us now."

Magda clenched her fists in utter despair. Jaelle said gently, "When we reach the Guild-house, you may lay your case before the Guild-mothers; it may be that when they have heard all, they will decide that your claim does not violate the oath, and send someone in your place to ransom him. There would be time for that. But I am not empowered to make that decision."

Magda turned abruptly away. *So be it,* she thought grimly; *on your own head, Jaelle, even if I have to kill you.*

The other women came from the barn, laughing, chattering, talking of the ride ahead. Jaelle said, "The rest of you may ride when you will, but you must choose another leader; Margali and I must ride for Neskaya."

"Oh, Jaelle," Gwennis protested, "you took this mission because your brother is there, and you have not seen him in years! Appoint one of us to take her to Neskaya for you! I will gladly change with you."

Jaelle laughed, shaking her head. "Why, I just reproved Margali, reminding her that our first loyalty is to Guild, not kindred! As for my brother, a boy of ten has little need for a visit from a grown sister; I can see him at Ardais in midsummer, and anyway, no doubt dom Gabriel has taught him enough about the family disgrace that I am sure he would rather be spared my visit!"

Magda asked, "Is your brother a monk, then?"

"Oh, no! But he has been sent there, like many Comyn sons, to learn to read and write and to hear something of our history. He is Rohana's fosterling; I have seen him but once since he was three years old."

Pretending interest, she asked the nature of the mission.

"At Nevarsin, the monks keep the records of much knowledge lost elsewhere since the Ages of Chaos. They will not teach women, and we are not even allowed to stay in the guest-house, but we have leave to use their library. Our best scribes, a little at a time, are transcribing their books on anatomy and surgery, as well as those on birth and the diseases of women— books you would think they would turn over to us entirely, since the monks can make no use of them. We are allowed to have only two scribes there at a time; Rayna and Sherna are going there to change with two women who have been there for half a year, and Gwennis to keep house for them in the village, while Camilla will escort the others home."

Magda toyed with a bowl of the powdered porridge. She was curious, but asked no more questions. It went against the grain to pretend friendliness with a woman she might have to kill.

Soon after, the other women rode away, leaving Magda and Jaelle alone. While they were saddling their horses, Jaelle discovered that hers had a loose shoe.

"I wish I had discovered it before Gwennis left," she said. "She is no blacksmith, but I have seen her make emergency repairs. Well, we must stop in the nearest village. Just look at that!" She handed the shoe to Magda, who stood weighing it in her hand as Jaelle bent to examine the horse's hoof.

I could stun her with it and get away now. . . .

But she waited too long; Jaelle turned back and held out her hand for the shoe, dropping it into her saddle-bag.

It was a bright morning, almost cloudless, with a brisk cold wind blowing. Jaelle sniffed the wind, started

to throw a leg into her saddle—and at that moment
Magda heard a savage yell and two men rushed them
from the woods, knives drawn. In split-second shock,
Magda recognized two of the bandits from last night:
the black-bearded bandit leader, and the big man with
the mustachios whom Jaelle had wounded. Magda
heard herself shout a warning; Jaelle whirled, half out
of her saddle. Then she was fighting, backed up against
her horse, the two men almost hiding her from
Magda's sight. Magda thought, *Run! Get away now,
they're saving you the trouble of killing her*—

But already she had her own knife out, was running
toward them. Blackbeard whirled and Magda felt his
knife graze her arm, a pain like fire, as she plunged her
own knife deep into his chest; felt it turn on bone and
slip. He slithered, with a groan, to the ground. Jaelle
was still fighting with the other man; she saw that
Jaelle was bleeding from a long slash on the cheek.
Then she heard Jaelle scream with agony as the bandit's knife drove down toward her breast; she fell to
the ground and at that instant Magda felt her knife
sink into the man's back.

He fell with a harsh sound, air escaping from lungs
already no longer breathing. Slowly, feeling sick, she
pulled out the knife.

*I haven't fought anyone since combat training, ten
years ago. Now I've killed one and wounded another.*
She looked at Jaelle, unconscious on the ground, almost under the body of the man Magda had killed. *Is
she dead?* The thought did not bring relief, but a
wrenching agony. *She fought for me, last night. And I
would have betrayed her. . . .*

Jaelle stirred, and Magda knew that Jaelle's life still
stood between her and her mission. She was still holding the bloody knife with which she had killed the bandit. She saw Jaelle's eyes move to the knife; she lay
still, looking up at Magda without a word. Magda suddenly knew that she could not kill anyone in cold
blood; above all she could not kill this woman who lay
bleeding and helpless in the snow at her feet.

What good is Peter's life if I buy it with another death? I will save him honorably if I can; not otherwise.

She knelt beside Jaelle. Her face was covered with blood; more blood was soaking through her shoulder. She lifted the sticky clothes clinging to the wound.

The bandit's knife had gone under the collarbone and sliced down toward the armpit; a bad wound, painful and dangerous but not, Magda thought, necessarily fatal. She got out her knife again and cleaned the blade, saw that one of Jaelle's eyes was open—the other was clotted shut—and that she was watching the knife. Magda said irritably, "I've got to cut these clothes off so I can stop the bleeding." She slit Jaelle's tunic and eased it gently away from the skin; Jaelle gasped with the pain but did not cry out. She only said, wetting her lips, "Did you—kill them both?"

"One is surely dead. I don't know about the other, but he isn't in any shape to harm us," Magda said.

Jaelle said, her breath coming loud, "Bandages ... in my saddlebags. . . ."

Magda got up, edging between the dead bandit and Jaelle's horse, which, smelling the blood, shifted its feet uneasily. She led the horse away and took down the saddlebags, hunting in them; she found two or three rolls, and what looked like a small, primitive first-aid kit. *That cut probably needs stitches, but I can't do it.* She made a pressure bandage, strapped it around Jaelle's shoulder, turned her attention to the long, hideous gash along Jaelle's face; it had laid her cheek open to the bone. Jaelle said, in a hoarse, frightened voice, "Can't see out of . . . this eye. . . ."

Magda went to the well behind the shelter, dipped up the icy water, came back and sponged the dreadful gash. The eyelashes parted; a little more sponging showed that the eye had only been stuck shut with blood from a small nick in the eyelid. Magda pushed the eyelids open; Jaelle gasped with relief.

"Can you walk? You can't lie out here in the snow." Magda knelt, slipped an arm around the woman, man-

aged to hoist her to her feet; Jaelle tried to walk, but
collapsed against Magda. Magda managed, somehow,
to get her inside the shelter and lay her on one of the
stone benches. She started to build a fire, put some
water to boil, thinking that some bark-tea, or some of
the Amazon grain-brew, would do them both good.
And if Jaelle was in shock—and she looked like it—
she had better be kept warm. Not knowing how Jaelle
had stowed her own blankets, Magda got out her own
and wrapped Jaelle up in them; shoved one of the
stone slabs into the fire, thinking she could heat it,
wrap it in something and put it at the hurt woman's
feet. When the water boiled she poured it on the bark
for tea, and went out to put the animals away—they
wouldn't be going anywhere right away. The second
bandit was definitely dead. She had to drag him out of
the way to get the horses and her pack beast into the
stable again.

When she came into the shelter Jaelle was conscious.
She whispered, "I thought you had gone."

Remotely, like something someone else might have
thought, it occurred to Magda: she could have escaped. After doing her best for Jaelle, she could have
left her here to recover, and felt no particular guilt.
Now it was something she could never have done. *I
swore to treat every Amazon as my own mother, sister
or daughter. . . .*

She fumbled for words, saying, "We are oath-
bound—sister."

Jaelle put out her hand, a groping gesture that made
Magda's heart ache, remembering how quick and skillful those hands had been. She whispered, "I told
you—oath-mother and oath-daughter exchange gifts. I
did not ask for such a gift as this."

Magda felt embarrassed. "You'd better not talk anymore. Are you cold?" She got another blanket, put the
hot stone at Jaelle's feet, propped her up to sip a little
of the boiling tea. Jaelle touched her sleeve. "Tend
your own wound."

Magda had forgotten it. "It's only a scratch."

"Just the same. Some mountain bandits ... poison their blades," Jaelle said with difficulty. "Do as I say."

By the time Magda had finished Jaelle was asleep or unconscious again. And asleep or unconscious she remained all that day. Magda made herself some soup from dried meat, late in the day, and tried to rouse Jaelle to eat, but Jaelle only moaned and muttered and pulled away from her hands; Magda knew that she was feverish. Once she woke and asked quite clearly for a drink of water, but when Magda brought it she was stuporous again and would not swallow.

Are there injuries I did not see? Or were the wounds poisoned after all? Magda found that she was fighting terror and dread. *I don't want her to die! I don't!*

By nightfall Jaelle's skin was blistering hot, and Magda could not rouse her even for a moment. Jaelle muttered and flung herself around; once she began with her free hand to tear at the bandage on her face. Magda pulled her hand away, but a few minutes later Jaelle was clawing at the bandage again. Magda, thinking that if she got the bandage loose she might hurt herself, make the scar worse, took a roll of the bandage and tied Jaelle's hands at her sides. She was not prepared to hear Jaelle begin to scream: wild screams of panic and terror.

"Oh, no, no, no, no, no ... don't chain my hands, don't— Mother, mother ... don't let them ... oh, don't ... oh, no, no!" and the thin tearing screams again. Magda had never heard such terror. She could not bear it. Quickly she cut the bandage, lifted Jaelle's hands one after another to show that they were free. Somehow that penetrated Jaelle's delirium; she stopped shrieking and lay back quietly. About an hour later she began restlessly to tear at the bandage on her face again, but Magda had no notion of repeating whatever had terrified her so; instead she took the unconscious woman's hands firmly between her own and held them tight. She said quietly and firmly, "You must not do that; lie still, you will hurt yourself. I will not tie your hands, but you must be still." She repeated this over and over, several times, with variations.

Jaelle opened her eyes, but Magda knew she did not see her. She muttered, "Kindra," and later, "Mother," but let her hands rest in Magda's without struggling. Once she said, to no one present, "It hurt. But I didn't cry."

Most of that night Magda sat beside Jaelle, listening to her delirious mutterings, holding her hands tight whenever she tried to tear at the bandages or, as she started to do later, to climb out of bed, under some agitated impression—Magda gathered from her raving—that she was needed somewhere else, at once. Magda had nothing to give her for the fever; there were some medicines in Jaelle's saddlebags, but Magda did not know how to use them or what they were. She sponged her several times with the icy water from the well, and tried to make her drink, but Jaelle pulled away and would not swallow. Toward morning she sank into quiet; Magda did not know whether she was asleep or had lapsed into a coma and was dying. In either case there was nothing she could do. She lay down at the unconscious woman's side and closed her eyes for a moment's rest; suddenly the shelter was full of gray light and Jaelle was lying with her eyes open, looking at her.

"How do you feel, Jaelle?"

"Like hell," Jaelle said. "Is there some water, or tea, or something? My mouth has not been this dry since I left Shainsa."

Magda brought her a drink; Jaelle gulped it thirstily and asked for more. "Did you stay by me all night?"

"Until you fell asleep; I was afraid you would tear off your bandages. You tried."

"Was I delirious?" When Magda nodded, Jaelle said with a wry grin, "That explains it; I dreamed I was back in the Dry Towns, and Jalak—well, it was frightful nonsense, but I have rarely been so glad to wake up." She put a tentative hand to the bandages.

"You will have a dreadful scar, I am afraid."

"There are some women in the Guild-house who think their scars a good advertisement for their skill," said Jaelle, "but, then, I am not a fighter."

Magda had to smile at that. "I should say you were quite a fighter."

"I mean, not a professional fighter. I do not normally hire myself out as soldier or bodyguard," Jaelle said, and shifted her body uncomfortably. "I don't remember much after you cut off my tunic."

"I'll tell you more after I dress your wound," Magda said. Jaelle had run so high a fever that Magda feared to find infection; but there was at least no renewed bleeding, though the edges of the wound looked ugly. Poisoned? Jaelle said, "I have some *karalla* powder in my saddlebags; it will keep the wound from closing too soon with rot beneath." At her directions Magda sprinkled the wound with the gray stuff before rebandaging it. Jaelle was exhausted and pale, but coherent; she ate some of the dried-meat soup, with Magda's help, and drank more water.

"You killed both of them? That does surprise me!"

"It surprised me, too," Magda confessed.

Jaelle uneasily fingered the bandage on her face. "I am not one of those who make a fetish of displaying their scars, but I may have to pretend that I am. Better scarred than buried—or blind! Camilla told me, once, that there were some men who found knife-scars on a woman irresistible." She sank back wearily against the rolled saddlebag under her head. "It was a fool's wound, really. Gwennis, or even old Camilla, could have driven them both away without taking a scratch."

She closed her eyes and slept again. She was somnolent, or sleeping, most of that day, but the fever did not return. Magda had little to do, after the animals had been tended. She thought about burying the dead bandits, but that was a task entirely beyond her strength. She stayed near Jaelle, in case the wounded girl should need anything. The sight of the bandage on Jaelle's face troubled her deeply. *She was so beautiful! In the Terran Zone they could repair that ugly slash as good as new; here, I suppose, she will bear that terrible scar until she dies!*

It occurred to her again that now, with Jaelle well on the way toward recovery, she could make her escape, leave her to recover at leisure, and not even have the other woman's death on her conscience. But by now the thought was very remote.

On the next day Jaelle was able to get up and walk about a little, moving her arm cautiously; swearing at the pain, but moving it, nevertheless. "I don't want the muscles to freeze and the arm to lose its strength," she said irritably, when Magda urged her not to risk tearing it open again. "I know what I am doing." Now that she was no longer somnolent with shock and exhaustion, she was in a good deal of pain, and it made her irritable and restless. Late in the afternoon Magda woke from a brief doze to find Jaelle staring at her as if trying to remember something. *Does she remember thinking I was going to kill her?* She remembered, with some shock, the moment when she had stood over Jaelle, not yet sure herself what she intended. Jaelle had been as still as a wounded animal awaiting the hunter's death-stroke. . . .

Jaelle said quietly, at last, "I did not expect you to stay with me, Margali; I knew you took our oath unwillingly. It is customary for oath-mother and daughter to exchange gifts; you have given me my life, I know."

"Don't!" Magda could not bear to start thinking again about her indecision. She got up and went out of the shelter, looking at the lowering gray sky, heavy with unfallen snow. Midwinter was only a few days distant; and on that day Peter Haldane would meet a dreadful death, suffering the penalty of Rumal di Scarp's blood-feud with the Ardais clan. Magda leaned against the outside wall of the shelter and gave herself up to helpless, desperate weeping.

After a long time she felt a soft touch on her arm; Jaelle stood there, looking very pale and troubled.

"Is he so dear to you—the kinsman of your mission?"

Exhausted, struggling for self-control, Magda could only shake her head and say, "It is not only that."

"Then tell me what it is, my sister." Jaelle took Magda's hand. She said, "Don't stand here in the cold."

More because she remembered that Jaelle herself must not be kept in the cold with her unhealed wound, Magda let herself be led inside. Jaelle stumbled, fell heavily against her; Magda caught her, eased her down on one of the stone benches.

"Now tell me, sister."

Magda shook her head, exhausted. "I told you all."

"But this time," Jaelle said, "the truth, will you not? I do not understand you, Margali. You were lying when you took the oath; you were not lying. You were telling the truth; you were not telling the truth. Even your name—it is your name; you have another name. Tell me."

Magda's defenses were down. "How did you know?"

Jaelle said, "I was born daughter to the Comyn; I have some *laran*." Magda did not know the word as Jaelle used it; it usually meant a gift or talent. "I have not had the training to use it properly. Lady Rohana— she is my mother's kinswoman—wished me sent to a Tower to be trained in its use; I would have none of that crew. So my gift is erratic; I cannot use it when I would, and when I would not, it thrusts itself on me, undesired. It was so when you took the oath; I could feel, within myself, that you were torn two ways, and in such fear ... there was no need for such terror as *that*. And now I can read your thoughts, but only a little, Margali—if that is your name. You are oathbound, but so am I; as you are sworn, so am I oathbound to you, never to hurt or betray you. Tell me, my sister!"

Magda said wearily, "I was born in Caer Donn. My true name—the name my parents gave me—is Magdalen Lorne, but the Darkover children with whom I played could not say that name; they called me *Margali*, and that is my name as much as the other."

"The—the *Darkovan* children?" Jaelle whispered, and her eyes were wide, almost with fear. "What *are* you, then?"

"I am . . . I am . . ." Magda struggled, the words sticking in her throat. This was basic. *You never tell any outsider who you are. Never.*

Jaelle is not an outsider. She is my sworn sister. Suddenly all conflict was gone. The lump in Magda's throat dissolved, and it seemed that she drew the first free breath she had drawn since she first entered this shelter several nights ago. She said, and her voice did not falter, "My mother and father were Terrans, subjects of the Empire; I am Darkovan, born in Caer Donn, but I am an Intelligence agent and linguistics expert for the Empire, and I work from Thendara."

Slowly, Jaelle nodded. "So that is it," she said at last. "I have heard something of the Terrans. One of ours in Thendara Guild-house—an *emmasca* who can pass herself off as a man: they all can, but many of them will not—hired herself out with the workmen among those building the spaceport, and she told us something of your people. But I did not know the Terrans were human, except in form."

Magda smiled at that way of putting it. She said, "The records of the Empire say that Darkovan and Terran are one stock from the far past."

"Does Lady Rohana know you are *Terranan?*"

"Yes; she saw me first there."

"This explains why you had to appeal to her," said Jaelle; she was just thinking out loud. "Your kinsman, is he Terran, too?"

"Yes; but taken prisoner by Rumal di Scarp because of a chance likeness to Lady Rohana's son."

"He is like Kyril? That will not endear him to me," Jaelle said. "I love Rohana well; Kyril is another matter entirely. But that does not matter now. You love this man so very much? Is he your lover, then?"

Magda said slowly, "No; although for a time we were"—she hesitated, used the Darkovan word—"freemates. But it is more than that. We were children together, and he has no one else. To my superiors in Thendara, he is—expendable; so I took this duty upon myself to save him from death and torture."

Jaelle bit her lip, frowning, idly fingering the bandage on her cheek. She said, "I must think. Perhaps—you are in the employ of your service, under bond for a legitimate service? A Free Amazon is bound by law to fulfill any work she hires herself of her free will to do, and it could be legally said you must complete this pledge and honor your conditions of employment." Again, she was thinking out loud. "You say you do not love him. How *do* you feel about him, then?"

"I don't know." Magda searched her mind; surprised herself by saying, "Protective."

Jaelle looked at Magda with that intense, frowning stare which made Magda wonder if the girl was really reading her thoughts. She said, "Yes; I think no man has ever meant more to you than that, not yet. You have, I think, the true spirit of an Amazon, and if you had been born among us, I think you would have come to us in the end. This must have been what Rohana saw in you."

She was silent for some time, thinking; suddenly she laughed.

"There is only one man living whom I love less than Rumal di Scarp," she said. "I would love to cheat Rumal of his prey! And you are oath-bound to obey all lawful commands of your employer. And there is a life between us; and it is required of me that I give my oath-daughter a gift. I will come with you, Margali, to Sain Scarp!"

Magda said, again with that sense of conflicting loyalties, "Jaelle, I can never thank you for this, but first you should know: it will cause much trouble for you in Thendara. Lorill Hastur has forbidden anyone in the Domains to take part in this affair."

"You do not listen very well," Jaelle said. "I do my own thinking, not the blind will of Hastur. Like all people, I must obey the laws of the land; but the whims of Hastur are not yet the laws of Thendara, and

Lorill Hastur has no right to forbid any Free Amazon, under the Charter, to accept any lawful work. Lorill Hastur is my kinsman—though the only time he saw and spoke with me he seemed not very eager to accept the relationship—but he is not the keeper of my conscience! The Free Amazons owe no allegiance to any liege lord, even if he calls himself the son of Hastur. And it seems to me that if the Terrans could give you, a woman, and born in Caer Donn, the strength and spirit to venture alone into the Hellers, and the—" She hesitated, looking away. "And at the same time, the integrity to honor an oath, even under such conditions of strain, then it seems to me that these *Terranan* might have something to teach even a Hastur, and that the Free Amazons should be their friends and allies. So I will give you leave, and I will help you, to rescue your friend."

Magda said hastily, "It must not be known that Peter is a Terran!"

"No, indeed! Rumal would take delight in hanging him from his castle wall that same day!" She held out her hands to Magda and said, "I think I can ride tomorrow; we will ride, then, for Sain Scarp."

Chapter

ELEVEN

Before leaving the shelter, next morning, Jaelle insisted on stripping the bodies of the dead bandits; an unpleasant task, as they had frozen hard in the bitter cold. They dragged them away from the path. "The *kyorebni* and the scavenger wolves will do the rest," Jaelle said cheerfully. "We could never have buried them with the ground frozen hard, so they can do our work for us."

The day was overcast and grim as they set forth, and Magda was anxious about Jaelle; exposure to cold, with an unhealed wound, could be dangerous. Yet once the pass of Scaravel was closed, no amount of haste could bring them to Sain Scarp before midwinter-night.

They made good time for the first three days; but on the fourth day it began to snow in earnest, and Jaelle looked troubled as they began to ride upward along the road to the pass.

"If we get through before dark, there is nothing to fear; Sain Scarp is a two-day ride beyond it, and there is nothing else so high as Scaravel. But if we are delayed today, or if we have to pass Scaravel in the darkness . . ." She was silent, frowning, obviously worried.

Near midday they came to a little village on the

mountainside, where they bought some hot soup at a food-stall, and bargained for fodder for their animals. They were about to ride on when the lashings on Magda's pack animal suddenly gave way, and the pack slipped; the beast snorted and neighed, frightened by the bumping of the heavy pack hanging under its belly. Magda slid down and ran to free it from the swaying, bumping burden, but the frightened animal kicked and reared, and it was half an hour before, even with Jaelle's help, Magda could quiet the creature enough to get the remaining strap unbuckled and the pack off. Then they had to find a harness-maker who could mend the strap or make a new one; and when Jaelle came back after talking at length with the harness-maker (his dialect was so thick Magda could not understand him), she looked grave.

"Lady Rohana, with her escort, crossed Scaravel three days ago, on her way to Ardais," she said, "and the pass was open then; since then, no traveler has climbed toward the pass. We may find it blocked already; if not, this storm will surely close it till spring-thaw. Come what may, we must cross Scaravel tonight, or we cannot reach Sain Scarp in time. Let us find some more of that woman's good bean soup before we take the road; we'll get little warm food tonight."

Less than half a mile out of the village, Magda looked back down the trail and saw that the thickening snow had already blotted out the lights behind them. Jaelle wrapped a fold of her scarf across her bandaged cheek; her voice sounded muffled through it. "If these folk were not all living in the very shadow of Sain Scarp—and probably in their pay, or at least in fear of them—I think I would have left the horses here and tried the pass on foot. But I would not put such a strain on their honesty. There is a saying in the hills: 'Don't trust your bone to another man's dog.' "

It was less than an hour before they had to light their saddle-lanterns; the small lamps, fueled with resin, cast dim light for a few feet in every direction, but beyond that the light scattered into fog against the curtain of the falling snow. The trail was beaten deep between rocks, and Magda was glad, for the snow blotted out landmarks, and they might stray from the trail and never find it again. But when she said this to Jaelle, the other woman laughed through the muffling of the scarf.

"Just keep going up until there's no farther you can go! Myself, I'm glad of the snow; so near to Sain Scarp, Scaravel is no pass to travel alone in good weather. I have no doubt that is how your friend was taken! But on a night like this, even a bandit would be home by his own fireside!"

Higher and higher they rode, and Magda began to feel the dull, internal ache in ears and sinuses, born of the high altitude, which no amount of yawning or pressing her fingertips against her ears could completely dispel. The cold was bitter, and they began to feel the wind of the heights, which set the thick snow streaming almost sidewise against their faces and heaped it under their feet till they sank knee-deep in drifts and they had to dismount and lead their protesting horses. They moved slowly against the wind, each woman isolated in her own cocoon of darkness and silence. To Magda the world had shrunk to a circle less than ten feet wide, containing herself, the front half of her horse, the tail of Jaelle's saddle-horse just ahead and the soft crunching of the antlered pack beast that plodded along on his broad hooves after her lantern. Outside this narrow circle was nothing; only darkness and a wind that screeched like all the demons of Zandru's legendary ninth hell. Up, and again up, with the protest of knee muscles with every step, and her breath short. She wrapped her thick scarf heavily over her chin, and felt the wind freezing it, from the moisture of her breath, to an ice-mask.

She felt herself bump into something hard and soft at once, recoiled from the intrusion of something else into her private cocoon, and discovered it was Jaelle, who had turned her horse somewhat so it stood sidewise of the trail to block it. She put her head close to

Magda's and shouted, "Let's stop for some food; it seems hours since we ate, and higher up it's dangerous to stop!"

They formed the animals into a triangle, nose to tail, and stood at the center of this crude windbreak, chewing on some dried-meat bars and fruit, which were the first things Magda could find at the top of the saddlebags. The world had shrunk so small that Magda found herself staring at the small pattern of blue birds knitted into the back of Jaelle's woolen mittens, and wondering if Jaelle had knitted them herself.

Then above them, sweeping down from the heights and even drowning out the shrieking wind, came a shrill, eerie cry; a long, paralyzing howl that made Magda's ears ring and almost physically paralyzed her. She gasped with the sound, then knew what it must be, even before Jaelle said: "Banshee. I was afraid of that; let's just hope the wind distorts its sense of direction. And remember it would rather have the horses than us, so keep in their shelter."

Magda had heard about—but never actually *heard*—the shattering, paralyzing scream of the great flightless carnivores who lived above the snowline and were attracted by the warmth and movement of their prey. Again the ghastly screech came, and it seemed to her that the meat-bar she was chewing had turned to leather in her mouth.

Jaelle was trying to make herself heard above the howl of the wind again. "What, Jaelle?"

"This is where we have to decide. I'm not an expert on Scaravel, but I *have* been over it in daylight, and I gather you haven't. Above here the trail narrows, so we can't turn around, and there's not even a level spot to spend the night. Beyond here, we're committed, because there's no stopping till we're on the other side. But it seems to be open now. It's a risk either way, but it's *your* risk, and your neck. Try it in the dark, or wait here? It's not a particularly good trail even by daylight."

Magda thought of the narrowing trail, the terrible

carnivores of the heights, her own aching legs and wind-burned face. And Jaelle, beside her, was not really well enough to travel. *It's not Jaelle's mission at all. If I lead her to her death . . .*

"What would you advise?" Magda asked.

"I wouldn't advise; I'd try not to get into such a spot. But being in it, I'd probably go on. Just the same, I didn't want you to go at it thinking it's easy or safe, because it's not. This is your last chance to lose your nerve."

And this was the last chance. If they did not make it across Scaravel tonight, and it proved to be blocked by daylight after the night's snow . . . She said, "But what about you, Jaelle? You're still not strong—"

"There's almost as much risk to turn around here and go down," Jaelle said, "and if we stay here, we might freeze. I can make it if you can."

Magda was not so sure; but having come so far, she was unwilling to retreat or give up. She swallowed the last of the dried meat, and said, "All right, then, we'll try. Want me to break trail? You've been doing it this far."

"From here on we don't break trail; we let the horses do it," said Jaelle, "and we stay between them, in case any banshee is prowling around looking for a midnight lunch!"

The trail was really steep now, but between the two saddle-horses, crowded together on the narrow path, the howling of the wind reached them less fiercely. The snow crunched hard underfoot, and they clung to the saddles on the horses to keep their footing. The trail twisted and turned between great rocks that gave some slight shelter from the wind, but now and then Magda caught, between the horses' legs or over their backs, a faraway and eerie glimpse of great chasms and cliffs, of dizzy gulfs of space dropping away from the trail; and, hastily turning her eyes back into the enclosing world—the horses on either side, Jaelle pressed close against her elbow—she was glad of the darkness that concealed the giddy heights to either side. They struggled along side by side, so close that Magda could hear the other woman's labored breathing; again and again, from the heights above them, they could hear the eerie, demoralizing banshee cry. The horses stirred and stamped; Magda's horse tossed its head, and she hauled on the bridle, trying to calm and quiet the frightened animal.

"Won't the saddle-lanterns attract the banshees, too?"

"No, they're blind," Jaelle said. "They sense warmth and movement, that's all. I remember—"

Magda never heard what she remembered. In the next moment there was another high, chilling banshee scream—this one almost on top of them—and a screech from the pack animal behind them, and Magda's horse reared, struggling, at the very edge of the cliff. The pack beast went down, screaming, plunging, kicking in the snow, and over its struggling body Magda caught a blurred glimpse of a huge, naked, buzzardlike head, an enormous ungainly body, the beak plunging into the pack animal's soft underbelly and rearing up, dripping gore. Magda pulled out her knife, backing away, waiting for the moment to strike. The naked head whipped around in her direction, weaving, darting, and Jaelle caught her wrist and dragged her back.

She said in a harsh whisper, "Let it eat! It's too late to save the animal, and if it's full it won't turn on us!"

Magda knew that made sense, but the screaming of the dying beast, the terrified screams of the other horses and the foul stench of the great predator turned her sick. She covered her face with her hands as the wicked talons struck down, scraping, raking, and the evil beak plunged down, again and again, as the banshee gorged his fill. Jaelle pulled Magda down behind the horses, and the women lay there concealed, trying not to hear or to see as the creature ate with little growling clucks and snarls.

God, those talons! One blow from them almost ripped the animal in half! Magda thought.

It seemed a long time before the banshee jerked up

its huge head, darting it from side to side without interest, then plunged back once for a final tidbit and lumbered heavily away. The talons left great sloppy prints of blood and filth on the snow. Magda, struggling to control her sickness, got up slowly. The antlered pack beast lay almost still, and—this was the ultimate horror—whining thinly, still alive. Magda could not stand it. She bent swiftly, drew her knife across its throat, and with one final twitch, it lay still. Behind the horses Jaelle was lying in the snow, retching weakly, helplessly.

Magda went to her. "Come on! Help me get the pack off that thing, and onto our horses! And then let's get the hell away from here before all that thing's brothers and sisters come around looking for another helping!"

Jaelle came, wiping her face on her sleeve. Her face looked grotesque, red and blotched. "Oh, that was horrible—horrible—"

"It was. But it could have been a lot more horrible if it had grabbed one of us instead," Magda said, and bent over the dead animal to cut the straps that held the pack to the half-eaten carcass. *The same strap we so carefully had replaced in the village!* With Jaelle's help she managed to haul it off the dead animal, though their hands were slimy with blood and entrails before they finished. Magda hoisted it to the back of her horse. "We can divide up the load tomorrow," she said. "Right now we'd better get moving."

Numbed by fatigue and horror, the women stumbled upward, higher and higher; and suddenly, rounding a curve in the deep-beaten trail, they were not climbing anymore. They stood in the top of the pass of Scaravel, and there was no way to go but down. Magda was too weary even to feel relieved. Jaelle was stumbling with fatigue and weariness, and Magda wished it were safe for her to ride. Certainly she could not go on much longer.

The going was easier now, although the horses had a tendency to slip and stumble; before long Magda felt the lessening ache in her ears that told they were losing altitude. She recalled hearing that banshees nested only above the timberline; when they reached the first clump of gnarled trees, thick wind-tangled evergreens, she could feel the tension running out of her like water. She stumbled along for another hundred feet or so, found a thick grove of trees where the horses would be a little protected from wind and the still-falling snow. Jaelle was dazed, out on her feet; she stood blinking, unaware what was going on. Alone, Magda tied the horses and blanketed them, managed to get up one of the tiny tents, got Jaelle out of her snow-caked riding-cloak and boots and shoved her into her blankets. She fell into her own without stopping to take off anything but boots. The tent was much too small for two— Magda had thought it was too small for one—but claustrophobia was better than taking the time to get up the other one; besides, they needed the warmth. She thought, as she fell asleep, *I'd bring the horses in if I could get them in.* Even the faraway wail of another banshee—or the one who had attacked them?—could not keep her awake.

The weather cleared in the night, and they looked on a dazzling white world, with evergreens bent almost double under their weight of snow. When Magda dressed Jaelle's wounds, they looked dull-white and macerated; they had been frozen, and this would make the scarring worse, but there was nothing to be done about it. She used some of the water she had boiled for porridge to try to clean them, but there was not much she could do. Jaelle ate listlessly, but she did eat, and Magda was glad; that glazed, numb look of exhaustion had frightened her. When she had done, she pointed to a low peak in the next range.

"Sain Scarp," Jaelle said. "If the weather holds we will be there tomorrow." Magda's eyes were sharp, but try as she might, she could see nothing but trees.

Jaelle laughed. "I doubt Rumal di Scarp will enter-tain us, so we may not have much of a midwinter-feast this year! But no doubt your kinsman would rather eat porridge on the open road than feast with Rumal! And if the weather holds fine, we might reach Ardais by midwinter; you cannot see it from here, though if you have good eyes you can see it from the very top of Scaravel. But I am not going back up to look now!"

Now that they were actually within sight of their goal, Magda found herself wondering about Peter again. How would he feel, to be rescued at a woman's hands? An hour later, as they rode down the trail through the melting snow, Jaelle voiced the same question.

"Your kinsman, will it damage his pride too much, to accept rescue at a woman's doing? Or don't the *Terranan* have that kind of pride?"

"Not usually. On other worlds men and women usually share the risks equally," Magda said. *But Peter was reared on Darkover, like me. And I found my Darkovan training too strong even for the Empire. Will it damage him, destroy him, as it might a Darkovan man?*

And suddenly Magda understood something about herself that she had never realized before.

Brought up as I was, at Caer Donn, only a Darkovan could have attracted me; they say the way you react to the opposite sex is conditioned before you're seven years old. None of the Terran men I knew seemed right, none of them had the right sort of emotional—or sexual—wavelengths for me. The sexual cues were all wrong. So Peter was literally the only man I knew to whom I reacted as to a male at all.

And when I was ripe for a love affair, he was the only man I knew; literally the only one. It wasn't that I cared more for him than others: it was that there were no others.

She realized that this might very well be the most important insight of her life, and resolved that she must somehow manage to hold on to it, even after she met Peter again.

Sain Scarp was an enormous fortress, isolated beyond a long rock causeway. The next day at noon the two women rode across the causeway, and Magda, at least, had the sense of eyes watching them from the tower at the far end. At the end of the causeway a big, rough-looking man stopped them, demanding their business.

Now. This is the culmination of it all; everything else that has happened—even the Amazon oath, dividing my life in two—was all for this. Strangely, Magda had almost forgotten that. She said, "I am the Free Amazon Margali n'ha Ysabet"—(how strange that sounded)—"come on a mission from the Lady Rohana Ardais. There is a prisoner and a ransom to be paid. Carry this word to Rumal di Scarp." They waited, shivering in the bright cold air, until the bandit chieftain came.

Afterward she could never remember what Rumal di Scarp looked like, except that he seemed a small man to carry such weight of rumor and horror tales: a small, wiry, hawk-faced man with fierce eyes. Behind Rumal, his hands bound, Magda saw a slender, familiar figure. *Peter!* He was thin and pale, dressed in shabby and torn mountain garments; a narrow fringe of coppery-red beard shadowed his face, but Magda knew him.

Rumal di Scarp came slowly toward them. "Well, *mestra*, I hear there is a ransom to pay. Who are you?"

Silently, Magda held out her safe-conduct; Rumal took it, handed it to the huge bandit at his side, who overshadowed him physically as much as the little man seemed to dwarf his giant companion in every other way. The man read it aloud to Rumal. "Lady Rohana Ardais . . . empowered to deal in a family matter . . ."

Rumal took the safe-conduct, crumpled it contemptuously and tossed it back to Magda. He said, laughing, "Gallant are the men of Ardais, that they send women to pay ransom for their menfolk! Why should I deal with you?"

Jaelle said, "Because I am the Lady Rohana's kinswoman, and if you do not honor your word I will spread it far and wide, from the Hellers to Dalereuth, that Rumal di Scarp does not honor his bargains. And then you may sit here in Sain Scarp and make soup from the bones of your captives for all the good they will be to you, since no one will ever again pay a single coin in ransom!"

Rumal made a gesture of contempt, signaled for Peter to be brought forward. "Well, there he is, heir to Ardais, whole and well, sound in wind and limb as a horse in spring market. And so, my ladies"—he used the intimate inflection, which made it sound even more contemptuous—"let us see the color of that ransom, then."

Magda knew her hands were trembling as she counted out the copper bars. Rumal shrugged, signaled to his giant henchman to wrap the ransom money in a cloth and take it away. "You have your kinsman. Take him away, then."

Jaelle looked at him defiantly, and said, "His horse and gear?"

"Oh, that," said Rumal. "That I kept to cover the cost of feeding him between snowfall and midwinternight, lest the ransom grow too great for one horse to carry." He said ironically to Peter, "Farewell, my Lord; fortunate is that man so loved by his kinsmen that they entrust him to a woman's ransoming. See that you repay these ladies well for their courtesy, my Lord, since no doubt it was only their pleas that persuaded the menfolk of your clan to ransom you at all. And now—" He made a deep, graceful bow, whose very courtly grace sent a shudder of horror through Magda, much worse than if he were ugly or deformed. "Farewell, dom; a safe journey and a fortunate homecoming."

Peter made him a deep, equally ironic bow. "My thanks for your hospitality, messire di Scarp. May I sleep the night in each of Zandru's hells in turn before I taste of it again."

"A churlish speech," Rumal drawled, "but the color of money is not brightened by courteous words—nor dimmed by boorish ones." He turned on his heel and walked away, not looking back.

Peter reached out and seized Magda's hands in a hard grip. His own were shaking. "It *is* you," he said. "I dreamed—I dreamed—" His voice caught, and for a moment she thought he was about to weep, but he managed to control it, clutching her fingers painfully hard in his own.

She said, and her heart was wrung with pity, "You are so thin and pale! Have they been starving you?"

"No, no, though the fare was not what I could have hoped for in the Hellers," he said, still clinging to her hands.

Jaelle broke in: "There is a horse for you at the end of the causeway; we traded for it in the last village. I thought Rumal would keep yours, as he did. I hope it suits you."

"*Mestra,* I would ride a rabbit, or walk from here to Thendara in my bare feet, it is so good to be beyond these walls," he said. "Come, let us get out of bowshot. . . . How came this to be? I had utterly lost hope that you would ever know where I was, or how, even, I had died."

Jaelle was studying him curiously as they came to where they had left the horses. "I cannot believe it! This is not a joke? You are not my cousin Kyril? Are you truly—*Terranan?*"

"I am," Peter said, and glanced curiously at Magda. "Who—and what—?"

"She is my friend and sister, Peter," Magda said quietly, "and she knows who we are, so there is no need for pretense."

Peter bent over her slender hand. He said, "How can I speak my thanks, *mestra?* Midwinter-night is too near for me to pretend I was not afraid."

Jaelle looked back, saw that Rumal and his men had turned to watch them from the end of the causeway. She said, with a hesitant laugh, "Now, indeed, I believe you are not my cousin Kyril. I think he would rather be hanged in fragments from Rumal's walls than confess himself afraid!" She added, after a moment, "No doubt they are watching and wondering why you do not greet me as a kinswoman."

From anyone else Magda thought that would have sounded almost unbearably flirtatious; Jaelle only sounded embarrassed. Peter said, "That will be my pleasure, then—kinswoman." He bent forward and made as if to give her a brotherly embrace and kiss on the cheek. Jaelle colored and lowered her eyes; suddenly, gently, Peter took Jaelle's slender hand up in his again, bent and laid a light kiss on her wrist.

Magda, watching, thought unexpectedly, *I'm free of him. Before, I would have been unendurably jealous—to see that look in his eyes, turned on any other woman. I nearly went mad when he danced with Bethany at a New Year's party last year. Now I do not care.* Her love, her guilt, her concern, had been a part of her so long that she felt cold, flat and empty. Now she looked at him with sympathy, with concern for his thinness and pallor. . . . *As if he were my brother, my child. But not a lover. Not now.*

Jaelle started to move away, then suddenly reached out and caught Peter's hand. She said, "I cannot believe it. You are so like to my cousin Kyril, and yet . . . let me see your hands! How many fingers have you?"

"Normal number," said Peter, "four and a thumb—oh, my God!" He was looking down at Jaelle's slender hand, lying in his own. "You have six fingers on each hand," he said numbly.

"Yes. The Ardais and the Aillard blood—those who bear it have the extra finger," Jaelle said. "Is it wholly unknown among Terrans? Rohana is Aillard by birth, and her husband an Ardais; and all of her children have the Aillard hands." She began to laugh hysterically. "If Rumal had—had bothered to count your fingers—" she got out between spasms, "you would now be hanging—in pieces—from his castle wall."

She could not seem to stop laughing; Magda came and tried to calm her, and at last, really frightened, reluctant but afraid that it was the only way to stop her, took her shoulders and shook her hard. Jaelle began to cry as hysterically as she had laughed. "You'd be dead," she got out between sobs, "you'd be dead—"

She has ridden too far; she is still not strong. Magda said to Peter, "Can you take her on your saddle? We must get away from here before nightfall," and watched as Peter tenderly lifted Jaelle on his horse, got on and supported the drooping girl, his arm holding her upright against him. Magda mounted her own horse, and took the reins of Jaelle's, leading it after them. And already—she realized a long time afterward—she knew then what was going to happen.

Part III

JAELLE
n'ha MELORA,

Free Amazon

Chapter

TWELVE

The ceiling was painted blue, with a border and a design of little stars in gilt. At first Jaelle could not imagine where she was. Then she remembered that she had slept in this room during her one extended visit to Castle Ardais, in her sixteenth year.

"Before you renounce your heritage as *Comynara*," Kindra had warned her, speaking more seriously than she had ever before spoken to her foster-daughter, "you must first know what it is that you are renouncing." So to Ardais Jaelle had gone, protesting, to remain a full half-year. She had not been happy there; she had felt, she told Rohana once rebelliously, like a fish in a tree.

But I am not sixteen years old anymore! Why am I here? She shifted her weight, and at the sharp stab of pain in her wounded shoulder, remembered. Where were her Terran companions? They had come late at night, she remembered, and she had told the servants at the gate to bear word to the Lady Rohana that her kinswoman had come to spend midwinter-night, bringing two friends. She remembered Rohana, graciously welcoming them all, and her dismay when she saw Jaelle's bandaged face. The rest was blurred.

Jaelle was lying in a big bed, wearing a long-sleeved nightgown, trimmed with lace at the neck and wrists. She supposed it belonged to Rohana, or to her daughter; she herself possessed no such garments, and it was too fine for a servant. One of the sleeves had been slit to accommodate the folds of bandage at her shoulder; her face, too, had been bandaged freshly. She looked around the room and saw a second bed near the window, and the Terran woman asleep in it, but at that moment Magda turned over and looked at her.

"You look better," she said. "When you were carried up here the night before last, I thought you were dying." Magda got out of bed and came to Jaelle's side. She, too, was wearing one of the lace-trimmed gowns, though she was so tall it came only midway down her calves. Her dark short hair had been washed and was curling around her cheeks.

Jaelle said, "I really don't remember anything after we got here; did you carry me here, or—" She hesitated, not remembering his Darkovan name, unwilling to use the Terran one where they might be overheard.

"No; dom Gabriel himself did you that honor."

Jaelle smiled wryly. "Poor dom Gabriel! How my kinswoman's husband dislikes me! Or, at least, dislikes having a Free Amazon in the family!"

"He seemed genuinely anxious about you," Magda protested, and Jaelle laughed a little. "Oh, anything belonging to Rohana he will treat kindly—pet dogs, Free Amazons, even Terrans, I suppose." She felt the smile stab ferocious pain through her bandaged face. "Does he know?"

"Rohana told him only that we were friends of yours," Magda replied. "She warned me afterward that the house was full of midwinter guests, and we must be careful. Of course, when dom Kyril met Peter, he was tremendously curious. He asked who Peter was, and Peter told him his usual tale—that he was born in Caer Donn, that he did not know his father's name. Dom Kyril said after that, 'Having seen you, I think I could put a name to your father's clan, at least.' And, like you, he looked at once at his hands."

Jaelle lay back, astonished at herself. *So weary, after sitting up only a few minutes?* Her shoulder throbbed as if it were afire. "Where is—where is he?"

"Asleep in the next room," Magda said, pointing to the connecting door. "Lady Rohana apologized that she could give us only these rooms; I told her that in any case you should not be left alone at night. You slept all of yesterday; you did not wake even when domna Alida came to dress your wounds."

"So I have lost a day," Jaelle said. Now she remembered, fuzzily, how they had come here. Rumal di Scarp would be expecting them to head at once for Ardais; would find it suspicious if they turned in any other direction. In any case, Scaravel was blocked behind them by the snow. Magda had felt that since Lady Rohana had arranged this mission, she had a right to know of its success.

Jaelle remembered, too, how Peter had ridden at her side, had helped her whenever they stopped to rest the horses. Much of that time, she had been in a daze of pain and weariness, but she remembered how when they stopped, he had coaxed her to eat, and how, when she could no longer sit in her saddle without falling, he had taken her again before him on his saddle and held her against him. All else was blurred, but she could remember, with a sharp tactile memory, the feel of his arms around her. She had been ashamed of her weakness and secretly a little glad of it, for it let her lean against him, rest her head on his shoulder through the swaying dizziness of pain and fever. . . .

She thought, with a sharp sting of guilt, *Appeal to no man for protection* . . . and closed her eyes, feeling tears of weakness sliding down her cheeks. She felt Magda's gentle hand on her wrist. "I will let Lady Rohana know you are awake," she said.

Rohana came before long, small and queenly in a fur-trimmed gown; she bent and kissed Jaelle on the cheek not covered with the bandage. "How are you feeling, my child? And how came you by this dreadful wound? Margali has told me very little, only that you fought for her."

"I suppose she did not tell you that she saved my life," Jaelle said, "nor that she is oath-bound to the Guild, and my sister."

Rohana asked very seriously, "Is this allowed, my child, that a *Terranan* should be accepted by oath into the Guild?"

"The Guild-mothers must give the final decision on that," Jaelle said, "but the Guild Charter excludes no woman; it is the oath, not the parentage, which makes an Amazon under the Charter. And my sister chose to honor her oath; to stay and fight for me, and to care for me afterward, when she could easily have abandoned me to die."

Rohana said gently, "Then she is kinswoman here, too, my darling." Relieved, Jaelle slipped back into exhausted sleep—or stupor—again, and over her head Rohana's eyes met the Terran woman's. "Someday you must tell me how this came about."

"I am not sure myself," Magda said with a troubled smile, "but I will honor my oath, whatever comes."

"For her sake? Only for friendship?"

"No. Not entirely. Perhaps—" Magda hesitated, searching for words. "Perhaps because I have two worlds to serve, and I think I can best honor both loyalties this way."

"And your husband? What will he say to this?"

"He is not my husband in law; we parted more than a year ago. Certainly he is not the keeper of my conscience."

"I thought—" Rohana stopped. Like all telepaths, she had a horror of seeming to intrude in any personal matter. But it had seemed to her, when she met Magda in the Trade City, that the Terran woman was wholly committed to her former lover; and she had had misgivings when she saw Magda in Amazon garb. It had seemed to her that in spite of the spirit and strength she had admired, Magda was all too feminine for the part she must play. It had seemed to her that Magda was much like herself, committed to taking a man's part for a woman's reasons.

She felt completely at a loss; and that was a new sensation for Rohana. It also roused questions she thought she had settled, completely and without any doubts, years ago. She was glad to put her self-questioning aside when Magda asked, "Is it right for Jaelle to sleep so much? Is she worse than I feared?"

"I do not know: Alida says that neither wound is healing as it should. She will know more today."

"It is my fault," Magda said, looking down at Jaelle with dread. Asleep or unconscious again? "She exhausted herself trying to help us."

Rohana's hands closed very lightly over hers. Magda did not yet know enough of the telepath caste to know how very rare a gesture it was, or what trust it indicated. "My dear child, don't blame yourself. Since Kindra died, there has been no one, no one at all who could make Jaelle do anything she did not want to do, or prevent her from doing her own will; so whatever she did was freely done." She looked down at Jaelle with a detached, sad tenderness. She said, and Magda felt that Rohana was not really speaking to her at all, "In many ways she is dearer to me than my own daughter. Yet I have known for many years that I must let her take her own way."

She turned to go. "Domna Alida will see her this morning; she is Tower-trained, and has great skill in such matters." She went away.

Shortly after, Peter came through the connecting door. "How is Jaelle?" he asked, in a low, troubled voice.

Magda repeated what Rohana had said, and he shook his head, dismayed. "I hate to think she would put herself in such danger for us," he said. "But listen to me, Magda; we have to leave here, as soon as we can. You know we can't stay here for midwinter, as Lady Rohana expects, when there might be someone here who recognizes us!"

"Rohana won't tell."

"Perhaps not. But among the household there are two or three men from Caer Donn who may recognize me . . . . remember me from the days when Terrans and mountain men could mingle freely. If they do . . ."

Magda was sympathetic, but for the moment another concern seemed more important. She said, "I cannot go without Jaelle's leave; perhaps I cannot go at all. Certainly I would not go while she is ill and needs me." She flung at him, in sudden rage, "Does an oath mean nothing to you?"

"Not one wrested from you by force," Peter said, "and in any case you had no right to give it. I know you were forced into it, but still——"

It was her own reasoning, and it made her angrier than ever, as he went on, persuasively, "I know you have always had a great love for pretending yourself Darkovan, and a pride in your skill at it. But there is a time to forget all that. Your first loyalty is to the Empire—do I have to remind you of that?"

He had taken her hands in his; she wrenched them away. "Then say I *chose!* I feel I can serve best this way, but if it comes to choice . . . !" She was trembling all over. He said, trying to conciliate, "I didn't realize you felt like that; you know I would never interfere in a matter of conscience, Mag. But why does this girl mean so much to you? It's not like you to have this kind of—this kind of emotional attitude over another woman. It's not quite—" He hesitated, unwilling to say it, and Magda, guessing what he refused to say, was angry again.

"Think anything you damn please! If you believe that, you'll believe anything!"

"Mag, I didn't say I believed——"

"You're a fool, Peter," she said in disgust. "Do you really believe no woman could be loyal to another woman out of common humanity and integrity? Jaelle saved my life; and do I have to remind you that if she had not risked hers to cross Scaravel Pass with an unhealed wound, you would still be counting the days to midwinter-night in Rumal's dungeons? And you want me to leave her, not even knowing if she will live or die, or be scarred for life?"

"Do *you* need to remain? I thought these people were her closest kinfolk!"

"Yes," Magda said, "but by oath she has had to renounce all her kinfolk; as her oath-daughter I am the closest kin she has beneath this roof." She said this with absolute certainty, knowing that, in spite of Rohana's deep affection for Jaelle, she would have said the same thing. Rohana had taken it for granted that Magda had a duty, and a right, to stay with Jaelle and care for her; more than Rohana's own right. Camilla had said, jesting, that Rohana was still ignorant about the ways of Free Amazons. But she had her finger on the very pulse of what they meant to one another; more, Magda knew, than she herself did.

Peter's anger had been short-lived, as always. He said, "Probably you know best, Mag; you usually do. And midwinter-feast is the time for hospitality; probably a couple of extra guests will never be noticed." He walked to Jaelle's side, and stood looking down at her.

"How beautiful she is," he said softly, "or how beautiful she would be, without that terrible scar! How could a woman like that renounce love and marriage?"

Jaelle opened her unbandaged eye; her vision was blurry and unfocused. She said, "It is not love we renounce . . . only marriage . . . bondage. . . ." she stretched out her hand, and Peter knelt beside the bed, taking her hand in his. Her eyes fell shut again, but she kept hold of him.

He was still kneeling there when the door opened again and Lady Rohana came in, with dom Gabriel's sister, who had been described to Magda as a *leronis*. The title translated, usually, as "soceress" or "wise-woman"; Magda suspected it meant, in this case, "healer." Her name was Alida. She was a small, slight woman with flaming red hair, younger by some years than Rohana, and with a kind of indefinable arrogance which made Magda, for some reason, think of Lorill Hastur.

Lady Alida inclined her head in the faintest of courteous greetings to Magda. She ignored Peter. She pulled back Jaelle's blankets and began to unfasten the cutaway nightgown; then looked, in unmistakable command, at Peter. He had been brought up in the mountains near Caer Donn and understood perfectly well; actually it was even somewhat scandalous that he should have been in the room when Magda was not fully dressed. He let go Jaelle's hand, but she quickly clasped it again, opening her eyes.

She said, "I want him to stay!" She sounded like a child, and Magda wondered if she were delirious again.

Lady Alida shrugged. "Stay, then, if she wants you. But take her other hand, and keep out of my way." Peter obeyed, and Alida, with some minor help from Rohana, got the bandages undone to examine the ugly wounds. Even Magda could see that they were not healing properly, but were swollen and festered. The clean slash on the face had spread and reddened, the nick in the eyelid so swollen that Jaelle's eye was shut.

"This is a poisoned wound! How came she by it?"

Briefly, Magda recounted their fight with the bandits. Lady Alida made a fastidious grimace. "That is no work for women!"

Jaelle flushed with anger. She said pettishly, "I do not need to be told you do not approve of my way of life, kinswoman, but courtesy should prevent you from insulting my sister and guest before me!"

Rohana said in haste, "Alida meant no offense—did you, kinswoman?"

Alida paid no attention to either of them. "What has happened to *your* wound, *mestra?*"

After a moment Magda realized that she was being addressed, and pushed up the long sleeve of the nightgown she was wearing. "It is healing."

"But not as it should," Alida said, her light, cold fingers gently touching the red seam, still puckered and inflamed. "A cut like this should long be closed and sealed, with not even an itch remaining. This still gives you some pain, I can tell—does it not?"

"Yes, a little," Magda said. She had so little experience with such cuts that she had thought it natural. She saw Peter looking up, in surprise and consternation, at her bare arm and the red seam there, and she pushed her sleeve down to cover it.

Alida said, "Jaelle must have been wounded first, and got most of the poison."

Rohana sounded anxious. "Can you help it, Alida?"

"Oh certainly. I learned to treat such wounds at Neskaya Tower; it is nothing much. You were Tower-trained in Dalereuth as a girl; can you monitor for me?"

Rohana nodded. "Certainly."

But Rohana watched, faintly troubled, as Alida uncovered her matrix jewel. She knew she should send the two Terrans away. This, she knew, was one reason why Lorill Hastur had interdicted any serious contact between Terran and Darkovan; he was unwilling they should learn anything about the ancient matrix sciences. Yet, if she should make a point of dismissing Magda and Peter from the room now, she must explain why.

She had told no one here that they were Terrans, but she was sure Gabriel guessed. When he had seen Peter's almost unbelievable likeness to their son Kyril, and heard that he was the prisoner from Sain Scarp, he must have known; but he did not really want to know, Rohana realized, that she had gone against his wishes again. *Because then I would have to tell him, in so many words, that he is not the keeper of my conscience; and even now I do not think Gabriel wants to know that in a way he cannot pretend to ignore.*

And the woman, Magda, was Jaelle's oath-sister and had a right to remain. As for the man—she saw Jaelle clinging to his hand, saw the tenderness in his eyes, and knew what neither of them knew themselves, as yet.

"Put that away, Lady Alida. I will have none of your sorcery," Jaelle said weakly.

"I must, child. There is poison in the wound and it
is spreading to your eye; it can damage your sight. If I
do not treat it now . . ."

"I do not care," said Jaelle in great agitation. "I will
not allow—"

Rohana said sternly, "Stop it, Jaelle. You are behaving like a frightened child who will not have a cut bandaged! I had not believed you so cowardly!"

Alida's voice was kinder. "I know you were afraid of
me when you were a child, Jaelle, but I hoped you had
outgrown your fear."

"I am not afraid," Jaelle said, shaking with anger,
"but I will not have you meddling with my mind! Once
is enough for a lifetime!"

Suddenly Rohanna recalled what Jaelle was talking
about. On that single extended visit to Ardais, which
she had demanded before allowing Jaelle to take the
Amazon's oath, she had insisted that Jaelle be tested
for *laran;* Melora's child, and with the flame-colored
hair that marked the telepath strain, would surely have
one of the Comyn gifts. Jaelle had been frightened and
helplessly reluctant, but on this point Rohana would
not be moved. Alida had done the testing, and Jaelle
had come away white as a corpse and looking deathly
ill. It was the only time since her mother's death that
Rohana had ever seen Jaelle in tears. When Rohana
had sent her away, a little calmed and comforted, Alida had said:

"Yes, she has *laran;* I think she is a powerful telepath, but for some reason she is blocking it. I could
break her defenses, of course; but whether I could ever
put them together again afterward—that is another matter. And since you have allowed her to be fostered
among the Amazons, I think she would find life in-
tolerable in a Tower. Let her take her own way."

Rohana had left it at that. She had complied with
the law that every child of Comyn blood—legitimate or
illegitimate; and in law Jaelle was illegitimate—must be
tested. More was not necessary. She was sure it was
the shock of rapport with her dying mother that had

forced Jaelle to barricade her own *laran*, but she had not tried to find out.

But was Jaelle's fear still so acute? Domna Alida only said, unoffended, when Jaelle swore at her, "You are ill, Jaelle. You do not know what you are saying. Shall I really put you to the indignity of having your hands tied?"

Magda almost cried out: "No, you mustn't!"

"Jaelle," Rohanna persuaded, "you are not one of those Amazons who makes a great thing of swaggering and comparing scars."

Alida said coolly, "If she wishes to end her days looking like a battle-scarred veteran of the campaigns at Corresanti, that is her affair; I am only concerned about her eyesight!"

Peter was still holding Jaelle's hand in his. He raised his free hand to Jaelle's cheek, caressed the smooth skin below the red slash. He said, as if there were no one in the room but himself and Jaelle, "You are so beautiful. It would be so dreadful to let that beauty be spoiled."

Jaelle moved her other hand, clumsily, toward his; and Magda knew—they all knew—that she would not protest further.

That wasn't fair, Magda thought. *Jaelle is too vulnerable. Peter should not have done it. . . .*

Lady Alida moved her hand, and Magda could see the blue stone in it—a jewel? A brilliant flash, a twisting, sickening *glare* . . . Magda turned her eyes away, unable to endure the sight. The *leronis* said quietly, "You were too busy cursing me to let me explain, Jaelle, but I need not touch your mind for this. I am going to be doing some very delicate cell-reconstruction work, so you must lie as quietly as possible, and try to make your mind as blank as you can, so that your thoughts will not interfere. You can sleep if you wish; it will be all the better if you do. I do not think you will feel any pain, but if you do you must tell me at once, so that your pain will not blur what I am doing."

Magda listened, in amazed curiosity. Hypnosis? All that about making her mind a blank . . . ?

"Rohana, you must monitor," Alida instructed. "And you must warn me if I come too close to the nerves, or to the small muscles near the corner of the eye," Alida warned, and again the blue jewel flashed in her hand. Magda felt a little, twisting ripple deep in her body, almost a sickness. Alida looked up, her face now remote and masklike, looking at Magda without really seeing her.

"Do not look directly at the matrix, *mestra;* many people cannot endure the sight."

Magda turned her eyes away, but found them drawn back. *Fakery, nonsense; but what are they going to do to Jaelle?*

Rohana approached Jaelle, bending over her; ignoring Peter, who still knelt on the far side of the bed, holding Jaelle's hands. Jaelle's eyes had fallen shut again. Rohana ran her fingertips along Jaelle's face, not quite touching her; down across the bared shoulder and the swollen, horribly festered wound there. It seemed to Magda that a line of light followed Rohana's fingertips, began to glow along Jaelle's skin . . . . *As if I could see the bones through the skin. . . .*

Rohana said, —*No, not the bones, the nerve currents that lie among them.* . . . But Rohana had *not* spoken, not raised her head; she was bending intently over Jaelle.

Alida was holding the jewel stone before her eyes with one hand, her face set in an almost inhuman calm. Now Magda could see, around the two wounds, a dull pulsing, a kind of glow around the inflamed flesh.

Alida said, "Now," and Rohana began to move her fingertips along the wound in the collarbone and shoulder. She did not touch Jaelle, but as the small lines of light followed her fingers, the swollen flesh seemed to move and ripple, dull colors swirling inside it; to heave, tremble and change color, from angry inflamed red to thick festering purple and then, almost, to a dull black, the lights in the flesh dimming, pulsing. Magda caught her breath; was this some ghastly hypnotic illusion? Blood oozed from the wound.

"Careful," Rohana said tonelessly.

The rippling surface of the open wound slowly paled, turned purple again, and as the lights around it brightened, turned red, then a smooth, healthy pink. . . .

Rohana shifted her hands, drawing her fingertips above the repulsive open gash across Jaelle's face. Alida brought the blue jewel stone close, and Magda, seeing it without sickness this time, found herself caught up in what was happening. She saw with a curious double vision those nerve currents under the skin, the slashed and broken and infected layers of skin and muscle and escaped, oozing blood, the seeped poison around the eye . . . she *felt*, with an inner itch and tension inside her mind, what Alida was doing: lowering her consciousness farther and farther, *into* the cells, exerting the tiniest pressures (*How! How?*) on each cell, so that she actually *felt* the blood and poison as pressures against the light-lines of the nerves, sensed the tiny, delicate membranes, the pressures against them. . . .

"Careful," Rohana said again, a low soft neutral sound, but to Magda, deep inside Alida's awareness, it was like a shriek of warning; and with infinite caution, Alida eased the carefully intricate pressures, moved her touch away from a small ruptured blood vessel, felt and almost *saw* the tiny tensions of fluids so near the eyeball, the glowing inner mechanism of the eyeball and tear ducts, so near, dangerously near. *Ease up just there.* . . . Something in the back of Magda's mind said, *Psychokinesis:* the power of the mind to exert delicate cellular changes. Her consciousness seemed wholly sunk inside that light, bending pressure. She looked at Jaelle from a great distance. *As if I were up somewhere near the ceiling and looking down.* . . . Giddy shifts of perspective.

Magda thought, somewhere back in her mind, *I can do that, too,* and found her attention focused on the healing slash in her own arm, sensed the inner pressures, somehow *wrenched* them into consciousness, feeling a faint sting of violent pain, somehow *outside* herself, which vanished without trace. . . .

She shook her head as if to clear it. She was standing firmly on her own feet, and Alida had covered the blue stone. She blinked as if dizzy, and looked down at Jaelle in amazement and shock. There was now no hideous, festering slash crisscrossing Jaelle's cheek; only a narrow, bright red seam, still jagged and raw, from which one drop of clean blood oozed. The nick in the eyelid was gone, and the closed eye, beneath its fringe of lashes, was no longer swollen.

Alida drew a long sigh of weariness. Mechanically Magda pushed up her sleeve, staring in puzzlement at where the bandit had gashed her arm with his poisoned blade. There was no puckered red line there now; only a firm white scar, which looked long healed. *Did I dream it?*

Alida thrust the wrapped stone inside the front of her dress. She looked at Magda, with a questioning frown, but did not speak to her. "Jaelle?"

Rohana touched Jaelle's forehead lightly. "She is asleep, I think."

"Good; while she sleeps the healing will be finished," Alida said, and gestured to Peter. "Leave her."

He tried gently to withdraw his hand, but the fingers were locked around it. He settled himself into a comfortable position on the floor and said, "I'll stay."

Magda tiptoed to Jaelle's side and drew the nightgown up over the girl's bare shoulder and breast, covered her with a blanket, then followed Rohana and Alida out of the room. Alida stumbled, almost fell against the door; Rohana caught and steadied her on her feet. She said, "Go and rest, Alida. And I thank you for Jaelle's sake."

Magda's mind was whirling. It was *not* illusion! That terrible, festering wound, like a great open, oozing sore . . . and now, as she covered Jaelle with her nightgown, it had not even needed a bandage, but was clean and almost healed. There was also her own arm; it looked like a scar a year old. And somehow, with the aid of the blue jewel, this had all been done through the powers of the mind. *Psi power. I never believed in it, not really. But I saw it. . . .*

Rohana saw Magda trembling, reached out and gently steadied her as she had done with Alida. She said, "Rest, my girl, that is strenuous work. Why did you not tell us you had *laran?*"

And Magda could only stammer, confused and dismayed, "I don't even know what the word *means!*"

Chapter

THIRTEEN

On the eve of midwinter-day, the long-delayed blizzard swept down from the Hellers, a thick white wilderness of snow and howling wind that effectively damped the preparations for the festival. The house-party guests had already arrived, but Lady Rohana told her guests, with some disappointment, that the usual festivities would have to be suspended. Normally, everyone who lived within a day's ride would have visited Castle Ardais at some time during the day to share in the merrymaking there.

Magda expressed polite regrets for the spoiling of the holiday, but was herself secretly relieved not to have to face more strangers. She had no personal fear. Dom Gabriel would not make trouble for his wife's guests, whoever they were; and the strong tradition of hospitality in the Hellers made it unlikely that they would meet with any personal unpleasantness. But it might well mean that other Terrans, after this, would be more carefully watched and restricted in their travel.

Lady Rohana had holiday gifts for them both: long riding-capes trimmed with fur. She also tactfully offered them garments more suitable for the festival, pointing out that they had only traveling clothes with them, and those much the worse for wear. Magda accepted with relief, Jaelle with a wry laugh. She said when Rohana had gone away, "My kinsman is cowardly, to make Rohana do his errands! Margali, you are a translator by trade; see if you can interpret this as I do! l may not have the words quite right, but the music is very clear, and the tune is something like this: 'I refuse to have two Amazons in trousers at my banquet-table!' "

Magda politely refrained from comment on her host, but she felt Jaelle was probably right. Jaelle was up and around now, though until today confined to her room, but she was recovering so swiftly that Magda still doubted the evidence of her own eyes. But there it was before her: the healed scar on Jaelle's collarbone, the red line—perceptible, and a little startling, but no longer disfiguring—across her cheek.

It makes Terran medical science look primitive! Magda thought.

But if it was psi force, what was the function of the blue jewel? Was it only a focus? Magda knew she would never rest till she knew the answer to these questions. The key seemed to be the strange word *laran*, which was colloquially translated as an art, skill, gift or talent; she surmised that a *leronis* was one who used *laran*, and that the meanings of "wise-woman" or "sorceress" were ancillary. Jaelle verified this guess, adding that *laran* meant an inborn gift for psi power, and that while she herself had a little of it, she had not wanted to be trained in its use. When Magda repeated Rohana's remark—that she herself seemed to have *laran*—Jaelle shut up and could not be persuaded to say another word.

In midafternoon the promised festival dresses arrived, brought by one of Rohana's women. Magda's was a rust-colored gown with narrow sable fur trim, and trailing sleeves lined with golden silk; it was one of the prettiest dresses she had ever seen, and fitted her well enough. She felt a twinge of regret as she put it on and brushed her dark smooth hair, thinking of the silver butterfly-clasp that she would never wear again.

Jaelle said, "Among Terran women, is close-cropped hair thought a disgrace?"

"Oh, no. Most women in Empire service wear their hair little longer than men; but I have lived on Darkover most of my life, and kept mine long to be able to mingle unnoticed with women here, so I am accustomed to long hair," Magda said. "I had half expected to be told that Amazons were not allowed to wear women's dress! Is this simply a courtesy to dom Gabriel, then, Jaelle?"

Jaelle laughed merrily. She had put on the delicate green gown Rohana had sent her. She said that it had been made for her cousin, Rohana's seventeen-year-old daughter, whose name was Elorie but who was usually called Lori. With a little pinning at the waist, it fitted Jaelle beautifully. As she brushed her own hair into a burnished coppery helmet and fastened it with a pair of gold bar-clasps from her saddlebags, she said, "Oh, no! Do you think we wear trousers compulsively, like men, you silly girl? We wear them when we have to ride, or work like men, but in the Guild-house, or when working indoors, we wear whatever seems comfortable to us. We are not *required* to wear anything in particular; we simply refuse to accept the social rule that *forbids* women to wear any comfortable garment for reasons of modesty or custom. The only thing we *may* not wear—by our Charter—is a sword." Again, she laughed. "Kindra chided me, now and then, that I spent so much of what I earned on finery; I probably have as many pretty gowns as Rohana, or more, because I need not account to anyone for what use I make of my money!"

Magda felt a little relieved; she was not fond of fine clothes, in particular, but she would have felt strange to think of spending the rest of her life in rough and unattractive work clothes!

Jaelle said delightedly, when they were ready to go down, "I had no idea you were so pretty! When I first saw you, you looked like a half-frozen rabbit, and after that I have not been able to notice!"

Magda herself had been aware of Jaelle's astonishing beauty, even in rough Amazon dress; in the green gown, she was breathtaking. She saw her own opinion confirmed when Peter joined them in the hallway, outside their connecting rooms; he looked at Jaelle in delighted amazement. She smiled at him shyly, and lowered her eyes; Magda knew Jaelle was embarrassed at recalling how she had clung to him when she was weak and ill. Jaelle did not offer him her hand as she had done readily during her illness; strangely, the very omission seemed to create a greater closeness than the frank gesture. *She reacted to him as a child reacts then. Now she is very aware that he is a man and she a woman,* Magda thought.

Peter said softly, "I am very happy to see you recovered, Jaelle," and with something of her own constraint, turned to Magda, and offered her his arm. She took it, mostly because she sensed his embarrassment and tension and it was an old habit, to cover his indecision.

"Have you noticed how like our own celebrations this is? The halls decorated with greenery, the great fire, the exchanged gifts—even the smell of the spice-bread!"

She knew he was only saying the first thing that came into his head, to cover embarrassment; it roused an old emotion, a mixture of tenderness and exasperation, so familiar that she felt an old, inner trembling.

"You are lovely, Magda. But I miss your lovely long hair—" He put up his hand to touch the bare nape of her neck: a gesture of intimacy, permitted only to lovers. Magda felt embarrassed. She said in a low voice, "Don't, Piedro." She used his Darkovan name deliberately, to remind him of where they were. Yet she knew it had had exactly the reverse effect; it had recreated the old intimacy.

He said, "Margali," speaking her Darkovan name like a special caress. She saw Jaelle's eyes on them and dropped his hand as if it burned her, so that they went into the Great Hall side by side, but not together.

The kindled midwinter-fire burned on the great hearth, and dom Gabriel, Lord of Ardais, stood before it, a tall, soldierly man, with graying russet hair, dressed in green and scarlet. When Jaelle stepped toward him with a formal bow, he clasped her, briefly, in a kinsman's embrace, pressing his lips to her cheek.

"I rejoice that you are well enough to join us, Jaelle. A pleasant year to you, and all happiness."

"I thank you for your hospitality, for myself and my friends, Uncle," Jaelle said, and stepped along, to be warmly hugged by Rohana and to exchange greetings with her cousins. Magda and Peter stood before the Ardais lord; he bowed over her hand, raising his eyes to hers with a puzzled, kindly smile. Magda thought of what Jaelle had said: "Anything belonging to Rohana he will treat kindly—pet dogs, Free Amazons, even Terrans . . . !" It seemed to her for a moment that Jaelle had been hard on him; from the very touch of his hand she sensed he was a decent man and a kind one, if a little narrowed by the prejudices of his caste, and without much imagination. Anyway, if Rohana loved and obeyed him, he must have more virtues than Jaelle could see in him.

"Welcome, *mestra,* as my kinswoman's friend; a pleasant holiday to you, and a fortunate year."

Magda, recalling the New Year's greeting of her Caer Donn childhood, said, "My year will be brightened by the memory of your hospitality; may the fires of your hearth never grow cold, Lord Ardais," and saw the puzzlement grow in his eyes. As she moved on to exchange formal greetings with Rohana and her grown children, she thought, *He obviously knows we are Terrans. Is he surprised that we can manage ordinary politeness?* She wondered if the Ardais lord really thought that a race which could create a Galactic empire were all ignorant boors without any sense of good manners. . . .

Lady Alida, at one of the long tables, raised her

eyes, looked directly at Magda and beckoned; Magda could think of no polite way to ignore the invitation. The Comyn lady wore a festival gown of pale blue; her red-gold hair was coiled low on her neck. She gestured to Magda to sit next to her, and Magda felt the little prickles of "hunch" touching her again. Alida was a Comyn lady, a *leronis,* and gifted with psi power. A mere trace of this, in Jaelle, had given Magda away. How could she manage not to betray herself?

For a time, everyone's attention was on the small delicacies of the table: a clear soup with golden slices of some delicious mushroom floating in it; small, hot savory tidbits of different kinds; spicebread in all sorts of ornamental shapes, gilded and decorated. But as these were taken away, and the servants—in their holiday garments, and joining in the feast they helped to serve—brought the main courses, Alida turned to Magda and said, "While your sworn sister was ill and needed your care, I would not call you from her side, *mestra.* But now she is well," and she looked at Jaelle, laughing between Peter and her cousin and obviously teasing them about their resemblance. "I wanted a word with you. Have you never been tested for *laran,* Margali?"

"No. Never."

"But surely you were aware of your inborn talent, were you not?"

"No," Magda said again, and a faint frown furrowed the lady's high pale forehead.

"But surely . . . as you know, it wakes normally at adolescence; had you no hint of this gift? Or were you committed so early to the life of a Free Amazon that you did not ask for this testing?"

That would have been a good escape, but the lie was too easily discovered; it was a matter of record that she had only recently been made a Free Amazon. She fell back on the literal truth. "Until the other day, my Lady, I had no idea that I had the faintest trace of *laran.* It came as a great surprise to me."

"Well, when Midwinter Festival is over, we must

have you properly tested," Alida said, as if the matter were settled. How, Magda wondered, would she get out of *this*? With definite relief, she remembered something else. She never would have believed herself capable of putting this forth with positive pleasure. "After midwinter, Lady, my duties commit me to the Guild-house."

Lady Alida brushed that aside. "Something will be arranged. An untrained telepath is a danger to herself and everyone around her, and that would apply to all your sisters of the Guild-house." She said no more, politely calling her guest's attention to the musicians who had come to entertain them, and would play later for the dancing.

But enough had been said to ruin Magda's appetite. What was she going to do now?

When the meal ended, the older guests gathered around the midwinter-fire for gossip and reminiscence (Magda knew these house parties, held when the weather brought all outdoor work to a standstill, were reunions of friends who often did not meet from year to year) while the younger people descended into the lower hall for dancing. Magda had learned to dance as a child—a girl could not reach her eighth year in Caer Donn without learning to dance, and to dance well—and knew most of these dances.

Although she took part with pleasure when Jaelle and Lori drew her into a ring-dance with a dozen other girls, she did not know what the rules of Amazon etiquette were for dancing with men after the group dances gave way to dancing in couples. But after a time, seeing Jaelle laughing and flirting and dancing with all comers, she grew less hesitant. She accepted the invitations, enjoying it on two levels: the Terran agent making mental notes (But would she ever really be that again?), and, to her own surprise, the young girl she had been in Caer Donn, mingling for the first time with young men. It was, literally, the first time since childhood when she had felt herself actually in the company of her own kind.

Magda had never realized until this moment quite how much her curious, between-worlds childhood had robbed her of the ability to mingle with people her own age. Childhood in Caer Donn had prepared her, emotionally and socially, for adolescence and maturity in the same world; instead, before adolescence, she had been torn away and isolated in the Terran Zone with children whose background was only that of the Empire; and at sixteen she had been sent off-world for training. She had felt isolated and completely at a loss with girls or boys her own age in the Empire. Later, when she could mingle with Darkovans in the course of her work, there were many inhibitions against allowing any purely personal contacts; and in any case Darkovan women met men only in their homes and under the proper sponsorship of their families.

But now, as Rohana's guest, she could join in freely. *If I had been exposed to a little of this when I was twenty I would never have married Peter.* The thought troubled her for some reason, and she was glad to turn to a young man of dom Gabriel's household who came up to her, asking for a dance. After a time he said, "Is your name—Margali?"

"Yes, that is what they call me."

"I thought so! You had another name, but none of us could pronounce it, so we called you by that one. You are *Toroku* Lorne's daughter, are you not?" The title was the equivalent of "learned man" or "professor," and had been given her father by the local children. "I knew you when we were children; you used to have dancing lessons with my sisters, Tara and Renata. I am Darrill, son of Darnak."

Now she remembered Darrill, and his sisters. She had once spent midwinter-night with Renata when she was quite small; she had played with them, visited in their home, and brought them to her own home in the HQ. Darrill had been an older boy, out of their orbit.

He said, "I thought all of you Terrans had gone to Thendara and would not return to the Hellers. What are you doing here?"

"I am Lady Rohana's midwinter guest—or rather, the guest of her kinswoman Jaelle."

Darrill demanded, "Do they know who you really are? I am dom Gabriel's sworn man, and if you are here under false pretenses, Lord Ardais should know!"

Magda said, trying to control her inner trembling, "My true name and my purposes are known to Lady Rohana; you may ask her if you wish. And I suppose, since she knows, that dom Gabriel knows as well."

He said with a faint grin, "I suppose so; but if the lady knows, it does not really matter whether dom Gabriel knows or not, since it is well known from here to the Kadarin that the lady rules the estate, with dom Gabriel's assistance when he feels so inclined."

She asked after his sisters; he told her the names of their husbands, and how they fared. She wondered if it was really safe to spend time with anyone who knew who and what she really was. But it might be worse to make a point of avoiding him; that would be suspicious conduct indeed. His fear that she was a spy once overcome, he seemed to accept it as quite normal that she be here.

It ought to be normal! Darkovans and Terrans should have a chance to be together, then they will not have a chance to build barriers of ignorance and distrust! Lorill Hastur is wrong, wrong, wrong!

When he had left her—it seemed, with reluctance— she found herself standing next to Jaelle, who had paused, breathless, after a fast, romping dance.

"I think Camilla was right," she said, laughing. "There are men who find scars irresistible on a woman! I have never been so popular!"

"I had half expected to find that Amazons were not allowed to take any notice of men—after Camilla warned me so sternly not even to look at them!" Magda could laugh about this memory now.

"Oh, this is only when there is work to be done, or the men are such as might consider a glance some sort of—of invitation," and Jaelle. "There have been times when I worked with men and they took no more notice

of me than of another workman. We learn not to cause
trouble—you will learn it, in the Guild-house—so that
an Amazon can travel alone in a band of a dozen men,
and will be accepted as one of them. But I also know
how to behave when I want them to accept me as a
woman—at Midwinter Festival, for instance! Or midsummer, when the dances—in Thendara, for instance—go on all night, and extend into the gardens!
And you know the old proverb: 'What is done under
the four moons need not be remembered when they
have set. . . .' Although for my part I have never had
any taste for waiting forty days after, to see if I would
bear a child in the spring—" She broke off, saying
gently, "I am sorry—it is like talking with Rohana; I
forget sometimes that she has been trained to the po-
litenesses of women's speech. I did not mean to shock
you, sister!"

Magda had not, of course, been shocked at the
words; but she realized that she did not know Jaelle at
all, in this madcap mood. And she herself had been
brought up to observe the fairly straitlaced sexual taboos of the mountain women. This had been confusing
to her during her off-world training and had tended to
throw her, more and more, into the company of Peter;
he respected them, to some degree shared them.

Jaelle said, "In any case, no one cares much what
happens at such festivals; even dom Gabriel will turn a
blind eye to whatever happens in the galleries and dark
corners, or when the fires burn low. . . . Usually the old
people go off to bed early and leave the young people
to do as they please." She leaned close to Magda, and
whispered, her eyes glowing with mischief, "There is a
saying that you never master a language completely till
you have learned to make love in it! I saw Darrill looking at you—I am sure he would be happy to teach
you."

Magda felt her cheeks flaming, and Jaelle gave her a
gentle pat on the shoulder. "I should not tease you, sister. Someday you will know how to take our jests, too.
Here is Piedro, come to dance with you at last!"

Instead he took Magda lightly by the elbow, and said, "I want to talk to you for a minute." He guided her toward the refreshment table, dipped himself up some wine from the great cut-crystal bowl there. He said in an undertone, "What did Darrill say to you?"

"Only that he recognized me," she said, "and asked if dom Gabriel knew who I was."

"He asked me the same," said Peter. "I told him that since Lady Rohana knew who I was, I was quite sure dom Gabriel knew it also." He hesitated, about to fill her glass.

"No, I've had enough. I'm feeling a little dizzy," and she nibbled on a bit of cake instead.

Peter said, almost jealously, "I saw you dancing with Darrill. You certainly seem to be enjoying yourself!"

"I am. Aren't you? I've never had a chance to do this kind of thing before! And I've missed it!"

"It never occurred to me you would want to," Peter said. "I have gone to the Midsummer Festivals in Thendara these last three years; if I had thought of it I could have taken you. But"—he hesitated—"at the public festivals—not the ones in private houses like this, where everything is very decorous—but the public dances, where all comers mingle, the party sometimes gets a little wild. Dancing till dawn, pairing off in the gardens and all that; I didn't think you'd want to come."

Magda suddenly felt a violent resentment; he felt it was suitable to go himself, even if the party got a little *. . . wild.* Yet he had decided, without consulting her, that that kind of entertainment was not suitable for *her!* She said dryly, "You might have let me decide it for myself."

He raised his hand to touch the nape of her neck again; a suggestive touch, arousing memories she had tried to forget. He whispered, "I was jealous, darling."

She felt a sudden, almost completely irrational anger. How dared he make that decision for her? Had he felt free, then, to take a casual sweetheart for himself at these festivals—a privilege he felt himself justified in denying to her, as if he were her father or guardian?

He was still bending close to her, fondling her neck; she could feel his warm breath. He was a little drunk; not much. Like herself, he had been taught to take great care with alcohol or other mind-altering drugs, and he knew and watched his own limits carefully. He was a good agent, she thought, a gifted agent, and felt the old fondness surge through her, so that she did not move away when he put his arm around her and drew her into the shadow of the draperies at one side. He bent his head, murmured to her.

She tensed in his arms and said sharply, "Speak *casta;* have you forgotten where we are?"

He brought his lips down on hers and kissed her. "It's good to be alive!" he said violently. "It's midwinter-night—and I *knew* I was going to die. I *knew* there was no hope of rescue. Oh, Magda, Magda, Magda . . ." His voice faded out. He kissed her, hard enough to hurt. "And I'm alive, and you're here, and we're together again."

At first she did not protest, thinking it was a mere surge of gratitude, awareness of life instead of death; but his embrace grew quickly more demanding, more personal.

"Do you have any idea how much I want you, *need* you, how damnably I've missed you?"

Gently she tried to put a little space between herself and his demanding caresses, but he whispered against her throat, "You feel it, too, I know you do! You want me as much as I want you, or you'd never have come so far for me."

Against her will she felt herself responding; but a cold rational voice was saying in the back of her mind: *Now that you are free of him, do you truly want to start the whole miserable thing over again?* The excitement of the festival, a few drinks, the general atmosphere of license and the straitlaced rules relaxed for once, the fact that he'd been alone a long time and wanted a woman—that's what it was and that's all it was. She wouldn't be fooled into thinking it was more than that. Gently, but inexorably, she removed his hands from her.

"I'm sorry, Peter."

"Mag, Mag, I need you so. Don't you know we belong together?"

"I'm sorry, truly I am," she said with a sigh. "Until a little while ago, I thought so, too. But now I just don't feel guilty about you anymore. Now I'm just sorry I can't give you what you want."

"Is there someone else? That Darrill—"

"No, no. Nothing like that. Don't be foolish, Peter. I haven't seen him since I was nine years old!"

There had never been anyone else. Until now she would have sworn there never could be.

"Mag, you know there can never be anyone else, not for either of us, not on this world."

That, she thought, was partly true; they had shared the Darkovan childhood, the isolation from their peers, which had kept them from finding satisfactory mates elsewhere; drawn together by the knowledge that they were the only ones available for one another. Now she resented this; and resented, even more, how much he took it for granted.

"No, Peter. Whatever you're asking—no."

"I want you," he said, as if in pain. "I want you for always. I want to marry you again. And I want you now. Magda, Magda, come with me now! Our rooms are together, it's as if it had been intended—"

She said quietly, "You know I am not free to marry. Now."

"Oh, that! This Amazon game you are playing—"

"It's not a game." The very softness with which she spoke accentuated the finality of the words.

His voice was bitter. "Have you cut off your womanhood with your hair?"

"No," she said. "I don't think so. But I don't think womanhood means I have to go to bed with you just because you're lonely"—she had begun to use a ruder word—"and want a woman."

He touched her softly, intensely, and she hated her own arousal. He said, in triumph, "You want me, too. You know you do!"

"If I do," she said, suddenly angry, "that is *my* affair and not yours, unless *I* choose to make it so! Oh, God, Peter, why can't you understand? Do you want me just to be *kind* to you?"

He said, trying to hold her, "I'd settle for that," but she wrenched herself free.

"But I won't, and that's final! Peter, let me go. Jaelle is watching us!"

She moved away; only a few inches, but with such finality she might as well have been on one of the moons. Seeing the angry flush of offended pride lying along his cheekbones, she felt almost regretful; but nothing kinder would ever have made him believe her. He swallowed hard, and turned away; she watched him go toward Jaelle, saw the girl hold out her hand, with none of the shyness now she had shown earlier this evening. Peter took the slender fingers in his own, and although Magda could not hear what they said, she saw them move away together.

She watched them circle the dance floor, with a certain sadness. She was really free of Peter now. And suddenly, with her new dimension of awareness, she knew what she had done.

She had seen it, as they left Sain Scarp. Perhaps it was only chemistry, perhaps it was something more; but it had been immediate and unmistakable. Jaelle's weakness and collapse had misdirected Peter's response into protective kindness, self-effacing chivalry.

But it had been there, all the time, behind the kindness and the gentle, impersonal protectiveness. She had seen it again, when Jaelle had clung to Peter in her delirium. And now, feeling almost humiliated, she knew why Peter had come to her tonight; and it was not because he found her irresistible.

Peter was, first of all, a Terran agent; and he knew

the rules. And one of them, a major one, was this: never, never—*never*—get seriously and deeply involved with any native woman on any planet where you're assigned. Casual liaisons were condoned, if not approved (every spaceport in the Empire had a red-light district), but anything more serious was forbidden.

And whatever it was between Peter and Jaelle, it was very real, and it was serious. Peter had been trying, a desperate last-ditch attempt, to protect himself against this involvement which could be so disastrous to the rules under which he lived. Magda was safe, Magda was one of his own. And yet . . . not quite.

He's like me; his sexuality somehow got to be Darkovan, just as mine did. He doesn't react to other women. But I'm near enough so that somehow he can be content with me. As I was with him. For a while.

If Magda had come with him, tonight, he could have resisted his own powerful, and dangerous, desire for Jaelle. But Magda had driven him away, with a blow to his masculine pride; and Peter had gone straight to Jaelle to heal that wound.

Now, with sudden dread, Magda found herself worrying about them both. Peter could risk his career for Jaelle. And Jaelle—what would she risk? She was no girl of the spaceport bars, but a woman of the Comyn, and, if Magda was any judge, deeply in love.

Irritably, Magda tried to dismiss the whole matter from her mind. It was definitely not her affair. Jaelle was no child; she was only a year or two younger than Magda herself, and, judging by the way she had been talking earlier, quite sophisticated enough to take care of herself. As for endangering Peter's career, Jaelle was not free to marry.

But even while she stood and watched a group of men dancing with torches, an ancient sword-dance, she wondered where in the lowering shadows Peter and Jaelle had gone. . . .

Somehow, the savor had gone from the evening. At midnight or thereabouts, dom Gabriel, Rohana and

Lady Alida, with most of the older people, said good night and withdrew, hospitably bidding their younger guests to remain and enjoy themselves as late as they chose.

Darrill sought Magda out again, and urged her to accompany him into one of the long galleries where, he said, there were some very fine ancient murals. From the way he touched her, and spoke, Magda was perfectly sure that he had no more interest in the murals than she did herself. She made some tactful excuse, and when he had gone away, she wondered why she had not taken up the challenge. Peter and Jaelle had long since disappeared and not returned; she wondered what gallery *they* were exploring. From what Jaelle had said, Magda knew it was not regarded as particularly reprehensible to share a good deal of casual kissing—or more, if she wished—on midwinter-night.

Sooner or later, now that I'm free of Peter, I must find out how I react to other men. . . .

Then, angry with herself, she thought, *Damn it, before I complicate my life with another man, I want to know more about myself! I want to know what I am to myself, not always have to see myself through a man's eyes!*

A strange man came and asked her to dance again; she pleaded extreme fatigue, left the Great Hall and went up to the room she shared with Jaelle. Jaelle had not returned. Magda took off her beautiful gown, readied herself for bed and lay down. She expected to lie awake, worrying about Peter and Jaelle; instead she fell at once into a heavy sleep.

Hours later, she woke to see Jaelle standing in the doorway, barefoot, her face flushed, her short hair tousled. Her eyes were very bright. She came across the room and sat on Magda's bed.

Magda said lightly, "I didn't expect you back until later."

Magda could smell the girl's sweet heavy breath, and knew she had been drinking; was not sober now.

Jaelle said, "Oh, don't be angry with me, sister. I didn't want this to happen, I know how you feel."

"Angry?" Magda sat up and put her arms around Jaelle. "Darling"—the word she used was *breda*—"what right have I to be angry? Do you think—" Abruptly, it dawned on her just what Jaelle *did* think. "Do you think I'm *jealous?*"

Jaelle said with a nervous giggle, "This kind of thing is easier at midsummer when there are gardens. We have spent most of the night in the long galleries." Her teeth were chattering, whether with cold or nervous excitement Magda could not tell. "I—I should have gone with him as he asked me." She looked at the connecting door into Peter's room. "But—but I wanted to be sure, I don't like deciding things in a hurry and," she added after a moment, looking at Magda in appeal, "I did not want to—to tread on the hem of your garment."

Incongruously Magda realized that she was still making mental notes about the curious idiom. She hugged the trembling girl tight, and said, "Jaelle, anything between Peter Haldane and me was a long, long time ago." As she said it, she knew that it was really true. "Do you love him, *breda?*"

"I don't know," Jaelle said. "I'm not sure. I've never felt like this before."

Magda found herself wondering if Jaelle were a virgin. From her flippant jokes, and sophisticated comments, she had not thought so; but could an experienced woman be so uncertain? As if Jaelle had picked up the thought directly from her mind—and by now Magda was almost ready to believe that—Jaelle said in a low voice, looking down, "It's foolish, isn't it? I've come near to it many times. Before I took the oath, when Kindra saw that I liked to—to laugh with men and to flirt with them, she told me that before I bound myself, I should take a lover, test myself that way; she said that it might someday seem hard to me that I was bound by law never to marry. But somehow there was never anyone I could—could trust that much."

She added defensively, "So it never came to more

than laughter or foolishness. Nor did I ever leave any man wounded by my teasing, or heart-scalded. But now"—she looked and sounded forlorn—"I have no more laughter. I think I am more afraid now, when I—when I love him, when I want him, than when I was a girl and the very thought of giving myself to any man seemed frightening, an open door to bondage and slavery. . . . I don't know myself anymore!" Her voice was shaking and she was very close to tears. "I don't know what I want! Oh, Margali, Margali—sister, what shall I do?"

Magda felt wrung, helpless. *What can I say to her?* She could understand that to Jaelle, brought up as she had been among women close-bound to one another by oath, it seemed completely natural to turn to another woman for comfort or counsel. *I am bound to treat every woman as my mother, sister, daughter . . . but I've always lived by such different laws . . . God help me, I don't know what to say to her!* If one of her own friends in the Terran Zone—Bethany, for instance— had come to her with such a question, Magda could have turned it off with a casual or even a crude joke. But she could not do that to Jaelle.

What would Rohana have said to her? Finally, in a voice shaking as much as Jaelle's, she said, "Darling, I can't advise you. I don't know if anyone could. You must do what you feel is right." Then, to her own surprise, she found herself whispering the words of the oath of the Free Amazons: "I swear I will give myself to no man save in my own time and season and of my own free will. . . ."

There was a moment of silence, then Jaelle whispered as if to herself, "In my own time and season," and smiled, tightening her arms around Magda; and Magda knew that somehow, by instinct, she had hit on precisely the right thing to say. She felt Jaelle's lips against her cheek for a moment; then, without a word, Jaelle pressed her hand, and went, on noiseless feet, to the connecting door, which closed a moment later behind her. She did not return.

Chapter
FOURTEEN

Day after day the snow fell, pouring from gray skies as if it had forgotten how to stop. Then, ten days after midwinter, Magda was awakened by Jaelle, sitting on her bed.

"Wake up, sister, the sun is shining!"

Magda ran to the window. The sky was filled with thick, low, puffy clouds through which erratic sunshine spilled; in the courtyard below, pathways were being cleared by bundled men with long shovels; and horses, their breath streaming in the cold, were being brought around for departing guests.

Magda dressed hastily in her traveling garments, not at all sorry to resume them. Every day their stay was prolonged meant another chance of revealing who they were.

Jaelle began slowly to dress. Since midwinter, she had spent her nights at Peter's side, although she had been careful not to be found there in the morning by dom Gabriel's servants. When Magda teased her gently about what seemed like hypocrisy, she had said, "I do not care a *sekal's* worth what dom Gabriel thinks of me; he is not my guardian and I owe no man any account of my acts. I care still less what his servants think of me. The servants know, of course; they always know such things. But if no one of them sees me there, then there will be no one whose business it is to inform dom Gabriel. And although he probably knows, too— he is not a fool, and he has seen us looking at one another—if his servants told him in so many words, he would feel compelled to ask Rohana to reprimand me for putting the women of the Comyn to shame by sharing a commoner's bed. And for his peace of mind Rohana would feel she had to come and scold me, even though she and I agreed together when I was sixteen that she was not my guardian and no longer the keeper of my conscience. And she would try not to offend me because she knows that I am a grown woman and by law the mistress of my own acts, and I would try not to be rude to her because I love her. And when we had all forced ourselves to say all these things, I would still go on sleeping with Peter whenever I chose; so it seems to me wiser not to start all that in motion."

That reasoning seemed complicated to Magda, but she had to admit that it probably saved trouble for all of them. It was even possible that dom Gabriel, if it were brought directly to his notice, might feel compelled to call Peter personally to account. By the Amazon oath, Jaelle had declared her independence of his guardianship, but Magda had heard from Jaelle that some men still refused to recognize the Amazon Charter.

Peter joined them in the hallway; he took Jaelle's hand in his as they went down the corridor, and Magda, watching, thought that the trip back to Thendara, with just the three of them, was likely to be awkward in more ways than one. She did not grudge Jaelle a single moment of her happiness—and that they were happy, no one who saw them together could possibly doubt—but it *was* going to be awkward, and she, Magda, would bear most of the awkwardness!

The immediate family of Ardais, with a bare handful of the house-party guests, and estate officials, usually had their meals in a small breakfast room away from the Great Hall. As they came in they heard a burst of laughter. Dom Kyril was telling a funny story, which was one of the commonest midwinter pastimes, at this season when all outdoor work came to a dead stop.

"... And everybody had to carry around a little torch to thaw out what he said before he could be heard; and this man made quite a bit of money by gathering up all the frozen speeches in a barrow, and carting them around to their owners. Only he wasn't quite as careful as he should have been, to make sure that they were delivered to the right owners, and when the spring-thaw came, and all the words thawed out again, there was a tremendous amount of trouble. The mule-driver thawed out what he had yelled at his team, and found he had the words of an old lady talking to her pet birds; and the young mother scolding her little children got the mule-driver's, and the children cried half the day; and the young wife telling her husband she was to bear his first son, got what the Free Amazon said to the man who—" He broke off and turned a full red as Jaelle giggled. "My apologies, cousin!"

Jaelle said dryly, "Kinsman, I heard all the jokes there are about Free Amazons, before I had turned fifteen; and most of them I heard in the Guild-house from my sisters. I would share them with you, but most of them would shock your delicate male sensibilities." It was the turn of the others to laugh. "Finish your story, kinsman; this is one I have not heard."

Kyril tried to take up where he had left off. "The aristocratic lady entertaining her guests was delivered the chatter of the men from the lowest tavern in the village, while the Keeper instructing her youngest novice found herself hearing what the Dry-Towner bellowed at his minion. . . ."

"Enough," dom Gabriel said, with a glance at Lady Alida. "It seems to me this is a tale for the barracks, son, not for your mother's breakfast table." He glanced up to greet the newcomers, his eyebrows raising in question as he saw the women in Amazon clothing.

Jaelle said, "Uncle, with your leave, we will ride for Thendara today; it is a long journey at this season, and my sister has duties in the Guild-house."

"Impossible," Lord Gabriel said. "This is only the snow-break, my girl; tomorrow at this hour it will be snowing harder than ever. This storm will last another ten days at the least; only the guests who live within a few hours' ride are departing today. You would be well advised to remain until the spring-thaw, at least."

"You are more than kind, Lord Ardais," said Peter, "but we could not so long trespass on hospitality."

"You couldn't possibly travel more than a day's ride before the snow blocked you again," dom Gabriel said. "It seems to me nonsense, to spend the rest of the blizzard in a tent or travel-shelter when you could stay here in comfort."

Magda and Peter knew he was right. And indeed, the weather in the Hellers at this season was proverbial; from midwinter to spring-thaw, only the mad or the desperate ventured more than an hour's ride from their own firesides.

Toward afternoon the day darkened again, and the next morning the windows were a flurry of white snow, with the wind howling around the towers of Ardais like a banshee hard on the heels of its prey. And at breakfast dom Gabriel said triumphantly, "You see? You had better stay till spring-thaw, all of you!"

Afterward, Lady Alida drew Magda aside and said, "We should arrange for your testing, *mestra*, today; it should not be much longer delayed."

Magda was seized by such panic that she felt it must be perceptible to the *leronis*. As soon as she could get away she went in search of Lady Rohana, and found her in her private sitting room, working on the accounts of the estate. At first this might have surprised Magda; now she knew that every thread in the running of Ardais was spun through Lady Rohana's slender six-fingered hands.

"Forgive me for disturbing you, my Lady; may I speak to you alone for a moment?"

Rohana motioned her inside and dismissed the lady companion without whom, it seemed, she could not move half a dozen steps. "Certainly; this can wait till spring-thaw, if need be. What troubles you, child?"

Magda felt an overwhelming sense of presumption; she had come to a Comyn lady to complain about one of the lady's own caste! She said hesitantly, "The Lady Alida is determined to have me tested for *laran,* and I am afraid that if she explores my mind that way it may cause trouble for all of us."

Rohana looked grave. *This is my fault; I should have sent the Terrans away.* She said, "We were both surprised to find you in the rapport when we were working in the matrix. Have you been trained in these powers among your own people?"

Magda shook her head. "Among us, there are not too many who even believe that such powers exist, Lady. Those who believe in them, or claim to be able to use them, are thought ignorant, superstitious, credulous."

"I had heard that." Rohana knew that had been one of Lorill Hastur's reasons for the ban on too much mingling with the Terrans. *They do not believe in these powers; once convinced, they would be greedy to know all about them, and exploit them.*

Rohana said, "Belief or not, you seem to have this kind of *laran,* child. How came you by it?"

"I do not know, Lady. All my life I have been able to use hunches, but I believed it was simply that I had a talent for adding up things which were subliminal— just a little below the conscious levels of perception. And there have been times when my dreams were not—not nonsense, but told me things I did not consciously know; so I have learned to take heed of them."

Rohana leaned her chin thoughtfully on her hands. This meant they must reevaluate most of what they had learned about the Terrans. "Lorill is committed to a belief that Terrans and Darkovans are different races of beings, and that the Terrans are inferior; and he uses their lack of *laran* as proof."

Magda said, "My Lady, I am not supposed to tell this outside the Terran Zone, either; but the Lord Hastur is mistaken. This is not a belief, but a fact that can be proved; Terran and Darkovan are one race. It is known to us beyond question that Darkover was settled by Terrans long ago, by one of what we call the Lost Ships. In an age before the faster-than-light ships that we have now, there were ships that were sent out from Terra—it was not an Empire then—and some of them were lost and never heard of again. There is evidence from your languages that it was settled by a ship whose very name I could give you, and the names of those aboard. It is most likely that this knowledge was lost to you centuries ago, Lady—probably to keep the survivors from pining too much for their lost homeland—but your people are truly Terrans."

"Then psi gifts—you have them, too?"

"It is rumored that once they were more common than now; now they are very rare, and there was a time in our history when people used to pretend them, or feign them with clever devices and machinery, so they fell into disrepute and their use was considered charlatanry. But there seems evidence that once they were known."

Rohana nodded. "There was a time in the history of the Comyn," she said, "when we did selective breeding to fix these gifts in our racial heritage; it was a time of great tyranny, and not a time we are very proud to remember. It led to its own downfall, and we of the Comyn are still suffering the aftermath; not only in the distrust the common people have for us, but in that our fertility was lowered by inbreeding; and the gifts are linked to some dangerous recessive traits. But they are powerful, and when misused can be very dangerous. Which brings me to you, child. Normally, psi gifts waken in adolescence; when they waken later there are sometimes dangerous upsets and upheavals. Have you felt any strange sensations, any unexplained sickness without physical cause, any sense of being outside of your body and unable to get back, any wild emotional upheavals?"

"No, nothing like that," Magda said. Then she remembered the moment of altered perspective during the healing, but that had passed off quickly and of itself.

Rohana asked her a number of searching questions about her dreams and "hunches," and finally said, when Magda felt wrung out by the questioning, "It seems to me that your talents are slight, and that you have compensated for them very well. You could, if you wished, probably learn the use of *laran* with ease, and it would be interesting to see what use a Terran could make of this training. I would like to have the teaching of you; but it seems it would make more trouble than it is worth. You are committed elsewhere; and I have already gone against Lorill's will as much as seems wise. Yet," she added, almost wistfully, "if you demand this training, I could not refuse it to anyone with *laran;* and by law, birth and parentage cannot be used to refuse it to you."

Magda said firmly, "I think I have quite enough trouble without that!"

Rohana touched her wrist very lightly, that feather-touch Magda was beginning to guess was peculiar to telepaths among their own. "So be it, dear child. But if you ever have trouble with *laran,* you must promise to come to me."

She sat looking intently at Magda for a moment. "If Lorill is wrong—if it can be proved that what he believes about your people is wrong—I do not need to tell you what it will mean for both your world and mine."

To Magda, with her heightened sensitivity, the force of what she had always called "hunch" raising her perceptions, it seemed at this moment that she caught the very image in Rohana's mind: a great barricaded door, slowly swinging open between two locked-away worlds, two peoples; opening to give a bright and sunlit view.

Magda thought, *We should be one people, not two ...
I would do anything for that. ...*

Rohana said, slowly, more as if she were thinking
aloud than speaking, and yet Magda knew she was
meant to share the woman's thoughts, "Does it not
seem to you, Margali, that there is a design of some
sort in this? That of all the Terrans on our world, it
should be your friend, who could be so easily mistaken
for my son, who should be taken by Rumal di Scarp? I
myself, in a quick look, can still be deceived, and must
look at their fingers and hands to be certain, until one
of them speaks. Does it not seem fantastic to you that
of all the Amazons of Darkover, you should fall into
Jaelle's hands, and that the two of you should be so
tested that you have become sworn friends as well?"

Magda felt uneasy. She said, "Coincidence, Lady."

"One coincidence, perhaps. Two, maybe. But so
many, like beads strung on a necklace? No, this is
more than coincidence, my friend; or if it is coincidence, then coincidence itself is only another word
for a design intended by whatever force it is that
shapes the fates of man." She smiled, and seemed to
come back to the practical world, saying, "Now I
must ask something of you, child. Will you take
care in what you say to your friends, and to your superiors in the Terran Zone, at least until I have had a
chance to speak with Lorill?"

"Indeed I will," Magda said, smiling a little at the
thought of Montray's face if she should ever try to tell
him about the matrix operation that had healed Jaelle's
wound within a few minutes, or that Lady Rohana had
said that she herself had *laran*. If this was ever to be
brought up between Darkovan and Terran, she was
quite willing it should be someone other than herself
who should do it—and she hoped there would be a more
receptive audience than Russell Montray!

Rohana rose, and said, "Go now, Margali. I must
think this over and decide what to do."

Magda hesitated just a moment. "But what shall I
tell Lady Alida?"

"Don't worry about her. I will tell her that I have tested you myself," Rohana said, and her smile was droll. "Don't you realize that is what I have been doing?"

The blizzard lasted for another ten days—almost exactly as dom Gabriel had predicted—and when the weather finally cleared, the roads and passes lay blocked with drifts so deep that the three guests at Ardais were readily persuaded to remain for a few more days. Yet Magda had begun to brace herself, mentally, for their departure, and for whatever lay ahead. She could not return to her old life inside the Terran Zone, venturing outside it only in disguise; she knew the disguise had become her truest self. But what she could do instead—that she did not know either.

She found herself thinking again and again of what Rohana had said about a design in the chain of coincidences that had brought them together; even in the peculiar pattern that had drawn Peter and Jaelle together as lovers. If the Empire was to remain on Darkover indefinitely, sooner or later there would be—as on all planets inhabited by different groups of humans—entanglements, romances, liaisons, and eventually marriages, even children who belonged to both worlds. And someone had to be the first.

Of course, one day Darkover would be an Empire planet. It was inevitable. The Empire did not conquer; but once the contacted planet saw the pattern of the Galactic Empire, and what it could mean to be part of it, the rulers always asked to be affiliated. When that time came, Terran and Darkovan would all be Empire citizens, and such affairs and romances would concern no one but the two people involved, and perhaps their families. But now it could cause only complications.

Magda hoped their departure would not be too long delayed. Jaelle and Peter were beginning to be a little less careful, and Magda wondered what the end would be. Again and again, seeing them together, she felt the small, indefinable pricklings of "hunch"—or precognition. *Sooner or later, this meant danger. . . .* Yet how could she speak to Jaelle, warn her, without the younger girl thinking that she was jealous, or grudged her the happiness she had found with her lover? Still less was it possible to remonstrate with Peter. So she only watched them with growing disquiet and anxiety.

In anticipation of their imminent departure she began to sort and put together her possessions; Jaelle found her occupied by this, and suggested that most of their traveling clothes were in need of repair, and that they might profitably spend the day in putting them in order. Magda was surprised to find that Jaelle was an expert needlewoman; somehow this had seemed too feminine an art for an Amazon. Magda herself, accustomed to the readily replaceable, cheap synthetics of the Terran Zone, had never mastered the art; had, in fact, been taught to scorn it as being a pointless way of passing time for women who had no useful work to do.

When she said this to Jaelle, the younger woman laughed. "And so it is, much of the time! Last night in the hall, when Rohana invited us to join her women at the tapestry they were making for the hall chair cushions, I thought I should go mad! I love to embroider," she added, "but how Rohana can endure it, I cannot imagine! I myself should go mad, to sit there night after night, surrounded by those fools of sewing-women . . . stitch, stitch, stitch, gossip, gossip, gossip! Rohana runs the whole estate of Ardais, and does it better than dom Gabriel could do, and she sits in Council and gives advice to Hastur, yet there she sits among those foolish girls, and chatters with them as if she had never had a thought in her head more serious than whether to embroider the next cushion with a rainfish or a starflower! As if it mattered to anyone's backside what was embroidered on a cushion, as long as it was well stuffed!" But even as she spoke, she was setting small neat stitches in the torn fingers of her glove.

Magda, watching her, thought that it made good sense to learn an art of this kind, on a world like Darkover, where warm and durable clothing was a necessity of life. She said ruefully, looking at the mess she had made of the torn tunic, "I am even less skillful with a needle than a sword!"

Jaelle laughed. "My skill with a dagger is incidental," she said. "I told you I was no fighter, but for my first year or two among the Amazons I used to work at Kindra's side. She was my foster-mother and had been a mercenary soldier. And when there was peace in the Domains, she hired herself out as a bodyguard to escort travelers through the Kilghard Hills and the Hellers, and protect them against bandits, catmen and what-have-you. For a few years I worked with her; but I did not really like it, and gradually I discovered my real skill."

"What is that, Jaelle?" Magda remembered Rohana saying that the Amazons worked at any honest trade; but she was curious to know which of them Jaelle had made her own.

"I am a travel-organizer," Jaelle said. "People who intend to travel in the hills come and consult me. I can tell them precisely how many pack animals they will need for supplies for any number of men, for the length of their trip, and where to hire or buy them, and where to hire drivers for them, and precisely how much equipment they must buy—or I can buy it for them, on commission. Then I can advise them about how much of the different kinds of food they must buy to keep the men healthy, and provide them with guides and bodyguards, tell them what roads to take, how long the journey will last at the specific season of the year, what passes might be closed or what rivers in flood, and anything else they might wish to know. It is not a business to make anyone rich, but I make a good living at it. Some people only wish for an hour or two of advice, and I give it to them for a fee; others put all the preparations for the trip in my hands, and I do everything from buying pack saddles to choosing meals and equipment they can use at midwinter in the high passes."

"Tell me," Magda said hesitantly. "From what I

have seen of Thendara—are there many men willing to turn such responsibility over to a woman?"

"More than you might think," Jaelle said. "Rafaella, who started this business, told me that in the first year or two, her business was almost limited to providing escort service for ladies whose kinsmen had no leisure to escort them and would not trust them to strange men. Amazon bodyguards for women were much in demand because they knew the ladies would arrive unraped! But as it became known that the caravans we organized could take quicker routes, and arrive without running out of fodder, or having to live on porridge-powder for the last four or five days, the ladies themselves began to insist that we be allowed to make plans for their husbands' business journeyings, and so it has grown to a point where we have as much business as we can do."

"It still seems a strange business for a woman—here," Magda said. "I have grown used to thinking that a woman's life on Darkover was always so limited. Oh, *damn* this thing!" She broke off, sucking the finger she had pricked with an incautious stitch.

Jaelle laughed, saying, "Don't bother; give it to one of Rohana's sewing-women. They will be glad to have something to do, and it will give them pleasure to think there is something, *anything* they can do better than a Free Amazon."

Jaelle, Magda thought, was a puzzle; she was devoted to her sisters in the Guild of Free Amazons—and yet she could be so contemptuous of other women! She said, "Do you really think all women would be happier as Amazons, Jaelle?"

Jaelle put her mended glove back with its mate and began to sort out some small things at the bottom of her saddlebag. She said, not looking up, "No, I don't. I used to think so, when I was younger. And I do truly look forward to a day on our world when all women will have the freedoms that we—the Guild—have seized and declared for ourselves; when they will have them by law, and not by revolt and renunciation. But I know now that there are many women who could not be happy living my kind of life." She sat in the windowseat, her legs folded up under her chin, her short hair tousled; she looked like an adolescent girl. She had a bit of ribbon in her hand and was absentmindedly twisting it about her wrists as she spoke. "Rohana's women. They think of nothing but marriage; they are shocked and troubled at the idea of any other life than they live. It seems dreadful to them, to think of hiring themselves out, as men do, at any work for which they have the strength and skills, instead of serving for a time as waiting-women in one of the Great Houses, and then going home, as Lanilla is doing at winter's end, to a marriage arranged by their families. I asked her what her husband was like and she said she did not know, and asked me, 'Does it matter?' It was enough for her that she would have a home of her own, and a husband. Did you ever want to marry, Margali?"

Magda reminded her softly, "I *was* married."

"But only for a time—"

"I did not know when I married that it was only for a time," Magda said, with a twinge of the old pain. They had made so many plans for permanence!

"Tell me: if you had had a child, would you have stayed with him? Do you think it can be a bond between you?"

"My mother found it so," Magda said slowly. "She followed my father to four different worlds; then we came here, and I was born, and she always seemed content."

"Content only to make a home for him? Is that your way, in the Empire?"

"She was a musician," Magda said. "She played on several instruments, and she wrote many songs. She translated many of the mountain songs into the Empire's standard language; and she wrote music for some poems written in *casta*. But my father was always the center of her life; after he died, she seemed to lose all

joy in living, and seldom touched her music again; and
she did not live very long."

"Rohana married dom Gabriel when she had seen
him only twice," Jaelle said reflectively. "To me that
seemed frightful, to be given to a man I barely knew,
to lie with him, to bear his children. It seemed no better than slavery or rape made lawful! But when I said
as much to Rohana, she laughed at me, and said that
any man and woman, with health and goodwill, can
live together in kindness and make a good life for one
another. She said she thought herself lucky that he was
decent and kindly and eager to please her; not a
drunkard or a gambler or a lover of men, as so many
of the Ardais are. To me, that seemed like a man, who
has received a cudgeling, rejoicing that he had not been
horsewhipped as well. . . ." She was still absently twisting the ribbon around her wrists, looping and uncoil-
ing it. "And now he is truly the center of her life.
I cannot understand it, though I find I like him better
as I grow older. But there are times, too, when it seems
to me that Rohana has as much freedom as any of us,
that she does as she wishes and has given up little. . . ."

She drew the loop of ribbon into a tight coil around
her wrists, began to coil the loose end around her other
arm. She said, "Margali, did you want a child at all?
Why did you not have one? You are not barren, are
you, *breda?*"

"I did not want a child at once," Magda said. "We
were traveling together; I did not want anything to separate us." It had been a bitter quarrel; she looked away
from Jaelle, unwilling even now to relive that painful
moment.

Jaelle reached out to touch her hand lightly, saying, "I did not mean to pry."

Magda shook her head. "Afterward, when we agreed
to part, I was glad I had no child, to remind me always. . . ." *But would we have separated, then?* The
touch of Jaelle's hand suddenly heightened the
awareness, the contact, and she found herself thinking,
Is she pregnant? Does she think she is, does she want

to be? But all she sensed from the touch of Jaelle's fingertips was . . . loneliness, fear. *I thought Jaelle was so happy.*

Magda knew that from this touch she could use her awakened ESP—what Rohana had called *laran*—to find out if Jaelle were pregnant. The thought suddenly frightened her. She did not want to pry that way, to use this new skill to intrude. She let go of Jaelle's hand as if the narrow fingers had burned her, and found her hand caught in the ribbon Jaelle had been winding and unwinding about her wrists. Caught off guard, she demanded, "What in the world are you *doing* with that thing?"

Jaelle stared down at it, in sudden shock. She wrenched it loose, and flung the ribbon across the room, with a look of horror and loathing. As if, Magda thought, she had found a poisonous snake coiling about her wrists!

"Jaelle! What's wrong, sister?" The affectionate term came readily to her tongue now; but Jaelle's moment of vulnerability had vanished again behind a barricade of flippancy.

She said, "Old habits! A puppy you don't housebreak almost before his eyes are open will still be wetting the floor when he's an old dog. I've had this habit since I was a little girl; Kindra told me that it was just a nervous habit, and that I'd outgrow it. But I haven't, see?"

Magda knew there was more to it than that, but she knew she could not ask questions; knew it with that indefinable inner knowledge she was beginning to trust. Instead she asked something she knew to be safer.

"Jaelle, are you pregnant?"

Jaelle's green eyes met hers, just a flash, and then looked away. She said, and sounded almost desolate, "I don't know. It's too soon to tell." Quickly she jumped off the windowseat, barricading herself again. "Come on, let's find one of those silly women of Rohana's and ask her if she can mend your outfit, and make her happy by thinking she is superior to a Free Amazon!"

Watching the girl as she bundled Magda's torn traveling clothes together, Magda thought, *She's so young and vulnerable! If Peter breaks her heart, I think I'll want to kill him!*

What was going to happen to Jaelle? For that matter—if this involvement was serious and lasting, as Magda was beginning to guess—what would happen to Peter? Could he really sacrifice his career for a woman? And for one who was not, by oath, even free to marry?

It was easy to talk about the inevitability of liaisons, love affairs, even marriages between members of separate peoples on Empire worlds. Magda had thought of them as inevitable statistics, before this. But it was different—completely different—when you knew the people involved, and guessed what they meant in purely human and personal terms. No statistics could give you even a clue to that.

Is this my fault, too? By refusing Peter, did I bring this on both of them?

Chapter

FIFTEEN

The winter drew on; the snow lay deep over Ardais. To Jaelle this was a precious interlude, a time separated from anything else in her life, before or after. For the first time since her thirteenth year, she lived surrounded by ordinary women; she wore women's clothes, shared in the life of the household, and spent her days with women who did not live by the terms of renunciation and freedom of the Amazon oath.

She had tasted this life—but briefly, and unwillingly—when she was fifteen. Rohana had insisted that she must know the life she was to renounce, before she made that renunciation irrevocable.

But I was too young, I could not see it clearly.

And now it is too late. All the smiths in Zandru's forges can't mend a broken egg, or put a hatched chick back into the shell. I can never, never be one of them, not now.

I do not think I want to be. But I am not sure, not now. . . .

And there was the Terran, her lover. . . .

Like any young woman in the grip of her first serious love affair, it seemed to her that he filled her whole sky. The Guild-house and the life there seemed very far away. She knew this was only an interlude, that it must end, but she tried to live entirely in the present, neither remembering the past nor thinking ahead to the future, but simply savoring each moment as it passed.

But there were times when she woke in the night, held close in her lover's arms, and realized that she no longer knew what she was doing, or who she was, or what lay ahead for either of them. None of the thousand uncertainties could be answered in words, or even asked; so she would turn to him in desperation, holding herself close to him, demanding the one thing she could be sure about, the one certainty they shared. She had ceased to be cautious. She no longer cared to conceal what was between them. She knew that sooner or later this would precipitate a crisis, but in some indefinable way she felt that even this would be a relief from the terrible uncertainty.

And then, one night, when she woke, she heard around the towers the soft dripping of rain and running of melting snow, and knew that the spring-thaw had begun. Now reality would close again over their enchanted isolation; and whether anything would remain, she could not even guess. She dared not even weep, for fear of waking him. She knew he would have only one comfort to offer, and now even that was no comfort at all, before the knowledge of the inevitable.

When I took the Amazon oath, I believed I had made it impossible for any man to enslave me. Yet here I lie, bound in chains of my own making! What can I do? Oh, merciful Goddess, what shall I do?

By the time the sun rose, red and dripping behind the fog-bank, she had fought her way to calm, and was able to discuss their impending departure serenely. "I must cut my hair; it has grown too long here."

Peter came and passed his hand through the silky strands, long enough now to touch her shoulder blades. "Must you? It is so lovely."

"Nothing in the oath binds me to it," she admitted. "It is custom, no more; to show, when we work with men, that we do not seek to entice them with feminine wiles."

He put his arms around her, and held her close. "Must we part, then, my precious? I know you are pledged not to marry, but—is there no way, no way at all that you can remain with me? I cannot bear to let you go. Do you truly want to leave me so soon?"

She said, through the pounding of her heart, "I can remain with you for a time as freemate, if you wish."

"Jaelle, beloved, do you have to ask if I wish it?" He held her so tightly that he hurt her, but she almost welcomed the pain.

She thought sadly, *Have I come to this?*

"Don't cut your hair," he begged, caressing the locks at the nape of her neck, and she smiled and sighed.

"I will not."

He did not know, and Jaelle would not tell him, that Free Amazons who elected to remain for a time as freemate to a lover did not cut their hair; by custom, close-cropped hair was a sign among them of commitment to solitude.

She was dressed and ready before him. Since they made a point of coming downstairs separately, she started down to the small breakfast room. The sun, flooding in brilliantly through the stone-arched windows, would at any other time have given her pleasure, after so many dark days. Now it only meant the end of an interlude that could never come again. She might remain with Peter, but never again in such complete isolation, mutual self-absorption; the outside world would intrude, with other work, other commitments, and she grieved for the end of their brief honeymoon.

A hand on her wrist detained her; at a quick glance she thought that Peter had hurried after her, and smiled, but the smile slid off as she realized that the hand had six fingers, and simultaneously she recognized the voice of her cousin Kyril. *So alike, so different. . . .*

"Alone, *chiya?* Have you quarreled with your commoner lover? I should make a reasonable substitute to console you, should I not? Or did you turn to him because you so much regretted refusing me, when we were younger?"

She picked his hand off her arm as she would have removed a crawling insect. She said, "Cousin, we will all be leaving here very soon. For Rohana's sake, let us try to remain friends, for this short time. I am sorry for all our quarrels when we were not much more than children; don't torment me by bringing them up now that we are grown."

Kyril pulled her against him, in a mockery of a kinsman's embrace, and laid his cheek roughly against hers. "Nothing is farther from my mind than quarreling with you now, Jaelle."

Shocked and angry, she removed herself from his arms. She said, almost in entreaty, "This is not worthy of you, Kyril. I am your kinswoman and your mother's guest. Don't force me to be rude to you!"

"And is *your* behavior so worthy?" he demanded, "when you put our whole family to shame with this bastard from nowhere?"

Jaelle struggled to keep her composure. "If he is truly a bastard of Ardais," she said, "then the shame is in the misbehavior of his parents, and no fault to him. You were born Comyn, and legitimate, through no virtue in yourself. And as for *my* behavior—for the last time, Kyril, I owe *you* no account of my actions, nor any man living!"

He gripped her by the arms, his fingers digging cruelly into the soft flesh there. Through the touch her untrained *laran* gift—which she could never control but which, in deep emotion, thrust itself on her involuntarily —made her aware of his frustration and anger, and desire. He wanted her, crudely, sexually, and in a kind of intense, man-to-woman hostility that she had never known since—incredulously, she identified it as what she had sometimes sensed, without understanding, between her father and his women. It turned her physically sick; she thrust him away without trying to conceal her disgust. Her voice was shaking.

"Kyril, I do not want to hurt you under your mother's roof, where I am a guest. But you have known since we were fifteen years old that no Free Amazon trained in self-defense can be—can be raped. Don't put your hands on me again, Kyril, or—or I will have to prove it to you again, as I did then."

She realized, in shame and self-disgust, that she was crying.

When we were both fifteen years old, Kyril probably meant no real harm; it was a game he was playing, a game of adolescent pride: a little kissing and fondling, just to prove himself a man and my master. But I would not play that game with him then, and I wounded his pride more than he could endure. And I made him an enemy, and he is still my enemy.

"You bastard bitch," he flung at her, and his face was very ugly; the more terrifying because it seemed such a cruel caricature of the face of her lover. "By what right do you play the whore with this stranger, and then turn away from my touch like any chaste lady? By what right do you refuse me what you so freely give him?"

"You *dare* talk of rights?" Her tears gave way to flaming anger. "Rights? I *choose* my lovers, Kyril—and by what right, then, do you complain that I have not chosen you? I would not have you when you were an arrogant boy of fifteen bullying his mother's fosterling, and I will not have you now when you have grown into"—she caught back the crude obscenity on her tongue—"into her unworthy son!" She turned her back on him, hurrying toward the breakfast room, knowing that he would never dare make this kind of scene before dom Gabriel. She was not overly fond of Rohana's husband, but she knew him for an upright man who would tolerate no offenses toward a woman and a guest at his own table.

But Kyril followed close on her heels, gripping her from behind, his fingers digging into the bruises he had made so painfully that Jaelle cried out. "How dare you talk of my mother and your respect for her? It has not kept you from behaving like a harlot under her roof! Does my father know how you have shamed our kin by flaunting yourself in this stranger's bed? If he does not, my girl, then I promise you he shall know at once, and then your precious lover shall account to the Lord Ardais himself for how he has dealt with his kinswoman!"

"I am not his ward; I am a Free Amazon, and by law I am mistress of my own actions," she said, and again, with that frightening *laran* awareness, sensed that he took pleasure—an active, *sexual* pleasure—in the pain of his hands bruising her arms, in her uncontrollable sobs. She fought hard to get herself under control again. She would not, she *would not* feed that sick thing in him that found pleasure in her suffering. She said, breathing hard, but her voice calm and steady, "What has Piedro done to you, Kyril, that you want to hurt him this way? Why are you doing this? I had thought you his friend!"

"This has nothing to do with Piedro," said Kyril, and he was breathing hard, too. "He is a man; but you damnable Amazon bitches, thinking yourself free of all the rules for women, thinking that you can pretend yourself chaste ladies and demand that we treat you like chaste ladies, and then playing the whore when it suits you, flaunting your lovers— Zandru whip me with scorpions, but I will teach you that you cannot treat men that way!"

She turned her back on him, wrenching herself free of his hands, and went swiftly into the breakfast room. She was shaking so violently that she had to steady herself for a moment against the doorframe. Her heart was pounding, and the bruises on her upper arms, where he had gripped her, ached and throbbed. Magda was already in her place; Jaelle went and slipped into a seat beside her, nervously smoothing her hair. Magda, instantly aware that something was wrong with her friend, reached out her hand below the table, taking Jaelle's hand in her own.

"Jaelle, what's wrong?" she whispered. "You've been crying. . . ."

Jaelle clung to her friend's hand, but she could not control her voice enough to answer. *Do all men hate us that way? Can it really be true that all men hate us so much?*

Kyril had come into the room behind her; he said, "Father—" with a defiant stare at Jaelle.

"Later, my son," said Rohana. "Your father is very much occupied."

And indeed dom Gabriel looked angry and upset, staring furiously at the factor who managed his estate. "No, damn it, man, I'll not have it!"

"Lord Ardais, a thief is a thief, whether he steals copper coins or *sarm*-nuts!"

"Avarra's mercy, man," dom Gabriel said irritably. "Are you seriously trying to tell me that I should hang a hungry man who steals a few bushels of nuts to feed his sons so they can grow up to be my loyal servants?"

"If they steal nuts in one season, dom Gabriel, they will steal the trees themselves in another!"

"Then mark the trees you have ready for felling, and let it be known that any man who touches a marked tree will get a good cudgeling; and turn a blind eye when they help themselves to the downwood. If they cart it away to burn at their hearth-fires, it won't be there to feed forest fire another year! That last burn cost us half a year's profit in resins! But no more hangings, hear me? Or you'll find yourself hanging there beside them!"

The man grumbled, "You might as well paint up a placard at the edge of your forests, Lord Ardais: *Open to every thief in the Hellers, come and help yourselves!*"

"Don't be a fool, Geremy," the Ardais lord said. "No man can own a forest! My fathers have managed the lumber for centuries, and because they were clever at manufacturing resin and paint, and trading with the Dry Towns for sulfur to make book-paper, we have grown rich from the forests we did not plant! But I grew rich with the aid of the men who live there, and they have a right to feed themselves with the fruit of the trees, and warm their poor homes with the wood from the trees! The Gods hate a greedy man; and when I grow so greedy that I think I own the trees themselves, and the fruits of the trees, and even the men who live among the trees, then it is only a matter of time before these men take the law into their own hands and teach me the lawful measure of a man's ambition!"

"Yes. But, my Lord—"

Jaelle looked at dom Gabriel and shivered slightly; his face was dark with wrath, and she could see that his hands were trembling. It reminded her, faintly but frighteningly, of what she had seen in Kyril. He shouted at the factor, "Not another word, damn it! If you want to work for a bandit, and grow rich, go ask Rumal di Scarp if he needs a *coridom!*"

"Well said, Gabriel," Rohana said softly, reaching over to touch his sleeve. "But calm yourself. No one is arguing with you; we are all, I think, in agreement on that." She stared at the factor. "Are you not, Geremy?"

"Yes, my Lady, certainly!" the man almost stammered.

Jaelle thought, *Why does Rohana always try so hard to placate him? If he shouted like that at my table, I would give him shout for shout—yes, and blow for blow, too!*

Magda saw Peter slide into his seat—he had come in while dom Gabriel was talking—and as he met her eyes, she knew what he was thinking. It was an opportunity given few Terrans, to sit at table with one of the Comyn lords and hear him expound his decisions. She knew Peter was making mental notes for a report in Thendara; so in her own way was she. But would she ever deliver it?

The factor had moved to the question of how to mark trees for felling when the thaw had progressed a little further, and the scarcity of ax-heads and saws in recent years.

Gabriel turned to Peter. "You have lived in Thendara; what do you know of the *Terranan?*"

Peter froze, saw Lady Rohana raise watchful eyes to her husband, but the question was obviously innocent, so he answered, "As much as any man in the street knows."

"Can you verify a rumor for me? When they were here in the Hellers, back near Aldaran, I heard that they traded in metal from off-world; that the off-world metals were stronger than our native alloys, and would take a more durable edge. Is this true, or is it like the tales of men with wings for hands, and pots for breathing on their heads?"

"I have never seen any men with wings for hands, nor yet with pots for heads," Peter said truthfully, "but I lived as a child in Caer Donn, and I have seen the off-world metal. It is good solid stuff, and can be traded in bars for forging, and as finished tools, and the tools are probably better than what your smiths can make."

"Rohana, you sit in Council," said the Ardais lord querulously. "Maybe you can tell me why that donkey Lorill has prohibited such trade?"

Rohana said soothingly that she was certain that the ban on trade was only a temporary thing, that the Hastur lord only wished the Council to examine the consequences of their world becoming dependent on resources not native to this planet.

Kyril interrupted. "May I speak now? I have a serious complaint to make, about a breach of hospitality—and decency! This man from nowhere, this nobody, has abused our hospitality—"

Rohana's voice was sharp. "Kyril, I will not have your father worried with such trifles! If you have anything to say, then you may—"

"I was not speaking to you, Mother," said Kyril, staring angrily at her. "Let my father speak for himself; I am weary of hearing you reduce him to a nonentity in his own household! Father, do you rule this household, or does my mother?"

Dom Gabriel turned toward them, and his face was red with an anger that made Jaelle tremble. "I will hear what you have to say," he said. "But I will not tolerate insolence to your mother, my son!"

Kyril said, thrusting out his chin, "My mother, too, has failed in her duty, since she has shown herself powerless—or unwilling—to keep order and decency beneath this roof! Or are you unaware that Jaelle has been seduced by this nobody who calls himself Piedro, and that she has shared his bed from midwinter-night?"

Jaelle tensed, clenching her fists with mingled rage and distress. She felt Magda's hand close gently over hers, and sensed the mingling of fright and dread in her friend, as dom Gabriel's flushed face, red with rage, turned toward Jaelle. His eyes were squinted close, his mouth contorted.

He shouted, "Is this true? Jaelle, what have you to say for yourself, my girl?"

She opened her mouth angrily. "Uncle, I am not your ward—" she began, and Rohana said in a low voice, almost agonized, "Jaelle, *please*—"

The desperate dread in Rohana's voice somehow got through to Jaelle; she said, more gently than she had intended, "All I can say to you is that I am very sorry to give you offense, sir. I would not willingly have done it." She bit her lip and looked down at the plate in front of her, her hands shaking as she buttered her bread, struggling not to say any more. Rohana's quick, grateful look was reward enough, but it could not calm dom Gabriel now.

He bellowed, "Is this true? Have you made a scandal here in my house, with your love affairs?"

She swallowed hard and raised her eyes to meet his. She said clearly, "There will be no scandal, Uncle, unless you make it!"

Gabriel swung on Rohana, rising from his seat, turning angrily between Jaelle and Rohana. "What of this, my Lady? Did you know of this and say nothing? Did you permit your shameless ward to play the whore while she is under your care? What have you to say to this, Lady? Answer me! Answer me, Rohana," he bellowed.

Rohana had turned dead white. She said in a low voice, "Gabriel, Jaelle is not a child. She has taken the oath of the Free Amazons, and in law neither you nor I have any responsibility for anything she may do, under this roof or any other. I beg of you to calm yourself, to sit down and finish your breakfast."

"Don't you quote that filthy law to me," the man shouted incoherently, and his face was so dark and congested with fury that Magda wondered if he were about to suffer a stroke. "Jaelle is a woman of the Comyn! I forbade you to allow her to join these female scandals, and now do you see what you have done? A woman of our clan, seduced and betrayed—" He actually raised his arm as if to strike Rohana.

Jaelle, in horror, rose to her feet. "Uncle! Rohana is not to blame for anything I may have done! If you are going to shout and carry on like a madman, at least shout at me!" she said angrily. "I am a grown woman, and competent in law to manage my own affairs."

"Law, law, don't you talk to me about the law," Gabriel shouted, beside himself. "No woman alive is fit to manage her own affairs, and it doesn't matter what you—law—" He struggled to speak, as if his rage had swollen his throat completely shut, got out a few words of gibberish, then clenched his fists, swayed and came crashing down on the table, shattering crockery and chinaware, overturning a copper pot filled with some scalding hot drink that flooded the table, drenching the cloth. He struck his head hard, seemed to jerk violently on the rebound, and fell heavily to the floor, where he lay with his body arching backward, his heels drumming the floor in repeated, convulsive spasms.

Kyril, motionless with shock, suddenly leaned half across the table, running to lift him, but Rohana was already there, cradling the unconscious man's head against her knee.

"Let him lie till it is over," she said in a low, angry voice. "You have done enough for one morning. Go and call his man to help him to bed. Are you content, Kyril? Do you know now why I begged you not to provoke or trouble him? Do you honestly think"—she raised gray eyes, literally blazing with anger, to her son's—"that anything—*anything* goes on under this roof which I do not know, or permit?"

Jaelle felt a lump in her throat, obstructing speech. She had seen epileptic seizures before, but she had never before seen dom Gabriel in the grip of one. Now, looking at Rohana, kneeling and holding her husband's head, she realized exactly why Rohana spent so much of her life—foolishly, slavishly, she had often thought—in keeping dom Gabriel quiet and content, in averting his rage and calming his anger. Rohana's burden was far heavier than she thought.

Could I myself do so much for any man, however I loved him? And Rohana was given to him by her family, hardly knowing his name. Yet all these years she has managed it so that few outside the household even know his disability! She must have seen the warning signs, and tried to avoid any trouble. . . .

"Mother, I am sorry," Kyril begged. "I truly thought he should know of this."

Rohana swept him with a look of utter contempt. "Did you truly, my son? You cannot bear to think of any woman who does not obey you as if you were a God! And now you thought you had her at your mercy! How petty you are, Kyril! So to salve your wounded pride, and to revenge yourself against Jaelle, you have goaded your father into a fit; and he will be ill for days." She brushed aside his excuses without listening. "Go and call his body-servant, and help carry him to his bed, and no more talk. You have insulted our guests, and I will not forgive you soon for this!"

He went, glowering, and Jaelle came to Rohana's side. "Rohana, I am sorry—I did not realize—"

Rohana sighed and smiled at her. "Certainly not, child; you thought you were dealing with a rational man. You spoke more gently than I would have expected, and you said nothing that was not true. And I know that Kyril provoked you."

Her eyes rested for a moment on Jaelle's arms as if she could see the painful bruises there, and Jaelle thought, *Does she truly read my mind?*

When Kyril had helped to carry the unconscious man away, Rohana rose to her feet. She looked weary and worn.

"I know that you three"—her glance took in Peter and Magda, too—"were planning to leave today. Can you delay one more day? Today I must remain and make certain Gabriel is recovering as he should; tomorrow I can be ready to ride to Thendara with you."

"To come with us? Why?" Jaelle asked.

Rohana looked at Magda and said, "Because I have made a very important discovery; I must talk at once with Lorill Hastur. He is under a misconception which, if it is not corrected at once, can have the gravest consequences for both our worlds. So, if you will have my company on the road to Thendara, tomorrow morning I will be ready to ride with you."

Chapter

SIXTEEN

It was raining when they reached the travel-shelter at sunset, and as the party began to dismount, Rohana said, "I had hoped to reach Thendara today, but I have no great liking for riding half the night. It will be tomorrow for certain."

"I shall be glad to get there," Magda said, but then she began to wonder. Just what awaited her in Thendara? Even this one night's respite was welcome.

As she was unsaddling her horse, Darrill, son of Darnak, came up behind her, lifting the heavy saddle from her hands. She smiled and relinquished it, and stood beside him as he began giving their horses fodder. He waited until most of Rohana's guardsmen had withdrawn—Lady Rohana, as wife of the Lord of Ardais, could not travel without a considerable escort—then asked in a low voice, "Will you be glad to get back to your own world, Margali?"

She said, troubled, "I am not sure it is my world anymore, Darrill. I am sworn to the Free Amazons."

"But surely . . . Piedro told me that was but a disguise, a way of allowing you to travel in safety."

"Piedro does not know anything about it," Magda said, with unexpected sharpness.

"I don't think I understand."

"I am not sure that I understand it myself," she said. "It is true that I took the oath as a means to an end; not really aware of what it meant. But later I chose, of my free will, to honor it, and I will do so, whatever happens."

Slowly, he nodded. "I can understand that. But what will the Terrans say?"

That, she thought, *is the question. Will I spend the rest of my life as a fugitive from the Empire's justice?* "I will try to get a leave of absence to honor my obligation to the Guild-house," she said. "And after that I think I could work more effectively for the Empire. It would allow me to do many things that an ordinary woman could not do here, otherwise."

He said, very low, "Margali, when I first met with you on midwinter-night, I was very impressed with your courage and spirit. It seemed to me that no woman of our people could have so much, and I thought it must be only that you were a stranger, a Terran. Now there are times when it seems to me that you are even more like a woman of our own people. You are not like anyone I have ever known before." He raised his eyes, and looked directly into hers, and for a moment Magda thought he would kiss her. Then he swallowed hard, recalled himself, and turned a little away. He said, "Forgive me; I must finish with the horses."

As he went about his work, Magda found herself thinking, *If I am not careful, he will be falling in love with me. And that is a complication I cannot allow now. I must be very careful.* The thought made her a little regretful. *I discovered at midwinter that I must find new ways of relating to my world; but before I complicate my life with another man, I must find out more about myself!*

It might be flattering to have young Darrill in love with her; but it would be a cruel thing to test her new awareness of men by capturing his interest and perhaps his heart, when she was not free, could not make any permanent or serious commitment to anyone. Jaelle had defended her flirting on the grounds that she had never left any man wounded or heart-scalded by her teasing. *I must be very careful to avoid that, too,* Magda thought.

Inside the travel-shelter, which was one of the largest, the guardsmen, and Peter among them, had made their fire at one end; Rohana with her ladies, and Magda and Jaelle, at the other. As usual, Rohana sent word that Peter should come and join them at their meal. When they had finished, she looked at Peter and Jaelle, close together, their hands linked in the shadows, and said to Magda, "In common humanity, I think we should leave them alone for a few minutes." She raised her voice slightly. "Come, my ladies, I think the time has come to visit the guardsmen at the other fire and see if they are content with their rations and their comfort."

Rohana's maid, a fat and sentimental old woman, looked back with an encouraging smile at Jaelle, as they went toward the other fire, and Jaelle felt herself blushing. Then she forgot the woman, as Peter drew her into his arms for a long, passionate kiss. She sank gratefully into his arms, blessing Rohana for even this moment or two alone with her lover; it would not be more than a few minutes, but while it lasted she could reassure herself. . . .

Finally he loosed her. "I am dizzy with wanting you! At least it will not be long; we reach Thendara tomorrow. Do you still love me, Jaelle?"

She looked up, laughing, into his face. "Can you doubt it?"

"But you avoid me."

"Avoid you? Of course not, love," she said, with a little flicker of laughter. "You certainly do not think I could lie with you in the presence of a half dozen guardsmen and all of Rohana's maids!"

He looked away, uneasy at her directness. "That is not what I meant," he protested, "but we could be together more often on the road; you could ride at my side, spend more time in my company! All during this trip you have treated me like someone you might have met at a public dancing-class, not like your lover!" He used the word in the inflection that made its nearest meaning "promised husband," and she smiled, pressing his hand.

"You are my beloved," she said in a whisper, "and soon we shall be together as much as you wish. But I am an Amazon, Piedro. I have not told you much about our laws and customs, but one of the things we are taught is that there is only one way in which women can travel among men without causing trouble and dissension. And that is by behaving as human beings; not as sexual creatures, women whose major business in life is to attract men to protect and care for them."

"Oh, come, surely Lady Rohana and her companions—"

"Rohana is the wife of their lord, a sacred trust they must safeguard with their lives. And her ladies are covered by her—her special charisma. But I am an Amazon and I have renounced my protected status as *Comynara*. And I am working among them; I organized this journey. So I must not come among them as a woman who is—is free to be desired. Can't you understand?" she begged. "If I spend much time with you, show myself as your lover"—she, too, used the word in the inflection meaning "promised wife," and he pressed her hand—"then I show myself to them as a woman. And they begin to think of me as a woman, and before long they begin to compete in small ways for my favor and attention, and to show themselves before me as men, and soon there is dissension among them all, and ill feeling. So I must be just another worker, one of themselves. They must feel at ease with me, not temper their speech to a woman's ears, or feel compelled to give me their lightest work."

She did not shade her words with the faintest reproof, but Peter recalled that a few days ago she had frowned at him for helping her, unasked, with a heavy load.

He said, "Are you trying to tell me that there is no work which is beyond your strength?"

"No, no indeed!"

"I should think not," said Peter indignantly, looking at the slender girl. "And what do you do, proud Amazon, when you find something beyond your strength?"

She smiled and said, "Precisely what you do among men, when you find something too heavy to lift, or a task needing four hands to accomplish it. You are not a tremendously strong man, I imagine; when a task demands more strength than you have in your arms, I suppose you simply say to one of the other men, 'Come here and help me lift this before I strain my guts!' Well, that is exactly what I do. If I have made it obvious that I do not shirk any work within my strength, then they will help me as they would help another man with a task too heavy for him, and not with any thought of a woman who must be sheltered!"

"I hope you do not always intend to treat me that way!" he said, and she laughed and raised her hand to touch his cheek lovingly.

"When we are alone, beloved, I shall be so fragile and demanding that you will sometimes think I am Lady Rohana herself, who is not by law permitted to move as much as a day's ride without her maid and her lady companion and half a dozen guards! But you must not expect me to be anything other than I am, my love." She stood on tiptoe, pulled his head down and kissed him quickly. "Enough for now. Rohana and her women are coming back, and tomorrow we will be in Thendara."

"And tomorrow night . . ." Peter said, smiling at her, and for a moment she held herself against him, not at all unwilling to let him know she shared his eagerness. Then, sighing, they moved apart as Rohana with her ladies returned to their fire.

They rode down into Thendara a little after noon. Rohana said as they came through the gates, "What will you do now? Jaelle, you must go to the Guild-house, I know, with Margali."

Magda felt a small clutch of fear. *It's here. There's no more delaying. Oh, God, I'm frightened!*

Certainly, within my lifetime, Darkover will be a part of the Empire, and it will make no difference. The usual time from first contact to affiliation is about fifty years, and that's almost half over. But will that come too late to do me any good? Must I be exiled from one world to the other?

She thought this, not knowing that Darkover was to prove unique in the history of the Empire, and that not only her own lifetime but many lifetimes would pass before Darkover and the Empire were reconciled. Just the same, the curious little flash of precognition iced her blood again, and she pulled her fur-trimmed riding-cloak—Rohana's midwinter gift—about her shoulders.

"This is idiotic!" Peter said, looking back to make certain they were out of earshot of Rohana's women and the guardsmen. "You can't possibly do that, Magda. Somehow or other, we've got to get you out of that nonsense of spending half a year in the Guild-house. I'm sure you'd find it interesting, but we can't possibly afford to lose our only resident female expert. Come back with me now to the HQ, and let the people there think of some way to get you out of it."

Magda said, in exasperation, "Peter, you don't understand. I am oath-bound, and I will honor my oath. I will try, after, to make it right with the Empire authorities; but the obligation must be met nevertheless!"

"Oh, that," he said in contempt. "You know as well as I do that an oath taken under duress is not valid!"

Jaelle looked at him in shock and dismay; and Magda, with that new, devastating sensitivity to thoughts, knew that Peter had just shocked Jaelle to speechlessness. *An oath is sacred. What kind of man could ignore it? And if he had no awareness of what* the oath meant to Magda, how could he possibly know what it meant to Jaelle?

Can he ever know, Jaelle thought with desolation, *that it is the very mainspring of my being?* It was only a moment, then her love began to make excuses for him; soon, soon he would understand. She smiled gaily at Peter and said to Magda, "We shall have to teach him better than that, will we not, sister?"

Rohana interrupted, sensing the strain: "The best way is for you, all three of you, to be my guests at Comyn Castle tonight. There is room in the Ardais suite for a dozen or more; and you, Piedro, can send word to your Terran supervisor that tomorrow we will all meet with Lorill Hastur. Both of them will be eager to know how this affair has ended."

They agreed to that compromise, and an hour later were all settled in comfortable quarters in the Ardais suite. Magda was tired from the long journey, and lay down for a nap, but she knew that sleep was simply another way of avoiding, for a time, the unendurable conflicts. Tomorrow, at whatever cost, they must be faced.

Peter stood for a few moments at the door of the room the women shared. He said, hurt, "Jaelle, you are avoiding me again!"

"No, my love. In a day or two we shall declare ourselves as freemates, before witnesses," she promised, standing on tiptoe to kiss him with a passion that swept away his doubts. "But just now I am Rohana's guest in Comyn Castle and for her good name I must abide, under this roof, by her laws and rules of conduct rather than my own. But I love you. Never doubt it, promise me, Piedro, promise."

"I promise," he assured her, then, in surprise, bent to wipe the tears from her eyes. "My love, my darling, why are you crying?"

"I—I don't know," she stammered, and although he knew she was evading him, there was nothing he could say. "Even though I am a Free Amazon, Piedro, you must sometimes just let me be a woman, and not always reasonable. . . ."

When he had gone away, and Magda had fallen into an exhausted sleep, Jaelle wandered, restlessly, around the Ardais suite. At this time of year it was deserted; Rohana and her guests seemed to rattle around the empty rooms and corridors like a few pods on a tree stripped by a storm. At last Rohana sought her out.

"Come and sit with me for a little while, Jaelle. It may be a long time before we can spend time together like this; at Council season I have little leisure to enjoy your company, and it may be many years before you can pay me another visit at Ardais."

They sat before the fire that had been kindled in Rohana's room. For a time they said little, but at last Jaelle got out of her chair and came and sat on the hearth-rug beside her kinswoman. She laid her head for a moment on Rohana's knee; hesitantly, Rohana stroked the soft hair. As a girl Jaelle had never permitted caresses and Rohana had quickly learned not to offer them, but for once she seemed to invite them.

At last Jaelle said, "I did not tell you this, but you probably have guessed. Piedro has asked me to remain in Thendara as his freemate; and I have consented."

Rohana looked down at Jaelle with a distant sadness. *She loves him so much; and I know I cannot really understand.* Rohana herself had been given in marriage very young, had obediently married the man chosen by her family, without question, and had never been touched by this kind of passion. At last she asked, with a hesitant tenderness, "Have you ever regretted your oath, Jaelle?"

"Never before this, never for a moment," Jaelle said. Then, forcing the words out, "Just the same, I think you were right, years ago, when you said I was too young for such a choice."

That struck to Rohana's heart, almost with physical pain. *Merciful Goddess, I gave her freedom, the freedom that had been denied to me. Was I so wrong?* For a moment time slipped out of focus, past and present blending together, and it seemed to Rohana that it was again the last day of Jaelle's long visit to Castle Ardais, in her fifteenth year. Rohana had known Jaelle was not happy there: she detested Kyril and had no great liking for Rohana's younger son and daughter; she thought Gabriel a petty tyrant; she had chafed at the need to wear skirts even for riding; and on the last day of her visit she had come to Rohana like this and told her, defiantly, that she would take the Amazon oath on the very day she was legally free to do so.

Rohana had foreseen this, but had still been dismayed by the actuality. She felt Jaelle had as yet no idea what she was renouncing.

She had said: "Be very sure, Jaelle; very sure. This is no game, it is your whole life. Don't throw it away like this!" And then she had begged: "Jaelle, will you give me three years, more time, as you gave Kindra, to prove to you that my life is no less happy than hers?"

She knew Jaelle was remembering, too (Or did the girl's awakening *laran* share her thoughts?), when Jaelle said softly, "Three years seemed a lifetime then; longer than I could bear to wait. And—forgive me, Rohana— you wanted to prove your life was happy; and yet I knew *you* were not happy. So it seemed—hypocrisy."

Rohana bowed her head. No; she had not been happy then, but she thought she had concealed it more carefully from Jaelle. She had felt harried then, trapped by the life she led, after her brief taste of freedom. She had been much beset with her adolescent children, and with the three-year-old Valentine, who was at the most active and troublesome age. And at that time she had been pregnant again with a fourth child she did not want; that had been the price she paid for Gabriel's final forgiveness. And though she had not wanted the child, Rohana was too much a woman to bear a child for most of a year and see it die without anguish. So when it had been stillborn, she had grieved as bitterly as if she had longed for it. But she had carried the child, that year, in anger and desperate rebellion, feeling that perhaps she had paid too high a

price for Gabriel's goodwill and peace in her home.
Now, before Jaelle grown to womanhood, she bowed
her head and said, almost inaudibly, "You were right; I
was not happy then. Now I feel more guilty than ever
that because of my unhappiness you rushed to take the
Amazon oath."

Jaelle laid her cheek against Rohana's hand. "Don't
blame yourself; I don't think it would have made any
difference. Even Kindra said I was stubborn and head-
strong; she, too, urged me to delay a little. Perhaps"—
she smiled fleetingly—"I am my father's daughter,
too, though I do not like to think so."

Never before this day had Jaelle spoken her father's
name in Rohana's hearing. She had some idea of what
it had cost Jaelle to say this. She was silent, asking after a long time, "Then you will stay with your Terran
lover?"

"I—I think so."

But she is not sure. "Is it fair to any man, Jaelle, to
give him so little of yourself as a freemate gives?"

"Rohana, I give him what he wants of me! The Terrans do not make their women slaves to their will!"

"Just the same—don't be angry, Jaelle—it seems to
me that a freemate gives little more than a prostitute."
She used the coarse word *grezalis*, knowing that on her
decorous lips it would shock Jaelle into listening. "It
seems to me that it is no marriage unless you commit
yourself to a man for all times: good and bad, in happiness or misery. You know that when I was wed, Gabriel was nothing to me but a burden I had to bear, because I had been born Comyn, and the laws of my
caste required me to marry within my clan and bear
him children with *laran*."

"And you can call *me* whore? When you were sold
like a slave for your family's pride of position, and I
choose to give myself freely to the man I love and
desire?"

Rohana put out a hand to stop her. "Jaelle, Jaelle
darling, I did not call you a whore, or anything like it!
I said: this was how my marriage seemed at the begin-

ning, a grave burden I must bear for my family's sake. Yet now Gabriel is the very center of the world we have built together. A freemate says to her lover, because of this storm of desire, I will remain with you while it suits my pleasure; but if we lose our happiness I will leave you, sacrificing the happiness we have had and the good times that may come in the future, all because of the unhappiness of a year or two. There is no obligation to remain together and work to turn the evil times into good again."

"How can you do that? Do you not live with constant regret for the years of unhappiness you had to share, with no possibility of escape?"

"Not really," Rohana said. "It has taken us a long time to outlive unhappiness, but we have forged a bond that will last till death. And beyond," she added, smiling, "if there is anything beyond."

"You say this bravely," said Jaelle, "but I think . . . oh, Rohana, I do not want to make you angry."

"The truth could not make me angry, Jaelle. Only remember, darling, that it is *your* truth, and not necessarily *my* truth."

"Then I think," said Jaelle, "that because it is too late for regrets, you tell yourself you have never had them. I think you simply would not give up your power and position as wife to the lord of the Domain of Ardais."

"Perhaps," said Rohana, unoffended, "a marriage is spun of many small threads. Gabriel is only a part of my life, but not a part I would willingly renounce now. I did not love him when we were wed, but it would rend my heart into a thousand fragments to be parted from him now."

Jaelle, remembering Rohana's face as she knelt beside the unconscious man, knew dimly that this was true; but it seemed to her that this was only slavery to an ideal, and nothing like the overwhelming passion that had caught her up, almost unwillingly, into Peter's life. She said, trembling, "That is not what I call love!"

"No, I suppose not, dear," said Rohana, taking the

small cold hands in hers, "but it is real, and it has lasted."

"Then you think love—love as I know it—means nothing? It seems to me you think marriage can be made by any two, however they feel about one another, as if"—for the first time in a dozen years, Jaelle spoke her mother's name—"as if Melora and Jalak . . . as if my mother, even in rape and captivity, could have built lasting happiness."

"Even that, under some circumstances, darling. But I went consenting to my marriage, with my family's support and blessing; Melora was torn by force from all her kin. But even then; had Jalak and Melora chosen one another, had she run away with him of her own will, or even, afterward, had he loved and cherished her for herself, and not as a pawn to his evil pride, and a memento to his hatred of her folk of the Domains— even then, perhaps, she could have found some peace; not happiness, perhaps, but content."

"Even in chains?"

"Even so, my darling. Had Melora loved Jalak, and willed to please him, she would have known that the chains were a game he played for his pride before all men, and she would have worn them to play the game with him, willingly. . . . Jaelle, if your Amazons made up an army and marched to free the women of the Dry Towns from their chains, no doubt there are some who would hail you as their saviors; but there are others, I am sure, who would bid you turn around and march home again, and not meddle in their affairs. Would you not wear chains to please your lover, Jaelle?"

She said, "He would never ask," but dropped her eyes, remembering her play with the ribbon; the fantasy game she had played as a little girl in the Dry Towns. She said, angry at the memory, "Had you no pity for my mother?"

"Only the Gods know how much," Rohana said. "I risked the anger of Hastur, and came near to destroying what happiness I had found with Gabriel, to bring her away before she bore Jalak a son; and to set you free, because she said she would kill you rather than have you chained in Jalak's Great House. Do you not remember that?" Her eyes flamed with the beginning of anger.

Jaelle took her hand, and after a moment kissed it. Rohana said quietly, "Jaelle, many women wear their chains as I wear the *catenas*." She thrust out her arm, showing her the ceremonial marriage-bracelet, whose twin was locked on Gabriel's arm. "A token of something that would be locked upon my heart forever, even if I refused, as you will refuse, to wear the outward symbol."

Jaelle said softly, "The Amazon oath binds me not to marry *di catenas*. I never thought I would want to," and her head went down on Rohana's knees, the slender shoulders shaking with the violence of her sobs. "I don't, Rohana! I don't!"

Rohana thought, *Then why are you crying so?* But she did not say so, sensing, through the feel of the girl's head against her knees, the very real heartbreak. She only stroked Jaelle's soft hair, tenderly. At last she asked, "Are you pregnant, darling?"

"No—no. He has spared me that."

"And do you really want to be spared, my precious?"

Jaelle couldn't answer; she was unable to speak. At last Rohana asked, very gently, "Will you stay with him in sorrow as in joy, Jaelle?"

Jaelle raised her flushed face. "I feel now that I would," she said in anguish, "but how can I be sure? How can I know he will love me in the evil times that come to everyone? How can I even know what *I* will be then? And yet—it seems that it is worth even this. Did you never love anyone, Rohana? Did you never want to give up everything—everything, your pledged way of life, your honor, *everything* because you could not—could not part from—" She put her head down on Rohana's knees, and cried desperately again.

Rohana's heart ached for her, and for a long-healed wound that Jaelle's words had torn. *Yes, there was a*

*time when I would have given up everything: my chil-
dren, the life I had made for myself, Gabriel—yet the
price seemed all too heavy to pay.* At last she said,
faltering, "There is nothing in this world that is not
bought for a price. Even Kindra; she never regretted her
oath, but she grieved to the day of her death for the
children she had abandoned. It seems to me that is the
one flaw in the Amazon oath; you women who take it
guard yourselves from the risks all women take willingly. Perhaps it is only that every woman must choose
what risks she will bear."

Jaelle listened, and the words fell heavy on her
heart. *I came too young to the Amazon oath; most
women make these renunciations in grief, knowing that
they are real privations. To me it seemed only that I
renounced slavery and embraced freedom. I did not
weep when I took the oath. I could never truly understand why so many women made the oath only with
tears. . . .*

"You love Piedro. Will you stay with him?"

"I—I must, I cannot leave him now."

"Will you bear his children, darling?"

"If he—if he wants them."

"But your oath binds you to bear them only if *you*
want them," Rohana said. "You must choose, and perhaps it is that which I feel so wrong; that you women
claim the right to choose."

"I will never believe that," Jaelle flared at her. "A
woman not free to choose is truly a slave."

"But even the freedom to choose does not always
guarantee happiness," Rohana said, capturing the cold
hands again and caressing them. "I have heard old
Amazons lamenting their childlessness, when it was too
late to change their minds. And I—" She swallowed
hard, for she had never said this to any living being;
not to Gabriel, not to Melora, not to Kindra, who for
so long had shared her innermost thoughts. "I did
not want children, Jaelle. Every time I knew myself
pregnant, I wept and raged. You weep because you are
not to bear a child, but I cried more when I knew I

was. Once I flung a silver bowl at Gabriel's head, and I hit him, too, and I shrieked at him that I wished I had killed him and he could never do this to me again. I hated being pregnant, I hated having little children around to trouble me, I feared childbirth worse, I think, than you feared the sword that gave you this." With light fingers she traced the still-crimson scar across Jaelle's smooth cheek. "Had I been free to choose, I would never have borne a child. And yet now that the children are grown, and I see that they are a part of Gabriel and myself which will survive when we are gone—now, when it would have been too late to change my mind, I find I am glad that the laws of my caste forced me to bear them, and after all these years, I have forgotten—or forgiven—all the unhappiness."

Jaelle said hoarsely, not wanting to show how much this had moved her, "I think, again, that you know it is too late for regrets; so you tell yourself that you have none."

"I did not say that I had no regrets, Jaelle," said Rohana, very low, "only that everything in this world has its price, even such serenity as I have found after so many years of suffering."

"You truly believe that you have paid a price? I thought you told me now that you had everything a woman could desire!"

Rohana lowered her eyes. She swallowed hard, and for a moment she remembered a day, years ago, when she had looked into Kindra's gray eyes and known the price she would pay. She could not face Jaelle; she did not want to cry. She said, "Everything but freedom, Jaelle. I think that would have been too dearly bought. But I am not sure." Her voice broke. "Nothing in this world is sure but death and next winter's snow. Maybe I do not want to be sure. The price I have paid is my freedom. You have your freedom; you are oath-bound to take it even now when you no longer want it. But at what price, Jaelle?"

Chapter

SEVENTEEN

Magda woke at twilight, to see Jaelle sitting on the foot of her bed. She looked pale, as if she had been crying; but she was calm.

"Sister," she said, "I know that you took our oath unwillingly; in a sense it was forced from you. Normally that would not matter; but you are a Terran, and you took it without the knowledge of what it truly implied. Do you want to petition for release from your oath, Margali? If you do, I will speak for you before the Guild-mothers."

Magda knew that this would solve some of her deep inner conflicts; more, it would free her from the fear of Terran retribution, not directed toward herself alone, but toward those who had aided her to desert her original loyalties. She considered it for a moment, but then she was seized by revulsion. Go back to her life in the Terran Zone, and the narrow, sterile world she had lived there, circumscribed by the little work of importance that a woman could do? She realized now that even through her tears and terror when she had taken the oath, it had still seemed a major decision in her life; and more, a genuine decision. *Here is a way I can fol-*

low. This is what I want, whatever the price I must pay.

I was not forced to abandon Peter to death. Jaelle saved me from paying this price. But sooner or later I knew there would be a day of reckoning; and now I will meet it, whatever it may be.

She used the formal Amazon phrase. "Oath-mother," she said, "I told you: I chose of my free will to honor my oath, and I will keep it, until death take me or the world end."

"Even if it makes trouble for you with your own people, Margali?"

She said what she had said to Darrill on the journey: "I am not so sure they are my own people anymore." Her voice was not quite steady. "I have renounced allegiance to—*to family, clan, warden or liege lord.*"

Jaelle took her hands; suddenly she leaned forward and kissed her, as she had done when she accepted her oath. She said, "Allegiance for allegiance, my sister. We are sworn. But I think you must face the fact—we must face it together—that it may make grave trouble for you."

"I know that," said Magda, and could not keep from trembling a little. "If it had not been for Lady Rohana, I think Peter would have insisted on taking me to the Terran Headquarters, even if he had to do so by force, and under arrest."

"A beautiful reward for your loyalty to him," Jaelle said angrily, "But for you, he would be dead in Sain Scarp this moment!"

Magda felt compelled to defend Peter's point of view. "He is a Terran agent," she said. "To him, I think, loyalty to the Empire transcends any loyalty to persons."

"That is not right," Jaelle said, troubled.

Magda thought, *It's not a point of view any Darkovan can understand; so in many ways Peter is worse off than I. He is Darkovan in so many ways, he can never live at peace within the Empire; but he will never be free to renounce those very things which would prevent him from being wholly at home in Darkover . . . and he will always be torn, an exile. . . .*

"Jaelle," she said, "you told me once that the Free Amazons were allowed to accept any lawful work. If the Terran authorities would give me a leave of absence to honor my obligation to the Guild-house for their training, then when I had completed it, would I be allowed to continue the work I have been doing for the Terrans?"

"Do you mean that you would spy on us?"

"No, of course not," Magda said; the very idea was repellent. "But to build a bridge between our worlds; to help my people better understand all the small ways of your society, your language, your laws and customs—even if I did nothing more than my old work, to keep our translators from unwittingly offending against your customs; and I think I could do more, much, much more."

"That would not violate your oath," Jaelle said. "By our Charter you may accept any lawful work anywhere. That means that as a sworn Amazon you may work for the Terrans—" She broke off, as if she had seen a blazing light, and said almost in a whisper, "And so can I."

"How would that be arranged, Jaelle?"

"However you wish," Jaelle said. "By our Charter's laws, you must pay a portion of your earnings to the Guild. We renounce family and home, but this means that we have the protection of home and family always. Whenever you are sick, pregnant, unable to work or in a strange city, you can always turn to the Guild-house or to any Amazons there, and find a home where you can be cared for. Your tithes go to maintain the Guild-houses, and you have always sisters and friends there, and you have a lawful right to them. You need never live within a Guild-house unless you choose, although if you choose to live there you are expected to help with the maintenance of the house, to take your turn at housekeeping or gardening or whatever needs to be done. But it is our true home, where we come as others come to their family homes, wherever else we may go."

Magda had known no family life since her father's death; she and Peter had never seriously tried to make a home together. The thought of having a true home, a Darkovan home, to which she could go not as a stranger or a guest, but as of right, gave her a sense of warmth she had not known for years.

Jaelle said, "We can go there in old age when we are past work, or have our children fostered there."

"You bear children, then?"

"If we wish," Jaelle said, and the memory of Rohana's words brought a fleeting sadness to her face. "Did you think we took Keeper's vows? Our daughters can be fostered in the Guild-house till they are grown, when they can choose for themselves whether to join the Guild or to marry. Our sons are usually given to their fathers to rear, after they are weaned, but if your child's father is unwilling, or you think him unfit to raise your child, or if you do not know who fathered your child—then you can arrange to have him fostered as you wish; though no boy over five years old may live in the Guild-house." She was thinking out loud; suddenly she came back to the present. "Well, you will learn all that during your Guild-house training, sister."

Was it possible that she could share her two worlds? It seemed almost too good to be true. Magda said, hesitating, "You know that Lorill Hastur has forbidden contact between the Terran Zone and his people. It is easy to defy him in the Hellers, Jaelle; but here in Thendara?"

"Yes, that is one of the gravest difficulties," Jaelle said, "but Rohana is pledged to speak to Lorill. Her heart dwells in two worlds, too, and I think it is larger than either of them. And I think it is time that the people of Darkover, not the Comyn lords alone, knew something of the Terrans, and what they can do for our world. You heard Gabriel speak about Lorill's ban on trade. Hastur's will is not the voice of God, even to the Comyn! Let us find out what some of the others think. Will you come with me now to the Guild-house, sister, and see what we can do to settle this, before we meet tomorrow with Lord Hastur—and with your Terrans? Then we will know where we stand."

Magda hesitated. Then, knowing this was the moment of choice, she nodded.

"Yes, I will."

The next morning, the Lady Rohana sat beside Lorill Hastur in the small Council chamber, awaiting the arrival of the Terran coordinator. Peter Haldane sat across from them, looking both apprehensive and angry. Rohana could not read his thoughts, but she did not have to. This morning, Magda and Jaelle had vanished, and she was certain they had taken refuge in Thendara Guild-house. But they had left a message saying they would appear before Hastur at the Council, and it was not Rohana's duty to explain further when they had not.

Hastur leaned over and asked her in an undertone, "This was the man taken by Sain Scarp? Is he truly identical to Kyril? The resemblance is extraordinary; are we dealing here with Cherillys' Law?"

Rohana laughed. "I have not remembered Cherillys' Law since I was a psi monitor in Dalereuth Tower with you and Melora and Leonie," she said, "But no, it is not that; the Terran has only five fingers on either hand."

"Still, a remarkable likeness, and it goes to bear out what you said about a single race; although it seems fantastic to believe that our people could have come from another star, or that we would ever have permitted ourselves to forget such an heritage. And you told me that the woman has *laran*. May I ask how you found that out? I gave orders that no Terran was to witness a matrix operation."

"Jaelle was dying," Rohana said, "and her sworn sister had a right to remain with her. I can only imagine—" She frowned, trying to think it out. "Alida has the Ardais Gift; she is a catalyst telepath, and contact with her may have awakened latent *laran* in this woman. But if it had not been there, Alida could not have roused it. The man—Haldane—was there, too, and he showed no sign of being aware of what was going on. But whatever the reason, this woman has *laran*, and it means we must revise some of our preconceived notions about Terrans." She said "our" preconceived notions, but she really meant "your"; Hastur knew it and scowled.

He said, "Here is the Terran official, and his interpreter."

Rohana had met Montray before, and had not been impressed; she wondered if she had picked up some shred of Magda's contempt for the man. This time he was accompanied by a young man who spoke *casta* as well as either Peter or Magda, which was as well as any native-born Darkovan. He introduced himself as Wade Montray, the coordinator's son, and politely made himself known to each of them, while his father went toward Peter, glowering.

"So there you are, Haldane! Do you have any idea how much trouble you've caused? And where is Miss Lorne? She should be here! In fact, both of you should have reported back to the HQ last night for orders!"

Peter said rather stiffly, "I have not been informed that any charges have been filed against us. It did not seem proper to give offense to the Lady Rohana when she invited us to remain as her guests. I am certain that Magda will be here at the proper time." He turned toward the door, with an audible sigh of relief. "In fact, she is here. And the young woman with her was instrumental in saving my life, Montray, so you be polite to her, damn it!"

"Nice-looking girl," Montray commented, and Peter stiffened up again. "Montray, you've been on Darkover how long—ten years? If you haven't learned yet that it's not proper to make comments about a woman's looks, I suggest you put in for transfer as fast as you can, or never stick your head out of the Terran Zone!"

Magda had come into the room with Jaelle and

three strange women, and was quietly seating herself with them on the fourth side of the room. Hastur said sternly, "Jaelle, what is this? I gave you no authority to invite any outsiders to this conference!"

"I did not ask for it, my Lord." Jaelle spoke respectfully, but with none of the fear most outsiders displayed before a Comyn lord. "Lord Hastur, it seemed to me that our Guild is very deeply concerned in these matters that are under discussion this morning, and I therefore asked these representatives to come and state our position before you, and before the Terrans."

Montray demanded, "What did she say?" and his son began quietly repeating Jaelle's words, as Jaelle went on.

"My Lord, my Lady and respected off-worlders," she added, turning to the Terrans. "I wish to present to you *mestra* Millea n'ha Camilla, Guild-mother of Thendara House." Millea was a tall and bulky woman, conventionally dressed, and as feminine as Rohana herself, "*Mestra* Lauria n' Andrea, the head of the Independent Council of Craftswomen, and *Domna* Fiona n'ha Gorsali, Judge of the City Court of Arbitration."

Rohana thought, admiringly, *Oh, Jaelle, you are far more clever than I ever believed!* The women seating themselves in a dignified row across the room were no ordinary Amazons; they were three of the most powerful women in the city of Thendara. The Guild of Craftswomen had successfully fought for the right to be recognized among the city's businesses; *Domna* Fiona was the first woman ever to be appointed a judge in the history of Thendara. Hastur could not dismiss them as unimportant.

Jaelle said, "Will you grant us the right to hear your deliberations, nobles?"

Hastur looked a trifle annoyed, but nothing could ruffle his long discipline in diplomacy. He rose and bowed politely to the three women. "I will not welcome you to this Council, for you came uninvited," he said, "but this is no secret conclave to work tyrannies; no concerned citizen may be denied the right to hear, and in turn, be heard."

Montray said, his son translating, "We welcome the chance to be heard by any citizens of Thendara. Be welcome, ladies."

Hastur addressed himself to Montray. He said, "When you were last before us, we granted permission for your employee, Magdalen Lorne"—Magda, seated among the Amazons, noticed that he did not hesitate or stumble even slightly over her Terran name—"to venture into the hills and negotiate for the rescue of your employee, the man Haldane, held captive at Sain Scarp. As I now understand the matter, the Lorne woman encountered a band of Free Amazons under the command of Jaelle n'ha Melora, and was required, according to their custom and the laws of their Charter, to swear an oath of allegiance to their Guild. Is this an accurate account of the affair?"

The Guild-mother Millea said, "According to the reports we have had from our sisters, this is true."

Hastur said, "I do not quite understand the difficulty. It seems to me that this is a matter for private agreement among the parties concerned, or at least for the courts of arbitration."

Montray listened with an angry frown; he said something, and his son shook his head, refusing to translate it.

Hastur turned to Magda and said, "Miss Lorne, did you have these women brought here that you might petition, in the presence of all concerned, to be released from your oath?"

Magda's voice was low, but very clear. She said, "No, my Lord Hastur. I am willing to abide by the oath I swore, and to honor it till death. But I am not certain that the Terran authorities will allow me to do so. They may possibly hold that my oath is not valid, or that because of prior loyalties I had no right to swear it."

Montray said something again, and the young translator said, just audibly, "I told you so."

Rohana, watching, realized that Magda had done an exceptionally clever thing. In private, the Terran ambassador might state that he did not believe in the validity of a Darkovan oath. But if he said so, in the presence of Hastur and three Guild-mothers from Thendara, he destroyed the credibility of every Terran on Darkover for decades to come. And if he didn't know it, and judging by his expression he hadn't, he was finding it out in no uncertain terms, both from the young and expert translator, and from Peter Haldane! From the look of frustration on his face, Rohana could tell, even without need for a scrap of *laran*, that he was consigning all of them, especially Magda, to whatever his Terran equivalent was for the coldest of Zandru's hells!

Domna Fiona said, "The noble guest from Terra appears to find some difficulty in accepting the decision; may we hear it, with Lord Hastur's permission?"

Montray said, waiting for his son to translate, "The difficulty is this: Miss Lorne is extremely valuable to us. She is the only woman qualified to act as an expert on the Darkovan languages, and to advise us on women's customs and the laws governing social usage on Darkover. It seems to us that we cannot, for the moment, spare her to any other work, valuable as it may be, and highly as we may respect those who would welcome her among them."

Rohana knew perfectly well that the polite phrases had been added by the translator, and suspected that Montray's original had been more emphatic and much less courteous. She did not understand enough of the Terran language to be sure.

"If that is the only difficulty, it can easily be settled," *domna* Fiona said. From the voice, and something about the narrow body in the judicial robes, Rohana suspected the woman was an *emmasca;* but the robes were too bulky to be sure. "If your problem is a lack of adequate experts on women's customs and the languages, then I think we can offer assistance. Sister," and she turned to Jaelle, who stood up nervously.

Her eyes met Peter's briefly across the room. Jaelle said, "Say to the Terran official that if it is agreeable to your people, I will offer myself to take my sister's place in working for you. I speak both *casta* and *cahuenga* fluently, and I can read and write in these and in the language of the Dry Towns; and I think I can help you to fill in what gaps there are in your knowledge of the customs of Thendara. And I think there are others of my sisters who would be willing to do the same, to the limits of your needs. We have been told"—again, briefly, she met Peter's eyes—"that you Terrans have had trouble in finding workers for anything but simple manual labor, and that you have sought for them without success."

Montray said, "That would indeed be welcome." He bowed politely to Jaelle. "But we had heard it was the will of Hastur that the people of Thendara should not give us this kind of assistance."

The Amazon Lauria, head of the Guild of Craftswomen, said quietly, "The Lord Hastur speaks for the Comyn, and for their sworn followers and those who owe allegiance in the Domains. But the will, or the whim, of Hastur is not yet the law of this land. With all respect, Lord Hastur"—and she made a deep bow to the Comyn lord—"we do not accept the right of Comyn to lay commands upon the free women of Thendara as to what lawful work they may accept, or what their relations shall be with the men of the Empire from the stars . . . or with their women. By the will of Hastur, the only women who have been permitted to know the men of the Empire are the women in the bars and brothels near the spaceport. We do not believe this will give a true picture of our world to the men of the *Terranan*. So we have come here today to offer you our lawful services in fields more suitable for meaningful communication between our two worlds: as map-makers, guides, translators or any suitable work at which the Terrans wish to employ Darkovan workers and experts. And in return, knowing that you of the Empire may have much to teach us, we ask that a group of our young women be placed as apprentices among your medical services and other scientific branches of your knowledge to allow us to learn from you. Is that agreeable to you, messire of Terra?"

Of course it was agreeable, thought Magda, watching Montray's face; it was what they had hoped for from the beginning, what they had so obdurately been denied on Darkover. She had never realized—and blamed herself for her own insensitivity—that the women of Darkover would resent being judged, by the Terrans, only by the women their men met in the bars and brothels. She herself, with her knowledge of such respectable women as she could meet in the markets and public places of Thendara, had gone a little deeper —but not much.

It wasn't, of course, total cooperation. There weren't that many Free Amazons, and they were rarely in positions of such power as *domna* Fiona. (It was also the first she had heard of the Courts of Arbitration. *What a lot I have to learn,* she thought, *and what fun I'm going to have learning it!*)

And afterward she would work again for the Terrans, and be one of the first to come and go between the two worlds, helping them to find a way to one another. Two worlds: and she would belong to both! She looked across at Lady Rohana, and the lady smiled. Again Magda had the image of a great door swinging wide, both ways, an opened door between locked-away worlds. . . .

Jaelle was watching Lorill Hastur. He seemed not very pleased, but he capitulated with such good grace as he could. *The fact is, the Free Amazons just aren't important enough—or so Hastur thinks—that he can, with dignity, take any notice of what we do. But where we go, others will follow, for their own reasons.* She caught Peter's eyes across the room, and smiled; and it seemed that her heart stopped at his returning smile.

I have found an honorable way we can be together in his world!

Montray was answering Hastur's gracious words with

a little speech about friendship and brotherhood, carefully using all the wrong inflections while his son Wade carefully straightened them out and made them into the proper ones.

How will Montray get along without me to write his speeches? Magda realized, lightheartedly, that she didn't give a damn. She had more interesting things to do.

When it had all been settled, and Hastur and Lady Rohana and Montray—his son at his elbow to keep him from any too offensive mistakes—were exchanging amenities, Peter and Jaelle and Magda met for a moment in the doorway of the Council chamber. Peter knew the custom of the Domains too well to touch Jaelle in public, but his quick glance at her was like an embrace. But he spoke to Magda, with raillery:

"So you've had your own way, Mag, and made us all look like fools—doing what no man could manage to do! Have you really such contempt for us all, then?"

"Contempt? Not really," Magda said, but she could not help flicking a quick look at Montray, which Peter caught. "But he, at least, hasn't done so well with Darkover so far."

Peter said, "Everyone knew you were doing the real work of the coordinator's office, Magda. It's just the way the breaks run, that you couldn't have the title, too. Maybe someday you can have the job."

She smiled without bitterness and said, "No, thanks. Why don't you try for it, Peter?" She felt the strange little prickles of the hunch running up and down her spine as she spoke. "You'll make a good coordinator—or the first Legate, someday. I have something better to do."

"You've already done miracles," he said, clasping her hands warmly, and she shook her head.

"It wasn't I. It was Jaelle—and the Guild-mothers."

He said under his breath to Jaelle, "You are wonderful! I never believed you could do it!"

Jaelle said quietly, "I think you do not believe that women can do many things, Piedro, in spite of what

Margali has done for us both. But perhaps you will learn, someday. I believed, for a time, that women among your people were more free than mine. Now I know that there is really not so much difference between Terra and Darkover. My foster-mother told me, once, that it was better to wear chains than to believe you are free, and weight yourself with invisible chains." Then she smiled at him, a luminous smile. "But there is always hope, and I am committed to a day when we are part of the Empire from the stars, and when we are not all strangers and aliens, but all people are—are—" She hesitated, stumbled for a word, and Peter said, "Where all men are brothers?"

She smiled, caught Magda's eyes and said, "And sisters."

He said, "Well, politics can wait; you and I have other things to think of today! Magda, will you come with us when we declare ourselves before witnesses?"

"I cannot," she said, glancing at the Guild-mothers. "I am not really supposed to leave the Guild-house for half a year after I am sworn." Suddenly she held out her hands.

"Oh, Peter, wish me luck! Don't hold it against me!"

He gave her a brief, almost brotherly hug. "I do, Mag," he said, kissing her on the cheek. "Looks like you'll need luck with those old battle-axes! But it's what you want, so be happy, love."

She said, "Jaelle—" and impetuously Jaelle flung her arms around Magda, holding her tight. Magda whispered, "You be happy, too."

"I'll come and see you," Jaelle promised. "Thendara house is my home, too."

Peter said, "But you must promise not to turn her against me, Magda! Must I cope with all those mothers-in-law?"

Jaelle said, laughing, "No one could turn me against you. But you must learn someday not to speak so of my mothers and sisters!"

She's grown up, Magda thought. *I've always thought of her as a young girl. But she isn't. She's a woman.*

*And she isn't infatuated anymore. She knows him for
what he is. And she loves him anyway.*

He would never understand that there could be loyalties—certainly not loyalties between women—that
could go deeper than love. But he would do his best
for the world they all loved, and his best would be very
good indeed, And for that, if nothing else, Magda
knew she would always love him a little.

The Guild-mother Millea turned and beckoned to
Magda to join them. Magda kissed Jaelle again, and
said, "Be good to each other." Then, slowly, but without looking back, she went across the room to join the
three women.

Jaelle, standing and watching her go, seemed to
catch from her mind the image of a great, opening
door, swinging wide on a sunlit world and a brilliantly
lighted future.

DAW PRESENTS MARION ZIMMER BRADLEY

☐ **HAWKMISTRESS!**
Hers was the power to command the beasts . . . but the troubled humans of the Age of Chaos needed her talent more! (#UE1762—$2.95)

☐ **STORMQUEEN!**
"A novel of the planet Darkover set in the Ages of Chaos . . . this is richly textured, well-thought-out and involving." —Publishers Weekly. (#UE1812—$2.95)

☐ **THE HERITAGE OF HASTUR**
"A rich and highly colorful tale of politics and magic, courage and pressure. . . . Topflight adventure in every way."— Analog. "May well be Bradley's masterpiece."—Newsday. "It is a triumph."—Science Fiction Review. (#UE1744—$2.95)

☐ **THE FORBIDDEN TOWER**
"Blood feuds, medieval pageantry, treachery, tyranny, and true love combine to make another colorful swatch in the compelling continuing tapestry of Darkover."—Publishers Weekly. (#UE1752—$2.95)

☐ **DARKOVER LANDFALL**
"Both literate and exciting, with much of that searching fable quality that made Lord of the Flies so provocative." —New York Times. The novel of Darkover's origin.
(#UE1806—$2.25)

☐ **TWO TO CONQUER**
A novel of the last days of the Age of Chaos and the ultimate conflict. (#UE1651—$2.50)

☐ **THE KEEPER'S PRICE**
New stories of all the ages of Darkover written by MZB and members of the Friends of Darkover. (#UE1837—$2.50)

DAW BOOKS are represented by the publishers of Signet and Mentor Books, THE NEW AMERICAN LIBRARY, INC.